This book belongs to:

Jean Waldaff

To Chuck & Jean

I hope you enjoy the story

Frederick F. Meyers Jr.
September 9th 2002

The Jericho Gambit

Frederick F. Meyers, Jr.

© 2002 Gardenia Press

THE JERICHO GAMBIT
Copyright © 2002 by Frederick F. Meyers, Jr.

ISBN 0-9712525-1-3 trade paperback:
Library of Congress Control Number: 2002107559

This is a work of fiction. Names, characters, places and incidents are either the product of the author's imagination or are used fictitiously, and any resemblance to any actual persons, living or dead, events, or locales is entirely coincidental.

This book was printed in the USA.

For inquiries or to order additional copies of this book, contact:

Gardenia Press
P. O. Box 18601
Milwaukee, WI 53218-0601 USA
1-866-861-9443 www.gardeniapress.com
books@gardeniapress.com

For
dmr & mgm

Acknowledgements

I wish to express my sincere appreciation to Gardenia Press for the opportunity to bring this story to print. Also, my thanks to Debra Farley, my editor. I often wondered what editors did and now I know—they beat up writers! Debra improved the manuscript with her insight to the characters and refined the flow of the story by her constructive criticisms. To her, my sincere thanks and appreciation. To Dana Jane Carroll, assisted by Mark Dietrich, my gratitude for applying their talents in the creation of the cover layout and art of the book. My thanks also to Elizabeth Collins, President of Gardenia Press, who gave me the encouragement to finish the manuscript and submit it for publication. A "Wow" from her along the margin as the story evolved was both encouragement and high praise indeed.

To my mother who hounded me to "write a book about the Irish;" well, at long last Mom, it isn't about the Irish, but here it is anyway. To the too numerous to mention, especially including my three sons, I also say thanks for the critical encouragements, suggestions, and support through the several drafts and edits you all endured.

My greatest thanks and deepest debt of gratitude I reserve for my wife Donna. She suffered through every page of this story from start to finish—and then some. She was always there to help, to encourage, to edit, to correct my grammar and spelling and to support me. Without her this novel and my continued scribblings would never have started. Finally to you the readers, I hope you enjoy the story.

1
Wilmington, North Carolina —July, 2000

A gagging dryness in his mouth accompanied a dull throb at the base of Rabbit's skull. From a far away dreamy place, Rabbit remembered being lifted into a car. They had brought him here, where he was afraid.

The abduction was a professional takedown that attracted no notice on the dark waterfront streets. The trap was so well done that it left no escape route. These strange outsiders had taken both Rabbit and the Dancer quietly and without notice or noise.

Rabbit had revived of his own accord in this hollow sounding warehouse, a vacant metal prefab of some sort. While the night still held the heat of the day, Rabbit was chilled and cold. He was naked and tied, spread-eagled, to two of the metal ribs of the structure. His clothes were piled in a heap on the floor off to his right.

Opposite him, just six or seven feet away, hung the Dancer, tied onto what could serve as a heavy frame for a chin-up bar. The Dancer looked a little the worse for wear. There was a deep cut behind and below his left ear that had bled profusely, the blood blending with his sweat. His head lolled against his shoulder and Rabbit had the impression that he was in pain. But pain had never seemed to bother the Dancer. No, pain was an old friend to the bigger of the two black men.

As he came to, Rabbit moaned softly. He had wanted to cry out, but was frightened that if he did it would attract attention to him.

"This one awakens, Abdul," a voice from the gloom said.

In all there were five of them in the abduction team. They now scattered themselves about the interior of the hollow building and were dressed in loose fitting work clothes—blue jeans, T-shirts, the well worn and non-descript uniform of the waterfront. Four of the five men appeared young, between twenty-five and thirty-five and were fit—the fifth, the one they called Abdul, appeared a bit older and a bit heavier than the rest.

"Welcome back, my friend. You were unconscious longer than we expected," the voice said warmly. The statement came from Abdul, the one Dancer had earlier in the evening nicknamed "Levis."

A sudden and terrible urge to urinate overwhelmed his senses. Rabbit managed to slur out the words, "Who and what da fuck you think you doin'?" before rough hands yanked his head sideways by his hair.

"Be still. We will tell you when to speak," a new harsh but accented voice replied.

"Yeah, right. What the fuck is this?" Rabbit asked, trying to assess his surroundings.

"Do not worry. You will understand everything in a short time," the voice continued in a more gentle tone.

Yes, he thought, swallowing another retort. It would be better to be still and maybe this bad dream would go away.

Rabbit's capture had been the more tenuous of the two street abductions. Both finesse and experience had been displayed behind the tap of the sand-filled leather sap that had caressed the nape of his neck. The blackjack patted Rabbit just so, instantly turning his stringy running legs to *Jell-O*. The trunk lines of nerve endings and electrical impulse from brain to muscle were instantly disconnected and Rabbit crashed without ceremony to the concrete pavement. The collision with the harsh stone surface caused several brush burns and bruises. They were colorful and tenderer to the touch than the lingering ache where the blackjack had been applied.

Dancer had offered no resistance. The 9mm automatic that somehow appeared as magic in Abdul's hand was pointed at Dancer's forehead. The declaration in the Arab's suddenly

sober eyes and his very lethal looking expression convinced
the Dancer that resistance would be dumb if not fatal.

They were set up, he and Dancer. Rabbit admired profes-
sionalism. He also respected brute power. To accomplish this
feat on their home turf was no small task because both Rabbit
and Dancer had lived in Wilmington all of their lives and
knew the area as well as they knew their own names. But by
Christ, these guys were both professional and scary.
Nonetheless, neither of the two small-time crooks thought
they were in life threatening danger. That turned out to be a
gross miscalculation.

"Nabil, bring the light closer to the big one," the leader
instructed.

The one named Nabil sat a Coleman lantern on the concrete floor. It hissed and sputtered three feet from Dancer's
trussed-up form. The shadows it cast carved receding hollows
of light and darkness in a circle around the two bound men
and their five captors.

Leroy T. *Rabbit* Walton and Tyrone *Dancer* Benton were
a strange pair. Tyrone had known, protected and intimidated
Rabbit since grade school. The "Rabbit" had once, not so
many years ago, been a star field and track athlete. They had
played on the same high school football team, Dancer as a
defensive lineman, Rabbit as an illusive wide receiver. There
was a time when he'd been considered Olympic material, but
that was before he embraced the needle in his arm as an alternate source of fulfillment.

Dancer was a large solid mass of meat and muscle, a
Goliath. At six foot five and 260 pounds he dwarfed the
diminutive, drug-emaciated Rabbit. Years ago he had been
dubbed the Dancer for his dance after a backfield sack, just as
Rabbit had been tagged with his handle as the result of his
acceleration off the offensive line. Rabbit was thin and wiry,
quick and slippery.

Together, on the field and off, they made a good team. They

seemed to be bound together by the common interests of
pleasure and money. Then, too, they did fill each other's
needs. For Rabbit, Dancer was a protector and bodyguard, a
friend. For the Dancer, Rabbit was an ego builder, a fan club,
a surrogate little brother, a flunky to do his bidding. The
arrangement was a suitable and longstanding pact between
the two men. They combined their meager talents to gain as
much money as possible. Both subscribed to the philosophy
that honest labor was demeaning. They were entitled by birth
to the same things that others worked for—especially if it was
dark and they were unseen.

Each of them had his own peculiar pleasure needs.
Dancer's penchant was an uncontrollable lust for the warm,
wet spot between the legs of any woman he could find, willing or otherwise. Dancer had found many, though not all
were willing until, one way or another, he convinced them.

Rabbit's compulsion, by contrast, was not sex. Rabbit
could have jumped into a barrel full of titties, come out
sucking his thumb, and would not have cared. The smaller
member of the duo took his pleasure from the two hundred
dollar a day habit he had to feed. His drug-induced pleas-
ures, though more compelling, were no less fulfilling than
Dancer's needs.

Rabbit had been hospitalized several times with symptoms
of withdrawal when he couldn't score. His constantly sore,
runny nose testified to a corrosion of nasal tissue from snort-
ing anything he could fit up his nostrils. In truth, there had
been very few drugs that Rabbit had not tried in his twenty-
nine years. The results in his physique were more than painful
and clear. The needle tracks along his forearms and between
his toes had left Rabbit gaunt and wasted. He was a drug con-
noisseur.

Dancer indulged in a little toot now and again or maybe a
taste of smack, but he found by experience that drugs, at least
for him, inhibited sexual performance.

Dat shit don't work for me, man, Dancer had said. Anything that inter-
fered with sex was something that the Dancer just would not tolerate.

Rabbit and Dancer had both suffered pain to satisfy their habits. Once there had been a hot shot, an overdose that almost killed Rabbit. Dancer's experiences, though not as life threatening, were no less traumatic. They came at the hands of jealous husbands or large male relatives of his amorous conquests. Still worse, they came in hot burning urination two or three days after the clap had blossomed. Dancer had no fear of AIDS because, simply, he did not believe that he could catch it.

Together, Rabbit and Dancer had struck upon a modest source of income. They considered themselves "culture merchants"—an unofficial extension to the Chamber of Commerce. They enjoyed the prosperity and growth of the city as much as the city fathers and they offered a "life experience" of robbery and mugging for the inebriated and imprudent. The darkened back of a vacant lot on Market Street was their office.

Confirming that mugging and robbery weren't the easiest ways to make a living, sometimes the victim carried a weapon, at least a knife, and he would become a bit too much to handle—even for the Dancer. It was not an easy living, but it beat manual labor and they extorted sufficient funds to keep well supplied in their dreams of drugs and pussy. The waterfront bars, adult bookstores and massage parlors provided ample environment to practice their style of free enterprise.

Dancer was a salesman who sold vice that he would personalize for any client. Promises and descriptions of uninhibited, big titted women who "could suck a golf ball through a garden hose" were a lure that not many horny seamen passed up. If women didn't suffice, then other attractions, such as a high stakes crapshoot, card game or drugs, served as enticements.

"I can gets you whatever you wants," was the standard pitch the Dancer used, accompanied with a large grin. But the duo would part their patrons from their valuables, often before accommodating the mark's desires. Every once in a while they would pimp for one or another of the street-wise women when it proved to be to their advantage. Those who passed their "office" on Market Street, drunk or alone, were often offered a final opportunity to contribute to the Dancer and Rabbit without prior enticements. No great harm was done and the occasional waterfront strong-arm or robbery casualty or even death was an accepted way of life the world over. But that, of course, was before the Arab.

Bosheer had proven to be the exception. Though painful, Rabbit recalled that night's events.

That evening they had cruised the normal waterfront hangouts of Wilmington, looking for a mark from one of the several ships in port. To find a sailor not in the company of one or more of his shipmates was unusual, but every once in a while, fortune smiled. They had stumbled upon the Arab by accident.

Bosheer had a full eight hours to kill before his scheduled rendezvous with Abdul. He had completed his reconnaissance early. It was the first time he was unsupervised and removed from the safety of his companions. He was an easy score.

"My bro-theer," Dancer had said, approaching the Arab wide armed and grinning. "You lookin' for some action? Den I'm de man."

The Dancer became a new bar friend and suspicion dwindled soon, helped by more than a few drinks. Graphic promises of what Dancer could provide for just a slight commission brought both interest and a smile to the Arab's face. He listened in rapt attention to the crafted scenarios dangled by Dancer.

"I tell you, man, dis pussy I knows can't ever get enough, and she loves Arab men da best," he confided to Bosheer.

The embellished stories were transformed into very creditable lures as the line was dangled before the sixth member of Abdul's team. The Arab wasn't the first man who had let the little head between his legs do the thinking for his big head atop his shoulders. Besides, he had never had a non-Arab woman. The blonde American ones, he had been told, were the best. It was said they were the most creative and uninhibited when it came to sex.

A bit over an hour passed before Dancer gave Rabbit the signal. Rabbit left the bar moving off toward Market Street and the waterfront. The wait was short. The booming voice of Dancer announced their approach to the ambush site. Rabbit listened to the unsteady footsteps of the Arab, accompanied by the footfall of Dancer. He lay close to the sweet smelling, moist earth of the vacant lot, down low behind the forgotten shrubbery and debris. By design, Dancer walked closest to the curb, placing the Arab between the two of them. They were near now.

Rabbit tensed, the spring-loaded five-ounce leather wrapped knot of lead gripped tight in his right fist. The two men passed by, Dancer's right arm encircling the Arab's left shoulder. Rabbit was up and swinging the sap before they were three paces past him. With an arcing swing he tapped the Arab with just the right amount of force in just the right place, but the Arab failed to fall. Instead, he let out a shrill yell and sprinted away, a shot from a cannon. His action was far from expected, and caught the Dancer off-guard. Rabbit was flatfooted and it took him all of five or six seconds to recover. The Arab had already raced fifteen yards down the street and was gaining speed as he headed toward the lighted dock area. Rabbit darted after him. Within a hundred yards he was at the Arab's left hip, positioned a half pace to the rear.

"Heh, heh, gotcha now, suckah," Rabbit giggled to the panting Bosheer. The sap came up and struck again in just the perfect spot between skull and neck. The Arab stumbled, let out a loud groan, recovered his balance somehow, and again staggered forward. They were under the outer bank of lights at the very edge of the pier.

The Arab staggered on. He looked back to see Rabbit's once again rapid closing form. Rabbit held the homemade spring loaded sap chest high in his right hand. It swayed obscenely with each of his pumping strides. As they raced along the edge of the pier, the sap came up once again. The

Arab tripped and went down, at last.

Bosheer remembered the urgent, running thud of feet behind him just as he tripped. He hit the wooden fender of the dock with a thud, hung for a moment, and rolled awkwardly over the side and into the black water twenty feet below. There was a splash and the Arab disappeared. The sudden cold waters that swirled about him, submerging him, carrying him beneath their dark mantle, shocked the terrorist. The chill cut sharply to the warm inner core of his being and sobered him.

Bosheer could not swim, at least not well, and came sputtering to the surface. He tried to call out. A sudden flood of foul water into his mouth smothered his plea. Gagging and sputtering he began to cough, only to take more of the foul tasting water through his nose and down his throat. Struggling, the man felt himself being drawn down into the dark depths. The now soaked navy jacket, heavy layers of shirt and sweater, and faded, thick cord trousers tugged him down. His arms grew heavy and would not respond to his feeble beating attempts to draw his body up to the oily surface. An annoying ache in the back of his head grew stronger with every beat of his racing heart.

Bosheer flailed outward, struggling to find and reach the surface of the river. A thoughtless but frantic attempt to inhale resulted in more cold liquid being sucked into his lungs and stomach. Reflexively his body responded and he began to cough only to increase the desperateness of his situation. Reality burst upon his fogged mind, coming in a clear, quick flash.

This couldn't be happening. It was not Allah's will, not now, not when *Jericho* was so close, he thought.

There was a claustrophobic realization. Overwhelming. Compelling. There was so much at stake and he was suffocating.

"I'm drowning! I'm drowning," he tried to scream.

Bosheer panicked, whipping the water to get to the source of oxygen. So much depended on him. But where was the surface? It was so dark, there was no way to determine which way was up. There was just the overwhelming press and presence of water everywhere.

The roar grew within his head. Bosheer had to think, to keep ahead of the roar; it was hard to concentrate. He pounded at his wet surroundings. The movements of his limbs became more frantic, less coordinated. The ache at the back of his head grew yet stronger, more pronounced, the burning tightness in his chest more acute. The electrical impulses to the muscles of his body began to become confused as his brain called up its last reserves of oxygen. His furious thrashing turned into spasms. The nerve strings frayed and popped. Almost as a final conscious act, Bosheer's unseeing eyes bulged and strained at their sockets. The great muscle in his chest spasmed, thumped, and convulsed. The organ pulsated a final time in erratic staggered beat, straining futilely to full measure, willing the muscles of his lungs and body to respond. And then in unwilling surrender, it stopped.

Bosheer's last thoughts were of Abdul. Abdul would be angry with him.

The Dancer, who arrived a few seconds after the Arab had gone over the side, had not been at all happy.

"Wha's the matta wif you, you dum fuckin' nigg'r!" Dancer howled. "Dat mutha had bread, man, and it was in my pock't and here you done fucked it all up."

Rabbit cringed under Dancer's curses. He ducked and parried the blows Dancer aimed at his the head and shoulders. The outburst by Dancer was brief and the two black men scanned the area, alert for movement, searching the shadows for witnesses to the event. Dancer could not believe his bad luck. It was Rabbit's entire fault and he would later leave some bruises on the addict's bony ribs.

"Let's get the fuck otta here," Dancer instructed, making no attempt to find or rescue Bosheer.

The police picked them up for routine interrogation soon after the body was discovered amid the trash and debris washed along the shore of the harbor. The investigation was *pro forma* and without much interest. The town fathers had neither particular fascination nor interest in the incident. The Dancer, whom other witnesses had placed with the deceased at a bar earlier in the evening, talked some trash, but in the end the police could find no evidence of foul play. The victim had been found with wallet, watch and ring on his body. The slight swelling and bruises behind his left ear discovered during the autopsy were attributed to an unknown object that his head must have struck during his fall.

No charges were lodged and the accidental drowning was obscurely reported on the back pages of The Wilmington Star. The one paragraph story noted that Dancer thought he saw the victim fall from the pier and had been questioned by the police. Dancer clipped the article and carried it folded in his wallet. Dancer said that women always got the hots for the newspaper celebrities. A toothy yellow grin altered the landscape of his countenance as he contemplated the sexual prospects resulting from this notoriety.

"Heh, heh. I sho' nuf' gonna git me some good pussy from this," Dancer told Rabbit as he refolded the clipped article and placed it back in his wallet for the third time in as many hours.

Rabbit didn't believe it but said nothing. No one ever seemed to have the hots for Rabbit, even during the days when his track and field glories routinely had made the papers. But no big thing, Rabbit thought. He was just happy that the newspaper article was recompense enough to make Dancer happy and even forgiving. Rabbit saw no reason to pick at the scab of Dancer's disappointment in the encounter with Bosheer's lost cash. He did, however, comment that lack of public acclaim never before slowed the Dancer down when he went after a slice of damp. It just sorta worked out for him that it was somehow there whenever he wanted it. Only a few days later Abdul entered their lives.

*   *   *

Dancer had come upon him much the way they had

noticed the other Arab—by accident. Still early in what was a slow evening, around ten o'clock, the Dancer had wandered through two bars without any action and had just crossed to the west side of Market Street. Abdul at that moment emerged from the old storefront that housed one of the adult bookstore and peep shows. He looked up and down the street and then sauntered across to McGrady's tavern and entered.

McGrady's is best described as the seediest bar in a worse than bad neighborhood. Even the toughest of sailors recognized the pub as a "no questions asked" Wilmington refuge. The dark, boarded up storefront was close by the Wilmington docks and a convenient place where a lonely sailor might find companionship from one of the two or three well-worn hookers who perched on tattered bar chairs. They would take your money and give you a good dose of the clap—no charge for the clap.

Dancer smelled the money on Abdul.

According to Earl, McGrady's career bartender, Abdul had been in earlier and was already well on the road to a liquor induced forgetfulness.

"Humph. Wher dat suckah bin?" Dancer asked.

"Hell, how am I suppose to know" Earl growled in response. "Do I look like his fuckin' mother?"

"Jus' never seen him 'round befor, that's all," Dancer replied in easy conversation. "Yu getting' lot ah nuw faces in here, Earl. He a nuw regula'r?"

"Nah, said he was from Kitar or Guitar or somethin' like that—wherever in the shit that is. He's lookin' for some action though," Earl replied, as they eyed the medium built, swarthy sailor who sat alone at a table along the wall facing away from the door.

"Got some bread too," Earl concluded, picking at his teeth. For Earl anyone who paid his tab with anything bigger than a twenty had bread.

Armed with his new knowledge, contact by the Dancer had been easy. Before long a fifty-dollar bill was incautiously peeled off a large roll of bills and Rabbit hustled from the bar to lie in wait at the vacant lot.

Rabbit had not heard the two Arabs as they came up behind him nor seen their shadowy movement until the last moment. It had only been with luck and speed that he bolted from their trap. There was no one who could catch Rabbit and he quickly outdistanced the pair. Rabbit turned the corner at full tilt into the alleyway that stretched between Market and Riverside. The third one was waiting for him there.

The six-man cell was a composite of sleeper agents and student immigrants. The team had been activated with orders to assemble at Wilmington, North Carolina. Further instructions were to be provided at that time by Abdul, the team leader who was to arrive from Libya.

Abdul, a member of Salal's cadre team at his Southern Libya training base, owned broad authority to carry out his mission. When the first five members of the six-man cell met upon Abdul's arrival, he briefly outlined their tasks.

"You will gather current and critical intelligence in the local area, provide details on the facilities, photographs, blueprints, the location and strength of local police forces, their capabilities and reaction times," he said.

"Two of you will become members of the workforce at the Sunny Point Military Ocean Terminal. Gather information on the ammunition and explosive storage locations, the roads inside the terminal, the communications, weaknesses and strengths—you will be the eyes and ears of Salal's attack force."

Abdul often repeated the importance of their mission. "What you accomplish is critical to Jericho. Without you there is no chance for success. You will be the on-the-ground guides for the force that will attack Sunny Point and destroy it. Later you will guide your brothers to our other Arab friends who will assist the freedom fighters in their evasion and escape back to the Middle East."

The team worked with due diligence to organize rally points, temporary safe houses and transportation from the area through the clandestine network from Wilmington in the North to Myrtle Beach to the South, to Fayetteville and Lumberton in the West.

At Sunny Point, Nabil became a railway workman and Kirshid an administrative supply clerk. Both of these men were activated sleeper agents who lived in the United States and had no problems in taking on their new identities. Two more members of the cell gained employment with the assistance of forged papers. Trained as a mobile crane operator, Zayed worked at the State Port located in Wilmington and the fourth, Sa'id, a Syrian Arab, as a cab driver within the city. The last man to arrive, Bosheer, traveled to the United States as a deck hand on a Norwegian cargo ship bound for Wilmington, North Carolina among other US port destinations.

Abdul, the sixth member of the cell and its leader, had entered the country on a tourist visa. He'd gone underground upon clearing customs and disappeared from immigration sight. Being both alone and unemployed, Abdul had more time to explore the region and coordinate the intelligence gathering effort. As the sole communications link with Machmued, the second in command, and Salal, their leader, he alone possessed the passwords and communication tools for routing and linking to Salal wherever he was.

Abdul established his base of operations in a rented "safe" house in Caswell Beach, a summertime bedroom community. A modern yuppie adjunct to the staid, unchanged Civil War hamlet of Southport, North Carolina and relatively isolated, this small but popular resort community was close to Sunny Point Military Terminal. No suspicion was aroused in the transit community of summer sun worshipers by Abdul's seasonal arrival nor the late evening comings and goings of swarthy young men who never appeared on the beach.

When Bosheer had not appeared at the designated meeting place, Abdul and the team immediately began to search the waterfront. It had taken only a few hours to learn of the death of a foreign sailor and then two days of discrete inquiry to reconstruct Bosheer's steps. The discovery of his departure from McGrady's with the Dancer was an accident, but put the team back on track.

Abdul said that Dancer would weep before he died.

Dancer just laughed. "Dat gotta be som' kind o joke or sum'thin, you dumb fuck. Ain't gonna happen and you can take it ta the camel fuckin' bank, asshole."

The big one is arrogant but appears brave, but we shall see, Abdul thought.

Neither Rabbit nor Dancer had been impressed. Such talk was an accepted form of street intimidation—a way of projecting image, of just getting over.

At first, Rabbit figured maybe old Dancer had been servicing somebody's stuff and her old man found out. Dancer had a way with the women and had more than once been caught with his pecker in the wrong set of willing female drawers.

So maybe we're in for a thumping, a good ole ass whipping. Shit, I could handle that and so could the Dancer. It wouldn't be the first time, Rabbit silently acknowledged.

But that simple and easy explanation, this time, didn't go down quite right. Somehow, the exaggerated response of these dudes over a little pussy just didn't ring true. Nonetheless Rabbit took refuge in the fact that no one wanted to piss-off the Dancer. *It mays not be righ' away, buts I do gets even,* the Dancer often warned potential adversaries.

Nah, that Abdul guy, he was all jive talk, man. Just talking trash, Rabbit reassured himself. Dancer hadn't been foolin' with any foreign or any white quail in a long time.

Besides man, you don't do no brother just over a little piece of pussy. Maybe you whup up on his ass a little, but you don't do him, the Dancer had told Rabbit on many occasions.

"Deese brothers just ain't got de word d'ats all," Rabbit mouthed silently. "It was jus' a mistake."

Abdul stood in arm's reach between Rabbit and Dancer. He turned to each of them, a look of distaste on his face. He took Dancer's massive head and cupped it between his two hands, forcing Dancer to look into his face.

"Do you believe in God?" Abdul asked in a curious conversational tone in heavily accented English.

"Hey man, what kind of shit is this?" Dancer demanded angrily. "Does you no who you'se fuckin' wif? You donkey shit, moth'r-fuc...."

"Silence."

Abdul left no doubt that he was the leader. The word was enunciated with harsh preciseness. It was a compelling statement, delivered with indisputable authority.

Dancer stopped in mid-sentence. That was bad—and strange. The Dancer was never at a loss for words—especially when he was threatened. Everyone on the street knew that sooner or later the Dancer would get even—one way or another. He had his own way of revenge. Retaliation on the offender's family was not excluded. Parents, wife, sisters, brothers—none were off limits. When it came to getting even, Dancer just expanded the definition of an "eye for an eye" to meet his own personal needs.

Nope, Rabbit thought, nobody fucked with the Dancer.

"Bosheer, whom you killed, believed in God. He should be here with us," Abdul said, as he removed his hands from Dancer's head and quietly patted him on the cheek.

"But," he shrugged and continued, "now he is with Allah."

Abdul turned to look at Rabbit. The man's eyes penetrated through Rabbit's prickled skin.

"Bosheer was a good man," he announced solemnly. "He died at your hands."

Rabbit opened his mouth to protest but before he could form the words Abdul raised his hand as if in judgment.

"Do not deny it. I know this is true. It will be easier for you if you do not lie."

"Do you believe in God?" Abdul again asked. The question was addressed to both of the black men.

Dancer watched impassively as Abdul stared at each of

them in turn. The intensity of his gaze was hypnotic. It penetrated their beings; it shriveled and exposed them—their fears, their greed, their ambitions, their petty tyrannies. It demanded that they focus on Abdul's words, leaving them unable to resist his imperative to answer.

Dancer was the first to recover. He was visibly shaken, but still managed to display his combative attitude.

"You, man! Hey man, you'se fuckin' wif the Dancer an' I'll tear off your fuckin' head and shit in you moth'r fuckin' neck in 'bout 'nother two fuckin' seconds if'n I ain't cut loose outta here, man. Ain't nobody what fucks wif Dancer, man. Who de fuck you think you are? You ain't nothin' but a sand nigger. Dat's what you is man. A fuckin', raghead sand nigger! What is dis fuckin' shit?"

Abdul paid no attention to Dancer's outburst. Nothing of his manner betrayed anything except perhaps a slight annoyance at Dancer's liberal use of obscenity. There was no indication that Dancer intimidated him although he was only half the Dancer's size.

Silence echoed in the cavernous building. Finally Abdul spoke again. "Listen carefully," he said, "I shall not repeat my words a second time. I do not threaten you. I will tell you facts." Abdul spoke in soft tones—deliberately, as if in conversation with a difficult and recalcitrant child who, before being punished, was with patience being told why punishment was necessary. The explanation was that of a long-suffering, involved teacher to a thickheaded student.

"You are at an end. It is time for you to depart this life. It is the will of Allah, just as Bosheer's death was the will of Allah."

The pronouncement of sentence was an indisputable, objective reality—as sure as the sun is a source of warmth and heat.

"We shall be your executioners," Abdul continued, gesturing to the other men of his group. "There is nothing for you to say in this matter. There is nothing to discuss."

The judgment had been rendered. There was to be

no appeal.

For Rabbit, Abdul's voice had taken on an unrealness. He was speaking from a great distance through the hollowness of an empty barrel.

"I gotta pee," Rabbit said inanely, directing his words to Abdul, asking, as a small child would do.

The terrorist on his left laughed and said something to his compatriots in a fluid language, and they then also laughed.

Rabbit was having a hard time focusing; he could not shake the dreaming swim of reality. Everything was speeded up but somehow moved in a thick molasses of slow motion.

Must have rung my bell with that sap, Rabbit concluded distractedly, not wanting to admit to his acute and growing anxiety.

Abdul was talking again. "Before you die, I shall ask you questions. You will answer me with respect and dignity. If you answer well, I will permit you to die quickly, without pain. If you do not, then you will die very slowly, with the whimpering of a child, afraid in the night."

Rabbit, who had been cold, began to sweat profusely. He could smell his own thick fear. The odor of fear seeped from the pores of his body and ran in rivulets down to his groin. He was afraid that they too could smell it.

Dancer put on a good show of not being impressed. He laughed. "Fuck you, asshole. Wen I's loose fum here, you knows I's gonna whup you mutha-fuckin' ass, man. Maybe not today, but it comin' man and it gonna you hurt bad, mutha. 'Fore I'm done wih you, you all is gonna be talkin' with Jesus and dancin' wif Allah, you mutha-fuckers," Dancer blustered.

If Dancer could handle these dudes and wasn't afraid, then maybe it wasn't as tight a box as Rabbit thought.

Dancer's goin' get us out of here—I jus' know it, Rabbit told himself. He began to feel better.

Abdul turned and faced Dancer squarely. The silence between them was thick and heavy as the test of wills between the two began in earnest. With the slightest of nods it became

apparent that Abdul recognized that trying to talk to Dancer
was a lost cause. The only language that the Dancer would
understand was one of action and violence and, perhaps, of
long, deep pain. It was an unspoken communication between
the two of them. Dancer's challenge was taken in full measure
by Abdul, a clash of two strong willed men.

Dancer, in that instant, recognized, indeed knew, that he
would suffer this night. But he would suffer or die on his
terms and the terms would not be dictated to him. That
was the challenge he defiantly grinned to the smaller man
facing him.

Abdul pursed his lips and nodded slightly. He turned and
spoke to one of the four men and spoke in that soft tonal,
songlike language. The words were addressed to Sa'id, the
one who had so expertly taken Rabbit down in the alley. The
words were guttural, but not like German. The language had
a rhythmic quality to it. Rabbit wondered if these men ever
had been in the mosque on Campbell Street where others
seemed to speak in the same language. He wished he knew
what Abdul was saying.

In a half dozen unhurried steps, Sa'id, a good foot shorter than Dancer, crossed to the front of the large black man.
His steps echoed across the hollowness of the building, rising from the concrete floor. Sa'id reached out and gently,
almost lovingly, cupped Dancer's scrotum in his left hand.
A half smile played about his lips as he looked into Dancer's
eyes. Instead of withdrawing, Dancer with obscene intent
thrust his hips and pelvis forward, grinding it toward the
mustached assassin.

Dancer grinned. "Is you goin' give me a hand job o' jus
suck me off, you queer camel humpin' muth'r-fuck'r?"

A large ball of mucus and spittle erupted from Dancer's
throat. It caught Sa'id just above the right eye, running
down into it.

Sa'id did not react. The smaller man smiled and wiped his
face on his shirtsleeve. It was the smile that shook Dancer. He
knew then, at that moment, that this little man was the most

dangerous of the group and understood that there was nothing he could do to prevent the inevitable ... but continue to be defiant.

The assassin gave no warning, no anticipation in his motion, just deliberateness and practiced skill. There was a muffled swish as the nine-inch double-edged *khanjar* dagger slid from its sheath. The little man's right arm cut a short slow arch as it swung to, across, and up through the scrotal sac. The grin of defiance on Dancer's face was replaced with a grotesque mask of sudden, penetrating agony. Dancer roared in pain, not fully comprehending what had happened. The razor edge of the blade sliced with surgical precision through the sac, through the muscles that held the testes in place. It passed through the tubes that carried the semen to the shaft of the penis itself. The second stroke was a flash downward and Dancer's penis skittered across the floor. Blood gushed forth, splattering the assassin's gray cord trousers.

Sa'id made no move to avoid the dark red flow. His eyes never left those of the Dancer, his stroke guided and unerring, drawn as a violin bow across the cords of Dancer's manhood. He had emasculated the Dancer in two swift strokes.

Rabbit watched in horrid, fixed fascination. He wanted to turn away but could not. Sa'id lifted his blood covered hand to Dancer's face to display the soft pulpy flesh which he had dissected, opened his fingers and let pieces of the bloody mass fall to the cement floor. They hit with a wet slopping sound. The assassin smiled broadly as the realization of the mutilation penetrated Dancer's pain numbed brain.

Sa'id then turned to face Rabbit and slowly squeezed the remaining mess between his fingers, turning his hand over to let the remainder of tissue and blood slop to the floor with another soft, plopping splat. Sa'id wiped his bloody hand across the Dancer's chest, his eyes returning to Dancer's, the smile on his face unchanged. Only then did the assassin step back.

A stream of blood poured down the Dancer's quivering legs.

Rabbit was reeling. Shock from what he had witnessed broke over him in a swift wave. It came like a rogue whitecap robbing him of strength and almost consciousness. He struggled and fought to retain his wakefulness. Rabbit heard the sound of moaning that came from the Dancer's throat, the buzzing drone of Abdul's voice. Bloodshot, veined brown eyes bulged from Rabbit's head and he found his lungs were too small to provide enough air for his needs. The dank, musk odor of terror was strong and ripe. It rose from within him. Rabbit needed air—cold air. He was suddenly overwhelmed with an intense desire to lie down on the cool concrete floor and sleep.

God, I'm so tired, he thought. It was the onset of shock, but he did not realize it. But the relief and escape of unconsciousness were not to come. Abdul broke an ammonia capsule beneath Rabbit's nose and forced him to swim back to reality, to the gagging reflexes in his own throat at the sight of Dancer.

The assassin turned to face Rabbit and took two steps towards him. The bloody *khanjar* gripped in his right hand, the left reaching forward toward Rabbit's own shrunken sac. Rabbit could feel himself losing it. His sphincter muscle uncontrollably loosened and he began to soil himself. His mind raced ahead of events and he heard himself screaming at the pain that was yet to come.

Abdul uttered a command and waved the assassin to the side.

"Be still. Be a man, not a child," Abdul commanded Rabbit. The imperative iron demand, delivered with the passive impatience and authority of a father, quelled Rabbit.

"Hey man, please don' do me, man. Please man. I ain't done nothin' man. Please man, please," Rabbit begged as sobs broke from his thin chest.

Dancer groaned softly in the background. Fuck him, thought Rabbit. If it hadn't been for that son-of-a-bitch, I wouldn't be here now.

"Jus' tell me wha' you wants, man. Jus' let me go, man. I ain't done nothin', I swears. I'll do anythin', man. Just keep him 'way from me wif tha' knife, man. Cum'on man, please, man."

A growl tore from the Dancer's throat—a muffled, half animal sound. "Rabbit, shut yur chick'n shit, moth'r fuc'n mouth! Dey's goin' kill you anyway. Fuck'em, Rabbit. Fuck'em. Don't giv'em shit."

It was then Dancer lost it. Tears mixed with sweat and blood rolled from his swollen, shaven skull. It was too much for Rabbit and he too began to weep.

There was an exchange between Abdul and the knife-wielding assassin. Abdul turned to Rabbit.

"Tell me about the Arab you killed last week." The tone was casual, impersonal, and undemanding.

"It was an accident, man. We didn't do nothin'! We jus saw him all drunked up and all, man. We didn' do nothin' to him," replied Rabbit, now wanting the attention which earlier he had tried to elude.

Dancer had stopped his silent weeping and was pulling it all back together.

"You were seen with him earlier in the night. What did you talk about, what was said?"

The question was directed to the Dancer.

Dancer's head hung on his chest, his throat working to clear his mouth of the raw taste of blood. He tried to spit, but was unable. He worked his mouth in silence, seeking time to come up with an answer that would keep the knife and the assassin away from him. In the end he could not.

"Hey, fuck you, man," he rasped.

The assassin moved in a blur. Sa'id drove the point of the knife into Dancer's mouth, behind the teeth, into the hard upper palate forcing the jaws open. Dancer choked, gagged and tried to spit the knife from his bleeding mouth.

"Dey didn' talk 'bout nothin', man. Jus pussy, dat was all, just pussy," interjected Rabbit. Sa'id, on command, withdrew the knife from Dancer's mouth, and stepped back.

"I was ther', man, I knows. Jus' pussy, dat's all dey talk'd 'bout man, dat's da truth, man, I swears."

Abdul studied Rabbit with a new interest and nodded to the assassin.

Rabbit's bulged eyes followed each of Sa'id's moves as he lounged against the frame that supported Dancer's hanging weight. The other three men had not spoken a word through-out the entire proceedings. They formed an involved but dis-interested audience.

"This one, Sa'id, will tell us all we desire to know. Won't you?" Abdul knowingly asked Rabbit.

The interrogation took less than fifteen minutes. There had been questions about money, and cameras, and pic-tures, and who else the Arab might have seen, and what women he had been with through the good graces of Rabbit and Dancer, and how many others had accidents thanks to the two of them. Too soon, thought Rabbit, Abdul finished with the questions.

Bosheer had committed an act of carelessness to become involved with these two, a weakness of the flesh. The two knew nothing of the Arab's mission. But this was the only way that Abdul could be sure. He turned and walked away, down the length of the cavernous room, his hands to the back of his neck. The loss of Bosheer would make his mission more diffi-cult, but it could still be done. He turned and walked back to face his two hostages. Dancer had gone into shock and was still bleeding. The volume of blood from the gaping wounds between his legs continued but had diminished. Abdul was satisfied that the two men knew nothing of the operation. It was time to make an end of this bloody business.

"Kill them both. They can tell us nothing more. Do it quickly, Sa'id, and then dispose of the bodies," he instructed in Arabic. "Use the boat and make sure they are not found. Do not be seen. I will send word to Machmued."

Abdul turned to his two prisoners.

"It is time to meet your God. May he show you the same mercy that you Christians and Jews have shown to my Arab brothers."

Dancer had made a bad mistake spitting on Sa'id. The Arab's passion showed in his pleasure in using the *khanjar*. The pleasure consumed him. I shall have to speak to him about this, Abdul thought absently. Abdul turned to his companions and spoke once more in Arabic, then turned and left the building with two of the five men.

The instructions to Sa'id were enough. They would both disappear in the ocean, in small pieces. But first Sa'id would have his own short pleasure with them. The tracks on the skinny one's arms would find one more puncture from a needle. He would minister to the big one, the one who spat on him.

There was exquisiteness to death and Sa'id had learned to savor it slowly. He turned to the Dancer, his face lit in anticipation. There was wildness to his eyes. Abdul was gone; Sa'id could surrender to the lust. His entry into the world of pain as pleasure had been a graduated exercise. His fascination with death had occurred during his fifteen years of killing, of living in constant fear of being discovered and executed, of privation and torturing, of running from Israeli vengeance, of fleeing from Interpol and, often, from even his brothers in rival factions within the Arab community.

The terrorist was obsessed with death—drawn to it like a flea to a dog. Sa'id was entranced and aroused to watch the light of life fade from another human being's eyes—to know just at that last flicker his victim appeared to see something he could not. Perhaps it was heaven or maybe it was hell. The Arab wasn't sure, but felt there was something at the moment of death that his victims saw.

For Sa'id, observing death was a sexual pleasure, a cathartic experience that had grown in intensity over the years and was now overwhelming. He had a blood lust and derived a sadistic ecstasy from inflicting pain, but had not yet crossed the threshold to total madness. Sa'id could still control the impulses but he knew that each time he killed like this, it became harder.

Disappointed that Dancer had not stayed conscious longer, the knife wielder regretted he could not take his time with this arrogant pig.

Dancer recovered enough to see Sa'id coming for him once again. An expectant glow was in the smile that lit the assassin's face. Dancer could do nothing, could offer no resistance or defiance. Tired and faint, the big man was still not prepared to surrender.

"Fuck'em, fuck y'all," he said to no one in a final act of resistance.

Dancer felt the tickle of the blade's tip as the knife slid across the left nipple of his chest. The cutting edge tormented the furrows between bone and breast muscle but did not break the skin as it traced a thin razor line vertically down the Dancer's rib cage. At the fifth rib, it stopped and to Sa'id's savored delight, reversed course. The tip of the blade bit. Exquisitely the steel gained depth sliding into the muscled tissue between the fourth and fifth rib. The insertion of the blade was deliberate and smooth, horizontal in direction and wheedling almost painlessly into the lung tissue. Bubbled bright red blood began to ooze around the blade. The *khanjar* went deeper.

Sa'id's breathing deepened. The terrorist's respiration came in emotional labored pants, his lips a scant two inches from his victim's face, his eyes intently watching the pupils of Dancer's eyes. Sa'id twisted the blade of the knife in a rasping 60-degree turn as he eased it from Dancer's body. The withdrawal was accompanied with a soft hissing not unlike a tire with a slow leak. Vast foamy quantities of bright red blood bubbled from the expanded wound, coating Dancer's heaving chest and flank. Dancer began to suffocate as more and more of his life's fluid infiltrated into his ruptured lung.

Sa'id quivered with excitement, a huge throbbing erection straining against his trousers. He traced the *khanjar* once again along the ribs, this time deeper, leaving a slice in the dark skin. The blade traveled upward between the protecting fingers of the ribs, sliced through the lung tissue, and came to rest with the point cautiously massaging Dancer's pulsing heart. With deliberate pace, Sa'id eased the point forward, piercing the sac surrounding the heart, penetrating ever so slightly the rubbery muscle of the heart itself. With each pulse beat he fingered the blade a micro-millimeter deeper, savoring the pleasure, anticipating the final rupture of the heart wall, its expanding irreversible final hemorrhage that would bring death. The assassin was in a state of rapture by it and could contain himself no longer. The blade dug deep completely through the heart. As Dancer died Sa'id exploded in cathartic orgasm. The climax spread in a wet stain across the front of Sa'id's blood spattered trousers.

Rabbit looked at what was once Dancer. His remains were somehow shrunken and smaller than what he'd been in life. Rabbit wondered if he would shrink when he died.

Rabbit watched Sa'id, too drained to either cry or offer resistance. The other remaining man, Zayed, the one in the green T-shirt, removed a packet from his left hip pocket. From it he withdrew a ten cc syringe and a small plastic vial of colorless liquid. The vial was filled with pharmaceutical potassium chloride. The EMT trained Arab held the needle of the syringe to it. The needle pierced the rubber gasket of the vial to draw its liquid into the syringe, discounting the labeled warning requiring dilution of the liquid.

"Hold his arm still," Zayed requested as he approached the cringing man.

Sa'id grunted and pinioned Rabbit's left arm. Rabbit did not resist.

Zayed was none too gentle with the probing needle. It took three tries to find and thread the scarred collapsed vein in Rabbit's left arm.

An amateur, thought Rabbit from the sleepy somewhere of shock as he felt the familiar prick of the needle. The plunger slid down the casing of the syringe pumping the liquid into Rabbit's blood stream. Rabbit felt the heat. Molten metal was

coursing through his veins. The pain was unlike any he had
ever felt. Leroy T. Walton tried to scream but the intensity of
his anguish translated only into an eerie silent wail. Sa'id
could see the light in Rabbit's eyes dimming. The glow went
more swiftly than it had from Dancer's eyes. Rabbit convulsed
and seized in a contorted grand mal dance. His body was not
his own. The muscles became locked and rigid, hard as iron,
pulling against one another, trying to rip themselves from his
bones. Suddenly they relaxed; his eyes became flat and empty.
Rabbit's bladder emptied, the raw, strong smell of his urine
filled the air until it was overwhelmed by the odor of his feces
as the sphincter muscle relaxed and the remaining contents of
his rectum slopped to the floor leaving wet brown stains sluic-
ing down his buttocks and legs. Sa'id checked the dying
man's heart. The organ had ceased its beating.

At two-thirty in the morning two fishermen drew up to a
private dock along the Cape Fear River. From the rear of a
nondescript blue Volvo mini-truck they removed a large drum
and muscled it aboard a twenty-seven foot Wellcraft with twin
Evenrude 150 horsepower outboards. They let loose their
mooring lines and departed eastward down the river. Several
miles to the east in the twisting channel of the Cape Fear
River, but still miles short of its entry to the Atlantic, they slid
the barrel over the side into 35 feet of murky dark water. The
drum sank with a splash and a whoosh.

The two men left unseen except by the birds nesting along
the river's edge.

The only interest in the disappearance of Dancer and
Rabbit was by the robbery unit of the Wilmington police
department. They noted a slight decrease in the incidents of
muggings along the waterfront.

Machmued received the message from Abdul with a great
sense of relief. The key to success of Jericho rested entirely on
the element of surprise. The possible compromise of the operation by the suspicious death of a member of the reconnaissance and intelligence team was a matter of grave concern. If

security had been breached, it was vital that they know how badly the operation had been compromised.

It seemed, Machmued thought, that his life as an Arab nationalist had always been one of concern and worry, of looking back over his shoulder. The road had been a long and tortured one from then to now. Machmued's thoughts traveled back over the years to his own coming of age, to that first major operation when he was a young man – a few short years and a thousand lifetimes ago.

2

The Negev Desert, Israel
—Late August, 2000

Lieutenant Colonel Matthew Gannon, US Army, shielded the lens of his wide angled 8X40 binoculars and watched from the defilade position, which hid the Israeli V-100 wheeled light armor vehicle. The whip antennas mounted to the hull of the low profile carrier were all that could be seen above the horizon. The late summer heat of the Negev was oppressive and at its peak for the day.

"Here they come," he remarked to his host.

Dov Itshaki raised his glasses and looked to the southwestern horizon. Three converging shimmering plumes of dust five to six miles distant were the only indication of the movement of the first elements of the Israel armored formations. They rushed across the Negev desert in open online battle formation.

"I'm impressed, Dov. They've done a good job in moving from defense to offense. Moving to regain contact with an enemy force can be a dicey operation," Matt observed. The comment was based on LTC Gannon's own experiences. Matt was impressed by the rapidity with which the Red Force moved from the static and defensive position they had held just a few hours earlier.

"Yes. Now we'll see what they have learned," Dov responded to the Multinational Forces Observer and friend.

Matt was eager to volunteer for the observation assignment and pleased to be able to witness the exercise accompanying the Blue Forces. They were under the command of Colonel Dov Itshaki, a once US military interchange student. Matt and he had met and become friends a few years earlier when they were classmates at the Fort Leavenworth

Command and General Staff College.

Dov's reinforced infantry-armor battalion had been successful in breaking contact from engagement twelve hours
earlier in the exercise. Now the Red Forces were racing to re-
engage and prevent Dov from establishing a solid line of
defense. The seeming invulnerability of an onward closing
armored force has its own demoralizing effect. Matt knew of
which he spoke, having commanded a tank company in the
Third Armored Division as it had chased Saddam's vaunted
Republican Guards across the northwestern reaches of Iraq.

The Israeli Defense Force, the IDF, had come a long way
since its inception with the creation of the state of Israel.

"What a change eh, Matthew, since those first days when
our tanks were nothing but buses with some bolted scrap
armor plates?" Dov asked, sparing a quick glance at his friend.

"I'm sure it's been a long, tough road," Matt replied.
"The IDF has become a world class fighting force since those
first few years."

*We recognized in '48 the danger of dependence on foreign
sources for defensive armaments,* Dov had explained during a
pre-exercise briefing, *so Israel moved as fast as we could to
establish our own military armaments. We borrowed, modified,
created and in some cases, just stole whatever technological
advancements we could use to improve our defensive force capability.*

Eventually, Dov had continued, *our capability evolved from
an essential cottage industry in the 1950's to the multi-billion
dollar complexes of Israel Military Industries Slavin, Israel
Aircraft Industries, El-Op Industries Ltd., Soltam, Ltd. and
Elbit Systems. Now we also have a host of indigenous modern
arms producing and supporting manufacturing efforts. We still
need help, but we are no longer the beggars of outdated, cast-off
equipments.*

"You're up against a pretty aggressive commander over
there," Matt remarked, looking across the flat expanse of
desert. "And his machines are a hellava leap over the old

M60's we've both bounced around in," he added as he turned and grinned to his companion.

The Red Force consisted of a newly activated armour battalion. The exercise in which they were engaged concluded the battalion's final field work-up trials, before being added to the standing IDF. They had done well in the defensive phase of the exercise and the commander had become a bit cocky as a result of his success.

"There is more to being a good commander than just being aggressive," Dov acknowledged with a smile. "Watch and learn my friend. Perhaps we can teach you some Israeli tactics."

Dov Itshaki was an acknowledged master in the art of defense and well schooled in the art of tactical warfare. The Blue Force battalion task force was arrayed for a classic trap.

My defense will be based on Soviet Airland Battle Doctrine, he had earlier explained to Matt. *My goal is to construct a deceptive defensive labyrinth that destroys the enemy's equipment and disrupts his offensive timing while exhausting and bleeding his formations.*

To the Soviets and to the Israeli Colonel Blue Forces commander, the defensive battle is a battle of attrition. Defense, to Dov, was a temporary measure marked by a stubborn insistence not to give ground and by an accelerating tempo of continual fire to inflict heavy losses on the enemy.

I will construct a 'fire sac,' Dov had explained earlier, pointing out the defensive area on his tactical map. *We will make it about five or six kilometers wide and four or so kilometers deep. The wadi here*, he had continued, jabbing at the dried riverbed on the chart, *will be at its center. We will lure the Red Force into us.*

Itshaki had picked his ground with an experienced tactician's eye.

Well back from the edges of the ravine, and on what little high ground existed, Dov deployed almost all of his battalion's Sabra MkII tanks in a 270-degree arc. Dozer blades, mounted on four of the tanks, had dug hull defilade positions as close to 2,000 meters to the ill-defined edges of the oasis. The sloped glacis plate turret silhouettes of the Sabra MkIIs were well broken and concealed. As targets, their profiles melted into the terrain and were reduced. Two platoons, eight tanks, he held two kilometers back on the left flank of the wadi, hidden in the dry bed of an ancient river that paralleled and protected that flank from envelopment.

From their hasty but well-camouflaged fixed positions, Itshaki knew that his tanks, with deliberate firing, could defeat two to three times his own number. The main guns of Dov's dug-in Sabra MkII tank force were but scant inches from the sandy earth and left little room for downward deflection, but they retained their elevation capability so as to deliver deeper range, plunging fire to the rear of the attacking formations. They also retained a 360-degree traverse capability that gave them optional flanking fire. Little could be done about the position signature resultant from the displaced cloud of sand and debris from the muzzle blast of the 120mm tube.

By then, Matthew, Dov had reasoned, *it should be of little consequence. The surprise of the ambush will remedy any disadvantage.*

Dragon Anti-Tank Guided Missiles, or ATGM's, and wire guided TOW anti-tank missiles were echeloned between five hundred and three thousand meters in front of, between, and behind the dug-in tanks, and thickened the defensive position.

The Red Force rushed on, the distant dusty plumes now more distinct as the tracks of the tanks churned through the dry rocky and sandy soil.

The Red Force outclassed Dov's force of earlier generation tanks. The Red Force commander was equipped with the new Merkava MkIII Main Battle Tank. This third generation of the Israeli designed and manufactured tank was the pride of the Israel arms industry. As an armored vehicle it is on a capability par with the latest M1A2 Abrams tank of the United States.

Israeli tank commanders called for a design to improve

survivability and the Merkava incorporates the latest concepts
of modular spaced armor into its manufacture. Spaced armor
provides an open area between two layers of composite material to dissipate the energy of an anti-tank weapon. The mod-
ularity feature permits quick field replacement of damaged
sections. A unique forward-mounted 1,200 hp diesel engine
acts as additional armor.

An advanced fire control system provides the newest IDF
tank with the ability to engage moving targets while on the
move itself. Fitted with a very capable day/night stabilized
panoramic sight, the Merkava has a hunter/killer capability.

The 1,200 hp air-cooled diesel Teledyne engine gives the
MkIII's fifty-one ton weight a top speed of over 40-mph. A
positive air pressure environmental control internal filtration
system conveys a defense against Nuclear, Biological and
Chemical, or NBC, weaponry.

In short, it was a world-class tank that brought the latest
designs of 120mm gun technology, three 7.62 light machine
guns, a 12.7mm machine gun and a 60mm mortar system to
the battlefield in a highly survivable package.

"There's no doubt about it, Dov," Matt said, musing as he
watched the approaching force, "there's nothing like the
shock power of an armored force comin' at you to pucker
your ass."

They could now make out the distinct silhouettes of two
of the Merkava tanks in the battalion scout element, accompanied by a trailing vee formation of three older M-113
Armored Personnel Carriers. Matt watched as two of Dov's
Sabra MkII's moved to take up overwatch positions on the
flanks of the wadi's beaten path, their 120mm main guns and
coaxial mounted 7.62mm machine guns swinging obliquely
to cover the immediate exit routes. The lead elements of the
center armor company of the Red Force, with its cross-
attached infantry component, closed on the scouts and were
moving unopposed well inside the throat of the ambush.

Itshaki had drawn the center out from the onrushing Red
Forces by creating an illusion of confusion and disarrayed

retreat with his own covering forces. Dov's opposite number took the bait and assessed the oasis as a seam between two defending units, an ill-defended gap that served as a possible coordinating point in a hastily constructed defensive line. The Red Force commander saw the wadi as a natural high-speed avenue of approach by which he could rupture the defensive line. Once through the breach, he would pivot his forces and exploit the advantage by piecemealing the destruction of the Blue Forces ruptured line of defense while destroying the blue command's logistic, control, and communication centers. Rightly, the oncoming force relied on the Merkava's inherent offensive advantages—superior armor and speed, its on-the-move 120mm firing capability, and the incorporated technology of an advanced fire control system.

But in the areas of force cohesion, training, skill, and actual combat experience to the rapidly changing conditions of combat, Dov Itshaki had the clear advantage.

The Merkavas' attacked three companies abreast with the command and logistics elements in trail striking for the weak seam, centered on the wadi. Little of its combat power was kept in reserve, the commander opting for the shock action of maximum power forward.

As they swept closer to the oasis the ground became broken and uneven. The right flank company of the attacking force found itself pinched against abrupt soft-bottomed sand washes that slowed its coordinated advance with the center tank company. The left flank company meanwhile had raced into a labyrinth of well placed mine fields. The umpires ruled four tanks disabled and it cost valuable time before the company could reorganize and bring flails, rollers and other mine clearing gear forward to extricate themselves.

As planned, the Red Forces were being slowed, channeled, and attrited even before making contact with the main line of resistance. The attack was losing some of its momentum even while the center company—still unmolested—continued in the lead, outrunning its flanking units and distancing itself from its follow-on supporting forces. Matt watched the disintegrating coordination of the Red Force attack as the Blue Force commander lifted his radio handset to his lips and spoke.

"Gideon One," he said, using the radio call sign for the two platoon mobile defense and counter attack force, "Esther now." 'Esther now' was Dov's two-word command. The coded message directed the receiving commander to commence movement to the left flank of main line of engagement.

Matt waited and watched the approaching force. It seemed only a few moments had passed before Itshaki again spoke into the microphone.

"Gideon, Gideon," he called across the battalion's command and control network. "Execute," he said.

The wadi ravine exploded in simulated munitions firing from the camouflaged positions on three sides of the exposed armor formations, taking the center company of the attacking forces by complete surprise at point blank ranges. Sensors—attached to the hulls of the vehicles and the web gear of the individual infantry soldiers—began their shrill beeping tones designating a hit and rendering the vehicle or player out of action. The umpires threw red smoke grenades on the chassis of the simulated destroyed tanks.

The commander of the company on the right flank saw with alarm the rapid engagement of the center company. The inexperienced young officer assessed the situation and made a tactical decision. Unfortunately, it was the wrong decision.

The attacking tanks positioned on the right flank of the ambush buttoned up. The company pivoted to their left so as to attack, in echelon, thus rejoining and bringing relief to the now stalled and rapidly being destroyed center company. The maneuver exposed the attacker's flank to the line of Itshaki's two mobile platoons, which had advanced up the riverbed at the "Execute" command. They appeared from their defilade position at a point behind and on the flank of the wheeling Red Force company.

With visibility reduced, the buttoned up Red Force never

saw the perfectly executed tank sweep coming from its right until it was too late. The two platoons caught the Red Force focused on the battle to their left front, off guard. The Blue Force tanks, at less than half the strength of its opponent, punched through the misoriented wheeling Red Force like a scythe, leaving 70 percent of its strength assessed as destroyed with no losses to themselves.

In fewer than fifteen minutes, the Red Force reinforced armor battalion had been better than two-thirds destroyed. The defense had turned the Red Force attack into a turkey shoot. The defending Blue Forces had eight tanks amongst the soft rear of their enemy's command and logistics elements and were about to engage the one remaining company of the attacking force, forcing it back into the minefield from which it had just emerged. At this point the umpires called a halt to the exercise.

Matt turned to his counterpart and smiled. The Red Force commander had reacted exactly as Matt would have in his position. It had been a learning experience.

"Well done, Dov."

Dov Itshaki turned and shrugged, not, Matt thought, without a slight degree of smugness.

"They ran to the sound of the guns," he said simply. "One man's audacity is another's foolishness. It is a common mistake and a fine line. They learn, so it is a valuable exercise for all of us."

The exercise critique that Matt attended wrapped up his official duties as part of the Multinational Forces. Returning to the MFO Northern base camp at El Gorah in the Sinai, Matt rendered a brief oral report on the exercise to his boss, a three star Norwegian general who commanded the international force.

Over the fifteen months he served in the Sinai, Matt developed a broad network of friends from the thirteen nations that composed the Camp David Accords force. Each of the nations brought unique skills and methodologies to the desert peacekeeping mission and he benefited in being able to build on the knowledge he had acquired during Desert Storm. His now greater exposure to the planning side of combined and coalition operations, as well as sensitive political negotiations in dealing with the Egyptian and Israeli governments, gave him a new respect for what went into making the Desert Storm coalition a success.

Matt was well received in the Multinational Force and developed close ties and warm friendships in both the Israeli and Egyptian camps.

Matt had been told there was a magic about this Sinai desert. There was, and it could not be explained. The solitude, the silence and vast empty beauty of the desert, its different rhythm of life, had brought about an evolution in his thoughts and actions.

The year had given him the time to sort through his life—to redefine and see better who he was, where he was going, what he was all about. He had come to know himself better and was more tranquil and at rest, more mature and more accepting—less rapid to jump to conclusions and to judge.

Maybe it's just a function of age, he thought. Maybe I'm just beginning to mellow. Too bad it's taken so long.

His one-year tour had been extended to fifteen months after the Force Commander made a personal request to the US Army Chief of Staff. But now it was time to move on. He found himself both anxious and reluctant to depart. The command selection board was meeting and he hoped for a shot at command of an armor battalion, perhaps at Fort Hood. A bit senior as a Lieutenant Colonel for another battalion sized command assignment, he had a good record. Promotion and future command at the brigade or group level were reasonable expectations.

At Ben Gurion airport, 12 miles southeast of Tel Aviv, he caught the TWA flight to New York, via Paris, then Delta to Atlanta and continuing to his final destination of Melbourne, Florida. There he was scheduled for three weeks of leave

prior to reporting to his yet to be announced new assignment. The fact that Matt had not yet received orders to his
new duty station was unusual. Successive assignments were
announced, as a general rule, six to eight weeks in advance of
new postings. The three-month extension of his one-year
tour in the Sinai, Matt knew, had knocked his slated assignment into a cocked hat.

The Boeing 727 commuter from Atlanta to Melbourne
International Airport nosed down into the afternoon haze
that hung in the September sky. The shimmering sun bur-
nished the starboard wing as the plane began its final lazy turn
to line up with the tarmac of the runway. The swaying palms
of Florida passed beneath the belly of the aircraft and the
brick and concrete of the terminal buildings slid past to the
left, reaching for the descending airplane.

Matt Gannon squeezed at the bridge of his nose and
scrubbed at the grit he felt under his eyelids. The sixteen
hours from Tel Aviv in the cramped economy class seats had
been tedious. Rarely had he been able to sleep on a plane.

As a rule most members of the US Armed Forces do not
travel in uniform on international flights. Matt avoided trav-
eling in uniform—even on domestic flights—whenever possible, preferring the relaxed comfort of an open collared shirt
and stonewashed soft blue jeans to the more conspicuous and
less comfortable requirements of a uniform. Air travel did not
enhance one's appearance nor contribute to setting an example to the trainee graduates who populate most major airports
enroute to first or new duty stations.

While Matt had taken the habit of casual dress, his general demeanor contradicted the image of his attire. His off-
handed manner and clothing style did not disguise his natural Type A personality. Under the exterior veneer of calm
casualness was a spring-loaded energy searching for a direction of release.

The still young Lieutenant Colonel was built on a five foot
eleven inch frame, albeit having been put together a bit

wrong. The muscles of his upper body had been designed for a shorter man. Nonetheless he carried his one hundred nine-ty-two pounds well, distributed across broad shoulders, a modest waist, athletic narrow hips and strong, heavy thighs and legs. The true strength of Matt's body was focused in his lower torso. The dimension and development of the muscles in his legs and hips would have well served a two hundred and thirty or two hundred and forty pound man. The meat and strength of muscle to drive and smash forward on the short yardage downs was evident.

Matt had thought about football during college but had been declared too small for varsity play. He'd been cut during the first week of tryouts for the defensive line, and was just too slow for the backfield. This was not a great disappoint-ment, for the fact was that his was a passing interest, a pedes-trian addiction to the game. The college years witnessed his athletic prowess to the friendlier strife and mayhem of the intramural fields.

That had been a long time ago, he thought.

All in all, he had worn well. Age wise, he could still pass for five or maybe even six years younger than his actual age. Of course, that was with the assistance of a soft light that did not betray the thickening web of crowsfeet around the corners of his eyes. Overall he was, at thirty-seven years of age, in better physical shape than most of his college classmates. He could and usually did hold the pace with troops ten to fourteen years his junior during the more vigorous morning runs and physical training drills. Matt reluctantly admitted though, that he had slowed a pace or two, and had begun to feel the effects of fifteen years of field soldiering. Still healthy, active and in his prime, he realistically acknowledged that the best years would soon be past.

During Desert Storm, he had taken three pieces of shrap-nel around his knee and the lateral muscles of his right hip. The pain reminded him of his frail humanity; the ache, a gauge of his aliveness. A regime of thrice-weekly racquetball became a thing of the past due to the increasing numbness in the leg and swelling of the knee. The three to five mile daily runs were now a bit slower, but they were still continued as part of his personal fitness program.

The fair Gannon coloring was a legacy of his Irish heritage but years of exposure to the sun and wind had deepened the pigmentation of his skin. The healthy bronze of arms, neck, and face marked Matt as one of those who preferred an out-of-doors existence to an air-conditioned office. The sun had also bleached lighter blond tones into his thick brown hair that was clipped short in the traditional Army style. Some premature gray, he noticed, was beginning to sprout and creeping into the lower reaches around his temples. Still, the cowlick that defied the occasional comb and the comma of hair that escaped to rest somewhere closer to the right eyebrow continued to convey a bit of youthful vigor.

Matt Gannon was satisfied and contented in what had been the pattern of his life. While several of his college classmates were well on their way to amassing all the trappings of success, he was nonetheless contented without all the signs of great visible wealth. His choice was to become a professional soldier; he had no envy for those who had taken different paths. Still, the choice to wear a uniform was not all peaches and cream. There had been many lonely moments and more than one second thought as to his choice. Loneliness and hardship, realities of a soldier's life, just somehow went with the turf.

Passed from his parents and even their parents were hereditary gifts that included a bright mind and a gift for detail. The glib tongue associated with his Irish father's ancestry was not Matt's forte. In contests of banter and repartee, he preferred an observer rather than a participant's role. That was not to say that he was not without a well developed if non-specific charm. When he focused the full range of attention on a specific woman, it could and—indeed on occasion—had led to an exhausting night of physical give and take that left the object of his consideration worn, weak, and quite satisfied. But those times had been infrequent and very selective.

The cabin caught a shadow from the banking wing and

chased a ray of sun in a circle about the interior bulkheads as the Boeing tilted and completed the turn onto its final approach. A single chime issued from the public address system and the "Fasten Seat Belt" signs lit up. Matt stretched, gave a shuddering yawn, and extended his legs as best he could, given the confines of the seat. His body acknowledged the ache of being in one position too long. He levered the narrow, uncomfortable seat upright.

From the small window two seats to his left, he saw the interstate traffic easing off to the east. The taste of stale food and unbrushed teeth crept along the edges of his mouth. His face was stubbled by a day's growth of beard and his eyes felt gritty and irritated from the prolonged exposure to the closed atmospheres of pressurized airplanes. Somewhere over the Atlantic the dryness of his sinus evolved into a throbbing headache that now pierced the sockets of his skull. Discomfort, while not apparent, hovered about his person with the same irritation of a pair of tight fitting jockey shorts.

Customs clearance had taken place on landing in New York, the first United States port of call. The customs clearance line Matt selected, while the shortest, proved to be the longest. The customs officer exercised his powers of meticulous search in the luggage of a rather attractive Israeli tourist. Matt lost patience and switched to a faster moving line, only in doing so, he attracted the attention of one of the floor men who mistook his impatience for nervous anxiety. The subsequent review of his luggage and person became reason for more delay.

Released from the customs hall, Matt manhandled his two heavy grips, the folding suit bag and the ever-present briefcase through the isolation area and into the noise and bustle of the unrestricted section of the New York terminal to find the gate for his onward flight to Atlanta.

Fifteen months ago the Pentagon was home. Four years had been consumed on that tour of duty—two on the Army Staff and then two with the Organization for the Joint Chiefs of Staff or JCS as it was called. Being the junior J4 Logistics member of the JCS Crisis Action Team, or CAT, was demanding duty.

In today's Army, officers were required to be competent in at least two specialties. Matt's primary qualification was in armor and his secondary in transportation and logistics. The two seemed to him to fit together and he had as much logistics experience as time in an armor unit. Consequently, as a lieutenant colonel he was qualified to command at battalion level in either of the two type organizations. His duties as a logistical planner on the CAT had brought him back into contact with General Brandt. Unknown to Matt, Brandt had been watching the young officer, whom he had first met as a senior Captain when Matt had commanded a company of M1A1 Abrams tanks during Desert Storm.

Matt was a cynic. Perhaps the tendency to discount good intention had always been a part of his nature, but it had grown in leaps and bounds with his CAT experience. His exposures on the CAT had given him insight to the decision-makers in the Department of Defense—the flag officers and presidential appointees who from great distance made the decisions that were life or death to the field soldier. The loss of innocence reinforced Matt's cynicism. With few exceptions, it seemed the more authority and power, the more petty, jealous and self-absorbed one became; and, ultimately, the faster and harder came the fall from grace. Clinton and his crew in the White House proved that point as did, he thought, several of his peers and superiors who pandered principle and honor for a shot at a star. Heroic or honorable figures that would sacrifice self-interest for the good of the whole were too few in number.

Brandt was one the few.

From General Brandt's commitment to "Duty, Honor, Country," Matt Gannon learned – and in his learning, gained both respect and admiration for the man. Matt placed great store in words of strong meaning, such as friend, promise, trust, love, and used them with caution so as not to dilute their significance by casual abuse.

With the few who were called friend, there was the realization that honesty and total candor were essential parts of the relationship. As these were immutable virtues to him, Matt was cautious in accepting these obligations. In friendship, there were no shortcuts and the commitment, once given, was total and irrevocable. These promises did not diminish with time or distance or age but, in their mellowing, only grew.

These qualities, which factored into his success as an officer, were the same causes for the destruction of his marriage some nine years earlier. For him it had become too much to accept cadre assignments and watch men four and five years younger than himself march off to "see the elephant" of combat. Not content to be left behind, Matt sought out the tough and dangerous assignments as much as he could. Normally they were *hardship* or solo tours and the toll on his marriage mounted swiftly.

As a matter of due course, the "gunslingers" of the MFO Peacekeeping Force at first took for granted that fuel, food and water would always be there—just crank up the requirement and the logistics types would make it happen. Matt smiled to himself at the rude awaking they all, including himself, had undergone during Desert Storm. Both the company he had commanded and his parent battalion outran their logistics supply line. Chasing the Republican Guards, they found themselves 150 miles out in an unforgiving desert with re-supply birds grounded by sand storms and ground visibility and navigation an impossibility for their logistics trains. Vast expanses of desert, nothingness and unrelenting heat, broke men down.

There was no difference in the Sinai where the sand and wind daily scoured the war machines on patrol in the peacekeeping missions. Fatigue was rapid for both men and working metal parts. The learning experience for some came slowly, just as it had in Desert Storm, but an appreciation for expecting the unexpected and a respect for the adversary called nature did develop. Some even learned the importance of the supporting logistics tail to which they were bound. The peacekeepers learned valued combat lessons, and unlike some of their counterparts in Iraq, they did not die learning them.

While in the Sinai, Matt experimented with a few new ideas in arraying logistics support to the forces which were scattered over 200 square miles in the desert of the North Sinai and the mountains of the southern Sinai. Some worked and some didn't. Relearning the construction and delicacy of a fragile, easily interdicted supply line in a hostile environment was a challenging and worthwhile task. The lack of "experts" pontificating on procedures, requirements, and regulations, as well as the absence of petty bureaucrats to enforce them, was revitalizing. Matt's fifteen month sabbatical as a field logistician with the MFO peacekeeping force was rewarding—both personally and professionally.

There hadn't been much of a social life in the Sinai. Only a very, very few were permitted within the inner circle that truly knew him. Since his very short marriage and more abrupt divorce he'd successfully avoided serious romantic entanglements by melting away at the first signs of danger. Nobody got hurt – no foul, no penalty.

But that was before Megan.

3
Gander, Newfoundland
—December 12, 1985

Machmued wrung his hands, blew on his fingertips and stomped his numbed feet as he looked back through the dissipating gloom.

"To be a member of the elite *fedayeen* is not without sacrifice," he reminded himself.

He felt the blasts of frigid cold sweep down upon him and longed for the heat of the wasteland sand, the warmth of a fire in the quiet desert night. The arctic December winds spilled down from Newfoundland's surrounding slopes with the same chill endured by the Norsemen who explored these remote Atlantic reaches a thousand years earlier. The black shadows of night paled in retreat before the approaching dawn. An eastern morning sun penetrated the heavy fog, lifting the pearl gray blanket from over the landscape. Daylight hours were short in these northern reaches during the winter season.

Machmued stood beside a dirty yellow Volvo sedan, its engine ticking, a thin plume of vapor emitting from its exhaust. He huddled against the side of the car seeking relief from its weak shelter. The young Arab had been on other missions in Lebanon and Israel, but this was his first so far from his Middle East homeland. But the worst was now past and soon he would be back in the desert.

Gander was a young town of the air age with roots dating back only to the early 1950's. This aerial waypoint gained importance after World War II when aviation assumed a wider role in international travel. The air terminal itself found its beginnings as a strategic staging base used by the Royal Air

Force Ferry Command during the war.

Gander lacked many of Newfoundland's customs and dialects; tourism was a major contributor to its economic growth. Indeed, it was these considerations that enabled the terrorist team to blend into their surroundings without suspicion.

Five hundred feet above sea level, the winds scoured Gander's International Air Terminal and the plateau which held its two all-weather runways. The DC-8 about to taxi this early December morning was returning 248 men and women, each a soldier, to their Fort Campbell, Kentucky home. They had just concluded six long months of isolated peacekeeping duty in the southern reaches of the blistering Sinai desert.

The Sinai had been harsh and unrelentingly boring duty. The tiresome and monotonous work took its toll on the entire battalion. The offensive posture and spirit of the battalion eroded over the six months—compromised by yet another non-combat peacekeeping and observation mission.

The unit was scattered across an area of operations that ranged over more than 200 miles of rugged southern Sinai mountains and desert. Deployed to isolated platoon and squad sized observation outposts, many accessible only by helicopter, combat skills had rusted and routines of garrison life had corrupted initiative. Void of rigorous training schedules and demanding warfighting exercises, which were hallmarks of the elite US XVIII Airborne Corps, the cohesiveness of the battalion was compromised. The Third Battalion, Five Hundred and Second Infantry no longer held the sharp edge of an elite "quick reaction" Army unit. The time had come for the "Screaming Eagles" of the 101st Division to return to the United States to renew and rehone their rusted fighting skills.

Despite Gander's high percentage of weather reliability, the Sinai flight had been delayed. The crew of eight—pilot, co-pilot, engineer and five flight attendants—was anxious to leave this alien place. Prolonged sub-zero temperatures brought by the arctic winds caused a crack in one of the trunk lines of the terminal's hydrant fueling system. Repair of the line had taken three hours and delayed refueling. During the delay, a crystal icy rime had etched body and wingspan of the silent aircraft. Now, the whine of the DC-8's idling engines testified to the completion of the transfer of 2,300 gallons of JP-5 jet fuel to the plane's cavernous tanks. The aircraft nudged the upper limits of its designed maximum 355,000 pounds take-off weight.

The Arrow Airlines plane was an older version of the DC-8. Built in 1963, it was one of the 556 copies produced by the Douglas Airplane Company since the DC-8's first commercial flights in 1955. The plane's range and capacity made it a popular international carrier and this specific plane had seen extensive service on the transpolar route to Vietnam.

"Gander Tower, Arrow 1285 Heavy. Ready for taxi," the pilot requested in the curious jargon of aviators and air traffic controllers.

"Arrow 1285 Heavy, taxi to runway 22, winds 270 at 20, gusts to 40, altimeter 2992."

"Arrow 1285 Heavy, roger, taxi to runway 22," the pilot replied, acknowledging and repeating the instruction.

The raw power from the four big Rolls Royce CFM56-2-C5 turbofan engines spun into a roaring crescendo of noise. Matching vertices of horizontal snow swirled behind each of the engines as the DC-8 inched down the taxiway, stopping just short of the final turn onto the active runway.

"Whatta you think Jerry?" the pilot asked, twisting to face his companion in the right hand seat.

The co-pilot finished the ritual of completing the cockpit departure checklist, turned and gave the pilot a thumbs up.

"Engineer?"

"Good to go," he spoke into the intercom. "Everything's in the green, skipper. Let's do it."

"Tower, Arrow 1285 Heavy. Ready for take off."

"Arrow 1285 Heavy, after departure squawk 3710, turn

right heading 330, climb and maintain 5,000 feet and contact departure control on 126.5," came the tower's response.

"Roger, Arrow 1285 Heavy, climb 5,000 feet, squawk 3710, turn right heading 330, climb and maintain 5,000 feet and contact departure control on 126.5l. Request departure clearance."

"Arrow 1285 Heavy, wind 220 at 15 gusts to 25, cleared for takeoff. You are only traffic within a six zero mile radius. Have a safe trip," came the tower's crackled response.

Lumbering in graceless movement onto the 200-foot wide runway, the hard rubber tires of the tricycle gear squeaked forward over the frozen pavement. The nose-mounted radar pointed itself into the funnel of wind and gloomy fog shrouded runway. The entire fuselage trembled as it came to a full stop and the pilot set the brakes. The pilot scanned the instruments and pressed the radio transmit switch.

"Gander tower, Arrow 1285 Heavy rolling. Have a good day, Gander."

The cell of dispersed terrorists watched the DC-8 move along the taxiway toward its departure. *Fedayeen* strike teams such as this one were normally larger, but only three men, it was decided, were needed for this mission. The men were dispatched at staggered intervals to rendezvous in Newfoundland. They spaced their arrival over a total period of two months; the last two men, Machmued and Khleed, arrived three weeks apart. It was a well-educated team. They were fluent speaking in their native Arabic, but also comfortable speaking English, Hebrew and French. Expert in explosives, small arms and covert intelligence, they had cross-trained so that all could perform the tasks required of either of the other two. Each had already proven he was a dedicated Pan-Arab nationalist.

Compulsively, Machmued slid his hand into the deep slash side pocket of his parka for the fourth time in as many minutes. He again fingered the small, square black plastic housing of the miniature radio transmitter. The bomb—such as it was—was dual triggered. The primary trigger was a short range, extremely low radio signal, a prototype circuitry much akin in design to those used in the infantile cellular phone industry. The backup trigger was a mercury switch coupled to a miniaturized digital altimeter. The device was actually molded into the body of the plastic explosive itself.

Machmued looked over his shoulder seeking reassurance from the outlined form of Jahbad, the team leader, on the observation deck of the terminal. Jahbad was turned from him, facing the runway.

The pilot eased the throttles forward and felt the solid power of the four engines as they each spun up to the 2,200 pounds of thrust. He released the brakes and the tires began their rhythmic thudding, chattering charge down the glazed, concrete runway. The plane took almost the full length of the pavement in its takeoff roll before the pilot began his transition to flight and rotated the aircraft skyward. The nose gear slowly lifted off of the crusted surface and moments later, at the ten thousand-foot markers, the main gear unstuck and the earth began to drop away. It was as if a giant hand grabbed the aluminum canister and cast it with smooth certainty into the sky.

Jahbad had personally selected Machmued for this mission. Machmued was a young man, in fact, the youngest member of the team, passing his twenty-third birthday only two months earlier. Machmued's breathing was slow and unlabored, his frame relaxed despite this new and unfamiliar experience of the unrelenting cold. More than just a little could be discerned about the man's physique even buried as it was in a blue, pile filled parka. The man was of average height, roughly five-foot seven and about 135 to 140 pounds. Solidly built, the terrorist had the lean, thin contours of a swimmer rather than the sculptured physique of a weightlifter. The lower half of his sun darkened, coarsely pored face clung to a slackening fullness of adolescence. Machmued's chin, upper lip and cheeks were covered by patchy straggles of a young man's beard.

A lock of oily black hair escaped from beneath the green knit cap that clung to his forehead and covered his ears down to the nape of his neck. The inability of his body to rapidly adjust to the unfamiliar climate had taken its toll.

His countenance had taken on an unhealthy look. The scrubbing wind had transformed his otherwise unremarkable face into a sore and raw profile. His beaklike nose, prone to a constantly runny discharge in the cold air, was caked with internal crusted sores. The soft leathery texture of his desert-tanned skin was bleached to a washed out lemon colored stain. Pinched by the temperature, his skin was stretched taut against the bone of the skull beneath. His cheeks and brow, especially around the edges of his eyes, were tightly drawn, latticed with the still ill-defined soft wrinkles of squinting too long over bright and shimmering distances in the heat of the desert. The angular features of his jaw and high, chiseled cheekbones confirmed his Semitic ancestry.

Since he arrived in Newfoundland fifteen days ago, Machmued had lost a pound a day. He had not adjusted well to the Western food and had been in distress with bouts of diarrhea and stomach cramps. The nausea and dysentery had begun within 36 hours of his arrival and further complicated his ability to acclimatize himself to his new surroundings. His blood was too thin to accept the rapid change of temperature to which his body had to adjust.

Machmued watched the plane lift skyward. The DC-8 passed with an earsplitting unmuffled roar over the end of the runway, climbing out at 2,200 feet per minute, up over the flashing beacon lights already 300 hundred feet below.

It was good to know that Jahbad was close by, he thought. Jahbad was father, brother, and leader—an unchanging mountain of granite in the shifting sands of the Arab struggle. Jahbad personified the courage, the resolve, and the hate needed to continue the struggle.

Jahbad watched the rising airplane, aware of the yellow car

and its dismounted occupant in the near distance. Much had happened since he was in the lead armor elements of the Egyptian Army as it swarmed across the Suez in the opening hour of the Six-Day War. The terrorist team leader had escaped the destruction of not one but two Russian built T-62 tanks that were blown out from under him.

Jahbad was 53. The fire of his youth was replaced with a lower but hotter ember of banked flame in these, his later years. As both the oldest member and commander of the team he was a veteran. He winced involuntarily as a muscle spasm cramped his back. A rugged vertical scar, the by-product of white-hot spalling shrapnel and a field surgeon's scalpel, ran parallel to his spine. The scar overlaid a six-inch titanium rod, which fused three vertebrae in his lower back. Disfigured, but praise be to Allah, not crippled, he survived.

To Jahbad the peace that followed the fierce bloodletting that destroyed the elite Egyptian armored forces was a betrayal. His own physical wounds slowly healed. A never healing wound, however, was the death of his only son, a martyr who died in *jihad* against the Israelis. He had thought of his son, Mustaf, many times over the years. In point of fact, Machmued reminded Jahbad of him—invulnerable in his youth, an idealist in his vision, and a patriot in his beliefs.

Jahbad was a self-taught man, patient and stoic. His life was a confirmation of hard held beliefs. For him the war with the Jews was a simple matter of justice. Arab land was stolen and given to an ancient enemy. The greatest insult was the Camp David Accords. If a thief came in the night and stole, you did not bargain with him to return that which was yours. No, you found the thief and punished him. By holy Islamic law, this was your right.

"The Jews shit on the Arab people only because the Americans protect them. Sadat and his kind, the appeasers, represent the worst of the Arab people – fools at best, traitors at worst. They are naïve. None of them possesses the will to sacrifice, to do what must be done to drive the Israelis into the sea, to punish them, to chop off their hands," the

Hizballah, Party of God, recruiter told him.

Jahbad was an eager recruit. The same words that Jahbad had heard so long ago were since repeated by him to other young men, even to his own lost son.

Jahbad sighed.

It was so many years ago, but then the fight with the Jews had always been long—from the time of the pharaohs, the time of Abraham, Agar, the mother of the first born, Ismael, and Sara, mother to Isaac, the pretender, the thief and father to the Jewish people. There would be no end to the hatred between the Jew and Arab, until one was crushed forever under the heel of the other.

Machmued winced in discomfort at the roar of the DC-8's passing over the outer markers, its noise amplified by the frozen chill air. The cabin windows leaked yellow loops of light on the still shadowed snowbanks packed along the edges of the sinking runway. The eyes of the airborne soldiers on board strained through the fogged portals for one final glimpse as they roared away from the rising sun, in a race to the West, chasing the disappearing night. The plane began to shrink into the distance.

With slow deliberation Machmued deployed the short telescopic antenna from the side of the transmitter and flipped a button at the top of the packet from the OFF to the ON position. A green light registered that power was being transmitted from the small battery to the transmitter's circuitry. Machmued flipped a second switch. A second light, blinking red, appeared. The light pulsated with an increased rapidity as the receiver to which it was tuned reached its optimal distance.

The placement of the charge had taken a great deal of planning and a degree of risk to Khleed, the third member of the cell.

Khleed was the first member of the team to arrive in Newfoundland. As an early October tourist, he passed through immigration without incident. Within moments of his arrival he contacted sympathetic members of the local Arab community. A new set of identity papers witnessing his Canadian citizenship was provided and Khleed, the tourist, became Khleed the citizen.

Khleed was a handsome man who sported a full, well-trimmed mustache. A consummate actor, he was often favorably compared to Omar Sharif in both personality and visage. He was the mechanic on the team—the actual bomb maker and primary explosives expert. His tradecraft was learned by on-the-job experience. Until now, his skills had been largely confined to the several bombing successes in the street cafes and on the buses of Tel Aviv. There had, however, been one notable exception. On October 23, 1983, Khleed, in one stroke, had brought the American giant to his knees. Two hundred and forty-one U.S. Marines, sailors and soldiers had died in their Lebanon barracks as a result of his handicraft. The First Battalion, Eighth Marines and the American peace-keeping efforts disappeared in the dust and rubble of an undeclared war far from the shores of their home.

Two weeks after arrival in Newfoundland, Khleed secured a position as an aviation petroleum specialist with Esso Avitat. For the first ten days he studied his co-workers, their habits, their vices, the shortcuts they took in violation of the safety and security requirements for refueling the large jet liners that passed through the terminal. The bomb maker became the ever present, never complaining workaholic petroleum specialist. Within six weeks he was a familiar and accepted face on the ramps of the air terminal.

Scheduling himself on the early morning shift to assist in the refueling of the DC-8 had been a simple matter. Smuggling the C-4 explosive onto the ramp had been a matter of opportunity and also was without problem. The trick, however, was to get the package into a wing fuel cell without causing notice or arousing suspicion. It proved to be less difficult than had been expected. No objection was raised when he conveniently volunteered to handle the refueling hose connection and disconnection at the DC-8's wing. Flushing the package into the fuel tank with a stream of fuel was impossible due to the series of baffles and filters that inhibited its progress. Lodging the small package of explosive in the fuel flow pipe, Khleed deployed the coiled wire receiver antenna within the fill tube.

The wind inexplicably had ceased its howling as if in momentary anticipation.

The moment had arrived.

Machmued pointed the tiny transmitter at the departing plane, delayed the space of a breath and then pushed the small spring-loaded button, holding it in place. There was no immediate response. He had been told that such was to be expected. Still it was disconcerting. The terrorist waited, puzzling his brow in momentary concern. There was neither flash of light nor puff of smoke to confirm the detonation of the explosive in the starboard tank. The thought sped through his mind that he had waited too long. Had he indulged the moment a fraction more than he should have allowed? Had the cold somehow affected the power of the battery or degraded the signal to the receiver? No, he had replaced the batteries that morning, and the plane was still well within range of the low frequency transmission. Machmued released the button and jammed it down once again.

Slowly, in solemn genuflection, the DC-8 began to bank to the north, its nose upward, still reaching. A flash of orange light and a puff of black smoke appeared. The DC-8 began its descent, arcing its back and flank in an increasing, confused spiral, its silhouette disappearing into the quiet brightening dawn.

The silence was complete.

Then, as from a great distance, came the death shriek of straining engines, a muffled explosion and a spectacular orange blossoming fireball.

Then again silence.

Machmued stood mesmerized by the aerial display. The

wind began its howl once again and awoke him from his trance-like state. The killer collapsed the antenna of the transmitter, opened the door of the Volvo and threw it into the opposite seat as he slid into the warm interior of the car. He adjusted the lap safety belt around his middle, carefully put the car into gear and backed it onto the road.

Machmued glanced at his watch and then a final time at the glow that now lit a small sector of the distant horizon. He listened to the rhythmic ticking valves of the Volvo until the response sirens of the airport blasted an announcement of the disaster. He was surprised at his calmness. A grim smile of both relief and accomplishment formed about his cracked lips. His mission was complete—these "eagles" of the 101st "Screaming Eagles" Divison would scream no more.

And so a new heightened phase of international terrorism began. The fight for Palestine, for Arab self-determination, for a Pan-Arab state started its trek from the Middle East to the homeland of the United States. It was a fight that would carry the realities of death and destruction to the shores and interior of the Great Satan itself.

"*Allah akbar*, God is great," Machmued murmured as he shifted into first gear, slowly released the clutch, and drove away from the black plume of distant smoke.

4

Over Florida
—Early September, 2000

The pilot slowly reined in the 14,500 pounds of thrust delivered from each of the three muffled Pratt & Whitney JD8D-9A engines. The heavy-duty landing gear of the aircraft thumped down and locked. The Boeing slid from its 570 mph cruising speed to the 250 mph wheels down landing configuration for which the 300,000-pound machine was designed. A rush of air through the overhead vents and the whine of lowering flaps joined the concert of noise as the plane rushed and descended to Melbourne's International Airport. A quick, bright flash of light caused Matt to turn and squint into the sunset. Below, a reflection from one of the odd shaped antennas rising above the field's control tower caught a glare that amplified and reflected back into his eyes. The communication antenna passed under the starboard wing and the Boeing 727 glided the last fifteen hundred yards to settle onto the Melbourne runway. Matt's thoughts returned to memories and Megan.

Megan had broken down all the doors, all of the subtle and carefully constructed arguments Matt used to avoid any permanent relationship. All the logics and rationalizations he had worked out were shot to hell. In all too short a time, Megan became much more than just a comfortable warmth and soft breath on the nape of his neck during a restless night. Theirs was a communication of the unsaid between two people who grew together to the point that words were unnecessary. They had not discussed the future; each hoping, despite their misaligned stars, that they would somehow find one together.

They met in Tel Aviv at a British embassy party, one of the

ritual social events where one's presence was expected. Their six-month relationship had evolved from casual greetings at the *you-will-attend-and-have-a-good-time* political and social outings, to less formal picnic and sightseeing tours, to the intimacy of true friends and a very exclusive and intense couple. Together they toured Israel from the Golan Heights, ate Saint Peter's fish at the Sea of Galilee, and drove down through the Jordan valley past the hot mud springs to Jericho. They viewed the spot on the river where tradition said Jesus had been baptized. In a rented Chevy Blazer they traveled to the southernmost city in the country, Elat, and viewed the borders of Egypt and Saudi Arabia. They swam and floated in the Dead Sea and climbed the snake path up Massada to the Macabees last stronghold against Silva and his Roman Legions. They had stood under the waterfall at En Gedi, the oasis to which young David had fled from Saul. The weekends became discovery adventures and more—explorations for and of the two of them alone.

Jolting in the Boeing 727 on its descent Matt remembered their last time together, just a few hours and another world away.

Matt had received reassignment orders six weeks earlier designating his departure date from the Multinational Forces. His new duty station had still not been determined. On his last night in El Gorah, the MFO northernmost base camp, Matt called Megan and asked her to meet him at the MFO station in Tel Aviv.

Megan arrived at the helipad just as the chopper that ferried him across the Egyptian-Israeli border landed. They spent the night together in mock gaiety both knowing and regretting what the dawn would bring. Rain had come during the night. The clouds had swept in from the East, laden with the moisture of the Mediterranean. They passed over Tel Aviv and continued toward the ancient hills surrounding Jerusalem. There was some thunder and a random bolt of lightning but all in all it was not a fierce storm. In its wake followed a soft rain carried on a light breeze.

The metronome of the wiper blades punctuated the silence between them as the wipers swept the windshield in rhythm with the rain. At four-thirty in the morning, the orange sodium streetlights still attested that Tel Aviv slept. All of the flights to North America left early.

"Do you mind if I drive?" Megan had asked.

"Not at all, be my guest," Matt replied, tossing her the keys to the rented sports utility vehicle.

She drove silently through the deserted predawn streets with her usual aggressive confidence. The set of her jaw reflected considerable more concentration than demanded by either the infrequent traffic or the wet condition of the road. Her mind was far from the focus of driving. By instinct rather than memory or awareness Megan wound through the outskirts of Jaffa and entered the four-lane expressway that swept up to Ben Gurion International Airport and ended in Jerusalem. The heavy ribbed tires hummed over an occasional low spot in the roadway and sprayed the hood, fenders, and windshield with the scrub water runoff of the streets. The humming drone of the tires and the squeak of the wipers on the slightly fogged windows were the only sounds.

"Are you sure you have everything now? Tickets? Passport? Little black book of phone numbers for girls back in America?" she asked.

"Think so. Almost everything," he replied. "Everything but you, that is," he added silently to himself.

He tried to say it in a light, casual voice but it didn't come off that way. They each wanted a permanent relationship. Neither was willing to admit it to the other, nor to take the first step toward making it happen. Neither would acknowledge dependence, nor submit to needing or being needed. They had avoided the obvious, not discussed it and had somehow managed to get beyond it. Until now.

Matt cracked the side window two or three inches and inhaled deeply. The pungent smells of wet streets, damp concrete, and fresh earth were all there, mixed and muted by the falling gray mist. They were lost in the essence of Megan's perfume that hung in the warm interior of the Chevy Blazer. The scent that she wore was *Mystere de Rochas*, one that he had first given to her as a gift. The perfume had become one of her favorites and was a fragrance that he would now forever associate with her.

Matt avoided her glance and hunkered deeper into his seat. He tried to think of something to say that would keep away from open questions between them.

"Be careful going back. The roads will be slick. The crazies will be out," Matt told her.

"I am a quite competent driver, you know," she replied, trying to keep the conversation and banter light. "We Brits are trained from birth to drive on both the right and left sides of the road with equal dexterity."

"Just don't do it simultaneously," Matt quipped, trying to make a joke of it. Megan once told him that his was an unremarkable face—not one well remembered, nor which stood out in a crowd. His ego, unprepared for the abrupt bruise, was irritated by the comment. But the longer he thought about it, the more he realized and accepted how accurate the statement was. Some had commented that there was tightness about his mouth, but he would have said that if so, it came from biting his lip – an act in which he did not often indulge. His eyes, sometimes hazel, sometime blue, were where the sum of his being resided. His moods, disposition, likes and dislikes, weaknesses, strengths and determinations, his tenderness and absoluteness of will and his dry Irish wit were all reflected or, in some cases, betrayed in his eyes.

Having been a major part of each other's life for the past six months gave them both good insights into how the other's mind worked. They knew they were both running out of time. Neither, it seemed, was prepared to do anything about it.

Matt stole a quick glance across the seat.

"You have my Florida address?" he asked.

"Of course. Tucked away amongst the treasures in my book of bloody stupid memories," she responded with an edge. Her features were outlined in the shadows cast by the dashboard lights and the quickening dawn.

Six months earlier, Matt's initial impression of Megan was that she was one of the hardcore survivors, a tough, savvy if not a slightly jaded lady. Matt had concluded from a distance, that first night he had seen her at the embassy, that if she hadn't lived a worldly-wise life, at least she knew about it. He had been a little right and a lot wrong.

Megan was a curious piece of work and it was difficult to put her into any neatly defined category. Perhaps it was the challenge of her, the tough softness, that inability to pigeonhole her, that put her inside Matt's head and kept him coming back to discover more about her. He didn't know that he had fallen in love with her, but he had. The realization of it came to him as he found himself remembering her a bit more strongly and missing her a bit more often each time they were apart.

Maybe it was a defensive reaction or habit, or whatever, but Matt had a hard time accepting the knowledge that he loved her. Uncharacteristically, he was unsure of himself. Maybe he was just gun-shy. He was wary of commitment even though Megan seemed to fit so well and so warmly into his life. Matt felt there would be time—lots of time. But now six weeks had all drained through the hourglass and the moment of long distance parting was upon them.

"A little too soon," he said to himself quietly.

"I'll e-mail you my new duty address as soon as I have it. When will you go back to England?" Matt asked, breaking the silence between them.

"I don't know," she replied. "Perhaps in a month or so, or maybe later in the fall; only be for a holiday. October perhaps."

Megan's coloring accented a mid-European ancestry—a gift, he had learned, that came from her mother's side. She was a younger copy of Sophia, her mother. The strong, high cheekbones, the clear chiseled features, the hint of stubborn fullness beneath a soft shaped chin gave her a classic beauty that was muted by a distracting laughter in her blue gray eyes and a dimple in her cheeks whenever she smiled. Her smile was her very best feature. From her mother Megan also inherited a fierce, eruptive temper, a deeper, longer lasting and sublime beauty, a sense of wonderment, stubbornness, and a penchant for absolute independence. She also copied, in softer miniature, the stubborn expression and aristocratic charm of her British father. She had acquired from him the characteristic British reserve, the distance and resolve for calm when things were coming apart, the taste for literature and theater, the fine arts, and the more expensive and better things of life.

At most public functions early in their relationship, Matt had found that she could be distant. No, not distant, he had thought, that wasn't right. It seemed to Matt that there was an unfocused distraction within her. She was socially pleasant but subtly seemed to be gathering and sorting, waiting and looking for someone or something.

In time he discovered that her social behavior was all a camouflage—designed to hide and sometimes protect her naiveté and vulnerability. She accomplished the charade well excepting those unexpected times when, despite her best efforts, the real Megan snuck free in a laugh or a smile or, sometimes, in the way she tilted her head or listened with her eyes.

There was a curious unsophisticated innocence about her in those moments.

Matt had taken the time to really study and know her, to peel back the layers of self-defense and discover her. The hardness, the brittle edges he found were all bluff. She was soft and curiously untainted. The surprise was unexpected and complete.

When they first met, her hair was cut so that it fell just short of her shoulder. Her hair was a soft and fragrant chestnut color with natural highlights of red when touched by the sun in a certain way. The style became her. Megan had been thirty-five on her last birthday and stood a shade under five eight, only three inches shorter than Matt. Earlier in her life she had been uncomfortable about her height. She felt, wrongly, that she was too tall and athletically muscled to convey the femininity she would have preferred.

When she was younger she had tried to conceal these features by slouching and wearing flat shoes, disguising her stature by a deliberate and contrived slump in her carriage and a round shouldered posture. Now she wore her height with pride. The sensitivities of her stature were cast aside when she had reached early womanhood. She came to enjoy her physical strength and natural rhythms on the tennis courts, golf course and ski slopes. She gave up on girlish and dainty and settled for athletic and healthy. Still, she worked hard at keeping her weight under one hundred thirty-five.

Megan had all the womanly curves in all the right quantities just where they should be. She had good legs—muscular and feminine. She was confident and pleased that men noticed. Megan also had an air of self-assurance—a natural, athletic balance, but more than that. Her stride was a graceful rhythm with an indolent kind of energy that came from the way she set her wide shoulders. She was all woman and not coy or shy about it and she radiated an unashamed sexual vitality and personal vibrancy. The resulting demeanor was difficult to describe and it came off more of an attitude than a posture. This, too, became her and wore well in defining her person. In quiet confidence it asserted:

"Here I am. Take me or leave me, but this is me and I'm a nice package. I do not seek or need your approval. I am secure in who I am."

Their parting had not been a good one, but that, perhaps, had been inevitable. Megan was swimming in the cauldron of her own unhappiness; silently building it into a reflexive storm of anger, hurt and disappointment that Matt did not understand but knew would explode. She replayed the evening, the few short hours-ago memory.

The moment came upon them swiftly last night just after dinner.

"We need some time apart," Matthew began.

"Why?" she had replied, startled and suddenly insecure.

"I just want to keep things as they are for the moment," he slowly replied.

The feud began in cold, clear terms, without passion.

Megan's anger grew. She focused on the difficulty of separation and the damages it could bring.

"These open-ended arrangements never work, Matthew," she said in final appeal. "I am a touch-and-feel person. I grow when you are here and I shrink when you are away. Can't you understand that? I can neither nurture nor be nurtured by you when you are some 10,000 miles away doing God knows what with your bloody stupid army. We shall fade away from each other as certain as the sunrise. Is that what you want?"

She hesitated and then finally asked him her most feared question, the one she didn't want him to answer. "Is this your polite way of telling me good-bye, your farewell without rancor or hard feelings or blame, a way to 'sneak' out the back door?"

This kind of coward's departure had happened to her before and she trembled in apprehension of his answer.

Matt hesitated before responding. It was hard for him to admit this self-doubt, the personal vulnerability. He started slowly, with obvious difficulty.

"There was another woman once, Megan. I was as certain about her as I am about you. The marriage ended in divorce; neither of us was ready for a lifelong commitment. We thought we were. Christ, it was us against the world. It didn't last long. It hurt and left scars," he said softly but firmly. "I just can't go there again, Megan. Maybe it's selfish, but I need time."

She had no answer—then or really even now.

"I'll think about it," she had finally murmured when the silence between them had grown too long. She didn't believe it but they were the words that Matthew wanted—no, the words he needed right then to hear.

"Perhaps a period of separation between us is a good thing, Matthew. Perhaps you are right. We should each take some time alone to arrive at some conclusion about a future together."

The wipers squeaked across the windshield, the noise jolting her back to the present, to the only a few moments left time.

Tears puddled in the corners of Megan's eyes and rolled down her cheeks—undetected in the morning gloom. They had begun some twenty minutes earlier when the reality of his final leaving had struck her.

Megan rarely was stripped of the veneer of self-assertiveness, of assuredness and supposed self-directed purposefulness in her life. She needed and wanted a strong man to love and be loved by, although she would never admit it—even to herself. She also had a tender quality that only a scant number had seen or had bothered to care enough to discover. Matthew had been one of the few to pierce the armor surrounding that vulnerability—not to exploit it but to protect and care for her because of it. That, in and of itself, had indeed made him different from all of the others.

Damn! I'm not going to do this. I'm behaving like a stupid twit! Acting like … like some romantic, immature teenager, she chided herself. In fact, she had vowed that she would not cry aloud—both to him and to herself. The current exhibition, she realized, did nothing but make it all the harder on each of them.

Not that it mattered any longer, she argued in silence. Not that he didn't deserve a full measure of misery—particularly if I am to be miserable.

Might as well share a bit of it, she inwardly decided—even while acknowledging that their mutual uncompromising stubbornness had brought them to this unhappy conclusion.

Well, a few tears will give him something to remember me by. Megan shot a glance in his direction.

Matt still clung nearer to the passenger's door, looking out the rain spattered side window. His face was turned to the breeze of the partially opened window, his soundless thoughts off somewhere, masked by wet, green fields and flickering orange groves.

She tried to mentally reconcile herself to the worst, to losing him for good. She felt rejected, hurt and angry. How could he leave her? How could she adjust to a life without him by her side?

She was conflicted. It was selfish and vengeful, she knew, but it was emotionally easier for her to shift the blame for the current situation to him. Perhaps if it were his entire fault, she could deal with the loss better and she set out mentally to build her case.

The choice was his, she thought, right to this current and inevitable moment. He made his bed and now would bloody well lie in it. Well, given, of course, there being no other more acceptable, practical alternative. Becoming little more than his self-supporting mistress wasn't bloody likely!

Pride and stubbornness became her sword and shield.

"The bloody, bloody cheek of the man!" she whispered to herself, trying to misinterpret what Matt had said last night.

Her acquiescence of his arguments wilted in the brooding silence of the car. Bloody hell if she would let anyone—even her own father—let alone this *Yank* dictate terms to her.

"He'll not be bending me to his will! Bugger them all!" she said to herself. No man is worth the sacrifice in the long run, she concluded.

She had been down the road of hurt and loneliness one time too many. The silent figure in the far corner of the seat was no different, she was sure, than any of the others who had entered her life.

With men before Matt, it had always been an adversarial relationship. Perhaps it would always be so for her. In time, with other relationships earlier in her life, dalliances became a game of emotional one-upsmanship. Megan refused to address her own self-doubts, her own deep fears of permanence. There was a perversity to it. She came to embrace the philosophy that the final test of perfect love was sacrifice. Megan reasoned that if loved she was forgiven any sin, any transgression. Failure to sacrifice equated to failure to love. Based on this premise, she built a circular trap for herself.

Inevitably pithy tests became her undoing. She would icily cling to the men who loved her and, in doing so, reduce the intensity and purity of their love for her ... in the end driving them away. She would watch with growing dispassion as she withdrew to the distance of platonic disinterest as one by one they failed her brief tests. In pity, triumph and disappointment the relationship would end.

The façade of independence and assurance would melt and she would find herself sliding into a cycle of fear, rejection and loneliness. Then would come the remorse—the self-criticism, the mental crucifixions for being so shallow and self-indulgent as to make a game of feelings, of becoming involved in the first place—much as she had seen the evolved relationship between her mother and father.

Her father was the only one who had seemingly survived the test—administered time and time again by her emasculating mother. Despite all, Megan knew somehow, somewhere deep in his soul, her father still loved her mother.

The logics that drove her were faces of the same coin. They were emotional survival techniques that came from the toughest of all teachers—experience. The tests were the damage control measures, the defenses that kept her inner self at an arm's distance and which kept all from reaching into and touching her soul. And so she had callused herself, protected her being with iciness, that it prevented the spark of commitment from igniting within her. The mental chastity, the discipline of too many hurts, was well armored. The conditioned reflex was so well learned that no one until Matt had touched her tender parts in a long, long time. Still ... Matt had, perhaps, been somehow different.

He unknowingly haunted her and was, she would not admit, the key to her redemption. He had not been lacking, she admitted silently. Well, at least not very often. Lord knows she had set him through the hoops. A trace of a faint smile crossed her lips in cynical memory.

The tires whined on the pavement. The headlights captured the reflective lettering of the ramp that marked the exit to Ben Gurion. She flipped up the turn signal indicator and acknowledged the answering green flashing arrow from the console. Megan clutched expertly down through the gears, dropping speed as she maneuvered through the cloverleaf turns of the exit. The Blazer braked to a halt as they reached the first of the brightly lit security stations.

She turned full face toward the sentry. The silent tears kept falling. Can't let him see me like this, she thought.

The IDF guard peered at them through the rain-spattered window, flashed his light.

"Papers please," the guard said.

The lone sentinel flashed his light on Matt's displayed credentials and Megan's British passport and with disinterest waved the vehicle through the barricade.

Megan guided the vehicle through the serpentine course of concrete barriers and spiked roadway, shifting, building speed.

She remembered the many nights he had to be away from her, how he would call at the most God-awful hours. She would answer with a smile and always immediately ask:

"Why are you not here where you should be?"

The question had begun as a joke but over time, its repetition took on a new meaning. They became Megan's first words when he was away and checked in on her. The words became her shorthand way to say that all was okay, that she loved and missed him. The greeting was a signal between them that said she needed him in her life. Many were the times that Matt said, only half in jest that he was the best thing that could happen to her.

Perhaps he was right.

But now he was leaving—expectantly for the last time, for the United States, for his home, and without her.

In the end it seemed that she, not he, had failed her final test. Matt had denied her the opportunity to say "No" to a proposal. He had preempted her with his "rash decision" soliloquy of the previous evening.

"Sod all of them!" she said under her breath to no one. A quick romance, the filling of a temporary need for warmth, closeness, and appreciation. Someone to care about, to be cared for, but just for a time—not forever. For them both it should have been a temporary thing. That, she tried to convince herself, was what she signed on for. Neither of the two of them could call foul for flying false colors.

So be it.

Despite her best efforts at bitterness she was having a hard time carrying it off.

Stop it, old girl. A bit long of tooth to become the martyr, aren't we? Romanticizing? Creating a bit of fantasy, are we? Living in the past? Certainly the first signs of addled senility.

But she knew it wasn't true. This time, for reasons that she would neither accept nor admit, the arguments just weren't working. The nagging doubt, always before dismissed, this time would not go away.

"Well, how did we do? Have we cocked it up?" she asked finally, breaking the silence between them.

Matt did not answer.

The long quiet caused her to think that he had not heard. She was just about to repeat the question when he responded.

"Not too badly, I suppose. We could have done a lot worse."

"Shall I come over on holiday once you have settled in? Perhaps for Christmas or in the spring?" she hinted, with a lightness she did not feel.

"Now isn't the time to make those plans, Meg. I mean, I don't want…"

"Right! Well, there you are," she exclaimed. "Just chucking me out then, are you?"

"Let's not do this, Meg. If I'm wrong about us, by December I'll be just another memory on a long list of names. The one after Frank and before Mike, Pete, Filipe or whoever," Matt said dejectedly.

He sounded tired and defeated. Yet she knew he was angry.

"Do I detect a note of remorse there 'Yank?' Perhaps some self-pity for becoming involved with me?"

"No, not at all," he responded. "I don't want our last minutes together to be tired words and empty promises. Just ... just let it go, Meg."

"No. No, I won't let it. Dammit! I'm exasperated. I'm angry. Just don't walk away leaving things like this! Be honest with me," she demanded.

"Well, what do you expect? The guarantee of a full lifetime commitment no matter what?"

Matt knew it was a mistake before the words had left his tongue. There it was—out in the open between them—the question they had both so carefully avoided and now asked at the worst possible time.

Megan made no response, just sat there, tight-jawed, staring off into the new morning distance, watching the rain slide from the hood.

"You ask too much of me for it to work. You, you take too much for granted," Matt offered, wanting her to tell him that he was wrong.

"Up to you then, I suppose," she said, with a distant British reserve and mock disinterest. "If it's right for us, it will work; if not, well ... I'm not going to argue for something that we both, together, don't want. Lot of bloody good America does for me. You offer me nothing. America offers me nothing. I couldn't even very well be a bloody self-supporting mistress over there, let alone independent. Could not even get a stupid green card in all probability. I am certain that your colonial State Department would love to issue a work visa to a Brit – ha!" she rambled.

"Let's leave things the way they are, at least for now," he offered.

"Nothing ever stays the way it is, Matthew," she replied. "Either you grow or you diminish. You just cannot stop the clock or stay at the place that is best for you. You just go on. There is no control of it, no way to stop it. It's reality and we cannot pretend it away."

"If we try and it's wrong then neither of us will be able to find our way back, so all the caring won't be worth a tinker's damn. I don't want that. Let's, for now, just keep the options open."

"Right. Oh, yes, options. Well you've got a plane to catch, haven't you, Matt? No option there," she said.

She pulled into the parking lot, found a space, and swung the truck into it.

"Stop throwing up smoke screens, darling," she said, attempting a weak smile. "And make up your turned about, upended mind. It's as simple as that. You damn well know it and so do I. Marriage isn't what you want, it never has been. Neither of us is a trophy to take home, to be mounted over the fireplace and disparaged by the in-laws. We're both smart enough to know one does not get married because that is what somebody expects."

"But that's really the way it is, isn't it? Just a game to you," Matt offered.

The words hung there between them invading Megan's ordered world, touching her doubts, magnifying her insecurities.

Megan flushed in anger. "How dare you tell me it's a flippin' game. Especially when you've been playing it all along. You're no different than the rest of them—just a bit subtler, Mister Colonel Gannon. Damn you! I'll be my own piper, thank you very much. Knights on white horses are a myth and I'm a bit too old for fairy tales, Colonel."

She wore the armor of unreasonable anger.

"I'd rather grow old alone than used by someone who professes to care but really doesn't. Oh yes, it is a game—the user and the used. And I won't be the latter! When I give myself, and to whom I give myself, and under what terms and conditions I give myself, will be as I bloody well choose. Full stop! Isn't that how you men bloody well think? How you play the soddin' game? Isn't it?" she demanded.

Her fury wasn't only at Matt but at every man she had ever allowed into her life. She said it for all those who had repaid her affection and love with disappointment and abuse.

"Bugger you all! I don't need you. I don't want you anymore, Mathew Gannon."

Tears flowed down her face.

He looked at her ... in her fierce stubbornness and in her hurting pride, hearing her voice but no longer listening to her words. Matt felt her pain unwillingly; he took the responsibility for being a part of it, while not admitting to himself his full complicity.

After a time he lamely reached across the distance of the seat and put the back of his hand to the wet side of her face and tried to stroke the tears from her cheek. She snatched his hand away.

"Just sod off! Catch your precious plane and run off to your precious America and just leave me alone."

They were the last harsh words between them.

She stayed with him at Ben Gurion for as long as it took for him to clear through security and enter the passenger-only shielded and sanitized departure lounge. They talked empty words, avoiding the things they both wanted to say. She hoped that somehow the empty space now between them would close, but it did not. The last few moments remained crowded with unsaid words.

He'd cut off his blinkin' nose just to spite his face! He truly would. Why must it be his way or none at all? She could not understand.

At the last moment she turned to him. "Why must you leave this way? Why must it be so ... so final and hard?" she asked.

"I don't know. Maybe it's best this way, Meg."

She took both of his hands in her own and squeezed them gently. "Right, then. It doesn't change the way I feel about you, you know," she said.

"Meg, I care too much about you to become just your near and distant friend and—that's what we'll end up as—

sooner or later."

"I'm afraid, darling," she wept softly. "I'm so afraid you will get on that plane and leave my life forever – and I love you so much."

Matt touched her still damp cheek and looked softly into her puffy, tear swollen eyes. His love for her was warm and tender and for almost a second, his guard was down and in that tiny moment she saw his heart.

"Megan, whatever shall I do with you?"

He said it so softly that he wasn't sure if it had been just a thought ... a question to himself rather than to her.

"Oh, leave me I suppose," she replied, gathering herself together. She smiled a half-hearted, brave smile, resigned to the words and the now reality of their meaning.

"There, there, it's to have been expected. I suspect we have just run our course. It will hurt for a bit, but," she hesitated, "in time, it will be all right. I shall heal," she said, smiling bravely.

There had been a final almost pristine kiss, a tight embrace, and her quick smile. A swallowed, throaty "good-bye" and he was gone.

Megan stopped and fumbled in her purse with unhurried deliberateness, watching the morning sun peek over the cluttered skyline.

A silhouetted Boeing 747 appeared low on the horizon, trailing through her vision, straining for the safety of the brightening morning sky. The deep-throated roar of throttled up jet engines broke the morning stillness. She followed the airplane's diminishing shadow as it fled toward the sea.

She turned to stare at the spot where he had disappeared. A faint dizziness came over her. She recovered and walked stoop shouldered—as she had in her youth—from the terminal and crossed the street to the parking lot. She withdrew the keys, unlocked the door of the carryall, fumbled it open, and slid behind the wheel. The scent of him was strong in the interior of the car, or so she imagined. She sat there alone, quietly, her mind numb and unthinking, for how long she did not know. A distant siren distracted her, caused her to look up and listen to the stillness of the dawn.

She was alone—again. It was only then that she fully turned loose the tears. And they flowed freely ... for the first time, in a long, long time.

5
Libya
—April, 2000

A tepid Mediterranean breeze stirred briefly to caress the sun-whitened stones of Tripoli, its skyline shimmering in the cloud of boiling saffron humidity. The bedraggled fronds of isolated date palms, branches of the olive treed gardens and errant orange groves stirred for a brief moment and then drooped again in surrender to the pervasive heat.

Belching buses hidden beneath their burdens of humanity staggered and groaned over the pockmarked paving. They crept along next to smoking, square wheeled trucks that wheezed under cargoes far in excess of their capacity. Together they dispensed and churned a bank of dirty smog that blanketed the city. An unhealthy blue-gray haze of exhaust fumes from thousands of motor scooters and ancient, oil burning automobile engines identified the Libyan coast.

Tripoli is the city of Arab art and handicraft, the city of historic Islamic culture. Excepting the industrial pollutants, it had changed little since its founding in the first millennium. The sweltering coastal plain had long since turned the *souks* of the old city into sour smelling steambaths. Stretched canvas lean-tos, once brightly colored, shielded inhabitants from the penetrating glare of the mid-afternoon sun and trapped the stagnant air, reinforcing the smells of animals, excrement, sweat, open sewers, tanned leather and rancid garbage.

The muezzin's, or holy man's, wilted call to *asr*, the formal mid-afternoon prayer, wailed plaintively, scratchily amplified by loud speakers in the minarets about the city. The whine of vendors and mullahs offering their wares and prayers echoed and rebounded from the narrow cobbled and mud streets to create a cacophony of noise that was only partially deadened by the high stuccoed walls that surrounded the conference site. The soothing drone of the cicadas overrode and muted the background noises of the city that sought to invade the quiet of the courtyard.

Salal sat in solitude in the garden of the isolated villa awaiting the momentary summons of the Islamic Conference Organization's executive council. The successes of earlier operations against the Americans in Lebanon, in Saudi Arabia, and against the American embassies in Africa were important steps. The success of operations far from their home bases demonstrated the feasibility of Jericho while adding to Salal's credentials and stature before the council.

He wished Machmued were here. As he sat, waiting, his thoughts returned to the previous evening's discussion with his close subordinate. Machmued was a good friend and a good counsel as well. With Machmued, Salal could freely share his inner thoughts as with few others. They had shared much together and understood one another.

"The heat in Tripoli is different than the heat of the desert," Salal had remarked. "The heat of the cities, the hotness of this new and modern world of machines and schedules and timetables is oppressive. The fire of the city does not cleanse; it bakes dirt and putrefaction into the very soul of one's being. The new ways rob us of our faith; they dismiss our traditions and heritage. But the desert ... ah, yes, the desert, that is different," Salal continued.

Machmued listened to his friend and leader and nodded in agreement and then quietly responded. "In the desert, I can hear Allah whispering in the sunrise and sunset."

Machmued understood. They were of one mind.

Salal nodded his head and continued. "Our cities look to the West where the voice of Allah becomes lost in the rattle of wealth. Americans come to take the black oil from our earth and then corrupt our people. Oil has become a new God to us, just as 2,000 years ago the golden calf of the Sinai became the new God of the Jews."

"Perhaps, it will change," Machmued offered. "Perhaps Jericho will awaken the pride of our people and return them to Allah and away from the evil of the West."

Salal shrugged but then nodded in agreement. "Perhaps. *Enshallah*, as God wills," he responded and then, teasing his compatriot, added, "and so very much better than the cold of Newfoundland, no?"

Machmued smiled. His aversion to the cold was well known. "God's voice is lost in the cold winds and muffled by the snows of the North."

Machmued had matured greatly since that long ago mission in Newfoundland. He was an intelligent man, an educated man who had begun his terrorist life while still a student at the University at Cairo. He had become a thinker, a man who selected his words with caution, preferring to listen to the wisdom of others and only then arriving at his own judgments.

"Perhaps our past successes will weigh on tomorrow's decision, eh?" Salal offered, seeking reassurance.

"They will help," Machmued agreed. "The leaders know Allah blesses your labor."

He paused, knowing Salal was uncertain about the meeting the next day, and then continued reassuringly. "Men of the book, the Koran, do not contrive to mold their destiny, Salal. Allah has already done that for them. It is your simple task to live the *kismet* that Allah provides. Such is the true spirit of Islam and the devout Muslim. Beyond that life is only simple rules," Machmued continued, "to be simply followed."

A chameleon darted across the tiled atrium floor at the edge of the garden in the periphery of Salal's vision, disturbing his reverie, breaking the spell and startling him back to the present. The distraction vanished into the garden and Salal, sitting quietly on a bench in the shadow of an arch, retreated into the memories of his youth, quietly reflecting on his life. He absently wondered if his father would have been proud of him, the only son, as he sat here today. A shadow flickered across his eyes. A silent sigh escaped from between his lips.

No, he decided. Ka'mel l'Rahal would have shunned this particular success, this way of living.

"Perhaps, if my father had lived, things would have been different," he said aloud but to no one. He pondered the thought, rolling it around in his brain.

No, that was not true, he reluctantly admitted. It had been the will of Allah that had led to this moment. He knew in his heart that some things were destined by Allah, never to be changed by man.

For Salal, the Arab *jihad* for a Pan-Arab union had become a consuming passion, a purpose for being where before, no purpose could be found. A mandate from the Grand Mufti himself had been written in Arab blood and sanctified by Allah in *jihad*. The declaration was a simple yet difficult matter to be sure.

"Allah gave the land to his faithful servants, the sons of Ishmael, but the Jews have returned and stolen it," the *imams* preached.

It was a theme drummed into his consciousness even before the time of his father's death.

"The Jews and their American superpower ally stole the land. The Americans and their President, this Truman and all since then, are the dupes of the Zionists. Jewish politicians and Jewish gold control the Americans. They conspired with evil *djinns* against Islam," the Grand Mufti of Jerusalem had pronounced when Israel was born.

He remembered the words, the arguments from the first days of his youthful indoctrinations in the desolate refugee camps.

"If it had not been for the Americans, the Jews would not possess our lands, there would be no Israel," the *imams* railed.

The theme was an unspoken current in the river of Salal's life events that had led, those few months ago, to meeting with the council—when Jericho had first been outlined to them.

Now the wheel was about to come full-circle. Their time had come and he, Salal, would be the sword of Allah. His father, his family, his village, all of the Arab people would be avenged.

Vengeance was a way of life and the code by which Salal and true Arabs had always lived. A part of their culture, a part of their heritage as a people has always been the knowledge that the non-believers sought their destruction. The only recourse to redress these crimes was vengeance.

The criminals who had destroyed Salal's home and his father's way of life may not have been Americans, but the weapons supplied to the Jews that had taken away everything had been American. Justice was accomplished only by retaliation and justice was the goal of Jericho.

"The Americans gave the Jews the means to make the death of your family possible. The Jews and the Americans are equally guilty," his *imam* teachers had agitated over the years of his *fedayeen* education.

In that knowledge, Salal rationalized that his father would have accepted the destiny Allah had chosen for his son.

Salal shifted his body on the hard marble garden bench, averting his eyes from the direct glow of the afternoon sun. He rose, clasped his hands behind his back, and slowly began to stroll along the pathways of the garden.

In spite of his ruthlessness toward the enemies of Islam, Salal's personal moral code, indeed, his life was a living proof to the five pillars of Islam. A devout man, Salal sought to be *ahlu l-kitaab*, one of the true "people of the book," the ones who submit, which is the genuine meaning of the word Muslim. Salal did not drink alcohol, nor eat pork. He did not beat his wife or children—but then again, he was not married and had no children. As a faithful Muslim, he lived by the *shahadah*, the confession that there is but one God, Allah, and that Mohammed is the Prophet of God, and he made the five times daily performance of *salaat*, prayer. No matter how poor, ever since before the refugee camps of his youth, he quietly performed *zakat*, the giving of charity. Salal fasted, *siyam*, during the holy month of Ramadan and had twice made the *hajj*, a pilgrimage to the holy Ka'aba in Mecca.

Salal's face creased in concentration as he paced the garden walkway. His jaw worked in determined effort as he mentally rehearsed the remarks he would make before the council. He reached deep into his memory trying to recall a name.

The author of the Jericho operation strode up and back, and then back once more to the bench.

"Who was he ... the general?" he asked himself aloud. He searched his memory and finally called up the name from a long forgotten textbook.

"Ah, yes, MacArthur," he answered. That was the name. A great general in spite of being an American. So simply, so boldly he had spoken, but his government had not listened.

There can be no substitute for victory, MacArthur had said.

Yes, that was the phrase—no substitute for victory.

La, Yes. That was it. So very appropriate, Salal thought. He must remember to use those words today as he spoke to the council.

"Just one bold stroke," he said aloud to no one.

This, by far, was the most ambitious of their operations against the Americans.

Was it too ambitious? Too great a risk? Too far a bridge? Was he a moth drawn to the flame? Salal shuddered at the involuntary premonition. He wished the interview and briefing were over.

The doors at the end of the garden, opposite the bench to which he had returned, opened. A man dressed in a simple white cotton *dishdasha*, the loose fitting dresslike garment falling to his ankles, motioned.

Salal crossed the garden and entered the room. An unadorned table backed with a single chair was in place in the center of the chamber. An ancient fan languidly churned the heavy air above a dais. The members of the committee lounged behind a semicircular table in the traditional Bedouin fashion, seated against piled silk and tapestry pillows. Three silver bowls of sugared dates, fresh fruits and figs and carafes of *ahwa*, the thick black coffee spiced with cardamom were positioned along the table. Two of the men slurped at the demitasse cups that marked the seat of each of the twelve participants. There were platters of *shawirmu*, roasted lamb and rice, and plates of *gibna beyda min*, goats' milk cheese with pita bread. They were arranged within easy reach of the men at the table.

There were no smiles, no introductions, and no exchanges of the kiss of welcome. Salal made obeisance to his left, right and to the center of the dais. He wore a formal black sleeveless *Bisht* as was appropriate for the occasion. His head was covered by a matching *kaffiyah* that flowed to his shoulders and was held in place by a black twisted wool *Agai*.

"*Salaam aleikem*," offered Salal in traditional greeting.

"*Aleikem es-Salaam*," replied a voice from the table.

An extended arm gestured for him to sit.

"You may begin," the voice said without further comment.

A numbness settled over Salal. A calm from deep within him dispelled anxiety and nervousness. He was ready.

Salal began to speak in the rich tones of their ancient common tongue. The language in which Salal spoke, Arabic, conveyed more than just the meanings of each word. Unlike English, the meaning of Arabic words lies in their abstraction rather than in their surface communication. It is a language of ambiguity, subtlety and hidden meaning, which is constructed to carry more than just a declaration. The language passes with it a culture, a heritage, an awareness. Those who just learn the sound of the words do not grasp the rich vibrancy of their under flowing meanings.

"As you know we have called the operation Jericho," he said, "in honor of one of our ancient cities."

"But today I come to speak about more than just Jericho."

The silence before his next words stretched and filled the chamber.

"Abraham, our father, described and promised his sons a

great destiny, a seat among the giants. That, my brothers, was promised to Ishmael and his mother. We were to be a great nation of people, to sit, to lead at the council tables of the world. The time has come to claim that seat."

He warmed to his subject taking the indirect, polite route demanded by Arab culture.

"Abraham was the father of two sons, Isaac the Jew and Ishmael the Arab," he said, recalling to their minds what they had always known. "We, the Arab and the Jew, are both a Semitic people," he continued, "bound by the blood of a common father. But that is long past. The Jews fell from the grace of Abraham as they have also fallen from the pleasure of Allah. The Jews betrayed their heritage. They lost the right to a land of their own because they dishonored their covenant with God; they transgressed the teachings of their own sacred book, the Torah. They martyred their prophets. They even crucified the one called Jesus, the Christian, whom even Muhammad recognized as a great prophet."

Salal paused for effect.

"Their sins have cost the Jews their birthright. The Romans destroyed their temple and sowed salt into their land. This land was forfeited to the sons of Ishmael who have been faithful to God's words. Allah Himself gave the word of the law to Mohammad and he, in the Koran, has given them to God's Muslim children. But now almost two thousand years later, the Jews have returned. They come to steal back the land that had been forfeit, the land of Palestine. They spit on us as they ride high up on the backs of their American allies and kill us with weapons bearing the words 'Made in the USA.'"

His audience was attentive and quiet.

"Ours is a family quarrel," he said. "The *Americai*, or the *Ingilizi*, or the *Roosees* do not decide who owns the land or who is to live on the *dira* in Palestine. It is for us to decide. Allah took the land from the Jews and gave it to the children of Ishmael. Until the land is returned to the Arab people there can be no peace," he announced fiercely.

"A people cannot be asked to live without their heritage, without their dowry, without their land."

This is the moment, Salal thought, that I must convince all of them. They must stand united behind me. It would all depend on persuading them before other conflicting, confusing voices were raised. Those other voices, given the chance, would cause hesitation and doubts. Salal knew they would begin to change their minds, to question their own wisdom. They would cast another vote—one in favor of more talk and indecision. This was the way it had always been and which had led them to their past defeats and disunity. They would lose heart and will for the Jericho venture. Salal's voice was rich and deep as he spoke again.

"Radical change requires radical means. A homeland for the Palestinians is no closer today than it was fifty years ago. The Israelis defile us! They grow stronger while we sit at the *Americai* table of peace to beg the Jews to return a piece of that which they stole from us. This would not be the way of our ancestors. Now is the time to demonstrate our unity. Now is the time to take back our lands from the *kaffirs*, the non-believers. Now is the time to show the world that it shall not treat us as beggars and whores fit only for scraps from the wealthy that take oil from our soil. Now is the time to reclaim our Arab heritage!"

Salal spoke with the heat of deep conviction both as an Arab and as a Muslim. His eyes were bright, his voice strong.

"A small group of dedicated Arab fighters will do more in just a few hours than have all of the oil embargoes and sheiks and governments of the world. Ours will be a statement of action to all of our enemies. Jericho will once and finally prove the impotence of the Americans—on their own soil. They become timid when the cost is their own blood. Our success will bring the West to accept our terms on Palestine. They will withdraw their support from Israel. The action I have outlined to you at our last meeting will confirm the Arab destiny as a world power and it will bring the Israelis to their knees. All that is now needed is your final blessing."

"We will be branded outlaws by the nations of the world" one of the council members said.

"No," replied Salal firmly. "We will only be branded by those who now hold the reins of power. But the wheel of history is turning. The inevitability of destiny as taught in the Koran will bend all to the will of Allah. One day, and soon, those called terrorists will be recognized by the entire world, by all, as patriots and martyrs, as our own people recognize them now."

He searched his thoughts for an example to prove his point. Perversely a Jewish name came to mind.

"Just as Menachem Begin, a terrorist, fought the British, it is now the British who praise Begin as the statesman, Begin as a hero and a champion of Israel."

The logic seemed sound and it was, more importantly, what the council wanted to believe. Still, Salal knew that his words would not quell the inevitable dissent. There was a faction that worried over political repercussions and backlash that would affect significant financial investments in the Arab world.

"They will retaliate! The Americans are a sleeping giant," said the Iraqi delegate of the council.

Salal stopped, looked into the eyes of the Iraqi and then briefly surveyed the remainder of the executive council members, before responding to the statement.

"Against whom?" Salal asked. "Please do not take offense brother, but we are not the Army of Iraq. Our fighters are not a deployed force of tanks, or artillery, or jet airplanes. The *fedayeen* are like the wind, heard but not seen. They strike and disappear."

The faces of the executive leadership were impassive. Salal bluntly continued his argument.

"The loss of just two hundred and forty-one American Marines in Lebanon changed the Middle East policy of the West," Salal said. "Khomeini changed the political fortunes of an American president. Jericho, in one swift and certain stroke, will change the tide of history. The West will view us with fear and new respect," Salal promised. "The Americans do not have the stomach for a long fight. They count their losses, not in lives, but in dollars. Their God is wealth and self-interest. Political channels and debates have changed nothing, accomplished nothing. The Israelis only grow stronger, and our own voices in the world weaker."

He bulldozed on in untypical Arab fashion—direct and to the point.

"We are at war. We fight by whatever means are available. There are no neutrals, no non-belligerents. There are only those who are with us and those who are against us. The means we use to achieve victory are not important. Innocents will die, yes. But innocents always die. Just as our innocent fathers and mothers and daughters and brothers were taken from their homes and died in the displacement and internment camps for the crime of being Arab."

Salal paused dramatically, trying by the force of his will to draw the council members to agreement with his arguments.

"We must never forget the reason for our struggle. A homeland for all of our people and the greatness to the Arab nation promised to us by our fathers long ago. We are the chosen of Allah. We will humble the Americans and restore Israel as a homeland for the Palestinian people."

Salal leaned forward, his arms flung out before him.

"Now is the moment of our destiny, our history. Our heritage is at hand. You, our rightful leaders, hold the destruction of our enemies and the restoration of our stolen birthright—stolen from us by the Jews and the Americans –- in your hands. History will be our judge and bold men have always written history. There can be no substitute for victory!"

There were discrete nods of agreement around the table and Salal knew he had made his point, perhaps not with all, but with most. He had captured their hearts and minds—at least for the moment. Besides, they had earlier approved the concept of Jericho. Today's meeting was to confirm Salal's authority to transform the idea into operational execution.

"You know my mind. You know my heart. With respect, my brothers, I have finished my words on this subject. Let me now tell you how we have proceeded since our last meeting."

Salal turned to the details of Jericho—all excepting the location of the target in the United States. It was a simple matter of security. The labyrinth of plots, leaks and intrigues of the Arab world was too well known and betrayal too common, even within these confines, to display all of the details of the plan.

6
Washington, D.C.
—May, 2000

The dark gray 1999 Mercury slid out of the main stream of Washington traffic and glided to a stop at the iron gated entrance of the old Executive Office Building, adjacent to the White House. Rufus P. Brandt, the sole occupant and driver of the sedan, worried the battered end of an unlit cigar. The Deputy Chief of Staff for Army Intelligence, the DCSINT, as he was known on the Army Staff, was not having a good day. And now, to top it all off, he was again late to an important meeting.

Brandt looked more like an aged NFL lineman than a senior Army officer. The son of a West Virginia Irish-German coal miner, Brandt was something of an anomaly in the uniformed bureaucracy of the Pentagon. Physically, he was not an attractive man. He did, however, exude a sense of confidence and an unidentifiable aura of power. His thick biceps were outlined in the sleeves of his shirt and the back of his hands supported a thick sprouting of course black hair. The tailored shirt tapered to a 38-inch waist but the buttons strained just above the brass buckled belt of his dark green trousers. Unwanted pounds were beginning to appear at the General's waist. His hands were heavy powerful slabs of callused meat, which, in an affectionate and enthusiastic handshake, crushed fingers and bruised bones. His black hair was parted on the right, combed straight back and cut to a moderate length. Graying at the temples, it was beginning to thin and recede into a pronounced widow's peak. His shoulders were rounded and, combined with a thrice broken nose that upon close examination tilted slightly to the left, his features conveyed the impression of a boxer.

The rain that had snarled downtown traffic began to slacken. A line of thunderstorms had swept through the city turning the day sultry and oppressive. The window-rattling micro downbursts had drenched the streets in a wetness which suprised both tourists and residents alike. Potomac feeder streams rose from their banks and sent eddies into Rock Creek Parkway. The tourist trade T-shirt and food vendors had slammed shut the sides of their carts in a rushed effort to protect their wares from the intermittent downpours. Streets were swiftly emptied as tourists huddled in the refuge of the several buildings of the Smithsonian.

While the damp day was a brief respite to the high temperatures, the cloudbursts had added to the mugginess of the city. Washington, DC, built on a tract of bog and swamp donated by Maryland and Virginia for a new national capital city, always seemed to attract humidity in the summer. The evening rush hour, just beginning, promised congestion well beyond its normal aggravating limits.

The uniformed Federal Protective Services guard at the gate was distracted by the scurrying antics of a family of large brown rats. The rats had taken up residency in two of the several large shrubbery areas adjacent to the concrete barriers surrounding the entrance to the Federal Executive Office Building. Aberrantly they seemed to relish the pepper spray that he dispensed at them. In spite of repeated direct hits, the spray had not deterred their occupancy. The guard was the only one discomforted by the spray's lingering eye watering pungency.

The guard stepped forward from the small glass encased hut and examined the sole uniformed occupant of the sedan, smiled, touched the brim of his cap, and nodded perfunctorily.

The man who peered back at the guard from the interior of the sedan wore a long sleeved, light green Army shirt and regulation black tie.

Rufus punched a button on the armrest of the door and

the driver's window glided into its recess. He removed the cigar from between his lips.

"Afternoon, General," the guard drawled, his eyes drawn to the Class A green jacket with three bright silver stars on each shoulder. It hung on a wooden hanger at the rear of the driver's door. Six rows of colored ribbons topped by the Combat Infantryman's badge and airborne wings were visible over the left breast pocket of the blouse.

"David," the general acknowledged.

"Got your own car today, I see. What happened to your driver, sir?" the guard asked.

"Gave him the afternoon off. Don't know how long we're going to be here today."

"I must be working for the wrong outfit," the guard noted with a smile. He checked his clipboard access roster for the day for the familiar name. "You're getting soft in your old age, sir," the guard chided.

Although well known by those who protect the public and private meeting places of the powerful in Washington, the ritual of clearance had to be accomplished.

"Must be so, David," Rufus replied. "I'm turning into a real pussycat. Ask anybody."

Finding the name, the guard waved to the central security office that was observing the proceeding by closed circuit TV camera. The tire piercing spikes guarding the entryway retracted.

"Well, my shift is about over. If I miss you when you leave, have a nice weekend, General," the guard announced, as he waved the car through the entry of the iron picketed compound into its private parking lot.

"You too, David."

An old college friend of the President, Rufus was trusted on a very personal level by the man in the Oval Office. Despite their divergent political views, Rufus' often-sought advice was appreciated and weighed in spite of, not because of, his military background. The President needed well-reasoned, honest dissent and, for that, Rufus' candor was invaluable.

Importantly and at something of a dichotomy, Rufus commanded the respect of his civilian intelligence peers—no mean task given their diverse personalities, backgrounds, conflicting political ambitions and agendas. Brandt's respect among his colleagues was earned. They knew him from his Desert Storm reputation as well as his proven insight and accuracy in gleaning the informal networks, structures and workings of several major terrorist organizations. Personal contacts in foreign intelligence services and a rapport with out-of-power political elements led to an acknowledgement that Rufus was the Nosterdamus of U.S. Middle East intelligence. He was an accepted player whose influence on the decision makers in the inner corridors of power and national policy making was quietly felt. The entire intelligence community used his analyses. CIA and British MI-5 rivals parsimoniously acknowledged—by their plagiarism—superiority in his expertise and analytical ability.

Only Rufus, it seemed, had been able to cobble together a coherent Middle East strategy that appeared to work for all the conflicting parties. Without direct authorship but working with representatives from the State Department and the National Security Council, his suggestions had been translated in a series of talks being hosted by the President at Camp David. The talks held forth a promise of peace in the Middle East.

Brandt grabbed his jacket from its dangling hanger, slammed the car door shut and heard the remote beep of its automatic locking as he both struggled into the blouse and adjusted the tilt of his headgear. Fat raindrops snagged at his cap and spattered across his shaggy eyebrows, cascading down over the dark stubble of an almost day-old beard. He ran easily for the doors of the building. The bronzed cased entrance opened before him and he strode into the cool antechamber. Brushing droplets of rain from his uniform, he passed through the interior security screening point and by the guard without comment.

Lieutenant General Brandt's brisk steps echoed hollowly on the polished stone floor. Proceeding to the last elevator on the right, the General removed a plastic card from his wallet and inserted it into an ATM teller machine-like slot. The doors slid open. Rufus stepped in, pressed the button marked Four, and watched the flickering display of indicator lights as the car descended into the ground.

The call had come from Malcolm DeFore, the National Security Advisor to the President and pro forma chairman of the National Security Council's intelligence committee for the Middle East. DeFore's office had run each of the ad hoc committee members to ground and advised them of the unusual requirement for the three o'clock gathering. The meeting bode no good things for the weekend.

The elevator glided to a stop and he stepped out, turned left and entered the third door on the right of the brightly lit unadorned passageway.

Rufus Brandt had remained on active duty longer than he had planned. Private government consultant firms had made several lucrative offers, but he had declined them. Brandt recognized that most companies only wanted to buy his reputation, not his ability; and his reputation, like his integrity, was not for sale.

The President had asked him to stay and, all other reasons notwithstanding, he had agreed because he was a patriot. But now the time had come for him to go. His name, he felt, was too much in the public, he was becoming too well known to be effective. And, truth be told, he was beginning to tire. Time had come for him to leave the stage to a younger, more vigorous turk, one more attuned to the automation, the electronics, and the rapidity of the twenty-first century.

There were more than enough of them, each with his or her own reasons and motivation, just waiting in the wings for the opportune moment.

Rufus would retire as soon as the new administration had their feet on the ground. I'll do it the end of June, he once or twice had mused absently.

The room into which he stepped was not large. Bathed in soft indirect lighting that radiated from the edges of the low-hung ceiling, it contrasted to both the corridor and most of the offices of the building. The room was handsome in its appointments. Sound was muffled in the expensive deep mat of the gold carpet and absorbed by the matching, electrically drawn heavy, yellow drapes. The drape coverings shielded Plexiglas situation board maps of the current force deployments in the several ocean areas as well as Bosnia, the Middle East, Africa, Asia, and South America. A large opaque screen for rear viewgraph projections was built into the wall at the far end of the table. A red light above the center of the conference table indicated to the participants that the conversation in the room was being recorded.

Computerized voice identification programs, designed to encode voice signals into random frequency ranges, were active. The verbatim conversations in the room were taped, encrypted and, as necessary, would later be available to a very small, select group of authorized personnel should they desire to listen to them.

"Good Afternoon, Rufe," DeFore smiled at the late arrival.

"Malcolm. Gentlemen," Brandt acknowledged as he slipped into his usual chair along the right side of the table. The other five members of the ad hoc committee had already assembled. In addition to Rufus and Malcolm DeFore, there were Ed Jouver from the CIA, Ted Morrison from the National Security Agency or NSA, Joel Stevenson, Deputy Director for Domestic Terrorism, Federal Bureau of Investigation, and the number three man at the State Department, Deputy Secretary George Dwier. They represented the key "special interests" of the intelligence community of the United States.

"Sorry I'm late. I got tied up in a review of remarks for Congressman Adderson's budget hearings on Monday. Ran a bit longer than expected and then the showers backed traffic up across the Fourteenth Street Bridge. My apologies."

The silent omni-directional microphones set into the ceiling recorded the words.

Congressman Charlie Adderson, the diminutive five foot four inch North Carolinian had earned the Chairmanship of the House Intelligence Overwatch Committee by virtue of seniority versus ability. Adderson was generally acknowledged as a consummate politician and bureaucrat, which was by way of saying that he was an opportunist of the first magnitude. The committee recognized him as an uncontrollable source of leaks to the media on sensitive intelligence issues, but like it or not, he was a power to be reckoned with. The Honorable Mister Adderson was one of the limited few that could obtain uncensored access to the NSC data banks—including the verbatim minutes of this meeting. Each of the men who had gathered on this late Friday afternoon had, at one point or another, borne the brunt of Charlie's grandstanding, demagogic rhetoric in one or another too public forum.

The Intelligence community and Rufus, in particular, had become a premeditated target that the Congressman attacked at every headline opportunity. Eighteen months earlier, the DCSINT had taken on the chairman in some verbal fisticuffs during one of the televised intelligence committee hearings. In a very rare and long overdue display of anger, Brandt had taken Adderson to pieces in logical and well-documented response to several McCarthy-like conclusions that Adderson had made on sensitive intelligence operations. The General made the North Carolinian look foolish and petty. The hostile act was not forgotten nor forgiven by the pseudo-intellectual gnat from the Tar Heel State. Rufus had created a powerful, vengeful enemy.

"Not to worry, Rufe," grinned Malcolm DeFore, "we all know how much you enjoy the Honorable Mister Adderson's company and would not want to deny you the quality time you no doubt will be spending with him on Monday."

Rufus turned to the other five men arrayed around the table and shook his head in mock exasperation, his shoulders slumping under a ponderous imaginary weight. In return each of his contemporaries in the room sported large grins.

"Well, let's get started, shall we," said DeFore, standing at the head of the table. "First, I want to thank you all for taking time from your busy schedules and I apologize for the short notice to this rather, ah ... ahem, hastily called and unusual session. I'll try not to draw this out any longer than necessary, but we have an important matter to discuss."

DeFore glanced upward at the invisible ceiling microphones, screwed his face uncomfortably, and cleared his throat. There was nothing he could do about his remarks being recorded.

"Obviously, the subject of our discussions is to go no further than this room. Let me begin by telling you that we are meeting this afternoon at the direction of the President. He has already been briefed on the matters we will be discussing and I shall be speaking with him later this evening on the results of our deliberations."

He looked down the table at the upturned and somewhat puzzled faces. "I recognize that this is procedurally back asswards, but suffice to say, it is not without reason. Given the President's involvement in the recent Middle East peace negotiations at Camp David, and the sensitivity of the subject we will be discussing, it was prudent to obtain his advanced approval for this meeting. Based on what I told him, he directed that this meeting take place as soon as possible, thus the reason why we are here this afternoon."

The interest of the committee was piqued and an attentive curiosity replaced casual silence. The tape machines spun on, hissing in the quiet of the conference room.

DeFore paused, gathering his thoughts, took a deep breath and began.

"The talks between the President of the Palestinian National Authority, Mr. Yasser Arafat and Ehud Barak, the current Prime Minister of Israel, mediated by the President of the United States, have been much more successful than has been reported in the media. While specific details of the key features have not been released, the progress of these past few days has been extraordinary. They may have, however, produced an extreme reaction that was not fully anticipated."

"What in the hell does that mean in English, Mal?" asked the CIA representative.

"The latest concessions by the Palestine Liberation Organization at discussions held at Camp David these past few days..."

Ed Jouver interrupted. "Said PLO also being a distinct organization from the Palestinian National Authority, but not so strangely also headed by our good friend Yasser Arafat."

"... were apparently not coordinated" DeFore continued, "nor even discussed with the Islamic Conference Organization. The Pan-Arab camp is in a frenzy. They're calling Arafat's compromises another Sadat sell-out, and we all know what happened to Sadat when he made compromises without the approval of the ICO."

DeFore swiveled about and removed six numbered copies of a yellow and black slashed folder from his briefcase and passed them around the table, retaining the last one for himself. Across the cover against the black background was yellow lettering which read:

EYES ONLY. TOP SECRET
GAMBIT
NOFORN

The President's National Security Advisor was all business now, brusque and direct.

"In the package before you, gentlemen," said DeFore, indicating the Top Secret portfolio, "is the latest intelligence we have on the ICO, and the locations and strengths of networked terrorist organizations. Rufus has put it together over the past several months. So then, gentlemen, with that brief introduction, Rufus, the floor is yours."

Malcolm DeFore slid into his chair at the head of the table, fussed his tie into place, and sat back in relaxed anticipation.

Rufus sat forward and folded his hands on the table before
him.

"Even the Mossad," Rufus offered, "supported by
Benjamin Netanyahu's Sayeret Matcal anti-terrorism force
and the Israeli Jonathan Institute, ah, a group that studies terrorism and develops strategies to combat it, has been unable
to discover all that you will hear this afternoon. The ICO
principals, the phantoms who sanction all the plans, establish
priorities, and finance international terrorist operations, have
never been individually identified. We knew the ICO existed,
but that's about all we had on them till now."

DeFore held up his hand and motioned Rufus to momentary silence. "Connections, identities, relationships were all
whispers," DeFore interjected, "that evaporated at the first
sign of investigation. That was, until Rufus started putting
events together that appeared to be random."

The National Security Advisor paused dramatically before
continuing. "The ICO leaves nothing behind it but a vacu-
um of doubt, insecurity and uncertainty. Even its name, the
Islamic Conference Organization, or ICO, as we have come
to know it, is vague and nondescript. However, their international terrorist intervention over the years is credited for
more than one abandonment of internationally sponsored
peace initiatives. As for the U.S., well, ah, let us say that
uncertain direction and changes to our policy in resolving
Arab-Israeli differences have been our typical reactions to
ICO successes. There is only one known link to their strategies, a name—Salal. The man is a brilliant strategist, an
effective, elusive foe."

Rufus picked up the thread again, stitching another patch
into a growing quilt. "Bottom line, gentlemen, is that we now
have reliable information that Salal is active again. He is planning a major operation with ICO sponsorship," stressing the
point made by Malcolm's comments.

"Jesus H. Christ!" whispered Joel Stevenson. "The ICO
again?"

"We believe so," Brandt replied. "It ties together. They

have been quiet for quite a while. So let me, ah, just to review the bidding on this particular group, bring us all up to date."

"The last we heard of Salal was a confirmation on him in Frankfurt about twelve hours before Pan Am 103 took off. We almost had that bastard," Stevenson said.

"He's stacked up more American military bodies with small teams from *Hizvallah*, the Black Septemberists, the Sword of Allah, and the *fedayeen* than Saddam did with the fourth largest army in the world!" Ed Jouver volunteered.

"Yes, and we are now certain," Rufus concluded, "he also played a major role in the February '93 underground garage bombing at the World Trade Center."

Joel Stevenson nodded in agreement, having headed up the FBI side of the investigation of the incident.

"All financed and supported," Rufus continued, "courtesy of the ICO and funneled through Libya, Iraq and a few others to Salal."

The DCSINT had much more to contribute to the discussion, but not right now, Brandt thought, and not for all the ears who could access this tape-recorded venue.

DeFore picked up the thought. "… and that doesn't even begin to include the civilians and other mischief he's caused among our allies. Remember the El Al incident at the DaVinci airport in Rome?"

There were affirmative nods from around the room.

"All it took was just some damn good planning, a couple of automatic weapons and a few Arab zealots who were willing to die for their cause. Interpol is quite certain the killing of those El Al passengers in Rome was one of Salal's first international jobs and he's engineered a hellava lot more blood baths since then."

DeFore punched at a button located on a console at the head of the table and the screen at the far end of the room lit up with an organizational model tracing the ICO's roots.

The chart was one that Rufus had put together for DeFore at his request. The General had connected the dots and sorted what had appeared to be global random acts of terrorism, but which was, in reality, a strategic tightening noose of ICO sponsored terrorism.

By working at the edges, analyzing the details, looking at timings and individual terrorists, he had proven that at certain times, for particular events, there had been a coalescence, a merging of more than just a casual conversation between several of the terrorist groups. There was a single hand that coordinated the most dramatic and political of the radical actions of assassination and bombings, the ones of international scope, the ones that caused national policy shifts. Often they had a secondary message, not the least of which was to serve notice on the United States that it was not invulnerable.

DeFore continued. "The Islamic Conference Organization has no international standing, no recognition by any government, and no formal ties to any group in the Middle East," DeFore began. "Its roots flow from HAMAS, otherwise known as the Arabic *Harakat al-Maqawama al-Islamiya*, the Muslim Brotherhood, which was founded in 1928 by Sheik Hasan al-Bana. The organization, however, continues to evolve from new Arab realizations resulting from the 1948 establishment of Israel and the disasters of the 1967 Six Day and 1973 Yom Kippur Wars. The ICO is an *ad hoc* body that parallels the quasi-organization of American colonies that existed after the American Revolutionary War before the Constitution of the United States was written and ratified. There, however, the similarities with the American model end."

"I thought the Desert Storm Arab coalition we put together dissipated the ICO's support base. My sources tell me that they lost quite a bit of their punch," Jouver offered, injecting another CIA contribution to the discussion.

"Not as much as your sources thought, Ed," replied DeFore, and turned back to the group to continue.

"The ICO is a quiet collective influence. The organization is a pervasive, wisp like power within the Arab corridors that silently borders on the absolute. Even Saddam pays attention when it speaks. There is no leader or chairman of the ICO, no troika of power. A communal consensus decides on courses of action. In general, it becomes involved in terrorist operations only if the operation is to take place outside of the Middle East. Not to inform the ICO in advance is tantamount to a rogue operation and so is sanctionable. Whoever undertakes an action without their approval risks political and economic abandonment as well as the loss of safe haven.

"Unlike OPEC membership, the ICO does not identify itself to the political interests of any specific Arab state so it is not distracted by petty Arab nationalism. Collectively, this gang is only interested in those actions that affect the collective Arab whole. National self-interest and individual state sovereignty are suborned to the greater good of Islam and Arabia. As HAMAS, its parent, the ICO mission is to bind the Arab states into one. They seek the establishment of a United States of Islam, a single entity speaking for the entire Arab world."

"What keeps holding this group together?" asked Joel.

"Good question," Rufus replied. "It appears to be religious ideology. The coercive and cohesive force of the Koran is what drives them. The leadership is not Shi'i, Sunni, Druze, or Alawite. These zealots subscribe to a Koran based only on the book itself and the *hadith*, or sayings, of the first Muslims and Mohammed. Their power comes from a moral as well as a financial base and so is more appealing, compelling, and enduring to the common Muslim."

DeFore punched the button and a new slide flashed up on the screen outlining ICO goals.

"It garnishes support from across the full Arab political spectrum," DeFore continued, "for the removal of repulsive Western influence."

"Something along the lines of the Khomeini philosophy?" commented George Dwier.

"Perhaps, but more Sunni, I would say, than Shi'i, George. Not as radical or fundamentalist as Khomeini and his followers. I'd classify them as maybe johnny-come-lately fundamentalists with a strong dose of international political savvy. In

any event they're turning a Muslim brotherhood of basic
moral values into a power base that supports the political
achievement of strategic Arabic interests. These folks are the
worst kind of terrorists. They're idealists. They will use any
means to achieve the elimination of Israel as a nation state and
Western social influence. They are devoted to the protection
of Islam and the Arab culture."

Rufus tag teamed in on DeFore's comments. "Let me just
add a few words to Malcolm's thoughts. This gang is unique.
Unlike the other groups we've run into, once the ICO leadership decides on a policy or course of action, the decision is
supported by all."

"Just like our Congress," Joel Stevenson added with a
crooked smile, drawing grins from around the room.

"We have reason to believe," Rufus continued, "the ICO
comes close to possessing the power and the resources,
including an unlimited source of funding, strong enough to
just about overthrow any targeted Arab leader. They organized the support for the Yom Kippur war, the expulsion of
Egypt from the Arab brotherhood, and were the driving force
for the Arab sanctions against Egypt during the Sadat years.
But, and this is an important distinction, gentlemen, it was
only when a jury of *imams* had sanctioned Sadat's death
under Islamic law in the *uluma*, a council of religious elders,
that the ICO supported that Al-Jahid effort."

Rufus looked up towards the silent ceiling microphone,
grimaced, and continued. "Just prior to mounting his attack
on Kuwait, the ICO gave Saddam the green light. Seems
Kuwait was straying too far toward Western culture and
Saddam was the instrument the ICO used to bring them
back in line. They warned the rulers of the other Arab States
against all but token political support of Desert Storm
against Iraq, but there were some cracks and, as you know,
some of the Arabs went all the way with us. Of the latter two
events it was said that both were sins of the first magnitude—clear violations of Islam, the Koran, and the *hadith*,
the words of the Prophet."

"Any luck yet on identifying the leadership?" George asked.

"Some strong leads," DeFore responded, "but the men invested in the ICO leadership roles rarely meet as a group. There have been less than a dozen occasions for such meetings since 1948. This latest meeting was at a safe haven at Tripoli. They met that time in extraordinary session, to hear the details of a plan that they had approved in concept."

He paused. "The issue, we have since learned, was straightforward—its substance delicate and very dangerous—even in its discussion. Simply put, the matter decided was approval of a major escalation in the spectrum of terrorism—a major attack on the United States itself ... one with profound and lasting impact and more dramatic than any other before attempted. The advocate for the action, our good friend Salal, argued that the action would bring about an end to the Palestinian question by removing the United States and other 'foreign' elements from the equation. He convinced the leadership that the operation he proposed would most probably lead to the end of the current fifty-year dispute with the Jews over Palestine.

"That could very well lead to the establishment a new order in the Middle East," interjected Joel.

"Exactly. Salal advocated a major military attack somewhere here in the United States. Whatever they're planning, it's big—we think more than just another run-of-the-mill bombing. The ICO wants us to sit up and take notice, do something that will give them back their clout, their political advantage."

"They want to knock us back on our heels and demonstrate our vulnerability," Rufus summarized.

DeFore nodded agreement.

"Salal's convinced his backers that it would take us out of the Middle East game. He proposed that it would break our political will, much as it was broken in Vietnam. The ICO is looking for something spectacular—something that will resurrect Nassar's old Pan-Arab league, give them *de facto* leadership, end the current peace negotiations, and, in short, establish once and for all, a new order in the Middle East. They are putting it all on this one roll of dice. They're betting they can replace us as the broker in the peace process and in doing so dictate terms to Israel."

"I think you're overreacting," Ed Jouver interrupted. "With all due respect, Mal, let's not jump to conclusions. You're overestimating Salal's ability and the influence of the ICO."

There was no love lost between the National Security Advisor and the CIA. Ed was embarrassed and upset that the CIA had not acquired this information. Professionally he had egg on his face and so his immediate and hostile reaction was to attack the credibility of the briefer's sources.

Jouver continued, "I don't know if I can buy into this attack theory. At this point you're still working from a vast reservoir of ignorance."

Ed searched the room appealing to his colleagues for support of his stance. "Here, let me play devil's advocate for a minute. How do we definitively know that Salal is even planning an operation, let alone one in the United States—and one of the magnitudes you describe? Maybe it's another rogue operation. I have yet to be convinced either Gander or Pan Am 103, for example, were sanctioned by the ICO. You give them too much credit. The only link you ever had between them was a weak one and Salal is nowhere even mentioned on the Gander incident."

He continued, gesturing to the file before him that he had just browsed, "According to this, your source isn't even identified. How do we know his information is any good? There's a damn good chance that we're being manipulated. Your man may have been compromised, tricked, or just fed bad info to get us to react."

DeFore turned to the sandy haired, pinch-faced and freckled CIA representative, managed an insincere smile and responded.

"First off, Ed, you have already been told that the source

is too sensitive to be identified, even to this select group."
The remark drew Jouver up short and reminded him that
the CIA did not have the only market on human, or
HUMINT, intelligence.

"Only three people know who he is. Even his handler
doesn't know him other than by code name. Every bit of data
he has ever given us has been verified and was A-1. And as far
as Pan Am 103 and Gander are concerned, you damn well
know that he gave us an exact reconstruct of both bombings
with names, places, and suppliers, descriptions and files on the
three men who wired it up. The Pan Am operation was, I will
grant you, sloppy but both were sanctioned ICO operations."
DeFore paused and then concluded with somewhat of a well-
targeted barb if not indirect reprimand.

"That information, I might add, the CIA didn't have but,
as you may remember, was able to verify once that same
source told you where to look."

"I still don't buy it. You're reaching," Jouver said in a
defensive tone.

"Ed, we're talking about the same Salal who put together
the hits in Beirut on the Marines, and blew up the Air Force
barracks out in Saudi. Even if you are right, do you want to
take another chance like that?" interrupted Ted Morrison.
"This guy has done us too much damage not to be taken seriously. Speaking for the National Security Agency, we cannot
afford to discount Mal's conclusions. This information and
the threat it conveys must be taken seriously."

"I have to agree with Ted. He's right, but Ed does have a
point," injected Rufus. "The ICO as a power is running into
some difficulty. Remember that power is as much perception
as it is real. Right or wrong, belief is the stuff on which politics, alliances and regional balances are built. What Salal and
his sponsors are looking for is power. Besides, it's just too big
a risk for us to assume that he has not lined up an operation.
We haven't heard from Salal for over 18 months and he's
overdue. The ICO needs a triumph. Organizationally, they
need a big win if they are going to be successful in grabbing

enough clout to create a Pan-Arab coalition. To do that they have to apply pressure—get us into a 'lose-lose' situation by either overreacting or quitting the peace process altogether. Either way it reduces our influence and is a move that helps them."

DeFore, who had turned his attention to Rufus, swiveled his chair and re-focused back to the full group.

"If you would please open your folio, gentlemen, to Tab A, I think you will be surprised with what we have learned," he said and smiled in satisfaction across the table.

All but the grousing CIA Deputy, whose copy was already open before him, opened their folders and turned to the first document in the file. The top of the first numbered page of the file was titled *Background*. Tab A consisted of a three page point paper.

DeFore began by summarizing the document from memory. "In October, 1983, Arab terrorists attacked and destroyed a battalion of our Marines in Lebanon. In November 1985, a confederation of several different Arab terrorist organizations agreed on a single target and then carried out a strategic terrorist attack. They destroyed a US Army battalion at Gander, Newfoundland that was returning from peacekeeping duties in the southern Sinai desert. We know who did it and how. We can link the same group to the Pan Am flight that went down over Scotland, and more recently the TWA disaster off of the coast of New York."

Warming to his subject he continued. "The December 1988 destruction of PanAm 103 over Lockerbie, Scotland, killed two hundred and fifty-nine. The downing of TWA 800 in July of 1996 off of Long Island killed another two hundred and thirty people. Long story short, gentlemen, the ICO has demonstrated that they can export their brand of terrorism out of the Middle East and onto Main Street America with virtual impunity. Now that was quite a jump for them, in fact—a strategic leap."

He paused and ruffled through the sheets in front of him in slow motion like a run down clock. "Well, the list goes on and on. You can all read it for yourselves."

Malcolm paused, gathered his thoughts and let his words and the script of the point paper sink in before continuing. "Gentlemen, the ICO is becoming adroit at using terrorism as a strategic tool, one by which they can affect our foreign policy. Salal took a page from the drug lord's playbook of intimidation and organized the hit on the Director General of the Multination Peacekeeping Force in 1984. I can't seem to remember his name right now."

"Hunt," Rufus offered. "His name was Leamon R. Hunt. Went by his middle name, Ray. Assassinated on his wife's birthday in February '84 when he stopped to buy her flowers on his way home from the MFO headquarters in Rome. Very cold-blooded, professional job. Well executed," the DCSINT offered without emotion. "He didn't have the remotest idea that he was even a target. The State Department tossed him out there without so much as a set of waterwings."

George Dwier opened his mouth to object but thought better of it knowing what Rufus had said was true. The State Department representative turned sour faced and sat back, deeper into his chair.

"Sorry George," Rufus apologized. "Didn't mean to come on so strong."

Dwier made no response, only grunted.

"That was his name. Right," DeFore said. "How could I have forgotten?" trying to smooth over Rufus' tactless jab at the State Department.

DeFore continued with the briefing. "More recently the ICO engineered the hit on the Israeli Prime Minister Yitzhak Rabin. That was in '95. As you can see, they pick high visibility targets. That has the effect of putting the heat on us."

Again DeFore paused. A good speaker, he knew how to capture and hold his audience even though each of the men in this room had yet to hear something they had not already known.

"To date, their attacks have all been hit and run acts. Effective? Yes, very much so ... very difficult to defend against. Remember, they can miss 99 times out of a hundred but when they get lucky one time, we're on the front page with a lot of bodies scattered around and egg all over our faces."

"We've not been able to penetrate either the ICO or Salal's inner circle," Jouver admitted.

DeFore smiled like the cat that had swallowed the canary. "That is, gentlemen, until now – maybe," DeFore offered. "Take a look at TAB D."

There was silence as the members read the short but highly classified document which detailed the latest intelligence on the suspected attack.

The chairman broke in after a few moments. "Questions?"

DeFore acknowledged the FBI representative.

"When and, more importantly, where?" Joel Stevenson asked.

"We have some pretty good ideas," DeFore responded, "but frankly, I'm not satisfied that Salal has picked his final target yet. We're going to need your help on that. As you can see from the point paper, we think it will be before the end of the year and somewhere along the East Coast. Salal likes to work around the big holidays. Heavy traffic, more flights, more traveler panic, greater public sense of vulnerability. And, of course, he has had a history of successes in air attacks, piracy, and the kind of blood sport that makes good theater for the six o'clock news—good psychological warfare. That plays to their advantage. There are still lots of holes in the information, but everything we have been able to confirm has proven to be one hundred percent accurate."

"Where is Salal now?" interrupted Stevenson, clearly worried about the possibility that he had slipped into the United States without FBI knowledge.

"Good question. We don't know, to be candid. He's elusive—keeps disappearing from all the scopes just like he did after Lockerbie and the TWA flight 800 incident up in New York. I wish there were more to tell. But he just dropped from sight. Not a word, not a sound, not a trace. The last sighting, however," he referred to another section of the black slashed yellow folio in front of him, "was just a week ago. We had people who claim that he was on the Chad-Libyan border, but no confirmation was made at the time. We think he was headed for a base training camp in Southern Libya, but that's only a guess."

He looked up from the folder at Ted Morrison. "Ted, we could use some help in getting a positive ID on the camp. Do you think our satellite imagery might be able to give us a fix?"

"We'll get on it right away, Mal," was the reply. "We should be able to come up with something."

DeFore returned to the folder. "As to Salal, well, hell, he just as well could be in Iraq or Afghanistan with Abu Nadal. The important thing is not where he is now, but what he is planning to do and where he will be in the fall. We have been seeing key personnel drop out at virtually every guerrilla training base we know of. These guys must be going somewhere."

A thoughtful silence of painful memories and missed opportunities ensued but the mood was broken by DeFore.

"Take Salal and the ICO out of the game and I believe we have a much better opportunity to clean up the Middle East mess gentlemen. If we're successful, it will take the Arab and Muslim movements between five to eight years to recover. A lot could be done to stabilize the area and bring true peace to the Middle East in that period of time."

"Mal, I know Ed has already addressed this, but I want to be very clear. Are you quite certain of your information?" asked the FBI representative. To Joel Stevenson this was all new knowledge. DeFore was sure that more than one Deputy Director of the FBI would have his head handed to him when Joel returned to the Hoover building.

"Damn solid, Joel," answered DeFore, "even though Ed and I are in obvious disagreement on this. We ran our source for three and a half years. Every time we went to him, he came through with vital—repeat, vital—information for us. Our contact has friends within the old Soviet KBG and he has recently told us that the Russians are nervous over the ICO's shift in targeting. Since the Berlin Wall came down the old Soviets have had their hands full with internal dissension."

DeFore shifted position in his chair. "The Transcaucasian republics, Turkistan and Azerbaijan and so forth where the Muslim dominate," he continued, "are a tinderbox for them. The Soviets are very apprehensive about providing arms, which may eventually find their way back to Muslim dissidents in these regions. They do not see continued instability in the Middle East as being in their own best interest."

"The Afghanistan debacle proved that point to them," Rufus interjected.

"The Russians," Malcolm said, "recognize that the U.S. is the power broker in the Middle East and has to be a player if there is to be a peaceful solution. Comrade doesn't want to see us pick up our marbles and go home. The Soviets have independently verified a good bit of the information at Tab … ah, lets see, yep, here at Tab E."

"So why are we here?" asked the CIA representative.

"The Administration wants Salal," DeFore answered, "but as a matter of political policy we can't afford to go after him in an overt fashion. He's somewhat of a cross between a hero and a martyr to the Palestinians now. We don't want to add to that reputation. Remember that we still have to be the unbiased broker between the Arabs and the Jews. When we get Salal, we have to get him with his hand in our cookie jar— hard and dirty."

"And you think we can maneuver Salal and his bunch into a trick box?" asked the FBI agent.

"Yes." DeFore smiled. "I think we have here an opportunity to decimate the terrorist's front line para-military organizations, and to expose their political and financial backers, maybe even make the peace process work. And that brings me to the focus for this meeting. The President has decided that we can't afford to let the ICO continue to hold the initiative. No grandstand public announcement, just his classified personal executive order at… let me see… Tab G, to neutralize their operation and eliminate those responsible. By the way,

Salal named the ICO operation Jericho. We have titled our response effort *Gambit*."

Rufus cleared his throat and spoke. "If you'll recall, there were a few people at this table who said go after the ICO when those two hundred and fifty kids from the 101st were killed in Gander, Mal."

"What do you propose?" asked Ed Jouver.

"Surely something preemptory? A series of raids on Salal's training bases?" offered the NSA representative. "I think we'd be able to find them and give you everything you would need from our satellite imagery."

"God forbid." Rufus responded. "That's just the overreaction that the militants want. In the middle of peace negotiations we attack their *freedom fighters* and on their turf. Not a good idea."

"You're right, Rufe. The President was quite explicit on that point," DeFore added. "Nothing so direct or blunt. These are delicate times and require sensitivity in how we act. Let's not forget that. When we respond, it must be made unmistakably clear that we are the innocents and acting purely in self-defense. We have something a little more subtle in mind."

He continued. "The President wants us to take Salal down here on our turf, here in the US of A, at the last possible moment. Let them fully commit to their Jericho operation and then burn them. Catch them here where they lack the infrastructure to melt away in the general population. Just nail them hard."

"And just how are we going to do that?" asked the CIA representative.

"We're going to do that because when Salal shows up you will have told us where he will be and we're going to be there waiting for him."

DeFore turned to Brandt. "Rufus here will coordinate our efforts. Specific taskings for each of the agencies are in the documents before you. Questions?"

Rufus smiled, settled into the high-backed leather chair

and loosened his tie. Unless he missed his guess, there would be some lights burning in quite a few offices late at night over the next few months.

7
Portrait of a Terrorist

Salal's father, Ka'mel l'Rahal, was a district elder. Although only a minor official, he was respected for his sound judgment, absolute integrity and sense of fairness. He was a simple man of simple interests, simple needs and simple faith. In him there was an extraordinary toleration and respect, a tender concern for living things. Salal's father lived by the code of Islam. Ka'mel recognized the dependency of man on other men, their bond with one another. Uneducated, he was not so presumptuous as to call himself a wise man, but he held to basic truths as he saw them. *There is no God but Allah and Muhammad is his prophet*, was his mantra.

As a Muslim and as a Palestinian Arab he believed that his purpose in life was to be an instrument of Allah, to live well the *kismet* that Allah had chosen for him. His creed was the patient acceptance and inevitability of Allah's will.

As most Arabs in Palestine, Ka'mel was poor, but he wore his poverty with a quiet acceptance and almost perverse pride. Money was of no importance. His true wealth was in his family. His wife and children shared his philosophy out of necessity. What was given to Ka'mel, he believed, was given by a merciful Allah, a God that was the center of his very being as well as a living part of his family's daily life.

Ka'mel did not own the house in which he lived. In fact he owned no land, no property in Palestine. As most in the village of Dura, he rented the land on which his home sat. The village was better known by its Jewish name, Hebron. Everyone knew of Hebron. There Abraham and the other ancients rested in their tombs.

Living on the land of absentee landlords was a fact of life

for most Arabs in Palestine. The landlords owned vast properties. They lived the good life in France and other various locations in Europe, depending on the time of the year. As a rule, the landowners made few improvements on the land and no capital investments for its future value.

Once a year, Abaza al Folathi, a fat and very wealthy man, would visit Dura to inspect his holdings. He would smile at the villagers and their children, briefly indulge their complaints, shake his head in sympathy, and then collect and raise the rent.

On one such visit Ka'mel was selected to speak for the village. Borrowing the village's only second-hand, tattered but well-brushed Western suit, Ka'mel went forward, with speech in hand. To represent the village to their benefactor was a great honor and Ka'mel rehearsed what was to be said before approaching Abaza al Folathi with the village request.

"Your excellency," he began, "the village council has agreed that a generator and electric pump for the village well would be a very good thing. The people could use the water," he explained, "to irrigate the fields and small village orchard. We might even be able to produce a better crop."

Abaza waved his hand dismissively even before Ka'mel finished his words. "Enough!" he exclaimed heatedly. "Every time I come to this place, you ask more and more from me. I am not a wealthy man. This is an extravagant and shameful proposal demanded by an ungrateful village.

It is wasteful," he continued angrily. "There is no need for a pump or a generator. These are things that break and wear out. They are unreliable. Water has been drawn by hand forever. This is foolishness—a foolish request by a foolish man."

Ka'mel accepted the decision and said no more. "*Enshallah* – as God wills," he told the expectant council and people of his village.

Among other things, Ka'mel believed the struggle between the Arab and Jewish sons of Abraham was a test arranged by Allah himself. Unlike others of the *Kharijite* sect, however, he was not vocal in support for a *jihad* against the Jews. Salal's father was a non-combatant who watched the happenings of his world from the safety of his home, firmly convinced that Allah protected his family.

It was difficult, but suspicion from his Arab neighbors was outweighed by admiration for the sincerity of his beliefs. Devoted to a God who Himself decided the affairs of men, Ka'mel could not bring himself to become an active participant in the Islamic inspired forays launched from the village and surrounding hills. Advanced age and three unprotected daughters were Ka'mel's crutch, but the truth was that he lacked enthusiasm for the killing.

"I know the Jews are not men of the Koran," he would say when his opinion was sought, "but their fate is in the hands of Allah. Allah should render judgment; it should not be done at our hand."

He understood the logic of guerrilla warfare, but he could not reconcile it with his own sincerely held Muslim beliefs. He also could not accept *fedayeen* atrocities or the Jewish wholesale destruction of villages in retaliation—all done in the name of the same God who bore one name in Hebrew and another in Arabic.

Ka'mel lived by the word of the Koran and denied haven, bread and salt to no one, Christian or Muslim, Arab or Jew. He practiced moderation in all but one thing. His one constant and recurring prayer to Allah was to be blessed with a son. After three daughters, Allah granted Ka'mel his wish. Salal was born on the fifteenth day of May, 1946. Ironically, two years later the Jewish State of Israel was to be born on the same date. Both Salal and, later, Israel suffered in the pain and uncertainty of existence those first months. Both triumphed and survived. There the similarities ended.

Salal was born in the valley just southwest of Al Khalil. He was a frail child who struggled to outgrow his physical limitations. The first two years of his life were marred with recurring and disabling asthmatic attacks. But what he lacked in physical strength, he more than compensated for in curiosity and intellectual capacity.

Ka'mel, for his part, instructed his son in the doctrines of the Koran just as he had been so instructed by his own father. In the confusion and terror of the times and wars, the father tried to convey to his son his own belief in peace with the Jews.

Salal idolized his father and struggled to understand, but the fierce rhetoric of the young *imams* who passed through the village left him confused. His father, he thought, was timid. Still, the boy became a devout imitation of his father whose core belief, as his father's, was the submission to Allah's will. Prayer, *salaat*, at dawn, noon, mid-afternoon, sunset and the end of the day reinforced the presence of Allah in every place, in all things, at all times. By the time he could speak in sentences, Salal could recite the six basic articles of Islamic faith—the belief in God, in angels, in scripture, in prophets, in the Day of Judgment, and in predestination.

Salal knew these things before he comprehended what they meant. The words of the Koran learned amid the hundreds of other daily experiences tempered the steel of his youth and his character. Islam became as much a part of Salal's world and life as eating and breathing.

When Ka'mel could no longer answer his son's probing questions, he had sent the boy to Al Khalil. There he studied with an old *mullah*, a conservative *imam* whose life was the study of Islamic law.

Salal was twelve years old when the new *imam* came. This new prayer leader was appointed by the Grand Mufti of Jerusalem and was a rabid disciple of the Mufti's own radical views.

In the proliferation of this new teacher's extreme sermons, Salal began to question his father's submission and agree with the other young men of the village, who were more worldly and more knowledgeable. Through their eyes he saw a world different from his father's and felt the first pangs of shame and embarrassment for being the son of Ka'mel l'Rahal.

Years of poverty and discontent found focus in an attractive hatred for the Jews preached by the *imam*. He held that the Jews were an immoral people. He certified the Jews sought the destruction of the *purdah* code, the Islamic laws that provide for the protection, seclusion and segregation of women.

"They shame and defile Arab women by making the head to foot gown, the *chadry* or the *buryu*, a thing of the past," he preached. "The Jewish women dress as harlots; they wear the clothes of men and show their bare legs for all to see. Allah will punish this shameful indecency."

He spoke of Jewish treachery. Arabs who had lived as tenant peasants for generations were told that their status in life was the result of a Jewish plot to destroy Islam.

"Look around us," he said. "More and more of the Jews come, seeking to steal and possess all of our lands. It is easy to see that the Jews seek the destruction of Islam and all that our Arab way of life holds sacred."

Resurrecting a hatred for the Jews until it burned white hot was not difficult in the Arab world. It was fashionable.

In September 1958, the battles between Arab and Jew, to which Salal until then had been only a distant though biased observer, came to his valley. The poor who owned nothing under the existing Arab feudal system filled the ranks of the *fedayeen*. The Arab world rose as one to demand a seat at the table of power. Their new leaders cast the votes of their Arab constituents from the muzzles of AK-47 assault rifles.

Fiction became fact.

"All problems, all of our troubles are Jewish inspired," the *imams* sustained in a constant harangue.

Jewish plots plundered the Arab land, the Arab spirit, the Arab history. Absentee Arab Palestine landlords, acting without conscience, sold their Palestine interests to Jewish immigrants at outrageous prices then allied with the radical and intolerant Grand Mufti of Jerusalem.

Jihad, declared by the Grand Mufti himself, gave the Islamic war religious legitimacy. *Imams* and misguided holy men across Palestine and throughout the Arab world took up the cry against the Jews and their infidel supporters.

The *fedayeen*, better armed, better led and impatient, came more frequently and in stronger force to strike deeper into Israel from safe havens within the Sinai, Syria, Jordan, and Lebanon. Dura became a frequent marshalling area for raids on the Jews near Beersheva, and in Bethlehem, Jeruslem, Jaffa and Tel Aviv.

A group of Jewish children, themselves the sons and daughters of refugees from the pogroms of Eastern Europe, had been on a daytrip from a nearby *kibbutz* to Bethlehem. All thirty-one of them were between the ages of seven and twelve. Six members of the *fedayeen* conducted an ambush of their bus. The attack was bestial. Male children were sexually mutilated and at least three of the young girls were raped and mutilated as well. Twenty-three of the children and three of their adult escorts died brutally and without purpose. Grotesque pictures of their mutilated corpses were smeared across the front pages of international tabloids.

The Jewish retaliation was swift and blind. Beyond rage, they came to destroy, led by men of the Palmach and the Irgun—hard men with cold eyes and stone hearts, survivors of the Nazi extermination camps who had vowed "Never Again." The Jews came in force to the valleys around Hebron and the IDF extracted their own sightless biblical revenge.

They found the scent and tracked the six ambushers to Dura. There they isolated the inhabitants, throwing a *cordon sanitair* around the village, allowing no one in and no one out. Then the Israelis took their time. Two of the six terrorists had been wounded during their flight from the ambush site. One of the wounded men found sanctuary in Ka'mel's home.

The Israelis found him.

The convictions, for which he was respected, did not prevent Ka'mel, his wife, and Salal's three sisters' death. It was their *kismet*. The Jews destroyed Ka'mel's home, killed him, his wife and his three daughters, ignoring the white flag he held above his head. It was an eye for an eye and the reaction of the world to this further slaughter be damned.

They found all six of the terrorists. Then the IDF soldiers assembled the entire village and executed each of the six terrorists by firing squad in their full view.

But the Jews were not done.

There was no discussion, no appeal, and no mercy. The horror that the *fedayeen* had committed was beyond mitigation, truce or surrender. There was neither time nor opportunity for the villagers to ask questions. American-made tanks and light artillery pieces rained high-explosive shells on the town. Often they burst among the fleeing residents. With deliberate precision they bombarded the village, reducing it to rubble.

No explanations were offered.

The Jews killed with an irrational blindness—without discrimination, remorse or conscience. Israeli soldiers came with American-made rifles, flame-throwers and grenades.

When the IDF had finished, they dragged the bodies they could find from the collapsed homes into the street and stripped them naked. They tied them behind their American-made half-tracks and dragged them through the rubble-strewn streets, dumping the soiled, bruised remains without ceremony in the center of the village, near the well. They dynamited what remained, reducing damaged buildings to trash, crushing personal belongings with the treads of their tanks. The bodies and the smoking, fire-gutted ruins were left to serve as an example to others.

The few survivors of Dura wondered why there had been no report, no pictures and no outcry in the international press as there had been for the Jews.

Salal was spared. Fate had taken him earlier in the day to the village fields, entrusted with the communal flock of goats. He heard the firing and ran toward his home only to be stopped by the cordon around the village. Still he arrived in time to see the bodies of his dead parents and naked sisters, bleeding and torn, thrown about like meat, dragged behind the Israeli war chariots. There was no sympathy, no offer of consolation, no opportunity for a reconstruction of the world so abruptly taken from him. In one terrible and swift moment the Jews had taken all. The rule of Islam, the safety of home and the comfort of family, all destroyed. Amid the rantings of the religious radicals and the confluence of events in 1958, Salal delivered himself to his *kismet*, his destiny.

Salal was interned. In time he was released by the Israelis and found his way into the United Nations refugee camp in Gaza. The world crashed down on his unprepared twelve-year-old head.

The United Nations acted with noble purpose and good intent. The establishment of the Palestinian refugee camps was well received from a world shaken by World War II's inhumanity of man to man.

Unfortunately, the UN was ill prepared for the task. The camps became the domains of third world political hacks in which international corruption flourished. The mice, who had nibbled at the edges of power, now gorged themselves in the windfall of the UN's largess.

The camps became bureaucratic nightmares in which corruption and *baksheesh* were the mainstay of existence. In a place and time already irrational, desperate Palestinian refugees sought relief from UN warehouses guarded by Arab wolves. Accountability was non-existent, bookkeeping a myth. Millions of dollars and warehouses of supplies simply disappeared.

The old landholders made new private fortunes distributing the necessities of life. Gangs of otherwise idle young Arabs roamed the area and extracted their own forms of misery from the population. Stores clearly marked and labeled as UN Relief were sold in the marketplace *suks* by absentee landlord front companies or by partnerships formed with corrupt refugee camp administrators.

A small, elite, Arab middle class of well off arose from the dismal confines of the UN camps. A select and strong few lived well on the bones of their displaced poorer and weaker Palestinian brothers. There were some that cried for reform and reported abuse, but the lie was still accepted as the truth. "The Jews, it is all because of the Jews."

Salal was released by the IDF to the squalor of Gaza, a boy without a home, without a family, without love and with few of the skills needed to survive. There in Gaza he learned the meanings of abuse, neglect, poverty and the loss of hope. There he learned new meanings for the words "Arab" and "Muslim." Shiite extremism replaced Sunni moderation. Salal found a new set of beliefs, beliefs from which he could feed his own thirst for vengeance. *Jihad* became a practiced dedication, a purpose for living.

In Gaza he was carefully taught how to hate.

Ka'mel's son was taught the fine arts of weaponry, explosives, ambush and survival. When the time came, just after his thirteenth birthday, he became a member of the *fedayeen* and soon thereafter Ka'mel's freedom fighter son killed for the first time.

Allah had meant it to be so.

Soon killing without feeling became normal. Hate and terrorism were the only diet to which he had access. Bitter and lost survivors served it to him, pouring huge portions on his plate every waking moment, seven days a week, three hundred and sixty-five days a year. These were the men and women who, like Salal, had lost everything, except their lives.

In those homeless and hungry days, Salal no longer practiced the six articles of faith. He, as those around him, lived only for revenge, for the privilege of joining martyred mothers, sisters, brothers and fathers, of dying for the cause of Islam and the Arab brotherhood. They made a new dogma for Islam.

Salal's *kismet* became inextricably intertwined with defending Islam and the Arab world from its enemies.

"*Enshallah* – as God wills," Salal intoned.

The *fedayeen* became his home. A bright and quick learner, the refugee from Dura was a cut above most of his contemporaries. Attendance at the elite school for future Islamic terrorist leaders was decided by the *fedayeen* as his next stop. Salal was smuggled from Gaza to Yemen and there his education began in earnest.

The school was called the *Dar al-Hadith*, or the House of the Prophet's Sayings and Deeds. *Dar al-Hadith* purports to be a theological school—albeit one that propagates the most radical anti-Western doctrine of Islam, *Salafism*. The essence of *Salafism*, from the Arab word, *salaf*, meaning ancestor, is that Muslims must shun the corrupt ways of the modern world and return to the austerity and zeal of the Prophet Muhammad.

"The most dangerous enemies of Islam are Western life and culture – democracy, pluralism, tolerance and any kind of voting," the Mullahs taught.

The facility was located in the village of Dammaj in Yemen. The area around Dammaj is the best-equipped arms bazaar in the Arab world, which says much for a country in which the government acknowledges the existence of sixty-five million guns but has only an eighteen million population.

In addition to providing ideological training for the *talibs*—the seekers of Islamic truths – the school is the crucible for young Muslims destined to lead the Arab terrorist movement. It was and is today the incubator for the Islamic and Arab *jihad* against the United States, Israel, Christians and Jews, and, on occasion, even the advocate of punishment against the moderates of the Arab world, like Sadat.

Few outside of the closed world of Islam, excepting counterterrorism experts, have ever heard of the Sheik Muqbel Hadi al-Wadie. This seventy-year-old Arab radical founded the school. His hatred of the West makes the

Ayatollah Imam Kohmeni's disdain of things Western ama-
teurish by comparison. The Sheik has an all-consuming
loathing for Western modernism.

At the school there were no modern distractions for Salal
from the word of the Prophet—no newspapers, no music, no
women, and no education other than the study of the Koran
and Islam. Bushy-bearded, Kalashnikov rifle bearing radicals
who came from all parts of the Arab world, but whose only
loyalty is to Islam and Muqbel, guarded the entire area.

Salal became a star pupil and, through his displays of
courage and intelligence, soon came to be warmly accepted
by the Bedouin ruling class that still controls vast stretches of
land that arc along Yemen's fifteen hundred mile frontier with
Saudi Arabia. Through his education and circle of new
friends—all young Arab nationalists—Salal developed the
power base and support from which he launched his successful career. *Dar al-Hadith* was the crucible that made him as
dangerous as Carlos the Jackal.

8
Somewhere in Libya
—August, 2000

The operations briefing to Salal moved along well.
Machmued began with good news.
"Abdul has found the killers of Bosheer, the missing man
from the intelligence and reconnaissance cell. Bosheer's mur-
derers knew nothing of Jericho. Sa'id sent both of the assas-
sins to their Christian God on Abdul's orders. Their bodies
will not be found."
The briefing was long and complex. Salal dwelled on every
detail of the plan or so it seemed. For each question, for each
contingency, Machmued had an answer. Options were covered. Organization reviewed. Targets again and again reex-
amined and the assault and attack plans wargamed to detect
flaws in timing. Execution concepts for each of the three sub-
structured forces were redefined and clarified. The strengths
and weaknesses of the commanders, their background, experience, performance in training, and understandings of the
primary and secondary missions were all reviewed in detail.
Finally, Salal seemed satisfied.
The Jericho author took a deep breath and squeezed the
bridge of his nose between his thumb and forefinger. The
sound that passed his lips was a groan of relief. Salal stretched
and twisted his bony-thin torso, preened his moustache and
goatee, then moved from behind the desk.
"Enough for a time, Machmued. You have a gifted mind
and you tire me just by the effort of remembering all which
you have told me."
In total, the briefing had lasted a concentrated two and
one-half hours. The morning sun had increased in intensity as
it arched its way across the deep blue Libyan sky. In another

two hours the heat would sap all energy and work would stop until the hottest part of the day had passed.

Machmued rose and the two men walked to a foyer which doubled as a reception area and conference room. A pot of tea sat steeping on a small propane fired flame in the corner of the sparsely furnished room. On the small linen covered table next to the burner was a stack of three nondescript, chipped cups. Beside it sat a plate of fresh dates. Salal waved Machmued to the nearest of the three ancient chairs. Salal sat opposite him over a long, low wicker table. Salal reached for the cups, placing one in front of each of them. Pouring the dark, strong tea he took his cup in both hands and raised it in half salute.

"I am afraid, my friend, that I am, indeed, a poor host. I can offer you no sweet cakes. But perhaps a few dates. If you wish, I will send…"

"It is not necessary, Salal. The tea is enough. Do not trouble yourself further." Machmued sat back deeply into the well-cushioned chair, balancing the tea saucer on his thigh.

"We must prove that the *fedayeen* can strike at will—anytime, any place—with impunity," Machmued said quietly.

The planning chief paused only long enough to glance at Salal over the rim of his cup. Machmued wondered if his friend was listening.

"Our most powerful ally is the American press. No one exploits the vulnerabilities and mistakes of the ones who hold the reins of power better than the news media. We must be the lead story on the evening newscasts and in the headlines of the Western newspapers. Their news coverage gains us support, power, and credibility."

They spoke with the informality and casual open honesty of old friends who together had shared hardship and danger. They knew and trusted each other and were bound together by affection known only to those who had been through the crucible of imminent death and constant peril.

"La. No one exploits the mistakes and ineffectiveness of the governments of the Western powers, their frustration and indecisiveness and lack of direction, better than their own media," Salal agreed. "Still…"

Salal attempted to conceal his irritation. While Machmued's abilities were held in deep respect, Salal also recognized the weaknesses of his friend and subordinate. His second in command, Salal felt, had dangerously discounted American intelligence efforts. The discussion was one that the two men had had before.

"Never underestimate the Americans, Machmued. When they appear the most foolish, it is then that they are the most dangerous."

Machmued shook his head in respectful disagreement. "La!" he exclaimed. "If that is so, they are the most dangerous people of all time," he replied with conviction. "They are not to be feared, Salal. They die as any man dies. They are foolish and bound up in their laws and politics. They are not like the Israelis. We can bend the will of the *Giaou Americai.*"

"Umm, perhaps, my friend, but remember what happened in Granada," Salal cautioned. "The Americans' reaction was totally unexpected. Their coup made the Cubans look foolish and inept. The Cubans too thought the Americans were toothless."

Salal read determination in his companion's flinty eyes and knew his arguments were unsuccessful.

"The Americans are arrogant as well as naive," Machmued responded with emotion. "As they are strong and resourceful, they are just as often stupid and weak. They are easily influenced by the television, their magazines, and newspapers. They hide behind their oceans thousands of miles away; they do not dirty their hands but have others do their bidding as in Iraq."

Machmued paused only long enough to sip at his tea and gather his breath. His hatred for the Americans was strident and uncompromised.

"They are cowards who fight not with bravery," he continued, "but with machines, to do their killing. To *Americai* fighting is the airplane, the tank, the artillery, but they do not have the courage to look into the eyes of their enemies; they do not fight with a *khanjar* as did the *moujahadin* against the *Roosees*. They approach their friends and enemies with words and a pot of gold. They think they can buy anything—even a man's honor, his soul. With *baksheesh*, their bribes, they think they can solve all problems. The *Americai* are beneath contempt. Jericho will show them that their oceans are no protection. Soon they will the meet the *ahlu l-kitaab*, the true people of the book, and then they will learn what true courage means."

Salal listened, knowing that any effort to reverse his chief of staff of his dangerous miscalculation was in vain.

"Be careful," he warned, "that you do not choose to remember only the things that fit your purposes, Machmued. Once their President Kennedy placed a noose around the throat of Cuba and dared the Russian bear with a blockade, eh? Do you remember? The *Roosees* removed their missiles. Americans' greatest strength is their lack of predictability. No one knows when they will become inflamed and turn loose all of their strength. No one can judge what will arouse them to rage, but once aroused, they are most dangerous. No, never underestimate them, brother. They are not as simple as they or you would have me believe."

Machmued shrugged. "They are an immoral people," he said, "and care more for money than justice. They answer the call only of self-interest, of racist Zionists and the rich Jews in America. The only answer to American interference is from the muzzle of an Arab gun."

"Killing Americans has always been a simple thing. They are a strange and foolish people. They never think of security and believe that they are invulnerable," Salal agreed.

"The Americans are the Israelis' whores. They are *Giaou*," Machmued said—the derisive term used for foreign infidels, "and *Ra'iyai*,—human cattle, the lowest form of foreigner, beyond contempt. They are naive and stupid."

"But learn from our enemy, Machmued," Salal cautioned. "The Americans do not seek a fair fight. Only the underdog or the foolish man seeks a fair fight. The Americans, as the Jews, seek only to win. They attack from their strength. We must attack at their weakness, retreat from their strength. Do not let your enemy select the battle."

"Is this not the strength of Jericho?" Machmued replied. "Have we not selected the place and time for the battle?"

Salal was slow to reply. Machmued had missed the point. His second in command erred in crediting American inaction to fear, a lack of courage, rather than restraint. Machmued could better understand the Jews because their ways were not far different from the Arab way. The Arab, the Muslim, and the Jews, in their own ways, had a simple and direct relationship with their law. In many aspects they were alike.

For the Arab the law of Islam, the law of the Koran, applied with equal effect to their own as well as to the *kafirs*, the unbelievers, who lived amongst them. There were no appeals or technical legal arguments, no reversals on the grounds of a poor childhood, a disadvantaged youth, or a lapse of sanity.

If a man was convicted of thievery by the *ulama*, the council of religious elders, then his hand was chopped from his body. If he slandered, his tongue would be cut out. If he committed a violent act or adultery, his head was lopped off. These were the simple laws with simple punishments that found their basis in the philosophy of an eye for an eye. Such had been the way born to both Arab and Jew and in some perverse way, respected, since the very beginning.

Salal demurred, seeing no point in wasting further time in fruitless argument.

"I shall say no more on the matter," Salal responded tactfully. "But you too must remember that it is not the American habit to snatch defeat from the jaws of victory.

"But you are right my friend," he agreed, crediting Machmued's argument. "They are only men, such as are we. To make them more than what they have shown themselves to be is an equal danger.

"Only remember," he continued, slowly wagging his finger,

"fear is the first sign of wisdom, Machmued. Let us not rely too strongly on the Americans' ineptitude. All plans are good only until the first shot is fired."

"The Americans will bend," Machmued said with conviction.

"Perhaps, Machmued, perhaps," Salal replied, "either that or we shall surely unleash a whirlwind."

By ability as well as experience, Machmued was a logical and gifted planner. He took pride in his accomplishments and often spoke with open disdain for the *Americai*. Their empty threats of revenge were meaningless. Their pitiful responses and blustering were a joke and served to reinforce his arguments and contempt for the superpower.

He was second only to Salal himself who was acknowledged as the best operations organizer within the ICO. Machmued's forte was surprise and night operations and his reputation, as Salal's, was one of success.

The excitement and adventure of Machmued's youthful apprenticeship as a footsoldier in the *fedayeen* had coalesced over the years. Swift, violent, well-rehearsed strikes that inflicted maximum damage with minimum risk and cost were Machmued's planning trademarks. Operations that he planned and participated in had never failed.

Machmued took Salal's concept of Jericho and gave it life. While Salal was the author of Jericho, its spokesperson and designated commander, it was Machmued who had taken it from idea to plan, who had molded its flesh and muscle into the details of a terrorist strike. Six months had passed before the plan had achieved its now well-polished and final form. The effort had been done with patience, painstaking attention to detail and thorough analysis of each probable alternative.

Machmued had changed a great deal since that morning fifteen years earlier in Gander when he had grimly punched the transmit button and sent the first of his American enemies to their deaths. The years had turned him from a skinny youth into a large, pear shaped man. Now he bore the dark, desert-weathered complexion of arid places and the familiar hawk-like nose that marked the Semitic descendants of Abraham, Isaac, and Ishmael. His once scraggly youthful beard, now full and dark with tinges of gray beginning to appear, had become his single vanity. In these past few years it had become sprinkled more with tones of salt-and-pepper than the shades of reds which, in his youth, had stood in stark contrast against the darker brown, almost black wiry mat of hair which covered his chest and back. The heavy growth of facial and body hair coupled with his short, solid, two hundred twelve pound frame earned Machmued the affectionate nickname of *The Bear*. The name equally as well fitted his personality. The years had made him neither a handsome nor an ugly man, just big and rough finished—not unlike an incomplete but powerful sculpture.

Machmued was of two personalities. By preference as well as natural inclination, he was a gentle and compassionate man, thoughtful and warm to family and friend. The gentility, however, was underlain by the firmness of his beliefs. *The Bear* was a radical of the worst kind, a religious radical. Most men may fight for things, some die for ideologies. Machmued was one of the latter. God was on his side. In the justness of his cause, he could thus use any means to achieve the destruction of his enemy. Anything that he could do to hasten the end of the Israeli State or destroy his Jewish enemies became his vocation, his life's force. His was a staid conviction that Israel had but two alternatives. This new Jewish nation could cease to exist or it could become a vassal state in the Arab world. Machmued cared not which it was to be.

His second nature was of a gruff, powerful, compelling individual. A mindless thug he was not, but neither was he a diplomat nor a polished statesman. Machmued was intelligent, an educated scholar who had been recruited from the University at Cairo. Though neither as articulate nor as savvy in a political sense as was Salal, he was an introspective thinker who selected his words with caution. That having been said, however, he did not appreciate the strategies and relations of the international stage. His hatred for the Jews and their *Americai* protectors was so intense as to be a part of his DNA. His viewpoint was colored and clouded by heritage, education and experience. His convictions grew even stronger and deeper as he moved from refugee camp to refugee camp in Lebanon, in Gaza, in Egypt, and Syria. Arab people—men, women and children—had been expelled from their lands, put in squalid camps, hunted down, and even killed. As he saw the disease and poverty, the trampling and martyrdom of his people and listened to the *imams* of his faith, he came, as they, to blame it all on the Jews.

Machmued grew more harsh-sounding over the years but also more guarded. His experience, position and power had grown with each year since Gander, but he had changed. Now, about his person there was an awareness of strained self-control. Not unlike that of a dormant volcano, which bespoke danger when aroused, he had a temper that was matched only by his tenacity and resoluteness to punish and destroy, to inflict revenge with satisfaction. The earnestness of his beliefs, the brutality of his words was supported by his actions in the *fedayeen*. He earned the trust and respect of influential men within the ICO and throughout the radical Arab community.

Jahbad had been his mentor. Machmued's apprenticeship was served under him and he learned well from the author of the strike on the Israelis at the German Olympic Games. Jahbad was instrumental in developing the Iranian negotiating position on the American embassy hostages. The bargaining strategy that had finally contributed to driving the American president Carter from office was of Jahbad's design.

Jahbad taught Machmued how to conceptualize a plan, dissect it, reduce it to its most basic, elemental pieces, and then reassemble it. From his mentor Machmued learned to visualize options and alternatives. Machmued learned how to pay attention to the details, modifying the scheme of events to the point where the plan became a reality, where the thought and the reality became one in the same entity.

The hard-learned experiences of the field craft Machmued had learned were not wasted. Quickly, he became a master of planning methodology and terrorist operations in his own right, first planning and leading only minor operations but then larger, more complex ones.

9

Cape Canaveral, Florida —September, 2000

Jake, Matt's father, was waiting for him at the Melbourne terminal gate on the Space Coast of Florida. More was said in the embrace and handshake between them than could ever be said in words. They shared many of the same convictions, values and traits despite a thirty-year difference in their ages. Often they communicated without words, just relying on the comfortableness of companionship to convey thoughts and meaning to each other.

"Welcome home, son, we've missed you," was Jake's affectionate greeting. "Cm'on lets get your bags, your mother's all excited and has a big meal waitin' for you."

Matt spent the hours in his parents' home in quiet leisure. The days were cast in that lazy slowness of the southern summer, with family and quiet talk, snapshots in one's forever memories. They were seamless times that become inseparate and blended one into another. The routines of waking and sleeping, lazy swims and easy jogs, eating and laughing, noise and silence, combined into a single warm satisfaction. Time became measured in perfect mornings that melted into stressless and untarnished days.

Among other things Matt wanted to do, there was an opportunity to rummage through the stored personal effects that he had left with his parents upon his departure for the Middle East.

As a hobby long years earlier, Matt's father had taken up gunsmithing. By the end of his first week home, he and Jake spent an afternoon at the local range plinking and sighting in a newly scoped 30-06 deer rifle. Matt had taken along and

fired two old favorite handguns, a Colt .357 Python and a
Browning 9mm automatic. While Browning did a better job
on bluing and was the superior self-defense or combat
weapon, the Colt seemed to fit Matt's hand better, to have a
cleaner sense of balance and form to it. Jake had given him the
Python for his twenty-fifth birthday and he had since used it
for deer hunting. Prior to presenting the Python to his son as
a gift, Jake had worked it over and installed a wider serrated
trigger shoe for an extended gripping surface, toiling over the
sear until he achieved an unflawed smooth two-pound trigger
pull. Standard factory sights were removed, modified and
reinstalled. The front blade sight was altered with an international orange inset, while the notch of the adjustable rear
sight was detailed with a contrasting luminous white frame.
The difference and speed in lining up the sights in low light
dawn and twilight situations were dramatic.

Handloading was one of the things Matt's father had
taught him and they had shared and enjoyed it as a part-time
hobby. They'd experimented and had good success with some
hunting loads when they had handgunned deer. That began
before Matt had entered the service. But, both then and
since, whenever it was possible, they made a trek to Jake's
birth state of Pennsylvania.

Jake owned a little cabin in Elk County, in the upper
reaches of Northwestern Pennsylvania near the border with
New York State. It was here that Matt, tutored by his
father, had been nurtured in his love for the outdoors,
where he had learned how to shoot a gun, how to cast a
line, how to work a fishing plug, and how to appreciate
things wild and pristine. These times in the mountains of
Pennsylvania were quality and bonding times—events that
both men relished and savored.

Now cleaned and freshly oiled, Matt slipped a full clip into
the grip of the Browning and packed it in one of the suitcases
along with a box of fifty rounds of handloads that he'd done
up some two years earlier. The six and three-eighth inch bar-
reled Python, his favorite hunting handgun, he loaded with

158 grain three-quarter copper jacketed hollowpoints. He packed the Colt into a smaller blue carryall backpack in which he kept it stored.

Early each morning Matt would jog the two and a half miles to the deserted beaches at Hightower Park. There he would swim a mile or two parallel to the beach in the choppy Atlantic surf, dry out on the sandy shore for 15 or 20 minutes, and then set a leisurely pace, jogging back to his parent's home. Mornings until noon, he surf fished at the mouth of the Sebastian inlet or went out with Jake aboard the *Outrage* up the Banana River.

The morning beginning Matt's tenth day of leave started in smudged rose purple promises. A watery yellow sun peeked over the edge of the river, penetrating through the damp morning mist, suspending the twenty one foot Boston Whaler runabout between the growing dawn in the east and a full moon still hanging a darkened western sky. In the bent light of the awakening day a silent Great Blue Heron stood frozen at the river's edge.

The channel up the Banana river narrows, twists, turns and shallows from just north of Patrick Air Force Base up to the southern tip of Mosquito Lagoon, north of Port Canaveral. Although Jake was well familiar with the waters he kept one eye on the integrated Lowrance LCX-15MT Global Positioning System, GPS, and sonar. He had spared little expense on his "toy." In addition to an ICOM VCF Marine Transceiver, Jake also installed a Raytheon R10XX Raster Scan Radar atop a custom designed T-top which sported four "rocket launcher" rod holders and twin Lee fifteen foot skiff outriggers. The suite was finished off with a Penn 625 downrigger mounted on the port side of the transom. The walk-around design of the center console completed the package for a very versatile fishing machine, though admittedly a bit small for long-range Gulf Stream expeditions.

The big 225 hp Mercury UltraMax gurgled softly delivering just enough power to maintain steerageway along the channel shelf in the Banana River. A school of mullet burst to the surface of the silent waters like pebbles tossed into the stream as the silver flash of a rolling tarpon announced its presence. Two brown pelicans, disturbed by the invasion of their space, squawked indignantly, lifted their wings from atop their nested rest and eyed the two men.

Matt breathed in deeply and savored the moment. Jake applied power and an emerald vee blossomed in a frothy gray-green wake. Twin contrails of white foam churned the waters beneath and along the nine and a half foot transom of the boat. A pod of three curious dolphins appeared, surfacing playfully ten yards or so off of the starboard bow, drawn by the vibrations of the propeller and the noise of the engine in the water. It was one of those rare, long to be remembered perfect moments.

"Do you love her?" Jake asked casually.

Not much needed to be said. There was a rapport between the two men that went well beyond the usual father-son relationship.

"It's not the same as it was with Ann," Matt replied slowly. "Megan's different. But yes, I think so, Dad."

"Then you screwed up not bringing her back with you, son," Jake tactlessly observed. "There are no certainties out there, son. Learn by the past, but don't let it jade you, or direct your future," he advised.

"You may just need this woman, Matt. Both your mother and I can see you miss her. God knows, there is no shame in needing someone."

He was right, Matt admitted and suddenly, with that admission, everything in his personal life seemed to come back into balance. As if a fog had lifted, the temperature, the light, the time of day, the hum of the engine, the swish of the bow cutting through the water—it was all, well, just more alive, more right. Doubt blew away and he knew what he had to do.

They stopped fishing at about five in the afternoon and ran the Outrage through the Barge Canal over to the Indian

River and up to Corky Belle's just north of Cocoa and tied up. They glutted themselves on cold beer and fresh deep fried fish. Intrusive thoughts of Megan were the only interruptions to what was otherwise a lazy, carefree, charging-your-batteries, relaxed time. But Megan continued to sneak in with all the delicacy of a sharp needle in the eye—suprising him with a poignancy Matt now finally accepted. The taste of her not being there came without warning. Memories were sharp and crisp, like the chewed fruit of a lime slice in a glass of crushed sparkling icewater. Her smile nagged at him, it broke into his consciousness, distracting and diverting him.

The twilight evening run from Cocoa back down the Indian River was smooth and uneventful. The sheltered waters of the two rivers, the Banana and the Indian, unlike those of the ocean that paralleled it some two miles distant, were serene. The river gently embraced the Outrage on its homeward run. The clouds blushed fading yellows and oranges in the drawing evening quiet. They swept around Dragon Point making the final turn toward the Tortoise Island canal at the spent end of dusk. Both men were wrapped in the warm weariness that comes from a day of sun and ocean air and contentment, a result of those infrequent memorable times of pure pleasure.

Once home, the two men worked together cleaning up the boat, spraying off the salt, washing down the deck, running fresh water through the engine to keep the corrosion factor down, cleaning and restowing the fishing gear. The good life at home was marred only by the intrusion of what lay ahead and Matt could feel the knots of nervous energy building and searching for an outlet. His decision, finally made, on his future with Megan keyed him up.

As they walked up to the house from the dock, Matt's mother, Ruth, appeared at the door and waved to the two tired fishermen. "Matt," she called, "you had a call from Washington. They want you to call back right away."

For Ruth any call from Washington had to be an important call.

"Any specific message?" he asked as he gave her a kiss on the cheek.

"Yes, it's all written down next to the phone. They want you to come up there to see a general, the man said."

"Word on your next assignment?" Jake inquired.

"Probably," Matt responded.

Matt read the clear script of the neat written message. The content was simple and straightforward. Listing a 703 area code number, the message read, *Call Colonel Max Jackson at the Pentagon. General Brandt wants to meet with you.*

Matt looked at his watch. Colonel Jackson could be reached through the Army Operations Center if necessary. If it were urgent, there would have been more to the message. Matt decided he could wait till morning to give Jackson a call. The youngest of the Gannon sons wondered why Rufus Brandt wanted to see him. Meanwhile there was a more urgent requirement. He picked up the phone and placed an international call to Israel. He let it ring for a long time. There was no answer.

The Delta flight to Washington, D.C. and Reagan National Airport, Matt's final destination, was uneventful excepting the inevitable connecting flight delay in Atlanta.

Atlanta's Hartsfield International Airport terminal possessed the same confused efficient blandness, the same overpriced souvenir and bookshops, the same newsstands, the same stand up bars and the same cardboard cafeterias as others the world over. Even the carpeting and furnishings were the same. Over the years and travels in the United States, Matt had come to believe that if anyone died east of the Mississippi, his soul was routed to heaven or hell through Atlanta. Delay was accepted with grim Yankee humor, not that there was much of a choice in the matter. In the men's room of the B Concourse someone had penned on the wall.

"If you have time to spare, fly Delta Air."

It seemed to be an appropriate slogan to which Matt added a silent "Amen." Not that any of the other air carriers were much better.

Departure delays in Atlanta never failed. Murphy and his laws were alive and well – at least at Hartsfield terminal. Perhaps it was all a Southern form of revenge for the way the city was treated at the end of the Civil War.

The cute blonde flight attendant made the announcement of arrival with just the right touch of frayed enthusiasm. She was the younger of the two women who served as flight attendants in the economy class cabin. Her cheerful cautions to remain seated until the aircraft had come to a complete halt were lost on the bulk of Matt's fellow passengers. The conditioned reflexes took over at the sound of the bell announcing that the aircraft had arrived at the gate.

What always followed, it seemed to Matt, was a predictable and pointless race—a herd instinct. Sedated during flight, the voyagers took over in a lemming-like rush for the cabin door well before it was even opened. They rose as one to bully their way into the narrow aisle fearful of losing one meaningless moment in the debarking process. Rivalries for position were won and lost as the stream of jostling commuters fought their way forward. Always there seemed to be the one passenger who could not retrieve his or her bulky baggage from the overhead compartment and delayed the flood. The human stream backed up like a lake behind a great dam until the bag burst from the overhead and the torrent rushed forward again.

By force of habit Matt was one of the last few to deplane. Avoiding the aisle crush and an overhead-locker-door-smashed-into-the-head routine seemed to be a prudent alternative to the tangling sprint for the connecting jetway. Tolerating such moments with an occasional grimace, he preferred to wait the few additional seconds to avoid the contagious aggression of his travel companions. On occasion he did present an exaggerated courtesy and smile for the more inane of his coach class zoo mates.

Idly, he held back to observe the worthless race to the

carousel with its charging, pushing, shoving, bumping, and jostling for luggage. Matt's cynicism sprung to full flower. Everything and everyone, in Kodak moments such as these, it seemed, was cheerless, impersonal and plastic, distant, isolated and uncaring.

People were just no damn good and getting worse, he concluded to himself. Maybe it was just a mirror of how we live.

It's a life in the fast lane attitude, a play now, pay later, go to hell, "I-got-mine" philosophy. Too many people measure their life's worth by a figure in a bank account, a social stamp of approval or something as meaningless as a spot two steps closer in line, he had once complained to Megan.

Somewhat startled, Matt recognized that his was a jaded look at survival of the species. Worse, it was spreading to become an unconscious part of his observation of life in general.

The first of his two bags appeared in the initial batch dumped across the carousel but the doubled over hanging suit bag was among the last to appear. Matt gathered his grips and was turning to depart when he felt a hand on his shoulder.

"Colonel Gannon?" The inquiry came from a uniform clad Army captain.

Matt acknowledged the recognition and extended his hand.

"I'm Doug Howlett, General Brandt's aide. My friends call me Dougger—it's an old family thing," he said disarmingly. "General Brandt asked me to—well, actually, he didn't exactly ask—to come over and pick you up, sir. It was sorta along the lines of 'Dougger get your young ass over to Reagan and pick up Colonel Gannon and make sure he gets settled in.'" His grin spoke volumes.

"I've taken the liberty of getting you a room over at the Doubletree in Crystal City," Captain Howlett continued as he reached for one of the bags. "It's a good hotel and walking distance to the puzzle palace. Got a couple of nice restaurants and a great bar."

He reached out and took the larger of the two bags from Matt's burdened hands. Being met at the airport was an unusual Brandt touch, a way of saying he appreciated that the call had interrupted Matt's vacation.

"Great. Let's go," was Matt's short reply. What the hell, might as well take full advantage of the VIP treatment, Matt conceded.

"I've got a car out at the curb, sir," Dougger continued affably. "The General wanted to see you as soon as you got in, but his calendar went to hell in a handbag this afternoon so you're on for zero nine-thirty tomorrow."

The conversation with Colonel Jackson the previous morning had revealed very little. All Matt had been told was that he was to report ASAP to General Brandt's Pentagon office.

Rufus Brandt was noted for taking care of his people—in all senses of the term. A demanding Dutch uncle, Brandt guided and cared for the officers he identified as comers. These few selectees were mostly wildcard individualists who thought outside of the box and were creative to the point of rejecting Band-Aid solutions to tough long-term problems.

His unseen hand that guided and expanded their assignment opportunities witnessed the influence of the general's efforts on their careers. The group he sponsored, although no numbers had been set, was about fourteen to sixteen rotating officers and senior civil servants. There was neither formal induction nor notification. Indeed, the only indication that an individual had been singled out was an increase in demanding and more critical work and pressure assignments. Rufus Brandt did not waffle.

The standard of performance expected was simple—nothing less than one's best, one hundred percent of the time. Praise was hard to come by and affection, gruffly given, was genuine. Guardianship, trust and loyalty were unspoken pledges. His charges returned his trust with a ferocious loyalty. The general was proud of that.

The ingredients for selection were simple. The key criteria

included excellence, a desire to do better and do more, unflagging patriotism, loyalty, and an eagerness for hard work. Prima Donnas were not tolerated and membership was conferred and withdrawn by Brandt alone.

Rufus did not like sugarcoating and he did not suffer fools well. As his subordinates and superiors both knew, he could be undiplomatically savage and direct when occasion demanded. Tact was the one item of the required "Be All You Can Be" Army diversity training that he was not compelled to follow. Brandt's philosophy regarding expectations was simple. Nice guys and slow horses finish last. Do what must be done. In war, the second place finisher is the loser. His attitude was expressed in an irreverent and concise slogan that hung on the wall in a brass frame behind his desk. The motto read:

Lead, Follow, or Get The Hell Out Of The Way.

Matt was quietly appraised and his value measured on two occasions by Rufus Brandt. The first was when Rufus had observed him under fire during Desert Storm. Matt's tank company had run up against the dug-in positions of a Republican Guard combined infantry and armor force. His tank had been hit during the action and he had been wounded but remained in calm command of the situation until the enemy position had been taken and secured.

The second had occurred about nineteen months later when Matt had appeared as a Major, assigned to the Joint Chiefs of Staff in the J-4 Logistics piece of the organization. In an unusual move for a newly assigned officer to the Joint Chiefs, the Major was assigned as the point man charged with putting together a "hurry up" critical support package for a clandestine drug interdiction operation in South America.

The logistics piece of the operation was professional, well put together and delivered within a critical short period. For a second time Rufus was impressed with Gannon's thoroughness, his judgment and the calmness of his decision execution. Without fanfare or even his objective knowledge, Matt became a member of Brandt's select group of comers.

Crystal City is now more than the few casual motels and office buildings it was in previous years. Today it is a humming area of commerce and high tech industry office complexes. Located on a trunk line of the Metro rail, its large and growing underground mall provides customers and residents with direct access to the Washington district, all of Northern Virginia and Reagan National Air Terminal.

The trip to the hotel took all of fifteen minutes. Dougger was polite and non-committal, offering no insight for the purpose of the interview with General Brandt. Conversation centered on Washington, the Sinai, and the predictions for the Redskins this year. Nothing was said, if indeed it was even known, as to why Matt was summoned. Dougger dropped him off, gave him a phone number and unneeded directions to the third floor office of the Deputy Chief of Staff for Intelligence, and with a salute, was gone.

Matt took a long hot shower, grabbed a bite at the café and grill on the main floor, watched the bar TV for an hour or so and made it an early evening. The international call he placed to Megan went through without problem, but the phone rang unanswered.

Twice from Florida he had tried to call. The phone had not been answered. The forth time he tried it was two o'clock in the morning, Tel Aviv time. A masculine voice, familiar but elusive, answered and informed him he had the wrong number.

In a brief trip to the lobby for stamps and a post card, he picked out a picture of the Washington Monument and addressed it to the British Embassy in Tel Aviv. The message was a simple one but spoke volumes. *I was wrong. Why aren't you where you should be? Come now. Love, Matt* was all he wrote.

Later in the evening, having retrieved his hotel pressed Class A Green Army uniform, Matt went about the work of properly detailing it with the various badges, ribbons, and appurtenances earned over his sixteen years of active duty. The last bit of ornamentation applied was the silver leaf on each shoulder epaulet denoting his rank. The climb to that

simple bright ornament had been long and difficult and it
represented to him a great deal more than just the rank of
Lieutenant Colonel.

Matt knew that he was not one of those singled out to
someday wear a star. One of the largest warts of his being, a
flaw in character, was in too frequently missing the opportunity to keep his mouth shut. Too often he spoke with too much
candor, too much criticism and with too little refinement to
the wrong audiences. As most type A personalities and his
father's son, Matt had a reputation for bluntness which, at
best, was intolerant and, at worst, just plain rude. On no few
occasions Matt made a critical remark or two on the "dumb"
pet project of a self-involved peer or superior. Later, they
would vengefully remember and return Matt's largesse.

The trait had not helped his career and was one that even
his few good friends tolerated rather than fully accepted. Still,
this was an honest flaw of character. There was no preten-
tiousness in his appraisal of himself, his abilities, or his judgment of those around him.

At zero six hundred the alarm went off and Matt crawled
from his untidy bed. A two-cup pot of coffee from the service provided in the room was quickly brewed, and, having
skipped his normal morning run, Matt began the day with a
hot shower. The shower was a long abandoned luxury in
which to indulge. Water in the Sinai had been a highly valued
and scarce commodity. By zero seven fifteen he had downed
his first two cups of coffee. At seven forty-five he was enjoying a large breakfast in the Doubletree restaurant. American
coffee was a far cry from that which he had drunk for a year.
The thick strong and sometimes bitter taste preferred in the
Middle East did not sit well with him and was often declined
when offered. The brew this morning was a welcome change
and he lingered over it while reading the complimentary *USA
Today* paper that had been left outside his door. He returned
to his room, performed his morning rituals, picked up his
briefcase and by zero eight thirty hours was headed out the
door for the Pentagon.

10
Libya Base Camp
—September, 2000

Salal and Machmued departed Tripoli in the morning and flew 600 miles to the south-southeast. Their ultimate destination was the oasis at Ghat. The oasis lay just to the north of the Tropic of Cancer. Ghat is buried in the Tadrart and Akakus Mountains some 300 miles south of the old Roman outpost at Ghudamis, close to the Algerian border. A jolting two-hour ride by jeep was accompanied by the *Ghibli*, a hot, very dry sand-laden wind that raises temperatures by ten degrees Celsius in a matter of minutes. Their route took them to the east and south of Al Qatron.

The scrabbled, sand-scoured hardpan in the Idehan Marzuk Desert, part of the Sahara in the southeast corner of Libya, was the location of the Jericho base camp. A bare and austere home to the force, it was created exclusively for this one operation. The site had been a major consideration in selection of the camp's whereabouts. Buried deep in the hinterlands of Libya, the compound was distant from other local populations. The bivouac was also secure, by virtue of its remoteness and inaccessibility, from surprise land assault or air attack.

The training base was nondescript. To the casual observer and from a distance there was nothing to set it apart from the hundreds of Bedouin camps that populated the deserts of Northern Africa. The fine hand of Sheik Muqbel Hadi al-Wadie, his alliances and influence with the old Bedouin rulers was evident in the security of the base, both in its appearance and in access to its confines.

There were no neatly lined barracks, well-defined rifle ranges, obstacle courses or other permanent structures. The camp was a random of multicolored Bedouin tents scattered at infrequent intervals within a circumference of some fifteen hundred meters. Goats and camels and an occasional older pickup truck dotted the landscape. The camouflage was eclectic and it worked. Upon closer examination, however, one would find that the tents sheltered military stores and training rooms, weapons, explosives, supplies and equipments.

The inhabitants of the camp were also different. While a few women and children were in evidence, the population of 200 to 250 was overwhelmingly very fit and mostly young men. They came from all parts of the Arab world—from Pakistan, Afghanistan, Syria, Turkey, Saudi Arabia, the Arab Emirates, Lebanon, Morocco, Tunisia westward into Algeria and back across Africa to Asia and Yemen, Iran, Iraq, and Jordan. All of the men, at some point, had undergone various degrees and depth of training at the *Dar al-Hadith* in Yemen or one of its five satellite centers. But here, under the watchful eyes of Jahbad, they would undergo a rigorous military training unlike even the most seasoned veterans had ever accomplished.

All the members of the strike force subscribed to the philosophical base of the purist, militant stridently anti-Western *Salafism* dictums of Islam. All, regardless of nationality, were dedicated to the destruction of Israel and its closest ally, the United States. They were the elite of the Arab fighters and the core of its future. The Jericho planners knew they would be under surveillance, but there was little to be done about it. They maintained as low a profile as possible and hoped that the site would not be uncovered and highlighted until its purpose had been fulfilled. The camp for all intents and purposes was nomadic, appearing on no maps or along any roadways. The ruse was successful. The training base had only the appearance of another nomadic tent city to the all-seeing eye of the American satellites orbiting hundreds of miles in space.

No permanent or visible erections of buildings and facilities were undertaken. The only construction was "to scale" sandtable mockups of the facilities they would attack. The miniatures were updated from intelligence gathered by Abdul's team already in the United States that was reconnoitering and monitoring the attack area. Outlines, diagrams and layouts of actual distances, scales and shapes were also marked off on the sand and hardpan to provide realistic distances for movement during training drills.

Jahbad was responsible for the resident training of the force. The screening and selection of the men, the intelligence gathering on the target area, the logistical preparations, the transportation and supplies—these and a thousand other details had crowded his mind these past months and now they had come together. Already a good number of the fighting force of over two hundred volunteers had found their way to this remote patch of barren nothingness.

The purpose of the camp was not basic training; it was to forge an advance skilled single force. The men were all experts in the rigors of small unit guerrilla warfare but never before had worked together in a single consolidated unit. A new strength would be stamped in a standard operating procedure, or SOP, extracted from the best of the techniques the fighters brought with them. The men grew more efficient as the teams to which they were assigned began to gel in common routines and coordinated drills that grew more complex.

The command and control structure was kept as simplistic as possible. The men were divided into autonomous cells of six. Each consisted of a leader, two explosives and demolitions experts or sappers, and three automatic riflemen. Six cells were supported by their own 61mm mortar crew cell of four men. Emphasis was placed on intensive physical conditioning, night-fighting skills, communications, reaction drills, timed operation executions, advanced terrain navigation during darkness, and coordination of force sub-elements. English was a daily hour-long class. Compartmentalized escape and evasion information, including codewords, phone numbers, locations of safe houses and routes to larger metropolitan areas were required memorization drills.

The cadre of the force was the cream of the crop, drawn

mostly, but not solely, from the core of seasoned fighters of the *Tala'ah Ah Fatah*, the Vanguards of Victory. These men were well versed in their fields, the best both in the theory and in the experience of terrorist operations, the best that the Arab brotherhood could offer. They had time and again demonstrated that they were fully prepared to sacrifice their lives in *jihad*.

The cadre and fighters of the Jericho force arrived at Al Qatron in staggered intervals accessing the camp over four weeks, so as not to arouse undue attention. Their specific skills ranged from small arms instructors in the standard AK-47 Assault Rifle, the 60mm and 81mm mortar, to communications wizards, to linguists, to creative explosive and demolitions handlers and bomb makers, to advanced hand to hand combat teachers and escape and evasion experts. Each had been selected on the basis of his expertise and skill.

Some, such as aged and wise Jahbad, who was in charge of the base camp, and Khleed, who would teach explosives and lead the demolition team during the attack, were old comrades who knew Salal personally. Others knew him only by reputation and were both curious and anxious to meet him and discover the specifics of the mission for which they had been selected and ordered here by their parent organizations. All were screened volunteers who had no specific knowledge of Jericho other than it was to be a highly dangerous operation and would be conducted on the soil of the Great Satan itself. More than this they were not told.

The assault force was well armed. In addition to an AK-47 assault rifle, each man also carried five fragmentation grenades, a heavy bladed assault knife and extra ammunition for the heavier weapons assigned to his squad. The team leaders were also armed with a 9mm automatic pistol.

The force was organized into six man teams. Assigned to each team for the assault phase was a light machine gun from the heavy weapons section. Four two-gun 61mm mortar sections complemented the lighter weapons and provided the only indirect and heavy fire support to the force. Rocket

Propelled Grenades, or RPG's, and two American-made LAW rocket launchers per squad added depth to the firepower of the assaulting forces. The accompanying supply of ammunition was considered more than adequate to secure the initial assault objectives.

Salal spoke in simple and direct language with the men, a number of whom he knew personally from past operations.

"We have come a long way from the days of ancient, rusty rifles and makeshift fertilizer," he said. "You are now well equipped and you will be well trained. Our mission is with a soldier's purpose. It is not the random unorchestrated act of a thug. We will strike our enemy in his heart."

There were many questions about the target but wisely few direct answers were provided. Requirements and expectations were defined with special attention given to the security aspects required of all participants. Many had never before seen such a carefully prepared or detailed schedule of events for one specific operation. English instruction, intensive physical conditioning, individual and team weapons and explosive training, would begin immediately. Mind numbing rehearsal and practice on the mockups of the attack site would be the daily routine until each member of the force could perform his tasks and that of any member of their individual cell in his sleep. The goal was the creation of an integrated elite and lightweight fighting force, well oiled and honed to peak sharpness and efficiency.

Here in the desert, with these Arab brothers, Salal felt at peace with himself. The desert was a better place, the home of true warriors. The cities were places of treacherous liars and deceivers, dishonorable people who followed the foreign corrupt ways of the West. Satisfied, Salal silently thought that the old ways were, indeed, the best.

Salal and Machmued left the camp late in the evening two days after their arrival and traveled west by primitive road to Tajarhi. Twenty-four hours later they disappeared.

11
The Pentagon
September, 2000

Matt breathed deeply during the uneventful twenty-minute walk down Army-Navy Drive and felt well with the world. Megan, he thought, would enjoy touring the city and he made a mental note to offer her the opportunity. Reality of her absence was coming hard and more frequently upon him.

The Pentagon loomed in front of him. The majority of staff action officers in the squat concrete monolith felt they ran the building. Half in wit, half in wisdom, the Majors and Lieutenant Colonels who wore the Army Staff or JCS Identification Badge held the belief that only they challenged convention, thought creatively, or crafted military policy.

Curosity nipped at the edges of his mind. Matt could not help but wonder why he had been summoned by the DCSINT to Washington. No point in worrying about it, he thought. Brandt always had a reason.

Rufus Brandt's office window—the symbol of success to other Pentagon aspirants, was, in fact, a grim reminder to the General. Facing out over the rows of white markers that bounded the southwestern edge of Arlington National Cemetery, the scene served him as a poignant reminder of his responsibilities. The panorama up the slopes of Arlington was sobering—the final duty station for the indispensable soldier, an example and memorial for those men and women yet to come. The debt still owed to those silent voices helped Rufus keep things in balance and perspective. The knowledge of their sacrifice gave a sense of purpose to his labors. Too often he had seen the grim parade of muffled, black-skirted drums, and the formal blue dress uniform of the Old Guard bringing a soldier home to the garden of stones. One day, the caisson and drums, he knew too well, would be paraded for him. That knowledge was both sad and somber.

Yesterday's Arlington ceremony lingered in his mind. Rufus Brandt had seen too many good men put into the earth. Too young a soldier, or sailor, or airman returned to the sweet Virginia soil of Robert E. Lee's forfeit mansion. In recent years they were the products of terrorist killings in Yemen, or Lebanon, Saudi Arabia or Pakistan. Too soon, they joined the gentle hush of their fallen comrades on the slopes under the shadow of the Lee-Custis Plantation house.

Rufus turned from the window. I'm getting old and maudlin, he thought. The sheaf of papers, which contained the morning message traffic, he dropped into the out box at the corner of his desk.

With the exception of the Chiefs of the various Services and the tribes of political appointees, the suite space for ranking officers in the Pentagon was austere. Several of the spaces housing junior flag rank officers on the other floors of the five-sided building were little more than a broom closet. Only a doormat in the hallway, a replacement for the insider's secret handshake denoting the residence of a lesser, but nonetheless aspiring, flag officer distinguished those offices.

Offices on the third floor, E ring, the outer most ring of the Pentagon, were reserved for the elite of the Department of Defense's leadership. They were the most sought after and protected square feet of office space in the entire military establishment of the United States. Not that it mattered to him as much as to his staff, but Rufus had been awarded one of these offices. The outer office housed four members of Brandt's personal staff. The executive office space and the secretary's cubicle were tiny in size, little more than a small room sectioned by dividers.

The suite, as Max Jackson liked to refer to it, had one of the less desirable views, but more importantly it was E ring office space. Inside the outer door, decorated in the corridor hallway with its appropriate floor mat, a thick General

Services Administration gray carpet covered the cement underfloor, differing from the corridor hallway concrete floor, which was covered with a well worn, but highly wax polished gray asphalt tile. By manner unknown and question better unasked, Max Jackson insured that the DCSINT's space received a fresh coat of white paint at least every eighteen or so months. White made the space appear larger than it was.

The walls of the DCSINT's private office displayed a series of original sketches and oils from the Civil War period on loan from the National Galleries. The office was furnished with a credenza that served as a backboard worktable. An oversized well-used but immaculate cherry wood executive desk dominated the room. Against its forward face stood a matching eight-foot long cherry conference table that was centered and lengthwise abutted. Three rolled, low-backed swivel chairs flanked the table on each side. The table served as a convenient and informal briefing site. The surface of the console doubled as a repository for overflow documents during the day and as a workspace when needed.

Set somewhat to the side of the main area were a pair of burgundy colored leather settees and a matching oversized leather chair. In their midst was a dark, polished coffee table for use in a more intimate and less formal discussion over coffee.

As usual, Rufus Brandt was behind schedule. The General looked at his watch. The time was already zero nine fifteen. Brandt swiveled the leather executive chair from the console behind his desk just as his secretary, Mrs. Murray, opened the door from the outer vestibule that served as both reception room and administrative space for his personal staff.

"General" she began, "Lieutenant Colonel Gannon is here. I've given him a cup of coffee; he's fifteen minutes early. Would you like to see him now or have me hold him until zero nine thirty?"

The visitor game was one that she and Rufus had played for the seven years that she had been his secretary. Unless in the midst of reading a complex decision paper or on the phone or for some other pressing need, Rufus never kept people waiting. Unlike many of his Pentagon counterparts, he held little value in useless control and ego based upsmanship games.

"Send him on in, Eileen, and please ask Max to join us."

Colonel Max Jackson was a tall, well-liked black officer, one of the first black graduates of the Citadel. A South Carolinian, his family traced its roots to a great, great grandfather who once served "Stonewall" Jackson while he was still an unknown officer teaching artillery tactics on the faculty of VMI. It was from that Confederate leader that the family name of Jackson had been drawn. Max was the repository of knowledge for the office, responsible for its smooth running and the prioritization of the General's several demanding projects. Brandt was grooming him, too.

In an operational context, Max knew more than anyone else, excepting Rufus Brandt himself. As the DCSINT's Executive Officer, he had complete access to almost all of the intelligence efforts and projects in which the General was involved excepting a few highly compartmentalized intelligence intercepts.

Max, at the General's direction, tracked Matt down and snared preliminary approval for his release to the Gambit project. The Pentagon interview this morning with the General was a result of his coordination efforts.

Matt entered the office with Colonel Max Jackson just a step behind him. Matt saluted in formal fashion as the General rose from behind his desk and extended his hand in warm welcome.

"Matt, how are you, tiger? Welcome home. How'd you like the Sinai?" Rufus inquired, a welcoming smile in place across his rugged face.

Matt returned the handshake with a grin of his own.

"Great duty, sir. Learned a lot, saw a lot, but I'm glad to be back. I met Colonel Jackson just a few moments ago in the outer office," Matt responded, acknowledging Max Jackson's presence.

"How did you get along with Colonel Tomini out there?" the General asked, coming straight to the point while motioning Matt to a chair.

Matt was somewhat taken aback by the question. Brandt had just given him an open invitation to drop a dime on the old son-of-a-bitch.

Colonel Benjamin Tomini was the senior serving US officer in the Multination Forces out in the Sinai Desert. To get that coveted assignment he called in quite a few chits. In addition to the position of Chief of Staff of the joint force, he was also the commander of the American brigade equivalent assigned to the peacekeeping force.

Tomini was a man with a history. In 1954, at the tender age of fifteen, Benjamin Tomini illegally entered the United States Army. No one at the time questioned the illegibly scrawled signature that gave parental consent to the enlistment and certified his age as seventeen.

Tomini was a maverick who volunteered for Vietnam in '63 and spent a total of four years in Indian country as a combat infantryman and advisor to the emerging Vietnamese Army. Promotions, especially in the combat zone, were fast in the '60s and Tomini, by 1967, was a combat legend and had advanced to the rank of First Sergeant. By his battlefield survival and acumen, First Sergeant Tomini came to the attention of enough of his superiors to be recommended for Officer Candidate School at Fort Benning, Georgia. Completion of the course conveyed to the Army a highly decorated *new* lieutenant, but a very much old breed warrior— not much for paperwork, not interested in improving his education, not strong on minorities or equal opportunity, or gays in the military, or women in the Army. What he was good at was battlefield survival and leadership as demonstrated by his record of survival and the two Silver Stars and the Distinguished Service Medal worn on his ribboned chest.

By the late-eighties he was a dinosaur but somehow hung on in spite of himself. The transition to a technical, computerized Army came hard for him as he discovered while

commanding a brigade during Desert Storm. Being a good
warrior who led by example did not, Tomini found, guarantee success nor inspire better performance at higher levels of
rank where organizational skills weighed much more than
personal bravery.

As chief of the American contingent in the Sinai, Tomini
knew it was his swan song. He was not ready for the pasture
and had no place to go. He had no life but the Army, no family to call his own, and the thought of forced retirement was
odious. His peers had moved on to their star or to retirement,
but he had remained, stagnant and more and more disgrun-
tled with his fate. The old sergeant had sacrificed much and
now, with some basis in fact, the handwriting was on the wall.
Instead of reward for his service and loyalty, he was about to
be shit-canned. Swallowing a 9mm round was more appealing
than a bench along the sidelines.

A belligerent, abrasive individual to begin with, Tomini
hoped that somehow he could turn this last job around, get
his star and stay on active duty a few more years.
Unfortunately, it was never to be. On the political side of
the peacekeeping operation, the old Colonel was in over his
head, never understanding the nuances of diplomatic language. His duties were reduced to ceremonial inspections
of the several outposts and the Colonel was kept in the field
out of harm's way.

Resentment grew, nurtured by the isolation of the desert
and Tomini acquired a new intimacy with old friends and now
constant companions, Jack Daniels and Jim Beam, both of
whom he increasingly called upon to help him refine decisions
and conduct inspections.

Matt knew that stories of Colonel Tomini's excesses had
filtered back to the Pentagon. Some had called him an international embarrassment and sought his relief. The sharks were
circling and smelled a kill. Here was a sad story of a good soldier gone to seed, an old warrior who had nowhere to go but
to the bottom of a bottle. Here was a man who turned bitter,
who should have left at his peak, but sacrificed all including a

marriage to chase the illusive goal of a star.

For the most part, Matt, unlike Tomini, was content with who he was. Like Tomini, he, too, could be a shade too demanding. Perhaps it was a sin of excess. There were times when even Matt had to admit that he did not comprehend the full range of his drives. Sure, there was a pride in the self-knowledge of what made him tick, how he was mentally and emotionally put together, but he could understand why some like Tomini did not want to look into that mirror.

Matt measured his words with care.

"Colonel Tomini, sir, probably has more time in combat than I have had in the Army. He's a taskmaster and I learned a lot from him. He is a great field soldier and a professional."

The reply hung in the air. Rufus smiled. The answer conveyed much more than what was said. Rufus reaffirmed for himself by the question and its answer that Matt retained the values and qualities he sought in a subordinate. Smart, quick and not a backbiter – loyal. Reputation was important and Rufus knew Matt would not build his on any part of the ruin of others nor participate in tearing a fellow officer's personal reputation down—Gannon would do.

"You ready to get back to work?" the General asked, coming directly to the point.

"Yes, sir. Just need to know when and where. I take it, sir, that you, ah, have something in mind?"

"Matter of fact, yes, Matt. Maybe," he responded in an elusive voice. "Still working on it, but I think so. First off, I want you to get smart on some recent intelligence reports. The job I have in mind for you may be high risk. Some of it I can't fill you in on right now. You'll just have to trust me a bit. Interested?"

"Yes, sir. But you knew that before I walked through the door," was Matt's attentive reply. "This have anything to do with my assignment in the Sinai?"

Rufus eyed Matt speculatively. The question was realistic and expected.

"Maybe," the General responded. "Could tie in a bit.

When Max gets done with you and the folks over at Langley have you up to speed, you'll see a connection. The job—well, some of it's political—not in the partisan sense, but in an international context. I expect you'll be smart enough to see what I mean before it's all said and done. When you do, keep your conclusions to yourself. Don't bother to ask or try to confirm them. If you're wrong, you'll just end up stirring the pot and if you're right, well ..."

"For the next few days, we're going to build a cover for you by putting you on a selection board over at PERSCOM," Rufus continued as he glanced at Max. "At least that will be the story. Max will get you set up for some codeword briefings as soon as we get your clearances upgraded."

The leather of the overstuffed chair squeaked as the General settled in and faced Matt across the low coffee table. "Have you ever heard the name Salal?"

"Salal? No, sir. We had pretty good intelligence out in the Sinai, but that's not one of the names I heard. The Israelis kept us pretty current I thought," Matt noted, his curiosity piqued. "Is he a new player?"

"No, just not one who is very visible. And don't be too naïve about the Israelis, Matt," Rufus smiled. "They're a pragmatic bunch. They give us what they want us to have, not all they know. In the case of Salal, we don't think even they have got that much."

"Who does he work for, sir?" Matt asked.

"Take your pick; ICO, PLO, Nidal, Bin Ladin, one of the splinter groups—all of the above, and then some. We think that Salal is a *nom de guerre*, an alias, but there is no way of knowing for sure. Every time we think we have a face or a background to go with the name, we end up at a dead end. He's very good and very elusive. Right now we don't know much about him, but we're digging hard."

"It's just a matter of time," Max interjected.

"We think he's in his mid-fifties, give or take," Rufus continued. "He seems to have a hand in international incidents more than the local events. What we do know is that he's been the brain behind some very successful operations. Salal's part myth, part man and all hero to the Arab underground. From that group he has developed quite a power base and a loyal following. That in itself is a remarkable feat in the Arab world. The flesh and blood Salal is very, very savvy on the political scene and appears to have access to the power brokers."

"We can tell you," said Max, joining the conversation, "that he's not a cowboy—damn good operative who stays away from the limelight. Thinks it through. Has a number two man, Machmued, who is just as good. Between the two of them, they've put together a couple of operations that just made us look dumb. We have a file on Machmued that goes just about all the way back to Newfoundland. Got very little on Salal—not even a picture."

"This Machmued was in on the Gander crash? I thought the crash was an accident, an ice buildup on the wings or something like that. I remember there was speculation at the time," Matt remarked, "but it all died down when the Air Traffic Safety Board report came out."

"Don't believe everything you read in reports," Brandt responded. "At the time, public knowledge that this was still another successful terrorist attack on our military was, ah, shall we say, decided by the political powers not to be in our best interests."

Jackson chimed in, "Especially not following on the heels of the Marine disaster in Lebanon. The administration couldn't take another hit like Lebanon and that's exactly what Gander was – only closer to the USA shores."

"For unknown reasons, Americans are an obsession for Salal," Rufus continued warming to his subject. "His name gets linked just about every time we have an American facility or troops hit. His objective seems to be to put as much pressure on us as he can muster. Salal thinks he can get us to pull the plug on our Middle East involvement. There are those in the Arab community who want us out of the peace process."

"I'm puzzled that I've never heard either of these names,

General. Fish as big as Salal show up in intelligence files sooner or later." The consternation showed on Matt's face. "This Salal can't be that much of a ghost. These guys must know we have intelligence on them," Matt reasoned, directing his comment to both of the other men in the room.

"Oh, they know all right," Rufus responded. "Much of the time you don't hear about the real players. But Salal, well, he's one of the deadly ones."

Max broke in again. "We think he was born in Palestine; he has always kept a low, quiet profile. He's a behind the scenes broker and, we think, an insider. He'll take a group, set up an operation, hand it off, and let other folks grab the headlines. Salal is just a phantom who gets it done. Not out for a name or personal glory at all."

"We haven't heard from him in over a year now," the General continued. "Defense Intelligence Agency and CIA concluded that he's lost favor, but we've recently heard that is inaccurate. Through a classified source we've confirmed he's been lying out there in the brush putting this latest operation together. He's overdue."

Matt sat forward on the leather settee, his interest obvious. Rufus nodded to Max who picked up the dialogue.

"We know he's worked with both Abu Nidal and Osama Bin Ladin. Both of them, as you know, are strident, well financed, and very anti-American. But right now there is evidence to suggest that he's tied into an even larger Pan-Arab group," Max continued.

The general jumped back into the conversation. "Recently, there have been a number of random incidents which, though unconnected on the surface of things, led a few of us on the NSC to the conclusion that something very big is about to happen, bigger in a terrorist sense than anything we've seen so far."

The general continued without waiting for comment, now on a roll. "According to one of our sources, there was a very important, very unofficial meeting in Tripoli in late March or early April. Some of the people we know, some we do not. At that meeting, Salal is alleged to have detailed a plan for a strike on the US that he claimed will hang us out to dry. The code name for his operation is Jericho. Since that meeting, our sources report that some of the more experienced people in several of the active terrorist groups have dropped out of sight. They've just disappeared."

"At last count it was somewhere upwards of seventy of their best, most experienced terrorist soldiers," Max contributed.

"Right now," Rufus added, "we don't know where they are but we suspect they are together and working out of a new base somewhere."

"But only a speculation?" Matt inquired.

"Well, perhaps a bit more than that," Brandt replied without expounding further. "They've gone to ground somewhere to organize and train."

Rufus paused and leaned forward, locking his eyes on Matt's. "There are much larger scale political and international implications at work here … more than you can begin to imagine. They include the entire Middle East peace process and where the future border lines get drawn on the maps."

He hesitated only a moment before continuing. "We've known, and when I say we, I mean the NSC, that the extreme radical Arab elements have wanted a major strike in the US for a long time. We've made a lot of enemies in the Arab world, particularly among the ones who see the only answer as a continuation of Hitler's 'final solution.' Not all of the Arabs are that militant, but you have to understand them. They're a race of people with both a blood bond and an even more important religious bond that ties them together. The terrorist leadership may be radical but Arabs will not turn against Arabs over the Israel issue. They're too xenophobic for that."

Rufus paused. "Did you learn any Arabic over there, Matt?" he asked casually.

"A word or two here and there sir, enough to get by in the suks," Matt said.

"Too bad," Rufus observed. "To come to an appreciation

of how Arabs think, it's a great help to first understand their language. Arabic is very subtle, much more than English. The scholars and linguists will tell you that it is a language of truths more so than of facts. Now it's a fact that the Arabs support the Palestinians on the land issue, but the greater and more driving truth is that radical Islam still seeks revenge upon the Jews for refusing to accept Mohammed as a prophet and the Koran in place of the Torah. It goes back to the belief that Ishmael was cheated from his birthright."

Rufus shifted in his chair.

"Two thirds of the Palestinians who were around in '48 when Israel was created are gone. The gifted ones, the educated and the wealthy, moved on to other countries. Arafat represents a dwindling one-third of the original Arab populace of Palestine. Make no mistake, Yasser Arafat's support is real. It comes from Islamic fundamentalists who just hate the Jews. Don't discount or minimize the religious angle here. It plays a big role," Rufus cautioned. "The moderates may not like the Khadafi's and the Hussan's, but they won't go against them when it comes to Israel. You can take that to the bank. This Arab-Israel thing is deeper than the PLO or the Palestine issues; the fight is a cultural heritage. The one thing that unites the Arab world is a common hatred of the Jews. Take away Israel and they will turn to fratricide, cutting up Palestine among themselves. Study their history, their culture, their society and you will see my point."

"But how does that play on Salal's operations against us?" Matt asked.

"Salal is a unifier who can pull diverse factions of the Arab community together, give them a focus," Brandt replied. "But the larger point, Matt, is that one must understand what motivates your enemy if you are to successfully engage him."

"Point taken sir, but it's my understanding the terrorists don't have the support base or strategic reach to project any major operation against the United States."

"Don't kid yourself. Go outside this building and catch a cab. Go to New York or Chicago or Detroit. Take a look at who drives the cabs and fills the manual labor and blue-collar jobs. We've got one hellava Middle East population over here. They have homes and people back there in the Middle East. There is a fifth column here, a small one perhaps, but nonetheless a network. But even discounting the loyalty or sympathy from immigrants here, Salal doesn't need a big support base for the type of action we're talking about."

"Then how do we preempt them? We've got to get out of the reactive mode and take the initiative away from them somehow, I would think," Matt hypothesized.

"Well, first let's just speculate that our Arab radicals would be willing to take a substantial hit if the rewards were big enough. At worst, it's only a calculated risk and it could be an acceptable situation to give them the status and power they seek. Khadafi has already told us he has ten thousand ready to die in *jihad*. Death in holy war is a very honorable thing for them, Matt. Big rolls of the dice to gain their ends are not without precedence. The militants keep proving it on the bombings and other suicide missions."

There was a quiet knock on the door.

"You have a 10:30 with the Vice-Chief, General," Eileen said.

"Ah, thank you, Eileen," Rufus said, glancing at the Omega strapped to his left wrist. The General made movement to rise from his chair while continuing to speak. "You know about the increase in the terrorist incidents all across Europe and how the PLO has denied them?"

"Yes, but nobody buys the denials, sir," Matt responded.

"Well, we think the denials are true, Matt. Arafat's PLO may have known about them, but we don't think he had anything to do with them. Arafat wants legitimacy, wants to be known as a statesman, leave a legacy, maybe become the George Washington of Palestine. You don't get that by terrorism. The men who pull the triggers trace back to radical splinter groups. They're like a bunch of school kids on display, showing off, each trying to outdo the other and receive the grand prize. Only in this contest, the results are threatening the Middle East peace process. Nonetheless, believe it or not, we now have a better chance for peace over there than we've ever had."

"Then maybe Arafat isn't so bad after all," Matt offered.

"You've got quite a few folks who agree with you. Better the devil you know than the devil you don't, Matthew. Over the long term, the radicals have been having a tough go. First they had their ass kicked out of Lebanon, then came the Sadat move toward moderation and an Israeli accommodation. They need a big win if they want to keep their influence."

Rufus rose and donned his uniform jacket, picked up a thick leather portfolio from his desk and glanced once more at his watch.

"The radical element needs something that will take the peace process off the front pages and put them back on. Doing that lessens Arafat's lock on legitimacy and he loses credibility as the spokesman for the Palestinians."

"And you feel that this might be the end game for Jericho?"

"Possibly. That and taking us out of the game."

Rufus paused and turned as he walked toward the office door. "We'd like to give the terrorists a damn good taste of their own medicine. And that's what Gambit, our counter to Jericho, is all about. We want to nail Salal and his gang with their pants down and identify his backers while they have their hands in the cookie jar."

"How sir? We've been trying to anticipate them without very much luck since before the Lebanon massacre."

Brandt looked at him and winked. "Trust me. Gotta go."

To Max he turned and gave instructions. "Get Matt set up over at Langley. Tell PERSCOM we're going to keep him."

As he reached for the door he turned back to Matt. "Good to have you back home, tiger. We'll be talking more. Oh, and by the way, congratulations on your selection to command. You're gonna take over Sunny Point. The list isn't out yet, but Max will tell you all about it," and he was gone.

12
Washington, D.C.
—Late September, 2000

During his prior Pentagon assignment Matt had clearance for compartmented data, a restricted security level above top secret. He was well familiar with the limited access to this level of highly circumscribed information.

Compartmented intelligence was a very proactive and stringently controlled program. Only those who have the proper credentials, a need to know, and who have undergone a rigorous background security investigation conducted by the FBI could access the files. Right of entry to codeworded files was reviewed every thirty days and, once determined entry was no longer required, access was immediately withdrawn.

Matt's selection by Rufus Brandt as the new commander of Sunny Point and a key player in the Gambit operation opened doors to him that otherwise would have remained closed. The subsequent briefings retaught him that military intelligence is an imperfect science. At best it can describe intentions; at worse, its logics, when applied in an inaccurate context, can develop into misleading conclusions.

"The intelligence gathering community of the United States is the very best in the world, but even it has severe limitations," the Langley briefing officer had acknowledged to Matt and Max Jackson.

"While our electronic and satellite reconnaissance is unequaled, our Middle East human intelligence resources, or HUMINT, are just lacking. It's a blind side we are trying to work through at the moment," Max reluctantly admitted.

"What are our options?" Matt asked.

"Well, to be honest, until we can get a network in place

we have to pretty much depend on the Israeli Mossad. The Mossad, which is Hebrew for 'institute' incidentally, is the Israeli agency for HUMINT, most of their covert actions, and all of their counterterrorism efforts. Their Research Department, one of eight departments in the Mossad, heavily censors information before releasing it to us, so we're pretty much at their mercy right now."

The briefings at Langley, Fort Meade, the CIA and State Department had taken five very full days but, due to scheduling, were spread out over a three and one-half week timeframe.

The Langley NSA crowd focused their sophisticated satellite imagery on suspected guerrilla training and deployment sites. The CIA had HUMINT capabilities and the FBI had domestic and limited international linkages to Interpol and Scotland Yard. They had come together to round out and fill in blank spaces in the original DeFore briefing. Additional specific information on Jericho was, however, minimal.

The U.S. response to Jericho, *Operation Gambit* was, so far as Matt could tell, a clear military answer. Only federal agencies were involved.

"For national security reasons," Max Jackson explained, "no direct request was made to Israel for information on the Jericho operation. Our knowledge of this pending Arab action came to us from a private source in very deep cover. Even the Israelis are unaware of his existence."

"And we're not about to share him," General Brandt added from the corner of the room.

Matthew found that the General had been right. The potential of Jericho was dramatic. If the conclusions were right, it was a scary throw of the dice by the ICO and Salal.

"As you no doubt have deduced by now, Matt, we've arrived at several conclusions," Max tutored him at the final wrap-up in the General's office. "First, we're about ninety-nine percent certain that the ICO has sanctioned a major assault on one of our installations here in the USA. Second, we make their window of opportunity as being in either late

November or the first part of December timeframe, probably the latter. Third, it will be on the East coast and fourth, with a bit of a stretch, we think it's going to be Sunny Point, the explosives and special munitions port on the Cape Fear River."

"Well, if we're in the ballpark," Matt replied, "we should be able to get inside their execution cycle and be proactive in our response to any attack."

"Maybe, but our intel still has major holes," Jackson cautioned. "Any successful assault on the homeland of the United States makes a powerful statement, particularly if it demonstrated that even military installations on our own shores are not beyond their reach. Bearding the lion in its den sends a hellava message, especially to the next Arab generation."

To that observation the General added, "If they're successful, the attack will serve as a rallying point for new recruits. The ICO would restore and consolidate enough influence in the Arab world to significantly alter current attitudes toward peace. Power and support gravitate to success. A religious pan-Arab coalition, with economic and political sway far beyond even that of OPEC, is not at all impossible. The probability of success is high and the result could become a dangerous reality."

The conclusion that Sunny Point was the target Matt had to accept on faith. How the intelligence community or General Brandt divined that the explosives port was to be the target of Salal's efforts was not shared. It was presented to him as a given, a known. Much, however, was still not understood.

The intelligence summaries provided, while important, still did not define how an attack would take place. The date of the attack, the size of the attacking force, their access points, their dispersal and assembly plans, their weaponry, their knowledge of the installation and its vulnerabilities were all still unknowns.

Sunny Point, Brandt believed, was the perfect candy store for Salal. Destroying a major ammunition storage and transfer point met all of his political and military objectives.

Sunny Point was built without fanfare in the mid-fifties, although the planning had begun on July 18, 1944. Its creation revolved around an event at a place then called Port Chicago at present-day Concord, California. According to the file in the Langley archives, several ships were scattered across the Port Chicago anchorage. Some ships were already at berth, some swinging on their hook, waiting for space. All were being loaded in an around-the-clock operation to support American forces fighting in the Pacific. Two ships, the Quinault Victory and the E.A. Bryan, one a Liberty and the other a Victory class ship, were at berth on the ammunition pier. The ammo area and pier were completed only three months earlier. The entire operation was cordoned with marine guards, waterside patrols, underwater netting and million candlepower spotlights around the area of the berths. The area was considered impenetrable.

It wasn't.

At 10:19 the morning of July 17, 1944, the sky was lit by the detonation of three and one-half million pounds of flaked TNT. Seismographs at San Francisco indicated there were two explosions, seven and one-half seconds apart, but no one, even the uninjured, seemed to care. The whole of Port Chicago ceased to exist. The detonation leveled all structures for a thousand yards in all directions.

The Quinault Victory, the E.A. Bryan and three hundred and twenty lives vaporized in the mushroom of fire, noise, light and fragmentation. Windows were broken and plaster cracked at a distance up to thirty miles. The War Department released a statement that attributed the accident to a mistake, carelessness during the rushed loading. The local and national papers picked it up and the experts of the day speculated about a random spark, a fluke of static electricity, and a careless moment by one of the longshoremen.

There were a dozen theories—an electrical arc in a cable to a battery, a split in the insulation covering on a sparkplug wire, a snapped cable swinging a load of one thousand pound bombs. Perhaps it was a misjudged distance, a careless hand signal from a tag linesman to the winch operator, an act of God, but nobody ever knew for sure—publicly. Whatever had happened was too sensitive, too embarrassing during the war to release. Neither the extent of damage nor the fact that at least two enemy agents had penetrated the security was admitted. Just as in Beirut almost fifty years later, the operation hadn't taken much—just suicide tactics.

In 1953, nine years after the Concord incident and at the outset of another conflict, the Department of Defense directed the unheralded construction of a new installation—one dedicated in design and operation, for the movement of munitions and explosive cargo. Construction began in the sleepy rural backwaters of the Cape Fear River in Brunswick County, North Carolina. The location was ideal, built adjacent to the small hamlet of Southport, remote but close to rail, highway, and water thoroughfares. In the event of an unforeseen accident the low-density population and sparsely settled areas would not be the high casualty risk of the larger more populated areas as was Concord, California or larger, better-known eastern seaports.

Work and jobs came to an impoverished part of North Carolina where little had changed since the Civil War. The local economy blossomed. The facility was the major East Coast ammunition and explosives terminal that moved not three million pounds of explosives at a time, but sixty million at a crack. Ten years later, in 1963, it was ready. But by then the community was beginning to change.

Prosperity and mobility of the population were ingredients of a new America. The shorelines became summer refuges and second homes. Low cost housing complexes were built on new resort beaches. Kure Beach, a new resort area community, sprouted at the outskirts of the tiny, traditional Southern hamlet of Southport and urban sprawl was beginning to rear its ugly head. Now almost forty years later, Sunny Point had several neighbors, the population had soared and the area had been transformed into a potential target, a high-stakes stalking horse.

"We're taking a hellava risk," Brandt acknowledged. "Aside from the potential loss of life and damage, a successful attack on Sunny Point would put a terrible knot in our munitions resupply capability. If the terrorists get through, well, it could bring down the administration. And God help us all if it ever gets out that we had even an inkling of what they were up to and we don't nail them."

Bits of the conversation Matt had after the Langley briefing with General Brandt just before he'd left Washington drifted back. It seemed like months rather than just a few short weeks ago. Brandt had been talking about credibility and perceptions.

"There is a difference," he said, "between truth and reality. Truth is fact but reality is what people come to believe. The two are not always the same. Remember the Viet Cong Tet Offensive back in January '68?"

Matt nodded his head in the affirmative.

"Tet was total military victory for us. Now that was a fact. But the reality was a complete propaganda victory for the communists, a rout for the other side. We won the battle and lost the war over it."

"Point taken, General. But how the hell do you respond without giving them another set of martyrs?" Matt asked.

"Until Desert Storm, the military took flak in every sector of the media. The six o'clock news banged on us with things like Westmoreland's asinine "light at the end of the tunnel" comment. There was a shot in the foot. It was only when Reagan took office that we began to regain any credibility. What support we've gained, we lose when we cry that the sky is falling and it doesn't. On the flip side, it's just as bad when we say we have things under control, and we find out too late that we don't," Max offered.

"It's a tougher job today, Matt," Rufus explained. "When

we had the USSR as our enemy, we could identify and focus our resources against a defined threat; we could justify our requirements for men, materiel, an overseas presence, and the taxpayers could understand it. It's much tougher to justify a large fighting force against small splinter groups of terrorists, and smaller rogue nations. They are just as dangerous, in a different way, than were the Soviets. Today, it's just that it is harder to portray to John Q. Public the danger they represent. That's why we've got to proceed with all due cautious haste. We can't afford to have the 'light at the end of the tunnel' be mounted on the front end of a locomotive. We've got to position ourselves to either stop or blow up the Goddamn train before it runs over us. If we do Gambit right, we'll set Middle East terrorism back at least a generation."

"*If* they appear at Sunny Point, *if* the intelligence is good, *if* we know when they are coming, *if* we know what they intend and how many they are—there's a hellava lot of ifs to cope with," Matt responded.

"Right now we may still be talking '*if*,' but I know they will come," Brandt said. "*If* it was gonna be easy they wouldn't need us. And Salal will be at Sunny Point by the end of the year. That's why I want you down there."

Brandt knows more than he's saying, Matt thought.

After the briefings, there wasn't anything more to be immediately accomplished in Washington. Orders were cut assigning Matt as the new commanding officer of Sunny Point. Matt took a morning, a week before his scheduled departure, to browse through the late model BMWs and smaller Mercedes at the Mercedes dealership in Arlington and the BMW/Porsche dealership in Crystal City. He settled on a used, late model Titanium Silver 323i BMW with low mileage.

"Appearance," Rufus cautioned "is what we're all about at this point. Don't do anything that will call attention to yourself."

The detailed operational plans of Gambit were being developed by elements of the Special Operations Command at Fort Bragg. An old Desert Storm and Command and General Staff College counterpart, Colonel Jack Dalton, was responsible for both the handling and execution of Gambit. Matt's association and friendship with Jack went back eight years to their assignment days at Fort Leavenworth. Nancy, Jack's wife, had then served as matchmaker and sought to relieve Matt of his bachelorhood at every turn.

Max Jackson cleared Matt to receive a full briefing on Dalton's efforts. There was a certain comfort in knowing that Jack Dalton would command the Gambit reaction forces and Matt warmed to the thought of seeing his old friend and renewing the banter with his wife.

Matt made a call to Jack Dalton at Fort Bragg. He missed him at his headquarters but got him at home and arranged to stop by, enroute to Sunny Point, and spend a day or two. The two officers avoided talking business although Jack knew the true purpose of the call. Nancy jumped in on an extension and teased Matt with verbal abuse and threatened matchmaking with one of the cold-handed nurses from the Womack Medical Center. The call was upbeat and Matt returned the receiver to its hook with a smile on his face. Megan's image leapt into his mind.

Over the past few weeks he had succeeded in crowding her into a corner of his memory with the door only slightly ajar. At least that's what he told himself. He settled on yet another post card with the same old message.

Why aren't you where you should be? Hurry, Come Now, it read.

Matt sent it to her parents' address in England. Included was his soon to be new Sunny Point address.

He mailed it off. She should know how he felt. Maybe it would be enough.

Two days later Matt packed the BMW with his few possessions and headed south. The traffic was light and the weather good. He pointed the 323i toward Interstate 95, rolled the needle of the speedometer up to seventy-five, and punched the cruise control. His thoughts returned to Jack and Nancy Dalton.

Jack and Nancy were the epitome of mismatched lovers. Where Nancy was gentility and quiet sophistication, Jack was raw, unchallenged, profane and as unpolished as the occasion would tolerate. He had a knack for the ribald and a covetous eye for good-looking women.

"Hell, I'm married but I ain't dead yet," Jack allowed with a grin, needling his wife.

Such proclamations were always made well within Nancy's hearing. A response from Nancy was neither infrequent nor unexpected.

"You just remember buster, I don't care where you get your appetite, but you damn well better take your meals at home," Nancy retorted.

They both recognized it as a game and it had become a way of acknowledging to each other that they cared and still very much loved one another. Nancy was accurate in her confidence that Jack was wrapped around her little finger. She would smile a quiet smile and tolerate his ramblings with a pretended exasperation. After four kids and a dozen years, they still had something going for each other. They fit. Matt looked forward to seeing them once again. Maybe he'd have something like that someday.

Matt slid a CD into the deck, turned up the volume and let the car effortlessly gobble up the concrete miles through Virginia and into North Carolina, to Fayetteville, to Fort Bragg, Colonel Jack Dalton, and Gambit.

Matt grinned and wondered if he'd make it through the hangover that would result from an evening with his old friend.

*   *   *

As Matt rolled down Interstate 95, some four thousand miles to the east Megan sat motionless and gazed down upon the distant sea. Since she and Matt had parted at Ben Gurion airport there had been but few moments when she felt an inner peace or contentment. It had been close to a month since her return home. She had quietly come back on extended leave within days of his departure rather than the fortnight holiday planned for later in the year.

In spite of the layers of caution built over the disappointment of past encounters, Matt had penetrated her defenses to find and touch the warmth buried deep inside her. She needed time, space and the security of her parents' nest to wring out her emotions and get past her feelings.

Though she was a most welcome guest in her parents' home, the fact that she was a guest annoyed her. Unhappily she realized that this place was not her much sought refuge, nor, she realized, would it ever really be. While Megan's character over the years had come to be more and more influenced by her parents, she had now lived too long by herself, by her own rules and rituals, to return to a role as the submissive daughter.

Her extended absence from the British embassy in Tel Aviv passed slowly. The days seemed long and shallow. She felt an emptiness that wasn't there before Matt. The cold drizzle and dark clouds of autumn reinforced her gloomy spirit. She took long walks accompanied by the companions of sadness and regret.

She missed Matt.

She missed their life together. She also reluctantly found she had been in England long enough to recapture and rekindle all of the reasons why she had left and why she would never permanently settle in her United Kingdom homeland.

An on-shore breeze shook the leaves in the trees and she shuddered. Even in an October Indian summer such as this, she thought, the winds blew chill in England. Megan gazed over the English Channel to the shores of France and let her mind flood with the memories of her years. She sighed, shifted her position and wrapped her arms tighter about her long legs. Deep within herself she knew she would somehow cope.

She came from a long line of survivors—a long line of strong willed women.

Megan mused on these things as she sat on a bright chilly morning with the sun shining off of the white Dover cliffs. Strange, she thought, how one's life was just a series of captured moments, frozen in time, to be called up and savored. The warm glows, the brutal angers, the unrequited grief, the happy, sad, lonely, celebrant days of life—the treasured secrets, all replayed and relived to herself alone, all in the record of her mind.

"Perhaps it's all just bad karma. I suppose it was just not meant to be," she sighed, talking aloud to no one but herself.

She almost believed it, but in her heart of hearts she somehow knew that he was the one, that Matthew was destined to be a part of her life.

13
Somewhere In The Middle East
—October, 2000

"The ship fits our needs even better than we expected," Machmued said.

"Are you sure it will block the channel?" Salal asked.

"Yes, it is perfect." Machmued withdrew a cheap green notebook from the pocket of his washed out khaki shirt, and riffled through the pages. Salal's second in command found the appropriate entries and continued.

"Once she is sunk no other vessel will be able to pass to any port on the Cape Fear River. The name of the ship is the *Compass Rose*. The channel at the point where we will sink her is 410 feet wide and almost 40 feet deep. The ship is 601 feet in length, and 90 feet in beam. When we have loaded our final cargo on board she will weigh just at 15,700 tons and draw about thirty-four feet of water. She has been to Wilmington many times in the last few years so her appearance is not unexpected.

"What of her speed?"

"About seventeen knots for routine operations; twenty-four knots for short periods should it be necessary. Her silhouette is a good match for several of the ammunition ships that the Americans use for their European resupply. At night and from a distance she could be mistaken," he noted.

"A good omen, Machmued, but let us hope that our success does not turn on that fact alone. What of the ship's owners and crew?"

Machmued glanced at his notes before replying. "The vessel is owned by Abdul Sa'id Lazir, an Egyptian, sympathetic to our cause. The vessel has been chartered by many different companies. Lazir may suspect that it is being used by our cause, but he has been well paid. A connection back to us would be most difficult to trace. Even *baksheesh*," Machmued continued, rubbing forefinger and thumb together, "will take Lazir only to the outer circles. The company that he owns has several such ships and the leasing was done through a holding company—a broker of shipping in France, known for reliability and discretion. We have used him several times before to smuggle weapons into Lebanon. His people have also been used in the past to evacuate wounded fighters from Gaza to other safe havens.

Machmued paused and sipped at the tea in front of him before continuing. "We have arranged to replace the captain with a man of our own. We have also placed three of our men, all experienced seamen, including the radio operator, in the ship's crew over the past three months. There has been no suspicion. The captain knows only that they will take on additional cargo and passengers at Rabat. Nothing has been said to him or the crew of the operation, but he has been instructed to make necessary arrangements to accommodate them."

"How much does the captain of the ship know?" Salal asked.

"The captain is not a fool, but he is loyal to us," Machmued replied. "He knows what we wish him and the crew to know. We have encouraged them to believe that we intend to capture an American cruise ship. We have promised that all actions taken would be accomplished in international waters. Beyond this, they have been told nothing," Machmued continued, pleased that he had anticipated and prepared for the thorough questioning.

"What of the cargo?"

"Most of it will load in Alexandria. There will be four thousand tons of African hardwoods. There are also one hundred and thirty-two containers of manufactured textile and leather goods from African and Middle East sources. Several of the containers will be discharged in Rotterdam and others then loaded before we board the ship at Rabat in Morocco. The cargo has been funneled through a legitimate exporter.

All the appearances of the ship's voyage are that of a routine movement."

"Why have we changed the departure port? I thought it had been decided to leave from Oran. We have many friends and supporters in Algeria."

"True," came the reply, "but Oran is a very large port. There are too many foreign eyes and ears that are not friendly to us in Algeria. From Oran the ship must pass through the Straits of Gibraltar and can be observed by the British and the American fleet in the Mediterranean. Rabat is a minor port. This new port does not command as much attention as Oran. A departure from the Bou Regreg estuary on the Atlantic Ocean in Morocco gives us easier access and the trip will be almost two days shorter. Travel security for the fighters is better and easier to Rabat. The change does not affect our time table."

Salal accepted the rationale without comment. "This man, the exporter, what do we know of him?"

Machmued flipped through his notes. "His only son was one of our fighters. The boy was twenty-three when the Jews killed him in Lebanon. The broker has been told he is supporting a legal enterprise to gather funds for the Palestinian cause."

"What has he been told of Jericho?" Salal persisted.

"Nothing. And if he had been, even then he could not follow the thread back to us. There is no reason for him to be suspicious. There have been no questions. The entire matter has been quite routine."

Salal nodded his approval. "There must be no loose ends. No one but you and I must know the full details of the plan. All must continue to proceed as normal."

Machmued nodded his agreement. "Three ports of call are scheduled. Rotterdam of course is first, Rabat is the second, Wilmington is scheduled to be the third and, *Enshallah,* it will be the last. The strike force will depart in small packets of men from the training camp and infiltrate to meet the ship at Rabat."

"When will they begin to leave the camp?" Salal asked.

"The first of the men will depart in a week's time. They will travel in groups no larger than two or three, without weapons and with new identity cards. For some we have arranged wives or parents or children on the different legs of their journey. Some leave as laborers, others as businessmen. A very few will travel as students. They are being routed over many different paths through different villages. They will all arrive and reassemble at the ship beginning three days before her sailing."

"Will not such a large number gathered in one place cause suspicion?" Salal asked.

Machmued shrugged. "The men will filter into the port at a slow pace so as not to arouse any suspicions."

"You must tell them how important it is for them to remain inconspicuous."

Machmued acknowledged the comment with a nod. "It is already done. The men will slip aboard during the night. Their weapons, explosives, equipment, food and other provisions for the trip have been assembled and will be loaded as three of the routine containers of cargo. Our agents assure us there will be no difficulty."

Salal accepted the answer and then fired another question. "What of Doctor l'Alham and his companion? What arrangements have been made for them?"

"They were kept apart during the training. As you directed we have made special arrangements to transport both of them. They will fly via London to Washington, D.C. and be met and transported to the safe house at Caswell Beach. The doctor and his companion will meet you there."

"They are to leave only when all other elements have left, Machmued. Protect them at all costs."

Machmued bit down his natural curiosity and nodded in affirmation. The qualifications of l'Alham and his taciturn companion had never been discussed. They had one day merely appeared, personally cleared to the entire operation by Salal. Both were unknown entities, unrecognized faces in the company of freedom fighters. They were Pakistani and were both very well educated. They were afforded no special privileges in the training. They remained to themselves and made no efforts to socialize with their compatriots.

"These two I do not know, Salal, this l'Alham and his associate. They keep to themselves. They train, but they are not fighters," Machmued noted candidly.

He waited for an explanation or, at least a response. None was made. "The others are very good. All are tested under fire and well experienced. They know how to take orders and are loyal."

The briefing droned on. They had covered this ground many times before.

Salal seemed satisfied, smiled, and shrugged his shoulders in easy resignation.

Machmued squinted into Salal's worn face. Fatigue had etched its way into his eyes. The difficulties in holding Jericho together, in garnishing support, in keeping security, in trying to anticipate and counter the Americans, in preparing against the internal conspiracies and counter intrigues of his own contemporaries and more, were clear.

Security was still a major concern. Too many, Salal feared, knew that a large operation against the Americans was about to be launched.

Leaders from other Arab factions, the Sword of Allah, the *Al Fatah*, the followers of Abu Nidal, the remnants of the Black Septemberists, *Hizballah*, the Party of God, and the *al-Jihad* all sought a louder voice and a greater leadership role in the operation. All were disturbed by the involuntary contribution of some of their best fighters while they, the leaders, were excluded from the operation and knew little of the details. Jealousies, old rivalries and blood vendettas between the individual factions were beginning to appear as each jockeyed for more power over Jericho.

"Salal, my friend, you must cease your worries," Machmued said in a moment of unusual intimacy with his leader and benefactor. "All will be well. The ICO has

approved and will support the strike. We have trained and
rehearsed well. Our fate is in Allah's hands now."
    "Ah, yes, the men. Even they are a danger to us now," Salal
remarked.
    "They know only that they will strike in the devil's lair
itself," Machmued reassured. "The men know nothing of the
details. From the mockups they recognize the type of installation. More than this they only guess. The older men do not
speak of the target. They know that guessing is not of consequence. The younger men, the fire-eaters, they talk among
themselves. They speak of resistance and *jihad* and hide their
fear with brave and foolish talk."
    Salal paused for a long moment and looked into the
teacup as if searching for an answer to a painful and difficult question.
    "Do they know that the risk of capture and death is very
great? That once they have left the estuary there is no turning
back?"
    There was a long silence as Machmued struggled to frame
his reply with the correct words. When he spoke his voice was
somber and quiet.
    "Some things are not said. Words are unnecessary. Among
these people, Salal, there are no cowards. Neither are there
spies or fools. I have lived and trained with these men and
have come to know each of them, as I know my own brothers and my sons. The Jericho *fedayeen* are not the rabble of
dirty streets. They have come together during the training
and become as one band. Each has come to accept that this
will be a battle from which he may not return. Those who can
escape to the safehouses in America will know how to find
them. The ones who cannot escape will fight well and they
will die well. They have made pacts that no wounded shall be
taken. This battle is their *kismet*, this war, the will of Allah. To
say more is unnecessary."
    Salal nodded, satisfied and silenced by the answer.
    They sat in a comfortable peacefulness for a space of time,
slurping noisily at the warm, strong tea, lost in their own

thoughts and the brightness of the evening sky. Salal hesitated and then broke the stillness.

"To dwell on the bloodletting and the death of good men is not a good thing, Machmued. We gain nothing from such thoughts ... nothing is changed. I do not worry for myself; I worry for the success of the operation. But," he said with a final sigh, "Allah will decide if we are to succeed. Jericho is in his hands."

"Allah has decided for us to be the instruments of his people," Machmued replied.

Salal's sense of predestination, of a fate beyond his control was a strong belief that colored his life. The teaching was part of his Islamic creed, drummed into him since his youth. The tenet sets the Islamic people apart from all others. *Enshallah.* As God Wills.

"There has never been a question, Salal. The men believe in you. They trust you and will follow you. The plan is a good plan. There is no reason to believe it will not work well. We all believe this to be true," Machmued said reassuringly.

"Then we shall have a success. But enough, let us finish. How much longer will this review require?" Salal asked, rising to return to the desk in the small adjoining office space.

Machmued glanced down and picked up his small notebook that lay open on the table between them. He thumbed through the last few pages, following Salal back into the adjoining room.

"Not long, a final matter or two. Perhaps one hour," he smiled, "if you do not interrupt me with too many questions."

Salal grinned. Both men knew that it was not to be.

"I shall try to restrain myself, old friend."

"Perhaps so," Machmued replied, giving voice to the known lie. Machmued wetted his thumb and forefinger and flipped a page in his notebook.

The call to Salal from Sabri l-Banna to meet and dine with him in Tripoli was not unexpected. Salal was well pleased with

his address to the council earlier in the day. Tired old arguments were once more raised against the plan, but in the end
Salal's persuasive logic again made the difference. His agitated final appeal to the Arab sense of destiny and manhood provided a focus too strong to resist. The final efforts of the
counsels of patience and moderation were banished. Salal was
directed to proceed with the execution of Jericho.

Sabri was a man known to the Western World as Abu
Nidal. Salal shared much with Abu Nidal. They both considered themselves patriots. Both had grown up in the
refugee camps, in Gaza, and at one time had lived in Nablus
on the West Bank. Both were honor graduates of *Dar al-
Hadith* and dedicated disciples of Muqbel ben al-Wadie, as
was Osama bin Laden whose father, Muhammad, was a
Yemeni. All three were terrorists who believed in the destiny
of the Arab people, the Koran, and a Pan-Arabic state. They
had all devoted their lives to this cause and were prepared to
forfeit all they possessed to achieve this end. All believed
that the destruction of Israel, not a compromise, was the
only solution and that Israel's existence was dependent on
the support of the United States.

The meeting was affable and not unexpected by Salal, who
had his spies well placed within the Arab leadership.

"My brother," Abu Nidal began, as they reclined at the
evening meal, "I speak to you from the heart as an old friend.
You have achieved great victories in our *jihad* against the
West. We all know of your success in the American embassies
in Africa, in Lebanon, in New York and the Pan Am flight in
Scotland, eh? No one can doubt your courage but there are
strong voices in the council who have expressed concern over
Jericho."

"And what are these concerns, my brother?" Salal
inquired.

"If I may be direct with an old friend, they say that you
have not disrupted the Americans in the peace process by
any of your past efforts. They say that perhaps a different
leader is needed for this operation, eh, one who is better

known perhaps, who can rally our people to our cause."

Salal listened to the byzantine comments, knowing Abu Nidal's true intentions for this meeting but not acknowledging or directly addressing them. He also knew that the radical elements supported Jericho and that Abu Nidal wanted control of the operation. Nidal had met with the council separately and contended that his was the most experienced leadership; that when Jericho was executed, it should be under his direction. Salal's source told him that Abu was particularly persuasive with two of the council members and that they, in turn, had raised the question to the full council. Abu Nidal sought to steal control of the entire operation—even at this late date.

By vote, the full council had ruled against Abu Nidal. Still, he wanted to play a major role in the operation. The council had answered that it would be Salal's decision. Salal was to be responsible for the Jericho operation—its success or failure.

Salal marshaled his thoughts, knowing that he needed Abu Nidal's support The Jericho author could not afford to alienate him. Abu Nidal had too much power and would be a bad enemy.

Salal's rebuttal was couched in the indirect language of the Middle East, where one thing is said and another is meant. Salal had to find more than just a warm sponsor in Abu Nidal but without compromising Jericho. Salal was prepared to grant concessions but not to release Jericho to Nidal.

"Sabri, old friend," Salal began, using Abu Nidal's Arabic name, "once again, just as when we destroyed the Marines in Lebanon and the American army battalion at Gander after they had left the Sinai, we have left the Americans confused, frustrated. The lion roars but has no one to bite. They grope in anger but do not know where, or who, or how, for all their might, to strike. They are embarrassed and lose face. That is good and a measure in our favor. That they are baffled shall make Jericho all the more meaningful. To permit another success by our freedom fighters brings only greater discredit upon their leadership. I have demonstrated to you that I have the power and the ability to be successful for many years."

Salal pressed on. "The attack at Gander long ago proved our ability to carry out a strike far from our own homeland and support bases. We have planned well. With the successes like Newfoundland and Lebanon, the Americans are defensive. The Americans do what we wish; they refocus their efforts. They worry more now about where we shall next attack, not about their peace initiatives for the Middle East. When more American blood is shed for Israeli peace they will reassess their position and political options."

"Your logic is sound, I admit, Salal, but it will not stop the debate even though it is too late to stop Jericho," replied Nidal. "Still this is a very ambitious operation. We have never before devoted so many resources to one attack. This effort needs a more—how should I say without giving offense—ah, a more visible leadership, a person to whom all of the Arab world can rally, my good friend, one who is known. You have been a grand worker behind the scenes, but you are not well known to all of our peoples. There is too much at risk. The operation needs a known leader, one that the people trust and can turn to."

"The pieces for Jericho are in place my friend," Salal replied. "I understand your concern and appreciate your support but it is too late to make changes. The teams are formed and the training is finished. But perhaps ..."

Salal rose and poured fresh tea for himself and his host. "Perhaps, my friend ... a diversion?" he suggested. "An effort in conjunction with *al Qaeda* to focus the American's attention?"

Nidal considered the proposal. He had sought a different answer, but still – a crumb from the table with low risk or higher visibility could only enhance his reputation. If Salal failed but his piece of the operation succeeded ... the thought had value.

"Perhaps, Salal, perhaps. Maybe an attack in two far apart places," Nidal replied thoughtfully, mulling over the consideration, already jumping ahead and constructing alternatives.

"Perhaps something could happen to the American naval forces in the Gulf?" Salal insinuated with a smile. "I am told you have many friends in Yemen where the Americans refuel the ships of their fleet.

Of course," Salal continued with deference, "it would be entirely your effort, but strongly supported by all of us. You and I can coordinate, but only on the timing and in any other way we may be of assistance, my friend."

Nidal nodded his head, the cogs of his mind spinning as he warmed to the idea. The option was worthy of consideration, perhaps with the involvement of Osama bin Laden and his *al Qaida* fighters.

Yes, he would have to consider this alternative; perhaps this could be acceptable. It would serve his ends, he thought. He would give the American president a gift and present his credentials to the American fleet at the same time.

A smile crossed Nidal's face as he dipped his right hand into the platter of rice and lamb. Yes, it would work out well after all.

14
Fort Bragg, North Carolina
—October, 2000

"Well, it's about Gawd-damn time you got your ass off of that Mediterranean vacation and got back to work," was Jack's irreverent and profane greeting as Matt eased the BMW into the drive of Jack's Fort Bragg quarters.

He grinned, looked about for Nancy who was nowhere to be seen, and shot Jack the bird. The ribaldry between the two of them was born of a special regard in which they held each other. Their often exaggerated and outrageous behavior and freely exchanged insults were really but perverted demonstrations of affection.

Matt crawled out of the car as Jack walked from behind the now quieted mower and snatched at Matt's outstretched hand.

"Ah, hell," Jack exclaimed and embraced his old Desert Storm colleague, delighted at seeing him once again. Jack was a good friend and the absolute worst of enemies and he, too, valued loyalty as the highest of all virtues. They were warriors and shared the unique bonds of surviving several deadly firefights, losing close comrades, and wondering where the next shell would land.

"You still hanging 'round the little boy's rest rooms and drinking at queer bars, Jack?" Matt grinned.

"Hell yes," came the immediate reply, "when you're my age you take what you can get. Besides I'm getting too old to chase young, good lookin' women. They're all track stars now and I'll be damned if I haven't forgotten what the hell to do with one if I did catch her," Jack conceded.

They both knew nothing was further from the truth. Jack, though only two years away from the half-century mark, could and routinely did outwalk, outfight, outlast any two men half his age. Dalton had a wiry strength, which matched his slight five foot eight inch frame. His physical appearance in no way reinforced the tactical genius he was, nor the fact that he had won every medal for valor, excepting the Medal of Honor.

"Honest to Christ," Matt continued, "I go overseas for a couple months only to come back to find out that the Army has screwed up again. Not only do they give you eagles, but command as well. What happened, did the Special Forces folks find your birth certificate and discover your parents were married and throw your ass out?"

"Have a little bit more respect for the war wounded, fella," Jack said, smiling. "Hell, Special Forces couldn't keep up with me. As for the job, I can see the fine hand of General Brandt at work. The old man sat on the command selection board. I'm his latest secret weapon." Jack grinned. "I don't shoot bad guys any more. I watch them laugh themselves to death when I start to hobble up the hill."

"How's the chest feel?" Matt asked. Jack had taken an AK-47 round through the left side of his chest on a covert mission. The copper clad bullet had demolished two ribs, bounced around a bit, and then ricocheted into his right lung, collapsing it, and a creating a sucking chest wound. He was lucky to have made it out alive.

"It's fine, a bit of tightness and a little bit of pain when it rains, but okay."

Jack held Matt at arms length appraisingly. "Welcome back, you big shit. Tell me, those ragheads over there still have the same marksmanship instructors as before?" he asked, turning Matt toward the house.

"Yep, no change. Still couldn't hit the ground unless they put a round through their foot first. Damn but it's good to see you, you skinny old grunt. There's just no justice," Matt teased as Nancy appeared at the door. "You get older and balder and I just get better looking. How's my girlfriend?"

Jack just grunted. "Damn right I'm older and balder.

Skinnier too. Haven't you got the word, Colonel? This is the new Army. No dopers, no drinkers, no lard asses, and no brains running it. As for your girlfriend," he said, tossing his head toward the front door, "that's the saint who saved me from the wicked ways of fornication, drunkenness and lewd debauchery; you can check her out for yourself."

A smile lit Nancy's face. "Welcome back, stranger. What did you bring me?"

"Don't know if we should talk about it in front of your husband," Matt replied. "When are you going to leave this bum and run off with me?"

"Can't leave him now—promised that he would take me to Cancun for a week. Besides, he's behind on both the car and the insurance payments. Got to stay here and keep him healthy till he catches up and I can cash in on him."

She gave Matt a tight hug and sisterly kiss on the cheek, placed her arm around his back, screwed up her face in pixy-like fashion at her husband and guided him into the house.

"I'll be with you in a second. Just let me knock off this last little piece of lawn and put the mower away, just two minutes," Jack hollered, the last of the words lost in the eruption of noise from the mower.

Nancy twisted about, cupped her hands to her mouth and shouted in the direction of her husband.

Jack shut down the mower. "What?" he replied in mock exacerbation.

"I just said take your time." She smiled in deviled amusement. "I'll give him the grand tour of the house—starting with the bedroom."

"Hell, if he's the best you can do, have at it, kid. Just remember he's probably got a thing for camels."

Jack didn't wait for a retort but bent over the cord of the mower, starting it once again. Nancy turned to face Matt and contorted her petite features in mock exasperation.

"How 'bout something to eat?" she inquired. "Kids just finished up and are out playing. You'll see them later on. I was just about to call Jack in for lunch."

She didn't wait for a reply but began setting a place at the kitchen table. "We just got back from the commissary about an hour ago. Saturday is shopping day."

Nancy took a long motherly look at Matt, hands in tiny fists on her hips, standing there askance. "So how are you, Matthew Gannon? I mean, tell the truth, how are you?"

"Doing just great, can't you tell?"

"You need a good woman to sort your socks out for you and nag at you a little bit. Find any prospects over there?" she asked, as she turned to the refrigerator.

Forever the blunt loving mother, big sister and matchmaker, Matt thought. Maybe that's why she and Jack were so happy. She just took good care of him.

The microsecond of silence before he replied was enough to alert her. She cast a quick suspicious look over her shoulder.

"I'll be damned. You found someone, didn't you?" Nancy accused. She shut the door to the freezer compartment, dumped ice cubes into the glasses on the table and slowly eased herself into the chair opposite him, her interest now clearly piqued.

"Don't keep me in suspense, tell me about her. Give me all the dirt. Come on, spill."

"You're too much the romantic, Nan. Nothing much to tell. Found a good 'un. Even thinking about making her an offer, but ..."

"Not so fast, Mister. If you think I'm going to settle for that as an explanation, you've got another think comin'. I want all the details, buster. What kind of offer? What did she say? What's her name and where's she from?" Nancy insisted.

Matt smiled in spite of himself. Nancy's unabashed demands to parade his personal life before her was just part of her way. Neither pretenses nor beating around the bush with this woman. Blunt and direct—right to the point, just like her husband.

Matt found himself suprised that Nan was probably just the person to talk to about Megan. She was the right audi-

ence and would understand where both of them were
coming from.

"Well, her name is Megan," he began. "She's British.
Good looking enough to turn a few heads, well traveled, and
typically *proper* in the British sense. Catholic. She works for
the British embassy in Tel Aviv."

Matt knew the Catholic qualification would discount
Nancy's inherited disdain for all things English.

"How did you meet?" Nancy asked, settling in for a long
interrogation.

"I first saw her at one of the 'you-will-attend-or-else' functions at the embassy in Tel Aviv. We saw each other once or
twice after that and just seemed to hit it off pretty well. One
thing led to another, it got pretty serious. I was in damn deep
water and then, well, we just seemed to run out of time."

"What the hell kind of ending is that? You ran out of time?
What does that mean?" Nancy demanded.

"She wants permanency, a commitment and, well, perhaps in time I'd want that too ... but neither of us was willing to bend."

Nancy looked on expectantly. "Go on."

"Nothing more to go on about," Matt replied. "She's in
Tel Aviv and I'm here."

"What happened? You let her get too close to the soft part,
huh?" Nancy asked in prying affection. "You mean that's it?
Fini? The End?"

"Yep. Appears that way at least for now."

"Well, you'll get no sympathy from me, Matthew Gannon.
You big, damn dummy. Do you love her? I mean is this the
one you want to keep around to beat you up every now and
again, and have your kids kind of love?"

"For what it's worth now, yup, I suppose so. I tried calling
her, but no luck. I've written her, but no response yet. I may
have missed the boat," Matt replied, uncomfortably shifting
position in the chair.

"Anyway," he added defensively, "I can't honestly say that
I'm ready for that type of settled down life yet. I tried it once

before and botched it up pretty well. I'm not really sure I want to risk that happening again. What Megan and I had for ourselves was pretty good ... it wasn't pushy or binding on either of us."

"Men! You're all the same. Looking for guarantees and ducking out when you feel the constriction of responsibility around your feet," Nancy fumed.

The outdoor racket of the lawnmower ceased and Nancy redirected her attention to the front door. She knew that Jack, equally interested, would nevertheless raise holy hell with her if he found out that she had been giving Matt the third degree.

"We'll talk more about this later," Nancy said, her tone threatening. She artfully changed the subject and glanced toward the door. "Now I'd better get lunch on the table before the wild man gets in here."

The lunch was casual. Bantering with old friends, reminiscing over mutual acquaintances, past events and happy times, filled Matt with a momentary sense of belonging and satisfaction.

"Megan would really have enjoyed this," Matt said to his hosts. "I'm sure she would feel right at home with the two of you."

"Of course," Nancy responded, "just shows that except for you she has good taste."

Jack caught Matt's eye and signaled him outside. "Matt, what say we go on out and walk off a little bit of this lunch? I'll show you around the finer scenery at Fort Bragg," he said, sneaking a glance at Nan whose back was turned.

Winking to Matt he continued. "I'll show you where the good lookin' women hang out. They, unlike some others I won't name, appreciate us older bulls."

Nancy guffawed. "Go talk your business," she commented. "The only studs in this house are the two-by-fours in the walls. You two go on out and dream your little hearts away and if you do get lucky, let me know and I'll send an ambulance for the remains. Go on now, leave."

"Okay, babe," Jack replied and turned to Matt. "Let's get out of here before we get slammed with a skillet."

They walked perhaps a quarter of a mile in silence, close by the golf course, enjoying the last signs of a late autumn.

"I thought it would be best to talk out here. I know you've been briefed on everything except my part of the Gambit operation, Matt."

"Yep. For some reason the old man wanted me to hear what you were doing directly from you and not from the staff up there."

"Sounds like him. You and I are gonna have to be pretty tight on this one. The old man has a lot of faith in you, Matt. He told me he wanted someone he can count on when the shit hits the fan, someone who can keep a cool head. That's why he put you right in the middle of what he thinks will be the target and made you the commander of the installation."

They walked on in silence for twenty yards more.

"I'll have to admit that at first I thought the old man was reaching on Gambit," Jack offered. "But the more we spin it up, the less I think that way. I think he's right. Those bastards want a piece of us and are going to be in our knickers in pretty short order."

Matt said nothing in reply.

"How much did they tell you about Sunny Point up at the puzzle palace?" Jack asked.

"Pretty much standard fare. Admit I was a bit surprised when they briefed me that less than a handful of troops are stationed there."

"Yeah, I was too," admitted Jack. "But when you think about it, contracting the operation out to a DOD civilian work force makes sense. Saves money and gives continuity in what is pretty much an industrial type operation. It's the same route our big depots have taken. Put the guys in uniform in the foxholes and let the civilians handle the rear areas."

"Tell me what you think about Sunny Point," Matt

demanded casually. "You been down there?"

"No, not on the ground. I've done some aerial recons of the place. Big base, remote, spread out, low profile, lots of woods and swamp. A good target. The port operation is not all that impressive given what it does and how much munitions tonnage passes over the piers each year. Only has three piers and they are well spread out along the riverfront. Can berth two ships per pier but we haven't seen all the berths loading at one time."

"That's because of QED," Matt replied.

"QED?"

"Quantity Explosive Distance. Big fear in munitions storage and handling is sympathetic detonation that would move from ship to ship or bunker to bunker in the event of an accident. That's why things are so spread out. I got a look at the site maps of Sunny Point up in Washington. The administrative areas and buildings are a good eight miles away from the piers and all the buildings were blast reinforced when they were built. The number of folks allowed down range near the piers is pretty tight when a ship is on berth and loading."

"Hadn't thought about that but it makes sense," Jack noted. "The labor force, except for the security folks, go to their homes in Southport at night. The quarters for the military are off base too, and in Southport. Your quarters are about twelve miles from the base in the center of town, big old columned house right on the river. It's on the historical registry by the way, called 'Garrison House' and dates back to the Revolutionary War they tell me. Wide open and no security, so sleep lightly my friend."

They walked on slowly, savoring the crisp autumn afternoon while Jack continued in his casual assessment and impressions of the Sunny Point complex. "The stevedores that do the actual ship loading are union gangs that come out of Wilmington. Good ole southern boys whose pappy's, uncles, and cousins have been doing the same thing since Sunny Point opened. It's a pretty tightly knit small southern town and the terminal is a big employer for the locals. Of course, they're under military supervision all the time at Sunny Point. Then every once in a while they get a reserve unit in for training, but that's normally in the summer months. The southernmost pier has two gigantic cranes for loading containerized munitions. The other two piers can do breakbulk munitions cargo, vehicles, general crap as well as containers, just about anything if they needed to, but it seems the big workload comes off the south pier. The base is pretty well empty of people after six o'clock."

"Have you put any one on the ground to look around?" Matt asked.

"I've sent a few of my guys down to Sunny Point to do some very quiet and on-the-turf covert recons and identify the more obvious vulnerabilities. We've been in three times so far with UH-60's at night and never been spotted. The insertions, recons, and extractions have been good training exercises for us. Their internal security is petty loose, but then my guys are pretty good when it comes to covert ops," he concluded, without speculation.

"What do you see as the biggest threat?" Matt asked.

"Take your choice—I've got two dozen EEI, essential elements of information, that the intel folks haven't yet been able to answer for me. We're not sure of how many, how they are armed, how or where they will assemble prior to the attack, how they will disperse … still lots of vital unknowns to the entire situation. We're still working on it and if it can be had, General Brandt will get it. You can bet that whatever goes down, there'll be lots of noise from the bad guys and lots of publicity from our liberal media the next day."

"I plan on heading down to Sunny Point tomorrow. Nathan Michaelson, the current commander, has already moved his family out of Garrison House. We'll have the change of command on Monday or Tuesday morning— his show."

They walked in silence for a time.

"What kind of qualifications does the internal security force at Sunny Point have?" Matt asked after a bit. "You obviously know more about the place than I do."

Jack shook his head in apparent dismay. "Well, from the homework we've done so far on your people, and the ease with which we've been able to move around the facility at night, it's not very encouraging. You've got a couple fellas in the base security force that are ex-special forces types. They generally know what the hell they're doing. Most of guard force, though, is just there—men well past their prime looking for a second income or a way to get away from their old lady for the day. Average age is about fifty-three, fifty-four or so, a couple in their sixties. Not a hellava lot of enthusiasm about anything and certainly way over their heads in trying to handle any kind of serious operation directed against the facility. Pretty much just a bunch of watchmen. They do perimeter security with some random checks on storage bunkers and open storage areas at night. Small reaction force but not really very much to stop you once you get in."

"Gotta be something they can provide us," Matt said tentatively.

"Zip, nada against anything that we're looking at. Oh, they might bust a cap or two with some success if they were prepared and if we had the time to train them and get them whipped into some kind of shape. But right now my folks tell me that they pay lip service at best and not even very much of that. They're just no match for a trained terrorist force. They'd give it the ole' boy try but they'd take a hellava lot of casualties pretty damn quick. Don't count on much there."

"The General told me just about the same thing. Hope your guys didn't make a drill out of their presence or your interest. If the old man is right Salal's folks have a pretty good eye on the place already. They might even have someone on the inside."

"Not to worry. We're invisible. Nobody there has any idea we are anywhere around. The one thing that really bothers me though, is our response time."

"What do you mean?" Matt asked.

"Well, I've got a Light Infantry Special Ops force of about

four hundred men I can bust loose to you, but we're about thirty-five or so minutes away by UH-60. That should be more than enough time, but it could be bad news, too. Given forty-five minutes a well-trained and rehearsed force can do a hellava lot of damage. They are going to have to assemble somewhere and that will take some time. We should be okay."

"The General wants to let them come all the way in before we slam the door."

"Yeah, I know. Puts you and me on some pretty hard ground though. We'll do our best to keep the good guys out of the line of fire, but you should know there just isn't any way to stop a few of the civilians from getting hurt. I've got my folks standing by over at the shop to poop you up on what we've set up in terms of reaction and response," he said and pointed vaguely off to a group of fenced off World War II two-story barracks buildings.

They walked casually along the edge of the fairway in the direction of the cluster of buildings.

"The report I read on the *fedayeen* who have disappeared from the surveillance screens indicates they're up to something very, very big," Matt offered.

"Christ, it can't be any wilder than some of the ones the General's come up with," Jack noted. "It's right outta the ballpark, I guess. But for the sake of argument let's assume you could infiltrate a force of say, roughly 175 to maybe as many as 250 experienced *fedayeen* terrorists into the U.S."

"Brandt thinks they could do it," Matt replied.

"If they did, they could really hurt us ... do a damn good job, kill a shitload of civilians and make us look stupid in the process. I wouldn't rule out a one way suicide mission."

"Is that the way you are going to play it?" Matt asked.

"Yep. That's it. We've worst-cased it out. If they are going to make that kind of investment, what with the risks they take over here, they're going to want more than just headlines. We think it all ties in."

"Once you're on the ground at Sunny Point, I want you to quarantine off an area for me so I can insert a platoon or so at night every so often to familiarize themselves with the terrain. You can tell your folks down there that it's off limits because of the nesting season for an endangered species ... ah, what the hell was that name again, oh, yeah, the red-cockaded woodpecker. By the way, it's no lie. Tree huggers and fuckin' bird nests." Jack found his remark funny and laughed deep and loud.

"Dickless wonders and their Gawd damned fucking birds! What next?" Matt got caught up in the humor and had to laugh as Jack cavorted in the antics of a crane trying to take off.

"Oh shit," Jack said, wiping tears from his eyes. "Damnation." Turning serious but still chuckling under his breath, Jack pointed in the direction of his headquarters building.

"We've picked a site," he said, "for a clandestine insertion if we need it, down near the docks over at Sunny Point. Couple of alternates, too. I'll show them to you on the maps. I doubt anyone but you will ever know we are even in there."

"That will loosen the pucker factor some. Sounds good," Matt responded.

"General Brandt feels nothing will be going down for six-weeks to two months. That's the latest intelligence at least. Most of his colleagues up in the NSC are beginning to think he's overreacting. He's under some heat," Matt offered candidly.

"Where from?"

"The General told me that Congressman Adderson is starting to snoop around. He's ordered up a copy of the taped minutes of DeFore's meeting. That much interest is unusual for him. There's a leak somewhere in the NSC Middle East Intelligence Committee."

"Adderson, huh? That guys so damn crooked they're going to have to use an auger to dig his grave. Not good. He's a piss ant who would screw a snake if someone would just hold its head. He's dumb enough to bend a ball bearing."

"Yeah," Matt replied, "but you gotta hand it to him, when

it comes to headlines, he will do anything to get his righteous name in the papers. A real glory seeker."

"He'll blow the whole operation and make Brandt the scapegoat if he can," Jack offered. "He has no love for the General."

"I know and you're right from everything I have seen or heard. Adderson's an asshole, but in his defense, I just don't think he can help it. It's his nature," Matt offered with a grin.

"There's been a hellava lot of change down around the Southport area in the past fifteen or so years," Jack offered, returning to the subject of the Gambit operation. "It's not as backwoods as the people in Washington think. There's been quite a bit of urban development. Hell, I could paint you scenarios for at least five or six damn good targets right close by Sunny Point. Off the top of my head, let's see, there's a power plant, a large chemical factory, a damn important Air Force early warning radar and missile tracking site, a key Coast Guard installation, and that doesn't even include the port of Wilmington. Most all of our quick reaction support packages load out of either Sunny Point or the Wilmington civilian port facility. Damage to either one could put a real crimp in our ability to deploy and sustain our quick deployment forces from here at Bragg."

They had arrived at the double aproned, cyclone-fenced area. Jack pulled an ID badge from his wallet and passed it to the armed MP at the pedestrian gate.

Until now Matt's entire focus had been solely on Sunny Point as the target. No one had even speculated about alternate targets during his Washington briefings.

He turned to Jack appreciatively. "I understand. Well spread out targets and all of them vulnerable."

"Yeah, well, it's all too iffy, tough to rapidly react if they come in any force," Jack replied. "I guess we're on the right track with Sunny Point, but I wouldn't want to shoot the whole wad on one role of the dice hoping that's the only place they're looking at."

"And?" Matt prompted.

"Well, let's just say that we've expanded the Washington thinking a little bit. Ah, you might say that we've tried to achieve a bit more flexibility in our planning," Jack said, giving him a wink.

"Something tells me that Brandt is going to have our ass. Expanded, huh? Who else knows about this ah, flexibility drill?" Matt asked.

"No point in getting the folks topside all worried and upset," Jack replied, smiling. "Just my folks are in on this and now you. We have a few ideas of our own on where and how to meet any threat at Sunny Point, eh, or elsewhere within reasonable range, but I'm asking you to keep your mouth shut, Matt. Just consider the options we're gonna show you as *contingency* planning. Both our esteemed Honorable Mr. Adderson and the Select Intelligence Oversight Committee would piss their pants if it got out that we thought that damage to civilian facilities was a possibility and they weren't briefed. Congress and the media circus would have a field day, not to mention our balls. But come on into my parlor, mate, and I'll show you how we're wasting the taxpayers' money."

They were passed through the gate into the restricted area.

15
Caswell Beach, North Carolina
—November 2000

A gentle breeze whispered across the azure waters of the southern Caribbean and went unnoticed in the placid autumn southern Atlantic seas. A gust swept the tranquil surface leaving only a pebbled texture on the march of almost indiscernible swells that paraded to the horizon of sea and sky. The event was heralded only by the shrieks of wandering seagulls and witnessed in solemn dignity by a sole flight of echeloned brown pelicans as they glided southward on the gentle circle of rising air. A heated wind from along the coast stirred along the surface of the waters and sluggishly began to wind itself into the familiar counter clockwise rotation of a tropical depression. The breeze languidly continued to feed on the energy provided by the warmed ocean currents, gathering its strength in the nether reaches of the South Atlantic, and became stronger in volume, faster in its spinning gyrations.

Hurricanes are annual occurrences; their frequency and ferocity are based on a twenty-year cycle. The Coriolis force of the earth rotating under the moving air of its atmosphere, spinning through space on its canted axis, causes a bunching effect on the upper northern flowing air. However, when the conditions are right, masses of high-pressure cooler air sweep from the north and dissipate dangerous evolving winds. A shearing upper atmospheric effect occurs, robbing potential storms of their strength and resulting in tropical downpours. Alternatively, when the warm winds continue to strengthen, the circulation grows stronger and tighter, sucking moisture from the sea, feeding on its heat and a hurricane eventually forms. Toward the end of November the waters begin to cool as the earth moves further in its seasonal race from the sun.

As the orbit of the earth swings back toward the sun's heat, the seas again warm and in June the cycle of events for a new hurricane season begins.

On this day in the late fall, the swirl of ocean-borne winds grew stronger and tighter, sucking more and more moisture from the sea. Somewhere slightly to the south and far to the east of the Dominican Republic, the atmospheric event became well enough organized to be given the title of tropical depression. The mass of wind, cloud and rain was tracked by satellite and radar and as it grew a name was finally given, "Kate." This was to be the eleventh named storm of the season and was destined to grow into a full-fledged hurricane.

For the year there had so far been relatively little damage in spite of the six hurricanes that had wandered on their unpredictable tracks to the North. For the most part, they had spent their fury well away from the heavily populated Southeastern coast of the United States. Some speculated that minimal destruction and loss of life was El Nino's atonement for the damages of years past. In recent years, hurricanes had swept across the warm Caribbean waters through Florida, Georgia and the Carolinas, northward into Virginia and the New England states causing loss of life and damage into the billions.

The sun rose slowly, a giant orange blister rising from a tortured gray sea. The world brightened and roused. The ocean waters glistened, the gulls and pelicans and sandpipers awoke and began their daily ritual, preening themselves, foraging for another day's survival. A car door slammed, an engine growled to a start breaking the rhythmic cadence of gentle waves lapping on a silent sandy shore. Another day had begun.

Eleven miles from the front gates of Sunny Point, Salal sat at an oblong kitchen table sipping on a stoneware mug of dark, strong tea. Spread before him was a large engineering blueprint of Sunny Point. Abdul's intelligence team included a railway mechanics helper, Kirshid, who had smuggled the document out of the terminal complex. The report supplemented the aerial photographs the team had also acquired.

Soon, Salal knew, all three present members of Abdul's five-man team would awaken and converge to the table to huddle intently over the document. Each would speak in his native Arabic tongue. They would be alert, bright, and compete for his attention, eagerly seeking to please him with their words and work.

Together the men would dissect the militarily significant aspects of each feature on the blueprint, jabbing at this or that area, explaining its importance to their attentive leader as they drank their tea, ate the sweet rolls and smoked the American substitute for their strong, loosely packed Turkish cigarettes. Their critique would key to Machmued's method of assault, the manner by which the obstacles to the movement of the terrorist force would be overcome or bypassed. The role each objective played in the overall reduction of the terminal's facilities would be analyzed. There would be, Salal knew, few and minor deviations to the assault portion of the plan which had been so carefully and repetitively rehearsed by the strike force in their Libyan training camp, but the team would be reassured by one last personal review of the plan by Salal himself.

He rose from the table and stretched his arms high over his head, arching his back and rising to the balls of his Nike clad feet. Late last night Abdul received a call relaying the information that the *Compass Rose* was proceeding without incident and according to plan.

I shall tell them all of it this morning, Salal decided as he glanced down at the blueprint covered table, distracted momentarily by the sounds of rousing men, running shower water and commodes flushing.

Now began the waiting in earnest, looking for Machmued and the ship. There was nothing that could prevent them unless there was a breach in our security, he thought. Two sharp knocks at the door startled Salal in his thoughts and attracted his attention. He glanced at his watch. The time was

7:26. Doctor l'Alham, his assistant, and their two bodyguards were due to arrive.

Salal crossed the room, a heavy Walther 9mm dragging his right hand down along his side. The weapon was a normal precaution that he knew was being duplicated by the other three men scattered throughout the house. Sa'id emerged along the hallway, an AK-47 rifle trained on the front door. Salal peered out of the slight window, decoratively cut into the upper portion of the heavy door. Grunting his satisfaction, he motioned Sa'id back from the hallway, calling back towards the other bedrooms and two bathrooms.

"Do not be concerned," Salal spoke with relief. "It is only expected company." Salal opened the door, smiling broadly at the four men standing at its threshold.

"Salaam, Harun l'Alham. Welcome."

"Salaam, Salal my friend. The time since we have been together has been far too long, eh?" Harun nervously smirked in response.

"Yes, too long," Salal replied as he motioned the four men into the house. "Everything is all right?"

"Yes, yes of course." Harun glanced about the room, judging the accommodations. His bespectacled, handsome face reflected his satisfaction.

"Good. Come, have some tea, something to eat. The others will be with us in a moment."

They walked into the ample kitchen.

"You have not yet told them?" Harun asked.

"No, I thought it best to await your arrival so that they could have your excellent assurance to answer any of their more technical questions. So now the moment is at hand."

The members of Abdul's intelligence team drifted into the large room which served as a living and dining area and were introduced to the two newcomers, receiving them suspiciously despite the accompanying presence of their two returning companions who had served as couriers and body guards. More tea was brewed and breakfast taken.

"Salal," Harun asked casually, as the meal was concluded

and cups refilled for a last time, "have you completed your final reconnaissance?"

"But of course. I spent the past three days being an innocent tourist and explored the entire area. I have seen nothing that is out of the ordinary. They changed the commander at the military base within the last month. I do not think they would have done so if they suspected anything," Salal replied.

"Yes, I agree. Allah blesses our work. None of the difficulties we had expected have yet come to pass. This is a good sign."

"A sign that Allah is with us," Abdul offered.

"Perhaps, but let us not be lulled into a stupor of overconfidence," Salal replied. His words captured the attention of the entire team.

"I know you must be curious," he continued, "about the presence of our new compatriots," Salal said, motioning toward the two new arrivals. "It is now time to tell you that there is more for you to know about Jericho. You are to be members of a special team which I shall myself lead," Salal confided.

Gesturing the two newcomers forward to the center of the room, Salal began to roll up the blueprints of Sunny Point as he spoke. Harun unlocked his case and withdrew new, different schematics, not previously seen by any of the intelligence team.

"What team, Salal?"

He ignored the question posed by Sa'id.

"The suitcase?" Harun suddenly asked of Salal.

"In readiness and in a safe place. Delivered by boat through our Cuban connection two days ago. I completed all of the checks myself late last night as you directed."

Salal, clearly satisfied, turned to Abdul and placed his hands on the heavier man's thick shoulders and turned to face the men in the room.

"Abdul, and all of you, my brave brothers," Salal said, "Sunny Point is only a secondary target. The attack on the docks and ammunition bunkers is to be a diversion. To be

216 Frederick F. Meyers, Jr.

sure, it is an expensive and elaborate one but nonetheless, it is still only a launching point to our main objective, the primary target."

The air was pregnant with confused silence. All eyes were on Salal, the leader, and the author of the strike, the guiding force that had brought them this far with so much success.

"We shall destroy not one, but two targets," Salal announced. The Jericho leader looked into their eyes before speaking another syllable.

"We shall not only twist the lion's tail, we will rub his nose in the mud at the same time. The attack on Sunny Point will make the Americans and their powerful armies look foolish and inept in the eyes of the world. But even more than this, we will create a concern in the United States that will forever keep them from interference in our business in the Middle East. The principal target is the nuclear power plant two miles distant from Sunny Point. We shall destroy it and contaminate the entire area with radioactivity."

There was a silence of disbelief. The enormity of Salal's statement settled into the realization of what such an action meant. Salal savored the moment, looking from one face to another, judging their stunned reactions.

"Then why do we not use our entire force against this power plant? Is not the attack against Sunny Point wasted?" Sa'id finally asked, giving voice to the question harbored by each of them.

"No. Until now you have not been told of the entire plan. We must assault Sunny Point," Salal explained carefully. "Machmued's force must have a quiet place, a location not so distant from the power plant from which it can disembark from the ship and organize swiftly, without being observed. Sunny Point is ideal for our purposes. From the wharf our force can quickly deploy, cause the most confusion and the most damage while diverting attention from our primary target. The ship and then the ammunition dumps will be exploded by Machmued's force. This will provide us with the needed distraction to infiltrate the power station. Machmued will attack south across Sunny Point, with his main force, destroying all in his path, just as we have rehearsed in the desert, but he shall not form a defensive perimeter. The *fedayeen* will continue to attack toward the power facility drawing their security force toward the river."

Salal pointed to the map. "His attack and the detonations of the explosives there will attract all but a few of the power plant security police away from the reactor and to Sunny Point, in the direction of the river. This diversion shall focus and fix the Americans' attention. We, you and I," he gestured, "will go through the front gate of the power station and destroy the nuclear reactors."

Silence.

Diversion and deception were not foreign concepts to the *fedayeen* but the magnitude of what they were about to do was overwhelming. Doubts bubbled to the surface.

Sa'id broke the silence. "Even if we do get in, we would never get close enough. The security is too strong. The security at the power plant is not at all like the military base. At the military base everything is spread out. The security is not concentrated on just one or two buildings as it is at the power plant. We should strike at their weakness, not at their strengths," Sa'id argued.

Salal sensed the skepticism, the doubts, and the fears. Execution of Jericho was not beyond their resources but he would have to have the complete confidence of these few men if the ultimate goal of the operation was to succeed.

"No Sa'id. The Americans still have no idea when we come, or in what strength, or by what means. If anything they will appear even more foolish in the eyes of the world because of their failure to stop us," Salal responded. "Do any of you doubt the success of our force against the American base?" he asked rhetorically, addressing the entire team.

Heads twisted in agreement. In this there was no question.

"So then, neither do I have any doubt. Surprise will make them impotent. The credibility of the American Army will be destroyed, as will their promises to the Jews, and their meddling to betray our homeland. In one daring stroke, we shall demonstrate the futility of both the American imperialistic designs and their so-called military might. We will sow the seeds of fear and doubt in their allies. And then we will reap the harvest of the West's timidity. That is the final objective of Jericho!"

Salal took a deep breath. His eyes shone brightly with a zealot's conviction. His was a rapture physical in its intensity. "The world will see that we can attack anywhere," he continued unabated. "The Americans will know that they are unable to even protect their own homeland. The myth of their invincibility will be shattered, cast into the dust by a mere handful of illiterate Arab peasants."

Salal paused. A strange smile lit his face. Passing his hands over each man's shoulders, squeezing an arm here, slapping a back there, he paced the room. Back and forth, then back again. His movements around the room became a mirror of his intensity, his magnetism, his controlled, directed energy. His team sat mesmerized, attentive in now respectful silence.

"The destruction of a nuclear reactor, an American nuclear reactor, that, my friends, is the political masterstroke. Our enemies will fear us. If the strong, brave Americans could not defend this place," he gestured, his arm sweeping around the room, "even with all of their army and computers and nuclear weapons, then what chance do the Jews have against us, eh? The world will bend the Americans to our will. The Westerners—all of them—will listen to us. The Jews will die and Israel will be no more. Palestine will rise as a new nation."

He could sense the team warming to his arguments, gaining in their enthusiasm and support. "Do not doubt for an instant that this act is not within our power. The fact that we can even strike such a blow so far from our own homeland, that we have mounted such an attack, will awaken the West to our strength. Our success will bring the Arab states to the position of power in the world which we have been denied for so long."

Salal searched from face to face for agreement, for any sign of support. Enthusiasm and desire were found but still mixed with doubt.

Abdul, the team leader, spoke. "Salal, you know that I am not a coward and am willing to give my life for our people, but this is too grand a scheme. We few are not enough. We would never be able to carry enough explosives to destroy even one of the reactors. At this nuclear facility there are guards and closed circuit television and intrusion alarms and steel doors at each of the critical points."

Salal nodded his agreement. Now was time to play the final card, the ace of trump. His white teeth lit his aesthetic face in a mirthful grin. His was a look of pure glee.

"You of all, Abdul, should know what we can do and what cannot be done." Salal turned about the room looking at each of them collectively and in turn. "Who of you have ever known me to fail? Have I ever made a plan that did not succeed? Am I a gourd filled with stones to rattle in the wind? An empty buffoon who dotes on victory over empty shadows? No, each of you knows me better than this. If I tell you that it can be done, then it is so. The security is strong, yes, but not the problem you believe. I have already devised our way into the plant. These pieces of camel dung that are the security at the plant are old men, men who work only for money. They will run like rabbits before us.

"Until now we have always been dismissed by the world as wild-eyed madmen who come with guns and explosives then, afterward, take credit for their acts over the telephone or by letters to the newspapers."

The pitch of his voice calmed a fraction. "We shall have no need to do such things when Jericho is finished. The American pigs will all know with whom they deal and the price they must now pay. The best way is this way, the bold way. While Machmued and his *fedayeen* are attacking and destroying the military port and blowing up the munitions, attracting the attention of the Americans, we shall attack the power station and destroy it." Turning, he pointed with pride to the two non-team members, "With Doctor l'Alham's tactical nuclear bomb."

16
Machmued's Strike Force
—November, 2000

The 200-man strike force reassembled in Rabat in accordance with the prearranged timetables that had been distributed upon their phased dispersals from the Libyan training base. The necessary customs inspectors and dock police were well paid to look the other way. A handsome profit was earned by the low paid officials for not asking questions and, instead, disappearing from their posts when told to do so. The Rabat port officials had no idea of the true nature of the outbound cargo of the *Compass Rose*, preferring the cash revenue to knowing.

The cellular integrity and security practiced by Machmued's lieutenants were rigid in their enforcement. Members of the Moroccan Islamic support structure that housed, fed, transported and loaded the fighters aboard the vessel did not know the true size or ultimate objective of the force. Nor did they ask. Each, however, believed that his effort was the key to the total operation. This belief heightened each of the groups' own internal security measures as well. Each group had been allowed, indeed encouraged, to speculate that the *Compass Rose* was to conduct a cruise ship hijacking to publicize the plight of the Palestinian people.

So far as Machmued knew, the true mission of Jericho was still secure.

The final stow of the *Compass Rose* was checked and the last of the ship's papers cleared. They were delivered by Moroccan customs to the First Officer of the vessel at 8:33 in the evening. At 9:20 lines were cast free and a tug assisted the *Compass Rose* off of her mooring. In addition to the quantity of fuel oil taken on board in Rabat, the ship's log witnessed an entry noting a bulky generator on the aft boom.

The ship's speed was logged at seventeen knots and a course plotted for the next port of call—Wilmington, North Carolina. The slight chop of the protected channel to the sea changed to the deeper rolling swells of the Atlantic. The *Compass Rose* plowed her way south and westward into the broad expanse of ocean.

Further to the north in Europe at Bremerhaven on the fringe of the North Sea, a second vessel, very similar in lines and deadweight tonnage to the *Compass Rose*, cast loose its lines. The ship, the Atlantic Express, had the Military Ocean Terminal at Sunny Point, North Carolina as its next port of call. The vessel was a Department of Defense chartered munitions vessel built in the same yard and at the same time as the *Compass Rose*. The Atlantic Express began its return journey to the United States ignorant of the destination or purpose of its sister ship far to its south.

The *Compass Rose* rode the sharpening glassy swells of the North Atlantic with less authority this voyage. With a heavier load she would have carried herself a bit better, a bit deeper in the sea. The rise and fall of the bow would not have then been as noticeable, nor would be the tremulous roll as she slid corkscrewing down the next trough to slice into the next swell. Toward the end of the fifth day at sea, the march of waves from the south-southeast had become more compressed in their interval, greater in their marginal height. To the nautical ignorant *fedayeen* the slight rise in a heavier, warmer wind bore no significant signal or menace.

Kate had become more than just another tropical storm and was spinning her way to higher and higher winds, stacking the waves still steeper farther to the South. She now packed winds of ninety miles per hour and was still growing. The National Oceanic and Atmospheric Administration, NOAA, weather models were not yet able to be accurate in their prediction of her landfall. Later, well after she had passed and dissipated, the forecasters would note that she dropped eight inches of rain in just two hours as her eye passed over Fort Comfort on the Cape Fear River.

With the exception of the seasickness that had been anticipated, albeit not in the degree of its severity, there had been but minor trouble with the *fedayeen* task force for the seven days they were at sea. Aside from the few experienced seamen who had been recruited into the strike force to control the ship, the members of Machmued's force had become cruelly and disabling ill during their short stay on the water.

These were men of the desert, not the sea. The constant motion of the ship coupled with the inability to focus on a point of reference in the complete darkness had affected each of them to a different degree of severity. Those who had the strength cursed the sea and all ships that had ever sailed upon it. They cursed Machmued, the PLO, the Jews, the Americans, and the day they had heard the name Jericho.

The fervor of dedication, their esprit, their sense of brotherhood, the bonding between them created by danger and a cause, their tolerance and their camaraderie had all but disappeared. Squabbles and old blood feuds were remembered. Their devoutness to a single unifying cause lay on the floors and the deck plates of the ship amid the nauseous odors arising from what had been the contents of their stomachs. Several even now hung over the rails in the mounting seas, choking on the bitter taste of their body juices, voiding their aching bellies of all contents through raw throats, not wishing to ever hear about or think of food again.

The first few days at sea had sapped their strength, robbed them of their will, and made them regret the day they had been born. A few thought they would die and would have welcomed it. Still others were afraid that they would not and that the greenish-yellow cast to their skin and the waves of dry heaving nausea would become a permanent affectation. Three had become so weak from dehydration and the inability to even keep water down that they had been retired to their makeshift bunks deep within the ship. Liberal doses of Dramamine had, for some, diminished the effects of seasickness but had not provided a total escape. The results had been a chain reaction. Those not inclined to head for the rail due to their own immediate physical discomfort, soon became sympathetic participants when the foul odor of their compatriots' efforts reached their noses.

These, the best fighters of the *fedayeen*, had met their match and had to bear the unkind snickers and jibes of a seasoned ship's crew. To ambush a Jewish patrol was one thing, as was planting a bomb on a crowded bus or in a school or fighting an enemy hand-to-hand in the silence of a combat from which there could be but one winner. To endure with stoicism the sickness, the nausea that would not stop was quite another. The *mal de mer*, seasickness, lasted two or three days for the majority of them. The worst of it, despite the worsening weather conditions, was over and the force seemed to be on the mend and faring better as it acquired its sea legs.

Machmued, too, had suffered from seasickness, though not with as much trauma as some of his subordinates. Now, like most of them, he was becoming more accustomed to the deepening roll of the ship as it pushed over and through the Atlantic seas. Machmued could even tolerate the thought of food by the third day out and so knew he was on the road to recovery.

In the afternoon of the seventh day, Machmued lowered the binoculars through which he had been watching the open expanse of sea and distant shore and grunted in satisfaction. So far everything, with minor exception, had gone according to plan. In fact, the execution to date was too perfect, enough so to make one nervous. The support from their organization in Morocco had been superb. The decision to depart from Rabat was, in reflection, a good one.

A youthful voice called from below. Faiz al-Rashid, the boyish leader of the communications team, beckoned to Machmued. "It is Salal," he said. "He has joined with Abdul's reconnaissance and intelligence team in North Carolina."

Prearranged communications had been established with Abdul's team by the young college student, an electronics wizard, who was entrusted as the radio operator during the voyage. Faiz was Machmued's sole communication link with Salal and he knew he was the linchpin that held the widespread forces in contact. The young PLO recruit wore the position with a somber weightiness.

Communications with Abdul's team were maintained by encrypted burst radio signal and were to continue until the vessel had reached its destination. Although Faiz's three-man team was in a listening silence mode, Salal was notified by coded radio message each night as to the position of the ship in its voyage across the broad expanse of the Atlantic. All was proceeding according to schedule. Not even the approaching hurricane, the captain assured him, would delay the strike force's arrival in the target area.

"Is there more to the message?" Machmued asked.

"Yes," Al-Rashid replied. "Salal says that the doctor and his assistant have been delivered to the safe house without incident."

Faiz's eyes glistened in emotion and admiration of Machmued. To him, this burly man who led the strike force was the symbol of all of his idealistic dreams for Arab union. This mission was his first overseas and Faiz was fully prepared to not return from it. *Enshallah.*

"May your name, Machmued," Faiz blurted out, overwhelmed by the emotion of the moment, "live in our homeland so long as there are sons of Ishmael. May Allah welcome you to his bosom."

"Tend to the communications, Faiz, let me worry about my journey to Allah's bosom," Machmued grunted. "Salal may soon send another message." The wheel turns slowly, Machmued thought, remembering back to how he was the boy who then had so respected and depended on Jahbad during the Gander mission so many years ago.

After seven days at sea the *Compass Rose* arrived at the sea buoy positioned some two miles distant from the sandy coastline in the rising seas and fading light of the November evening. The buoy marked the seaward entrance to the Cape Fear River. Despite a late Indian summer, the ocean here had begun to put on her winter face. A tangled dark gray blanket of gnarled foam and blustering white caps witnessed the ocean's upset. Even the sprays were more violent, heavier in their lifting from the slashing eddies and cross currents. Swells climbed higher, the waters were darker and less forgiving as they flowed in steady march as hurricane Kate and the *Compass Rose* competed for entry into the Cape Fear River estuary.

The village of Southport lay just behind the sand-duned coast on the southern shore of the river. Seven or so miles further up the stream, also on the southern bank, lay Sunny Point, its two gigantic derricks poised like some prehistoric orange-colored creatures, overhanging the river on the easternmost of the installation's three double berth piers. Finally, at a greater distance, thirty-four or so miles up the serpentine channel lay the State Port of Wilmington.

The river, too, showed a change in her character as Kate approached. There was a foreboding about the river — a surliness and resentment of the summer's passing and Kate's invasion that she painted over the landscape. Even the mild but waning autumn could not deny the chill that now accompanied Kate's on-shore gale force winds.

Above the sound of the wind, the gentle hum and slight vibration of the generators and propellers were the sounds to be heard on the bridge. From Abdul's intelligence reports Machmued knew that the navigation of the Cape Fear River, their refuge and destination, even in the best of times was a difficult and hazardous task. The channel is passable for ocean going vessels for about thirty-seven or so miles inland to the port of Wilmington and safe harbor from the gathering, growing storm. Thereafter the river was blocked by a series of flood control dams along the river's 200-mile course.

Just to the south of the berthing facilities at the State Port of Wilmington, the river widens from its quarter mile span to, in some places, the distance of a mile and a half. The channel deepens to forty feet and begins to meander across the lower coastal plains while shallower, wider-spreading waters deposit a submerged alluvium delta outward to the ocean. In this latter, shorter distance, the errant and twisting channel, difficult in the best of times, often doubles back on itself, a live and thrashing thing, twisting in its contorted rush to the sea. The waters of the river twitch and bounce in a ten knot current from depths measured in inches at shoals that migrate each season, to the deepest part of the likewise shifting main channel. The betraying ruffling of bottom ripping, ship destroying snags, more often than not are lost in the wind whipped shallows—even for the most experienced who find their livelihood in the river's waters. The silted, muddy bottom was carpeted with the remnants of ships—pirates, merchantmen, Civil War blockade runners, men of war, private sloops, ships of wood and ships of metal, some of which date back to the river's discovery. They all mutely attest to the unrelenting and unforgiving nature of the river.

Entry and transit of any vessel the size of the *Compass Rose* required the services of a Coast Guard certified pilot. The acquisition and services of the pilot are a function of the ship's agent. The final coordination,—times of arrival, ship characteristics, final destination, rendezvous point with the pilot boat and so forth are provided by radio from the ship to the pilot's station in Southport.

The weather had deteriorated to a great degree as the day had progressed making the last six hours of the trip the slowest and most difficult part of the entire journey. Now, in the storm, there was a brief moment of respite as the ship approached the marker buoy rendezvous awaiting the arrival of the pilot who would guide the ship through the mouth of the Cape Fear River and up its treacherous and difficult mud silted channel. The oppressive winds that blew from the south had grown in ferocity and piled the dark seas higher and higher over the past hours.

In the semi-shelter of the westward headland the *Compass Rose* rode the interval between the oily whitecapped water, the height of which had decreased from fourteen to a lesser ten-foot swell. The sheets of pelting, horizontal rain had abated as if resting to conserve and renew their energy. The precipitation promised to begin again soon. The damp air was washed clean of the essence of the sea. The wind carried the smell of rain and wet earth from the distant shore. Somehow the sun had broken through the dismal gray overcast creating a deceptive, peaceful twilight. The western sky was beautiful in the afterglow of the dissipated sun—clean and crisp—clear in the spectrum of washed out reds and golds and pinks which contrasted against the boiling gray and black clouds which were even now again charging up from the south and east. The massive beauty of the skyline was quietly, tumultuously ominous. The hurricane was closing in on them with the speed and fury of a freight train.

Machmued stood at the stern of the *Compass Rose*, alone, inhaling the tranquil, menacing beauty of the diminished sunset. I wonder who of us shall see another twilight, he thought. Before another day is through there will be fewer of us.

The thought was sobering, a reflective postulation for the warrior. In his continued dismal, reflective musing, Machmued thought of the irony of it all.

"A poetic justice that an American military base will be the launching point for an attack that would change history," he voiced to no one.

Reality and circumstance forcefully charged back, drawing him into the present. His thoughts were interrupted by an urgent voice calling him to act.

"Machmued, the pilot boat has been sighted. There is also radio contact with Salal. You are needed on the bridge," the young guerrilla said. Machmued glanced at his watch. They were on time. Their preparations had been rewarded.

Machmued nodded, took one last deep drag on the strong Turkish cigarette, removed it from between his nicotine stained teeth, snapped it across the rail and watched it spiral downward into the sea to be lost in the spray and foam specked waters.

So, too, it shall be with each of us, he thought in the acceptance of his fate, if Allah so wills.

Machmued turned and strode after the messenger to the closest hatchway, two more of his men joining him in the companionway, striding behind him trying to match his pace. The strike force commander disappeared into the superstructure of the ship moving along the passageways and through the labyrinth of corridors with a sure familiarity. The winds stirred and the puddles on the steel plated deck were pricked by the first drops of the resumed rainfall. The storm revived and hurricane Kate turned landward to unleash her full fury on the North Carolina coast.

17
The New Playing Field
—Morning, November 10th

The conversation had taken place upon Doctor l'Alham's arrival when the orange sun was greasy above an oily ocean, just as the clouds had thickened and turned gray and heavy, pregnant with the rains and winds of *Kate*.

Disbelief, incredulity, bewilderment, and perplexity were all registered across the faces of the team. Salal's words had the effect of a stone dropped into a still and quiet pond when he made the announcement. There was a moment of astonished disbelief, of stunned silence. The unspoken challenges to the words were formed into silent questions as acceptance of the fact registered.

Salal responded only with a smile to Harun, comrades in a secret shared confidence. They, the two of them, held the true objective of Jericho—Salal, the terrorist, would-be militant leader of a new pan-Arab state and, Harun, the nuclear mechanic. Then a dam of questions broke over the two terrorist conspirators.

A nuclear device? How was this possible? How would it work? Where did it come from? How would they know how to operate such a weapon, to detonate it safely and live through the results? How were they to destroy the power plant with it? Who knew of the attack?

The questions came in a torrent from all sides.

Then, with Salal's slow answering rhetoric, came the acceptance, the recognition and meaning of their attack.

Almost in the identical instant, the same thought flashed into their individual minds. Yes, their success would be the turning point. They, the Arab brotherhood, the sons of Islam, would be a world power.

No longer would the West brand them as barbarians. They would be feared, powerful men, the warriors of a superpower, a nuclear superpower. They would be treated with dignity and respect. If this thing were true, if they possessed a nuclear bomb, then anything they set their will to was possible. Truly, Allah was with them.

Salal played the moment masterfully. He allowed time to permit his simple explanations and arguments to penetrate their minds, to dwell and mull their implications. Only then did he turn and point to Harun.

"This is Harun," Salal said and then, more solemnly, he pronounced, "or more properly, my friends, this is Doctor Harun l'Alham, a graduate of Oxford and the famous American Massachusetts Institute of Technology where he studied nuclear engineering. Doctor l'Alham is a gift to the *fedayeen* from Libya. For the past six years he has studied in China and Pakistan where he worked on their nuclear fission programs. This man, he is the father of the Arab nuclear program who built the first Arab reactor in Libya and has been the teacher for those in Iraq."

The team viewed Harum l'Alham with a new respect.

"Locked in his mind," Salal continued, "is the key to our success. Of all of us, he must be the best protected. The Americans must not take him. Is that clear?" Salal stared intently at the intelligence cell, assuring himself that they understood his meaning.

Satisfied, he continued. "I assure you my brothers, Harun has provided us with a proper nuclear device. The good doctor knows all that is necessary to put it in place and how to use it. That is why he is here with us now."

Their continuing wonder was clear as they turned to now study in detail the new member of their team and the new element in the equation of what had been a simple attack on an American munitions base.

"He shall tell you what must be done and how we shall destroy the nuclear power station next to Sunny Point."

Those words were Harun's cue.

He withdrew a small dark blue tri-folded pamphlet from a battered briefcase along with two other documents. They were a simple road map of Brunswick County, North Carolina and a hand drawn, to-scale map of the grounds and facilities of the power plant. He opened the pamphlet to its full poster sized dimensions and put his finger to rest on a simple schematic of the nuclear reactor consisting of the reactor vessel and building, the steam turbine, generator, step-up transformer and intake and discharge canals.

"Men of the book," he began, "what you see before you is a simple sketch of a boiling water reactor. This reactor is like the one at the power plant which we will destroy."

He had their undivided attention, their full interest.

"Commercial nuclear electric power generation in the West, unlike the Soviet Union," he explained, "is accomplished by the use of either a pressurized water reactor or a boiling water reactor. Since the one with which we will be concerned is of the latter type, I shall tell you of its specific and unique functions." His intelligent eyes peered over the rim of his glasses. He pushed them deliberately back up onto the bridge of his nose, the image of a teacher at his trade.

"There are two units at this facility which generate power by nuclear reaction. They appear to be of safer, more modern design than I have seen before. In fact, the reactors are quite large."

"Doctor," interrupted Abdul, "you must explain to us how this thing, this power plant works."

"Yes, be patient. The process of nuclear power generation creates tremendous heat, much more than is actually needed. This is why a great deal of water is needed for the reactor, to cool it."

l'Alham looked around.

"But what makes the material in this reactor different from that in a bomb? Why will it not explode as a bomb does?" Harun asked rhetorically.

"The uranium in the reactor is called U-235. For bombs we use U-238."

His students were lost.

"U-238 is ah, ah, what we call enriched uranium ... more powerful than U-235, more, ah, unstable, and much more difficult and expensive to produce. These reactors at this station have no need for such a material. Their function is quite different. They are designed to produce heat, not explosion. In fact, to produce the necessary heat takes about one hundred and twenty tons of U-235 uranium. The design of the reactor, as you will see, is really quite simple. This reactor is not like a bomb. It is quite different and will not blow up. The reactor generates heat, which, in turn, converts water into steam. The steam drives the electrical turbines. Water also keeps the reactor from overheating," Harun explained as he walked them through the elements of the diagram.

He sipped from his mug of hot tea that sat on the edge of the table.

"The danger from this reactor is that it is possible for it to become too hot. When it does, it can burn itself up. If such a thing were to happen, then radiation, radioactive gasses and waste could be released into the air which would kill the living things and destroy the soil on which it falls for ten, fifteen, perhaps even a hundred years. As long as the radiation is contained within the building which houses the reactors, what we call the reactor vessel, then the danger is minimal."

Harun returned to the pamphlet, a black felt tipped pen his pointer, confident in his knowledge of the subject and teaching ability, knowing that he would kindle and spark the attention, the enthusiasm of his audience to the subject. He had done so many times before in university lectures.

"The difference is the radioactivity. There is only one significant difference between this," he said pointing to his hand-drawn schematic of a nuclear core, "and the traditional generation of electrical energy."

The doctor paused gauging how much his audience understood what he had said. In his realm now, he continued much along the lines of a high school teacher offering the first basic instructions to his students on the subject of physics, chemistry, or any other of the mysterious natural sciences. He lectured for just over one and a half hours. At the end of that time each of the team had an elemental working knowledge of the theory and practice of nuclear generated electricity.

"Harun, explain the fuel rods," instructed Salal.

"They are simply cylindrical rods which, in this reactor, are about twelve feet long. They are made of pellets of U-235 uranium. The rapidity of the reaction, ah, the heat to boil the water, is controlled by a series of control rods located here," he said, pointing to the heart of the reactor. "These rods are made primarily of a compound of a material called Boron. This material absorbs neutrons and so controls the intensity of neutron bombardment on the uranium fuel pellets. They control the speed of the nuclear reaction and thus the internal temperature of the reactor itself."

"And you are sure, Harun," asked Sa'id, "that this room which holds the uranium reactor has walls twenty feet thick?"

"Oh yes, my friend, quite sure. The actual nuclear containment vessel is almost 75 feet high and weighs over 600 tons."

The men spread around the table listened appreciatively.

"What we shall do with this small nuclear device is destroy the control rods and the cooling system of the reactor as well as the building around it. The reactor will become so hot it will begin to melt and spread radioactivity into the air. This is what happened at Chernobyl. The reactor vessel ruptured in the initial explosion and it permitted radiation to contaminate for hundreds of miles around the area. At Three Mile Island to the north, in a state called Pennsylvania, there were two reactors that generated electricity. One of them had a meltdown, but they were very lucky. The vessel housing the reactors did not rupture and the radiation was contained in the building, so the surrounding countryside and the population were not exposed. The accident was not like Chernobyl, which ended up killing thousands with radiation poisoning and will kill and deform many more in generations still unborn. What we will do is rupture the vessel, destroy it and cause the reactor to melt down, releasing a fountain of radiation for as long as there is nuclear material in a reaction state."

The possible magnitude of the effects of their success stunned the team. Harun went on.

"The winds at this time of the year blow from the south and from the west. They will carry the radioactivity up along the eastern coast of the United States all the way to Maine and beyond before turning out into the Atlantic Ocean. Do you all understand what I have said?" He looked at the reflective faces of his *fedayeen* students.

There was a sober silence.

Abdul spoke.

"We are but simple soldiers. Most of us are men of the desert, doctor. We know about fighting and killing, but to destroy the land ... this is a difficult thing for us. You also ask us to understand these technical matters. This too, is not easy. There are many questions for all of us." The assenting nods of the team confirmed Abdul's comment.

Salal interrupted. "It is not important that you or your team know the technicalities nor to question what we must do, Abdul. The team must only provide us the time to place our 'suitcase' where it will do the most damage and rupture the control rods and the reactor's cooling system," he said chastisingly.

"Harun, his assistant Yuusuf, Abdul, and myself, will be the only ones to enter the reactor building," Salal said, addressing the entire group. "We must have at least fifteen minutes within the reactor building to position and arm the bomb. *You*," he motioned to the intelligence team, "must give us that time, if necessary, with your lives. This is why we have come."

"How large is this bomb, Harun?" asked Abdul. "What of the danger to us? How will we have time to get away?"

"How many do we leave behind to keep the Americans from removing or disarming it?" asked Sa'id practically. Cynically he knew that there would be a price to be paid to protect the bomb until it detonated. The room echoed with the silence of the question.

"I shall stay behind," Abdul slowly volunteered, facing his commander and then looking expectantly at the others of his group, knowing what this decision meant for him. "Who stays with me?"

Without hesitation all but one of the intelligence team, all except Sa'id, nodded their acceptance of the suicide mission to remain behind.

Salal did not comment nor dwell on the decision. Neither was there by word or inference by any of the men a disappointment or resentment that the last member of the cell had not volunteered. There was no question of Sa'id's courage, nor his loyalty, for neither of these was ever in doubt. Rather it was a free and personal decision as to how one chose to die and was accepted as just that. For Abdul and his four subordinates, including Widaad, who had replaced the ill-fated Bosheer, their decision was made as much from conviction and commitment as in the knowledge that their lives had been forfeit the day they had joined the *fedayeen*. Theirs was not a difficult choice. All knew that sooner or later each would die in the holy war, in *jihad*. Few of their brothers were given the opportunity to decide when and how they would die.

"Allah has brought us to this time, this place, and this decision," Salal said. "He has so destined since all time. We will be welcomed to heaven by Allah himself. It is not difficult to die. After all, is it not the ultimate reason for living?" he asked, not expecting an answer.

"Good. It is decided. The five of you—Abdul, Nabil, Zayed, Kirshid, and Widaad—shall be a sufficient force," was Salal's final comment.

"Tell us of the bomb itself, Salal. What must we do?" asked Widaad, the youngest of Abdul's team.

Doctor l'Alham responded. "The heart of our bomb is only ten kilos of U-238 uranium. The device has the explosive power of about one hundred thousand tons of TNT, about one-twentieth of the size of the bomb the Americans dropped on Nagasaki. But the blast will be sufficient to destroy the entire power station, the two nuclear reactors, and all buildings to a radius of two miles. Radiation and fallout will have their greatest effects out to as far as perhaps ten miles, depending on the wind at the time of the explosion. The whole bomb, including the trigger, the timing device, all that is needed, fits into a large suitcase and weighs just over ninety-five kilos, about two hundred pounds. As for radiation, you need not worry," he half lied. "The core of the bomb is shielded until just before the timer detonator is connected. We shall set the timer for one hour to permit those of us who must escape to be clear of the area when the bomb goes off."

"From where did this material, this ah, ah U-238 uranium come?" asked Abdul.

"From our friends," Salal quickly and simply replied, cutting off further questions on this sensitive topic.

Harun looked around the room questioningly and then at Salal, seeking and receiving his approval.

"Sa'id, for you I have another task. You will not go with us to the power plant. You will kill the Commander of Sunny Point and prepare the way for our escape. Come, we will talk alone."

18
Wilmington, North Carolina
—November 10th

Megan awoke at 8:30 in the morning, stirred by the muted gray dawn that slipped through a crack in the hotel room draperies. The night's sleep was deep and restful, no doubt because she was both exhausted and emotionally charged. The flight from London to Washington D.C. was uneventful. Megan rented a car from the airport Avis vendor and drove the eight hours to Wilmington, North Carolina without incident. This was not her first trip to the United States, merely the first to this part of the country. She enjoyed the rolling landscape that was much like the South of England. Interstate Ninety-Five was different from the roadways of Europe and the Middle East, excepting the German autobahns of course.

The drive and jet lag had left her physically drained. The excitement of her unannounced, surprise arrival charged her emotionally. She anticipated the meeting with an exuberant joy and she lived the moment in her mind's eye for nearly the full trip. What kind of life would they have together? How would it be to live in North Carolina? What would it be like—the places they would explore together, the trips they would take, the future they would have?

She realized she needed rest. She wanted to be at her best when they met and so decided to spend the night in Wilmington.

Matt's two postcards arrived at her parents' Chelmsford home on the same day. The first, after a dozen postal and diplomatic pouch errors it seemed, had been sent to the embassy in Tel Aviv and then forwarded. The second, bearing a much later postmark, was mailed directly to her parents' home eleven days earlier. Prior to their simultaneous arrival she had reconciled herself to not hearing from Matt and had decided to end her leave and return to the British embassy in Israel. The "Hurry, Come Now" comment served as an immediate catalyst for her to reverse her decision and instead travel to the United States. The e-mail with the address of his new posting arrived two days later, but she had not responded to it, deciding to keep her travel plans and arrival a surprise.

"Megan, this is so unlike you. This traipsing off to America is not well thought out at all," her mother complained. "Why on earth are you chasing after this 'Yank'?"

"Because he makes me happy and I love him, and he wants me for his own," she replied gaily.

Megan was as much surprised by her words as was her family, but she felt that the decision was the right one.

Arriving in Wilmington, North Carolina late in the evening, Megan had no difficulty in finding a comfortable hotel. She crawled into the welcome bed and quickly fell asleep. The next morning, as she lay in the enjoyment of a few extra minutes in the hot water of the tub, she felt particularly pleased with herself. There was, after all, no great hurry to race the remaining thirty-five miles to Southport. Matthew, unaware of her presence, would be at work until later in the evening, no doubt. She closed her eyes and let her thoughts drift back to Matt. She knew Matt missed her, but what would his first reaction be? She daydreamed in anticipation of the pleasure and joy that this new day would bring her.

The scenario Megan had mentally created for Matthew's evening homecoming envisioned his finding her quite naked, tucked into his bed, wearing only her most seductive smile. She rose from the tub, dried herself on an oversized towel and dressed in a loose fitting pair of white safari trousers and a bright red silk blouse.

Megan ate at the hotel restaurant. She had acquired a fondness for strong, black American coffee—under Matt's tutelage—and now almost actually preferred it to tea. Matt had teased that it was part of the Americanization process and she remembered his pointed, sometimes mocking, smug humor and smiled inwardly. She'd been doing quite a bit of that, smiling to herself, that was, since she had finally heard from him.

After breakfast she returned to her room and the mirror over the short dressing table that also served as a bathroom cabinet. Critically she examined the reflection, pouting at the soft roll of skin that had begun to fold from beneath her chin, creasing into her smooth neck. The first ruins of age were beginning to make their permanent inroads.

"I wonder," she said to the mirror, "if the rose is beginning to fade? No, not quite yet, but perhaps soon," she answered herself.

It was an acknowledgement that only a month ago would have sent her into the pits of despair. Now she was rather surprised by her own acceptance of this new reality. Still the piper had to be paid and so, rather than her normal flash and dab, today Megan took extraordinary time and care at preparing her makeup and hair.

Megan was gifted with a natural aptitude for both color and smartness. Her eye, by intuition and experience, told her those combinations that flattered her best features. There was no one "best" color—all were flattering, but blues and grays were her very favorites. Megan preferred her American cousins' call to casual and comfortable slacks, jeans and blouses although she was not quite so liberal as the sweat shirt and chewing gum set, both of which she personally thought to be vulgar and in bad taste. On a whim and in response to a teasing remark that Matthew had once made to her, she did buy a pair of high heels, pleased with the line that the three-inch elevation gave to the calf of her long legs.

In the selection of scents, Megan was a romantic. Each fragrance, she believed, conveyed a different meaning and was worn to match the purpose of the occasion. Modest priced French scents were more in keeping with her tastes than in the snobbery displayed by a pricetag or name. She had a particular liking for *Opium* by Yves Saint-Laurent and a Guerlain scent called *Chamade* as alternating daily favorites. Both conveyed, she felt, not only an air of femininity but also a sense of independence. There were others that she wore on occasion including an American fragrance by Revlon called *Ciara*. Her favorite by far, however, was *Mystere de Rochas*, that Matt had given her. She reserved Matt's scent for the best of times, occasions of very special significance. She dabbed it on today.

Some twenty minutes later she found that she was rather pleased with the results of her labor, gathered up the bits and pieces of cosmetics and stowed them in a small, gaily colored vinyl case.

"Still a bit of looks left in the old girl," she appraisingly thought at last. She cast about the room gathering her things, tossing them with a practiced ease neatly into her bags. With a look of finality, she surveyed the room a last time, lifted the two bags, deposited them in the hall, shut the door, and headed for the lobby.

"I say," she smiled to the desk clerk as he returned her American Express card "could you please direct me to the road to Southport?"

The clerk eyed her over the edge of his glasses.

"Yes ma'am, but most of the folks from that area are headed away from the coast. We have a hurricane coming this way and expect that it will hit land somewhere in the vicinity of the mouth of the Cape Fear River. Southport is just about ground zero."

"Yes, thank you, but it will be all right, I am sure," she replied.

"Well, ah, if you insist, ah," he hesitated, looking down at the registration card, "Miss Felton, you will want to take Route Seventeen two blocks down to the right." He examined her road map and oriented it for her, then marked the route with a yellow highlighter. "Cross the bridge over the river and go on about four miles to the intersection with Route 133. Southport is about, oh, I'd say about thirty-five

or forty miles directly down Route One Thirty-Three.
Southport's a pretty small town but right nice folks over
there. You can't miss it, runs right into the river." He smiled
his most engaging smile.

"Right. Well, thanks so very much, indeed," she said, gathering up her bits and pieces.

"Watch out for low spots in the roadway. We've had some
heavy rain and winds along the coast already. If the hurricane
keeps on track it could be pretty nasty down there this
evening. If it's as bad as they say, they'll be evacuating that
whole area before the day is through. Gonna get pretty wild
and windy out there. You would be much safer staying here
than being closer to the coast. Just thought I might save you
a trip," he said, smiling again.

"Can you tell me anything of a military base around
about Southport? I believe its name is Sunny Point," she
asked tentatively.

"Certainly. That's on Route 133 but pretty easy to miss.
Not very well marked. The terminal, well, it's really not much
of ah, ah, military base. Actually it's a large port complex
that's just owned and run by the military. If that's where
you're headed, look for the intersection of Route Eighty-
Seven with Route One Thirty-Three, perhaps thirty or so
miles on down here," he said, tracing out the route with an
orange marker on the map.

"The main entrance to Sunny Point Terminal is right
there," he said, circling the intersection. "Southport's maybe
another, oh, eight or ten miles beyond that. But the terminal's not, ah, open to the public, ma'am. It's pretty much off
by itself," he volunteered.

"You have a nice day now, Miss Felton. Thanks for staying
with us and y'all come back. Be careful now," he drawled,
handing her the receipt for her room.

Megan smiled, nodded a "Thank You" for a final time and
headed for the car. She'd come too far to let a little wind and
rain stop her now.

A weak watery sun groomed the morning with a slate colored sky. The day was overcast, but even the gloomy, diffused light of a mostly unseen sun could not dampen Megan's spirits. The bulk of the traffic was flowing away from her destination, but then Route One Thirty-Three, according to the map, was the major artery from the several beaches to the south of Point Comfort. A strong gust of wind occasionally rocked the car and spattered it with a fine mist of rain and sporadic heavier droplets as she maintained her course toward Sunny Point. Following the clerk's directions, by eleven o'clock Megan passed the Sunny Point cut off, electing instead to proceed directly to the address which had been provided on Matt's postcard. She pulled into the single Southport Exxon station, filled the tank at the self-service island, reached for her purse and walked into one of the two open garage bays to pay the bill.

"Would you know where I might find Riverfront Road?" she asked the acne-scarred attendant.

"Riverfront Road? No, I don't think so. What're y'all lookin' for? Maybe I can help you that way."

"I believe that it is a street somewhere here in Southport. At least, that is what I've been told. Let me see." She riffled through the deep purse and withdrew the postcard, handed it to the attendant.

"Here you see, Riverfront," she said pointing to Matt's scrawled address. The attendant reviewed the card and then spoke.

"Oh, you want the Garrison House. Yeah, sure. Down to the traffic light. Turn left. One block then turn right. Look for a big red brick house that sits on the bluff right above the river. You the wife of the new Army man they got themselves over there at Sunny Point?" he asked with the curiosity of all small town residents.

"No, afraid not," Megan replied while adding silently, "at least not yet."

"Well hope you stay around for awhile," the boy responded with a smile. "Uh, the way you talk, like maybe Australian, huh?" he asked bluntly, wiping a grease stained hand on the leg of his trousers as he peeled three one dollar bills from the greasy roll he had withdrawn from his pocket.

"Not quite – I'm British," she said walking to the car. Sliding behind the wheel she smiled, switched on the ignition, and slid the automatic transmission into gear. "Thank you for the directions."

Megan eased the rental out into the street. Garrison House was not at all difficult to find, but it was not in the least the way she had pictured it. The house was too grand for a mere Lieutenant Colonel. Four white Georgian columns ran to the thirty-foot height of the gabled porch roof. The view of the river, the distant light house, and the ocean beyond all too spectacular, all more than she had expected. A spacious well-groomed, three-acre front lawn ran to the river's edge marked with well-tended random beds of colorful flowers.

Megan parked in the small three car private parking lot adjacent to the south side of the house, slid from behind the wheel and walked up the herringbone patterned red brick walkway that paralleled the front of the house. The wind had begun to gust and carried a light spray, but with it the scented promise of heavier rain. She peered in the ajar front door, strangely, superstitiously reluctant to cross its threshold without invitation. She knocked noisily on the wood of the door.

A shade of doubt crept through her thoughts.

"Hello," she cried. "Any one there?"

"Yes, hello, come on in," replied Estelle. "I'm saved. Are you from the moving company? I've been waiting for you for the last twenty minutes."

She babbled on. "Thank God! And I'm late. I promised Colonel Gannon I'd be here for you to go over the inventory but I have a doctor's appointment that I'm already late for. That's what you get for doing people favors."

"Actually, I'm … " Megan began in reply.

"Look," said Estelle, swinging a light windbreaker jacket across her shoulders and heading for the front door. "I've just got to go. The damaged items are all in the dining room for

you to inspect and I've marked each of them on the inventory. Would you be a dear and just slam the door shut when
you're done?" She handed Megan a ream of papers. "Thanks.
Bye." And she was gone.

"Actually..." was Megan's unheard reply. She sighed.
"Right, then."

Megan retrieved her luggage from the rental car and
deposited the bags in the upstairs master bedroom. She found
her purse, riffled through its contents, no small task in itself,
and emerged with a pen and scrap of paper. She sat thoughtfully for a moment and then began to compile a list of needs
that, as the afternoon sped by, grew as she undertook the
most pressing of the items to be accomplished. She roamed
across the large main floor of the 200 year old structure. In
her exploration and wanderings about the large house she discovered a meager closet of cleaning supplies and a tiny larder
of food items.

"He's obviously been eating out," she concluded, as she
cast a speculative, jaundiced eye on one of the stack of frozen
dinners, examining and then returning a random sample to
the exile of the refrigerator's freezer compartment.

"And eating all the wrong things at that," she said
frowning.

So, there it was, she thought. The unstructured pile of
crates, furniture and boxes dominated the large living room
area and held the keys to his past. There was little he carried
with him in the Middle East, just the expected assortment of
uniforms and clothing, but nothing that really gave a hint to
him, the individual. Matt's former life, his life before she had
met him, had been a closed door between them, not locked
but pried open only with difficulty.

Megan paused in speculative reflection. Really she knew
very little about him, about those years before she had come
into his life. In Israel and in the Sinai, Matt had lived austere-
ly. The Spartan quarters he occupied at the MFO El Gorah
base camp in the northern Sinai gave no clue as to his own
tastes and his own trappings. The personal items he brought

to the desert were relatively few and modest, not at all in keeping, she thought, with the volume of packing cases and variety of furnishings she saw heaped before her. This was a totally new side of him, a new and unopened facet to be explored. In the boxes and crates were the secrets, the private things, the possessions he valued enough to keep. She fell on them with the eagerness of a child at Christmas.

Unpacking and unwrapping his things was a special time for Megan, a time of singular intimacy, to savor and reflect and imagine. The afternoon, during which she came to know Matt more intimately than ever before, passed in quick time. She opened each of the boxes, some with contents only cursorily examined, others examined in detail, speculated upon, categorized, catalogued for future inquiry, and then repositioned in the appropriate room of the two storied house. The major items of furniture had already been positioned throughout the house for the most part.

In a smallish cardboard box she discovered what were the important documents, papers, and mementos of his life. There were several picture albums that traced his growth into manhood and his career in the army, as well as pictures of family and what she took to be college friends. There was a faded color photo of a younger, scrawnier Matthew. He was sitting on the edge of a foxhole, clad in boots and faded green field trousers, shirtless with a helmet on his head, a rifle resting across his thighs. The younger Matt was smiling woodenly at the camera, the background a scar of ripped earth, jagged, torn rocks and sand, and oily black smoke curling to a blue, cloudless sky. Curiously there were no photos of women in the album other than those of his mother or older people or young teen-aged girls.

Odd, she thought in passing.

The corner of the box held a stack of small presentation cases, each holding a different medal or decoration. She opened each, touching the surface of the medal, running her fingers over the engraved name and date on the reverse of each of them, feeling the colors of each ribbon, knowing them to represent a presence of Matthew, yet not knowing the meaning of each.

She found his college diplomas, an ancient key chain with half of a heart attached to it. There was a well-used misshapen gold ring—the shank was broken and one could see where it had been mended. The monogram initials "MFG" were faintly etched across the thin, worn square that served as the face of the ring. There was a wine cork from a bottle of champagne, two holy cards that portrayed the Virgin Mary at Fatima, the reverse of which memorialized the name of Mary Bridgett Gannon.

She had just undone the rubber band from a large stack of documents when a long, blue legal protector fell free from the ream of papers. Megan suspected what it was immediately, his divorce decree. She touched it cautiously and then carefully began to unfold the blue protective cover that bound it. A picture slipped from the folds of the document and fell to the floor, landing face upward. The photograph was a miniature of his wedding portrait. Matthew smiled lovingly at a stranger, a beautiful young woman who returned his gaze with a shared understanding and intimacy. The impact on Megan was immediate and the reaction both physical and emotional. It was a totally involuntary reflex—unconscious, startling in its effect. All at once she felt as a thing alien, as one not belonging, as an invader who touched some valuable relic without permission, who had captured a secret, taken something to which she had no right. The feeling was strange, depressing and saddening, strong and sudden. She hurriedly replaced the picture in the document and closed the box, searching no further, no longer curious. She felt somehow ashamed, if not anxious about how he would feel about her less than innocent prying into the secrets and possessions of his life, a life of which she then had not been a part.

With effort she cast off her self-induced guilt and the depression that threatened to engulf her. She cast a thoughtful eye on the small box; intrigued by it but then turned away, respecting the secrets it held. Slowly but decidedly she moved onto the less personal heap of goods.

The furnishings in the master bedroom—quite nice at that, she thought. I'll have to find out what inspired him to buy a king-sized bed.

The major furnishings that required assembly or connection—the bed, the heavy dining room table, the washer and dryer, the entertainment center with television, VCR, stereo and tape deck—had all been accomplished. There was at least a place to sit and a work area from which one could begin to unload the boxes and crates of crockery and appliances.

First things, first. She returned to the bedroom to rummage for the packed away bed clothing which, when found, went straight away into the laundry.

The soft gray day rolled into a blacker afternoon. The rising river witnessed a growing sea gale that shuttled heavier rainsqualls through the front door of the house that, not fully latched, had swung open. The afternoon was unmistakably cooler, and Megan closed both the door and the few windows she had cracked open for cross ventilation. For a moment she debated laying a fire in the large fireplace for the evening, then set about the task from the stack of sheltered firewood neatly piled outside at the rear of the house. Megan hummed softly, happy as she quite contentedly spun her new nest about herself.

By six o'clock Garrison House had begun to take on more of a lived-in air, the makings of a home versus only a house or a residence. Megan, despite the first twitches of the warm and welcomed fatigue of physical labor, felt quite contented and pleased at the progress she had made. In reflection she found that the day had been more fun than work and the hours had swiftly passed. She glanced at the watch on her wrist and decided she had time for a hot shower to wash away the grime and glow of the day before the lord and master would arrive. She latched the front door, surprised at how dark the sky had grown. Heavy wind-driven raindrop splats now blew against the solid front oak door. There was an increasing growl that accompanied the wind with all the promise that it would be a terrible night to be out and about.

Dinner tonight, for no reason dealing with the storm, would be a bit late, if at all.

She smiled, half in anticipation, half in satisfaction in knowing what the night would hold for Matthew and her.

19
Sunny Point
Friday Evening, November 10th

Friday marked the last workday of the first full three weeks of Matt's official command tenure of the Sunny Point Military Terminal and Port. His government furnished sedan sat alone in the parking lot, its windshield shedding the deluge of rain that was now falling in fat, heavy drops from the darkened sky. Matt sat alone in the solitude of the vacant building that was his headquarters. The heavy rain wore itself into the soft pine trees, silently penetrating into the needle-carpeted soil. Hurricane "Kate" was coming, rolling up from the South. She was on time and would keep her date with the North Carolina coast tonight.

The projected weather conditions had prompted a great deal of concern by the workforce and Matt, shortly before noon, approved the early dismissal of all but essential personnel. There was little more he could do to improve on the safety or the exposure of the several thousands of tons of munitions and explosives secured in their concrete bunkers scattered across the base.

The high hazard cargo had arrived steadily by both highway and rail. The procedures for receiving shipments and segregating them into well-separated locations to prevent sympathetic detonation from a freak accident, such as a lightning strike, were sound and well established. Still, there was a vulnerability to the facility.

Excepting the new commander, there was not a sense of danger or threat among the community of workers, administrators, surveillance technicians and cargo handlers who daily worked on the wharves. Apathy and "it-can't-happen-here" was a mantle that resulted from several years of safe operations with no external threat. How to rapidly change that attitude without sounding like a shrill alarmist was Matt's immediate and major problem.

He glanced at the Seiko strapped to his wrist. The time was 5:45.

Might as well head home, he thought. He reached for the phone, plucked the handset from the cradle and punched zero for the terminal's communication center operator.

"This is Colonel Gannon," he said unnecessarily. "Give me the security duty officer, please."

A pause turned into a short silence and he absently fiddled with a pencil turning it end over end on his desk.

Only sixty more working hours until Monday, he thought idly. So very much still to learn and even more to be done just to become proficient in the operations of the port. And then there was the ever-present matter of security. There was just no way to learn or cover it all in the time he hoped he had before any trouble began.

The operator came back on the line.

"It's ringing, sir."

"Thanks, Jodi."

There was something to be said for the closed loop communications system of the terminal even if it was not the most modern of telecommunication centers. The Sunny Point switchboard still had the human element in it and Jodi, the switchboard operator, was just as efficient as any automated system and not nearly as high in maintenance requirements.

"Sunny Point security," a gruff deep voice reported.

"Mister Owens? Colonel Gannon. You've got the con. I'm going to pull the plug early tonight and head on home. Looks like your folks are going to have a miserable one. Keep tabs with the Coast Guard and let me know if they advise evacuation or any other extra precaution with 'Kate' off the coast out there. If anything else comes up, give me a holler at Garrison House."

"Yes, sir. No problem. Have a good evening," came the reply.

Matt hung up. Checking out with security was a habit, a ritual he had established the first night he had arrived. The base security officer always knew his off-duty whereabouts.

Matt rose from behind the desk, snapped off the lights of the office, and punched the lock on the doors to the carpet clad command suite behind him. He walked down the tile-covered corridor to the main entrance of the headquarters building and pushed open the door. The temperature had fallen through the day and now it was noticeably cooler. Winter was not far away.

The wind and rain slashed through his fatigues. Hesitating a moment in the shelter of the alcove, he watched the plump raindrops angle past the overhead lights which illuminated the empty parking lot. Sensing that it would not diminish, he dashed across the twenty or so feet of rain soaked pavement and jerked open the door of the military sedan.

Preferring to be his own driver, Matt had taken to driving the sedan himself rather than being provided with the authorized military driver. Besides, he felt it pompous to be provided with a chauffeur whose skills were better employed in shuttling the cargo of the terminal to its appointed places. There was another reason why Matt preferred the stripped down compact to the better-styled, more powerful BMW garaged at Garrison House. The reason rested in a console beneath the dash.

Housed under the dashboard was a military FM transceiver with which he could maintain communications with the security net of the terminal as well as military relay stations and aircraft. With the radio Matt had the capability of direct and instant communications with the terminal from as far as thirty-five miles away—even longer if he chose to route his message traffic through one of the available relay stations.

The short ten-mile ride from the terminal to Garrison House wandered down rural State Route 133 through the scented green pines and golden autumn of the North Carolina coast. Now, however, the ride was a bit longer and not nearly so scenic. Tonight it was a dismal, depressing journey that at its conclusion would be followed by a lonesome and empty house.

The daylong gathering clouds had thickened into an unbroken mantle of deep gray in all directions and shortly after one-thirty the forbidding sky had loosed a staccato of rain, which had increased in tempo throughout the afternoon. The rain, now falling in sheets, traced itself in an unending waterfall across the body of the car. The wiper blades, turned to their highest speed, could barely keep-up in shuttling the water from the windshield.

The latest national weather advisory had warned that "Kate" was following a line fifty miles offshore and scheduled to be opposite the Cape Fear area somewhere between nine and ten o'clock later in the evening. Severe beach erosion had already occurred and was expected to continue. The nearby resort areas of Kure, Caswell and Long Beach were ordered evacuated, as had been the low lying areas of the town of Southport proper. Small boat advisories had been posted earlier in the morning and gale-warning flags had been hoisted at the area marinas. On a bright note, however, unless an unpredictable turn to the West was in the offing, the worst appeared to be only heavy rains, gale force winds, and localized flooding for the Southport and Wilmington areas. The main force of the storm would remain off shore.

Matt's light vehicle was buffeted by the blasts of wind that swept the two-lane blacktop highway. The last three miles to Garrison House were driven in yet a heavier downpour and the main street of the old Civil War hamlet, then called Smithport, had already begun to flood.

Matt followed the twin headlight beams of the government sedan into the rear driveway entrance of Garrison House. The driveway, one of two, was behind the house, away from the waterside of the building, where Megan's unseen rental car was parked. The sedan slid to a stop next to the canvas covered BMW and Matt cut the engine. Lights burned in the kitchen attesting to someone's presence.

Probably Estelle had left the light on, he thought, to

prevent his stumbling about in the darkness of the house across the household goods still to be unpacked.

Withdrawing the ignition key, Matt fumbled on the ring and located the key to the kitchen door. He sprung from the car, slammed its door while on the run, and tried to dodge the wind driven cold drops that cascaded around him, pelting his head and shoulders with tiny pinpricks. The sanctuary of the building once gained, Matt forced open the door, and slammed it shut against the swirling chaos that attempted to follow him into the kitchen.

Rivulets of rain ran down the back of his neck and he shook himself like some great bear, brushing the raindrops from the camouflage uniform. As he looked about the spacious room he registered a level of surprise to see the unexpected orderly kitchen before him. Someone had put in a great deal of work in ordering the shambles of cartons that had existed on his departure that morning. Roaming through the rooms of the first floor Matt became more puzzled and pleased at the turn of events. Hearing movement upstairs, the Sunny Point commander was drawn more by curiosity than caution and mounted the steps. Darkness had fully fallen and the door to the master bedroom was a bit ajar, casting a sharp, narrow beam of yellow light from beneath the doorframe. The light reflected from the ancient planked floor onto the white hallway. The vague aroma of a distant perfume tugged at his senses. Matt opened the door and stepped into the room.

Megan stood before him, a towel wrapped about her, modestly covering her from shoulder to thigh. At first she started at the door's opening, but then seeing Matthew, her smile blossomed and the tension left her body, belonging, as she was, where she should be. Her eyes sparkled. A pixyish smile of delight and anticipation lit her face as she viewed Matt's complete confusion. That he was shocked and unprepared for the woman who waited in this place for him was clear. The look on his face betrayed him and left no room for recovery and Megan laughed at his bewilderment.

"Hi, soldier. Want to show a girl a good time?" she asked, as she unwrapped the towel from about her form, but holding it in front of herself.

Matt still had not recovered, but just looked at her, his mouth hanging open.

"New in town?" she continued in saucy, seductive fashion, letting the towel slip to the floor, revealing her nakedness. She walked across the few feet that separated them and into his arms.

"Megan. How ..." he began.

She kissed him. The kiss lingered soft and warm on his lips and he felt a completeness he had missed.

"Wait, I want ... "

She stifled his words with her eager lips. Her tenderness melted in the heat of urgency as she drew him closer, undoing the buttons of his uniform shirt, pulling at the brass buckle of his trousers belt. She put a silencing finger to his willing mouth and drew him down onto the bed beside her.

"Not now," she said. "No talk now. What's important is that I'm here ... with you. I love you, Matt, and I'll stay on whatever terms you'll have me. Talk is for later, darling."

Urgency engulfed them. The heat of need came sharp, physical, overwhelming both of them. Matt drew his head to Megan's neck, kissing it gently, moving his hands across her already sensitized body. She was warm and soft and smelled of the human scent of need. Megan positioned herself underneath his body. His hips felt the strong lock of her powerful legs embrace his thighs and then his lower back drawing him down into her wet warmth. She thrust upward with a deep sigh as she drew him deep inside her. Megan was wanting and strong, demanding and giving with no holding back. Without reason he found himself trying to hold back, wanting to match her giving, but somehow afraid to. She coaxed him with her body and caressed him with her touch until he could hold back no longer but joined her, locked in his own pleasure.

The storm peaked within them matching the frenzy and

power of the growing wind and rain that surged outside the house, peaking in an intensity that drained them both. When the need and passion ebbed, it left in its place a sense of wonderment, fulfillment—a tenderness in the ecstasy of being one, together. And then, without words, the need grew again and once more as before, they made love.

The second time was different. Not better, certainly not worse, but just different than anything either of them had ever felt before. They made love with a lingering gentleness, a fragile caressing of each other; much different from the urgency they had earlier felt. They recognized, each in the other, the need and love that dwelt and grew in the moments just past. Between them there was a giving of being, of total self to the other, a forever bonding.

They lay there together, resting in each other's arms, touching, holding hands—two innocent children as the darkness of the night and the storm raged outside. Matt for the first time talked about the past, the future, heretofore unshared intimacies, what they almost lost, what they meant to one another.

"I thought I had lost you, Megan," he said.

"And I, you," she added after a moment, fondling his chest. "I suppose that sometime we must be practical and talk all of it out, but not now, Matthew. Tonight let's not worry about tomorrow, or the day after or the day after that either. I shan't let you ever leave me again Matthew," she said seriously, "nor shall I ever leave you unless you don't want me anymore."

They lay side by side, enjoying the moment, savoring it in an afterglow of warmth and expended passion.

In time Matt roused and turned to Megan, a smile on his lips. "And what would you have done had I arrived with a good looking blond on my arm tonight?" Matt teased, trying to break the seriousness of the moment, frightened by it and now again finding himself holding back on his own final, irrevocable commitment, not wanting to make the surrender of his person, which Megan had already made in being here.

"Well, first, I would have kicked your Irish-German ass," she exclaimed, slapping at him, "and then I should have had a talk with the blond trollop, telling her what absolutely dreadful taste in men she had. The two of us no doubt would have gotten on quite well."

"I suppose I asked for that," Matt replied with a laugh.

"Are you hungry?" he asked glancing at his watch and noting the time. It was ten minutes before eight.

"We haven't been apart so long as for you to forget that I'm always hungry," Megan replied. "I didn't have much of a chance to do anything for dinner. Your larder is woefully inadequate. Unless you will settle for an omelet we shall have to find a grocer if you want anything fixed here tonight."

"This storm has pretty well closed everything down, but I know a super seafood place," Matt said. "I've eaten there quiet a few times and know the owners fairly well now. It's right up the road, less than a ten-minute ride away. I'm sure they will be closed, but I'll give them a call. Perhaps Sue or Hank will put something together for us. I'll run on over there and pick up dinner and bring it back here. We can have a glass of wine, a nice slow dinner and then make love for the rest of the night. What do you think?"

"Delightful," she replied. "I'm famished."

"Get moving, wench. I'll give you ten minutes to freshen up and repair the damages and then I'll be right behind you."

"Right," Megan said, sliding off the bed and moving to the bathroom. "I am quite hungry, Matthew," she remarked over a departing shoulder, "so you best be prepared to spend a few quid to replenish my strength if you expect to take advantage of me later."

"Umm," came the sleepy reply.

She would let him doze a few moments, she thought.

The night so far had been as she thought it would be. She studied her satisfied face in the bathroom cabinet mirror.

"Yes," she softly said, "it is the right thing—to come and be with him once again."

All, once again, was right in her world.

Megan dressed in short order, glancing but once at Matt's sprawled form, breathing deep and even, on the bed. She had just finished putting on her face when she heard the chimes of the front door.

20
Cape Fear River
—Evening, November 10th

The transfer from the forty-foot black-hulled pilot boat was accomplished without incident. Adeptly, the coxswain maneuvered the smaller vessel from a hundred meters astern of the *Compass Rose*. The pilot boat took a position on the port side, using the larger ship's bulk to shelter it from the wind. The captain issued instructions and a boarding ladder was lowered to assist in the transfer of the pilot to the larger vessel. The pilot, an overweight redneck, sensed an anxiety among the ship's crew but in error identified it as concern to put the ship to berth in safety before "Kate," in her meandering, made landfall and wreaked havoc.

"Evening, Captain," he said, entering the bridge. "Looks like we'll just about get you safely into the river before this damn hurricane hits," said the pilot, the words rumbling forth from somewhere deep inside his enormous girth and whistling across his decayed teeth and cigarette stale breath.

With practiced ease he took the con and guided the *Compass Rose* toward the Cape Fear channel. The surging ground swells abated as the ship moved deeper into the confluence of the river, past the protection of the shoals and low headlands that sheltered the tributary's mouth.

The *fedayeen* task force was hidden from view below decks amid the strange but now familiar noises of machinery and the vibration of the turning shafts and screws. The smells were of diesel fuel, mildew, gun oil, cordite, rust, tension and sweating men. The grunts and quiet movement of bulky shapes were ghostlike as they tended to their silent preparations. The click of magazines being locked into place in the AK-47's, of bolts drawn back, the snicker-snaps of rounds being chambered and the rap of bolts thrusting forward accompanied the last minute rustle of final adjustments to personal gear.

A minimum quantity of plastique would be carried ashore. The explosives would be supplemented with captured incendiaries as needed to destroy the wharves, cranes, railway bridges, and storage igloos. The locations of the appropriate stockpiles had already been determined by aerial photo and confirmed by their spy in the terminal complex. The men were ready and the waiting was almost over.

Machmued remained on the bridge, introduced to the pilot as a supercargo representative of the ship's owners. The Arab leader had returned from the fantail of the ship to receive final instructions from Salal just before the pilot was transferred to the ship. There was one more short communication from Salal with further instructions.

"As the ship completes the second of the 90 degree turns just inside the river's mouth," Salal explained, "you will be very close to the western bank of the river. A fishing pier extends almost 150 meters into the river at that point. Send three men. Sa'id will meet them at the pier with further instructions."

Machmued acknowledged the direction without question, identified the men, and gave them their orders.

"You," he said, speaking to the three experienced seamen he subsequently selected, "will go aboard the pilot boat. Kill the one who remains there now and secure the boat to the fishing pier at the turn in the river. Take your instructions from Sa'id who will meet you. Go with Allah, my brothers, and may he bless your work this night," he concluded.

Unknown to the pilot, Machmued instructed the radioman to request the pilot boat to come along side. The transfer of the three terrorists had been accomplished as the *Compass Rose* crept along in the narrow entrance of the river channel, maintaining only speed necessary for steerageway and maneuvering in the darkness.

The red and green channel markers that appeared every

quarter of a mile were swallowed in the swirling rains that seemed to part as the *Compass Rose* snuck forward up the river. Almost an hour and fifteen minutes after the pilot boat had disappeared bearing the three terrorists, the lights on the Sunny Point wharves appeared in the mist and gloom along the left bank. The routine thirty-minute trip had taken more than double its normal time due to the compounding effects of darkness and the storm that had grown in fierceness about them. A lighted piling close by the main channel bore down upon the ship. Tacked in place above the reflecting light was a fourteen-foot yellow square bearing three-foot high black lettering. Machmued wiped at the fogged window with his sleeve to read the words.

> RESTRICTED GOVERNMENT WATERS
> NO TRESPASSING
> VIOLATORS WILL BE PROSECUTED

"The time is upon us," Machmued murmured. "Jericho is at hand." Turning, he issued his first instructions in his native Arabic tongue.

"Khleed," he directed in quiet whisper to one of his lieutenants, "pass the word for the men to take their assault positions. Have the charges all been placed?"

"They have," Khleed responded.

"Good. Activate the relay switches to the charges. Bring the transmitter here to me. I want you to do this personally. Do you understand?"

"Yes, sir," the lieutenant replied and slid out the rear of the bridge to weave his way into the lower bowels of the ship.

Machmued turned to find the captain staring at him. "Ah, Captain may I speak to you in private for just a moment," Machmued asked, reaching out and steering the captain toward a far corner of the bridge.

"Captain," Machmued confided, "it is almost time for me and my men to take our leave of your ship. As soon as my men are off the ship you must position the ship in the channel as we have discussed."

The captain acknowledged his instructions and Machmued smiled. "Good. You are a brave man, my friend. Perhaps we shall meet again one day in paradise. Now please go back to your station and do not look so grim. After all, for you the worst is now over, eh?"

The captain returned to his position next to the wheel. Machmued moved next to the taciturn pilot who strained into the darkness seeking the next set of markers. Their two faces were lit by the reflected blue gray light of the radarscope that charted their flight down the black hole of the river.

"Pilot," he said in English, "the captain and I have conferred and we wish you to take the ship there."

Machmued pointed to the centermost of the now discernible three well-lit wharves, a little over a half mile off of the port beam. A slap of wind pelted the rain into the bridge windows. The visibility of the shoreline was momentarily obscured. Silhouetted where Machmued had pointed were two of Sunny Point's four giant fifty-ton gantry cranes. A red aviation warning light topped them, made almost invisible by the shifting blasts of rains and spray.

"With this weather and the visibility that's not a bad idea," the pilot replied, misunderstanding Machmued's intent. "That's not Wilmington, no sir," he chuckled, "that's Sunny Point, that's a government port—restricted area. No, can't go in there. No sirree. We still have another two or so hours up the river to the State Port. No need to worry none though, tough part's behind us now."

"You will position the ship to dock on the center wharf, there," Machmued said, pointing to Sunny Point.

It was as the pilot turned from the wheel to reply that he saw the vacant eye of the 9mm pistol pointed casually at the base of his chin. His eyes bulged. Machmued smiled. The pistol came up, extended at full arm's length.

"I am, sir, your very worst nightmare," Machmued threatened in exaggerated politeness. "And if you do not do as I direct, I shall be your executioner. Do you understand?"

The pilot raised his hands, palms outward, to his chest. His eyes focused on the barrel of the pistol, and he took three rapid steps backward to feel the outline of the telegraph pressing into his back.

"Are you crazy man? You gotta be, be outta your friggin' mind," he stuttered. "Even if'n I could put this ship at berth there we don't have the clearances, or the tugs, or the line handlers on the wharf to put us in snug like."

"We have no quarrel with you unless you make a quarrel with us," Machmued lied. "I assure you that we, however, are very serious. I beg your forgiveness, but in war, many of the innocents are hurt and killed. Such is decreed by Allah and it is foolish to struggle against one's destiny."

Machmued cocked the exposed hammer of the pistol, the metallic snick of the sear against the safety stop of hammer audible to the pilot. The vacant eye of the barrel came to rest at the point of junction between the bridge of the nose and the brow, slamming the pilot into a sudden wall of apprehensive submission.

"Make no mistake, my friend," Machmued said, "you will not be the last to die this night. I shall, however, give you the honor of having been the first if you do not follow my instructions immediately. Do as I have ordered. Do it now."

"They've already killed three of my men and he won't hesitate to kill all of us if you don't obey him," the captain lied, adding a fiction to the scene being played.

The pilot hesitated. His gaze swept around the red-lit bridge at the faces of the anxious crew. He saw determination in the eyes of three men who had appeared on the bridge, weapons in their hands.

"Shit," he said and spun the wheel hard over to port.

21
Strike at the Head

Salal's instructions had been clear.

Sa'id waited in the warmth of the Volvo, its engine purring smoothly, the heater on a low setting, blowing a soft warm stream of air against his legs, the defrosters turned to high to keep the windows from fogging. A cigarette dangled casually, carelessly from the corner of Sa'id's mouth. He had not shaven in the past two days and the smell of curry and stale sweat rose from the black turtleneck sweater and heavy black canvas trousers that were bloused into high-topped heavy, rubber-soled boots. Sa'id watched the approaching bulk of the *Compass Rose* and its deceptively lazy swing through the second ninety-degree turn. In the gloom he could just see the outline of the lowered gangway as he watched the running lights of the pilot boat match the ponderously slow progress of the *Compass Rose* and hold station at the gangway.

Sa'id opened the door of the car and stepped out to be hit by a blast of wind that rocked him back against the frame of the open car door, the cold rain stinging his exposed face like so many tiny needles. Bowing his head to the wind, he clutched at the railing of the pier and braced himself forward out onto its timbered surface. Waves crashed against the sea wall beneath the wooden pilings, the vibrations of their charge transmitted through the soles of his shoes to his feet and up the muscles of his legs.

Reaching the end of the T-shaped pier, Sa'id could clearly see one man in the bow of the pilot boat. The changing pitch of the twin engines was carried to him by the wind as the small black hulled navigation boat maneuvered, bow against the wind, crabbing toward the pier. A line shot out over his head, thrown by the man at the bow as the boat crept to within ten feet of the pier. Sa'id caught at it, missed, and scrambled to his left to retrieve the rapidly retreating whipped end.

There was a note of final surge of engine as the boat touched the pier and was made fast with lines fore and aft. Protective tires hung from the lateral stringers of the pier and fenders were put over the side of the pilot boat as well to protect it from crashing or rubbing the hull into the sharp, barnacle blanketed pilings. Spring lines were quickly crisscrossed and made fast.

Sa'id noted the proficiency in the teamwork of the three men with a sense of satisfaction. They had brought a strange vessel safely and efficiently to berth in a minimum of time. One of the two Arab deckhands motioned aboard as the last line was snuggled down. Sa'id gingerly half stepped, half leapt onto the vessel.

"*Salaam,*" he said to the two darkly clad men who stood on the deck.

They nodded their greetings and all three men hurried through the rain into the comfort and warmth of the tiny closed cockpit. A rush of cold salt air washed into the small compartment with them.

The confined space smelled of the sick-sweet copper scent of blood, the odor so strong that it could be tasted. In the corner, next to the wheel stood the third of the men sent to Sa'id by Machmued. Next to him lay the rumpled body of the vessel's only crewmember and skipper. His throat had been cut so deeply that only the vertebrae of the neck held the head, at grotesque angle, to the nearly decapitated corpse. Fresh dark red blood ran from the wound, soaking the victim's clothing and meandered under the assassin team's shoes. They walked in it, smearing it in distorted patterns on the gray asphalt tile flooring as it rambled across the deck to coagulate in a sloppy pool along the seam of the floor and the bulkhead.

Sa'id aimed his first instructions at his subordinate who manned the wheel of the bouncing vessel. He spoke in Arabic.

"You," he said, pointing to the terrorist at the helm, "will remain with the boat. Stay here until we return or until Salal himself arrives. Let no one else on board. There can be no delay in our departure when we return. Study the charts, here." He traced a course over the chart to a point thirty miles distant, south on the Intercoastal waterway.

"If there is any trouble, do what you must, but do not permit the boat to be taken. If you are forced to depart tell Salal we shall meet you here," Sa'id said pointing to a spot on the chart some three miles to the south.

"Do you understand?" he questioned.

A nod of agreement conveyed that the instructions had been understood. The twenty-eight year old Arab seaman would die before either he or the boat would return to the hands of the Americans. He would do what was required.

"Up there," Sa'id said, engaging the two men who were working the gruesome dead body into a length of heavy chain for later disposal, "is a white columned, large red brick house which overlooks the river from a small bluff." Sa'id tossed his head in the direction of an unseen gray shape looming off in the rain some five hundred or so yards distant.

"In it lives an American army colonel. He is to be eliminated. There is a woman there now. She entered much earlier today and has remained since. The colonel left early this morning before she arrived. He returned earlier and is in the house now."

"Is there anyone else in the house?" asked the taller of the two men who faced Sa'id.

"No, I think not, but it makes no difference," Sa'id said impatiently. "If there are others, they must also die with the man and the woman."

Sa'id continued in a most serious, businesslike manner. "We will kill the American Colonel first I think, and then, if there is time, enjoy his woman." He added as an afterthought, "But both must die."

Sa'id's eyes shone. His companions knew of his reputation. Even among the *fedayeen* he was known as a dangerous man, one who relished killing too much. Inflicting pain was something Sa'id enjoyed, extending it, becoming more excited by it. Sa'id, it was said among the *fedayeen*, was an evil but necessary man—one who was to be obeyed from fear not from admiration.

"We will wait here for thirty minutes until our comrades are closer to their destination. Throw this one over the side, the smell of his blood is offensive," Sa'id directed, kicking at the body with the toe of his boot. He looked at his watch. Casually he pulled the stiletto knife with which he had dispatched the Dancer from the waistband of his trousers. The knife was his toy, his mistress, and a sexual thing. To Sa'id, it had an unholy, evil life of its own. The balanced black handle of the knife rolled back and forth, slowly, sensually, across Sa'id's fingers. The knife's blade massaged the palm of his hand, an unconscious habit, which seemed to simultaneously draw together his brooding thoughts and excite him.

"I wonder if American women are as brave as Arab women, if they die well. I have never killed an American woman before," he said absently to his reflection in the window of the wheelhouse. "It will be ... different."

Staring out through the rain at the darkness and wind, present but somehow absent, remote from his companions, he glanced at his watch. Sa'id's fingers played with the heavy handled, well-balanced knife while two of his companions struggled the weighted body through the narrow cabin door. A blast of wind and rain flooded the cabin as they left, diminishing but not removing the copper smell of blood from the tiny warm area. In just a matter of seconds they returned, relieved of their burden. The shorter of the two men who would accompany Sa'id thought of the body now laying on the bottom of the river, of the crabs that would feed on it. A sudden chill trembled his body.

Sa'id consulted his watch. It was almost eight o'clock. He grunted and slipped the knife back into the sheath at the waistband of his trousers.

"It is time," he said. "Come."

The rain and wind fled from the cabin after them, leaving but a sole terrorist as the only occupant and guardian of the pilot boat. Three men, Sa'id leading, trod swiftly back up the darkened pier and disappeared into the night, the wind and the rain marching with them up the knoll toward the Garrison House, to the point of their destinies which had been determined by Allah even before their births.

22
Assault at Garrison House

What now, she thought. Who in their right mind would be
paying a call in this weather? Tromping around out there was
as dumb as, as, well as going out to fetch dinner, she admitted, noting the irony of it with a smile.

"Matt, get up, darling. Get moving. There's someone at
the door. I'll get it."

He swam back up to the fringes of awareness from the
semi-rest, semi-sleep, not registering the meaning of Megan's
words, but hearing the sounds. With reluctance, he pulled
himself into to a sitting position on the edge of the bed,
reached to the end of it and pulled a pair of cord trousers over
his naked form. He stood listening to her retreating footsteps
down the stairs, stretched and had started for the adjoining
bathroom when he heard her scream.

Megan had seen only Sa'id at the front door. She had
found and flipped on the front lights to the house and just
pulled open the heavy oak door, an anticipatory smile set to
her lips and the three had burst in. Sa'id grabbed at her, but
in reflex she had jerked back, into one of the other two who
had rushed past her. She was thrown off balance and
screamed. That was when Sa'id had hit her. The blow struck
her over the left ear sending stars shooting. She heard herself
scream a second time as she bounced off one of the overstuffed living room chairs and crashed, stunned, into the wall
and slid to the floor.

The intonation of the stifled, muffled but audible Arabic
halted Matt in mid stride, two steps down the flight of
stairs. Heavy booted feet smashed open doors and began to
search through the first floor. Matt knew they would be up
the steps to the second floor in just a matter of seconds.

The noise and voices on the first floor told him that there were at least two, possibly three of them. Retreating to the bedroom, he searched for the blue rucksack, cursing Megan for her neatness.

"Shit!" he whispered.

Finding the backpack at the bottom of the closet, he plunged his fist inside. His fingers closed about the grips of the Colt .357 Python, yanking it from the bag. Damn, he thought as he fought the pistol to free it from the pouch.

Matt knew that he was out of time. Rapid steps had already raced up the stairs. He sensed rather than heard the Arab hit the landing at the eighth step and make the ninety-degree turn to carry him up the remaining nine steps.

The damn hammer of the gun had somehow tangled and become hung up in a few loose threads along the edge of the bag's zipper. He stared with intensity at the half closed bedroom door, willing it not to move as he struggled with the bag.

The bedroom door slammed open into the wall.

From that point Matt could remember only a series of reactions—a strobe lighted progression of images, frozen in the flash of muzzle blasts from the door and the revolver in his own hand. The half shut door bursting open. The wide stance of the man in the doorway with the AK-47 leveled at the room. The surprised, unexpected look in the gunman's eyes as the Arab's brain recorded and reacted to the image that had been sent by the optic nerve. The slight squint about the corner of the Arab's eyes as he squeezed the trigger, how the muzzle of the rifle had arced in a tiny, jolting movement from left to right and how the floor six inches to Matt's left exploded in splinters. The flash of light as the bulb in the lamp exploded and the lamp cartwheeled to the floor plunging the room into darkness.

A searing heat shot through the fleshy part of Matt's left thigh as one of the copper-jacketed rounds found its mark. The shock slammed him back and spun him to his right, loosening his grip, nearly knocking the heavy magnum from his fingers as yet another round glanced off a rib and gouged a deep channel across his left side, leaving a meaty, copiously bleeding, but superficial wound.

The .357 in his hand came up of its own will. Matt could not remember clearing it of the bag nor thumbing back the hammer. Falling, twisting, driven backward from the impact of the two 7.62mm slugs that found him, Matt's shot was much more instinctual than deliberate, more reaction than aimed. But the fates smiled. His time to die would have to wait.

The sharp, deep bark of the magnum's report gave notice that the 158 grain jacketed hollow point was on its way. The gunman never heard the sound. The last thing he saw was Matt being hit and twisting from the impact of his bullets.

The slug took the Arab below the chin at just under 1,600 feet per second and traveled on an upward course. As the bullet ripped through flesh and muscle, it made the Arab's entire face balloon grotesquely. The soft-nosed bullet expanded and ripped its way through the Arab's lower jaw, tumbling into the base of his skull, and severing the spinal cord as it exited. The now misshapen chunk of lead, wrapped in its torn copper sheath, sprayed the hall wall into which it buried itself with chunks of skull bone and fragments of brain, blood, and muscle tissue.

Matt reacted before the shock of his wounds could set in and slow the engine of his mind and body.

They had Megan.

The cold logic of his training and combat experience kicked in and told him there was little he realistically could do about it right now. If she were not already dead, she would be soon.

A fury surged up inside him. Emotion and adrenaline numbed his wounds. His mind was clear and focused. Matt willed his next actions just as he had willed the door not to open until the Python was free of the bag. Staggering to his feet, he felt the shriek of pain through the torn muscles of his left thigh, but the leg supported his weight.

"Good," he thought aloud, taking inventory of his condition, "nothing broken." Both wounds looked much worse than they were. There was a warm stickiness running down his left side and gingerly he felt at the torn flesh over the ribs. "Ribs bruised, losing blood," he said, softly repeating the message relayed from his fingers to his brain. The wound was gory, ugly, but not fatal or debilitating. Pain blossomed again, making him gasp, making him dizzy, nauseous and unbalanced. If he didn't focus and control his body, he knew he would go into shock. Without conscious awareness, almost by instinct, he reacted.

Use the pain, make it work for you, he thought silently. Matt grabbed at the towel that Megan had earlier discarded to the floor and pressed it into the bloody, painful wound in his side.

"Got to move," he said to no one. There were others, he knew. They would be on their way to finish him off.

For some inexplicable reason, Matt flashed back to the one other time he had been hit and how he had then reacted. The wound had come during Desert Storm. The learned reaction of experience took over and sent the necessary messages, prompting him to action.

"Do the unexpected," his mind told him. "Don't wait for them. Go after them."

His body checked into the network, completing its damage assessment program. The overloaded circuitry to his brain telling him that he had been hurt began to clear. The various life giving systems reported into the human computer, networking to convey the electrical impulse message that they were still, though perhaps only temporarily, in the green. His body could still function and he was still in control.

Less than ten seconds had ticked by but already he had waited too long. Painfully he swayed across the room toward the door and the corpse in the hallway. There was a thud at the top of the steps. Matt spun to the near wall and rolled into the protection of the master bathroom that paralleled the center hallway into which the grenade had been thrown.

The explosion in the confined space overwhelmed him in its loudness and the impact lifted him from his feet and sent him sprawling across the room. The foot thick solid walls and ceiling absorbed the fragmentation and deadened the concussion as the grenade exploded. The immaculate white walls were painted with the blacks and charcoals of explosives and gouged obscenely by the hot razor sharp fragments of steel from the casing of the grenade. The air was sucked from the room and driven from Matt's lungs by the force of the blast, blowing out windows, numbing his hearing, distorting his balance and sending him into a slow moving dream world of distorted realities.

The heavy doors of the other three upstairs rooms were ripped from their hinges and the smell of cordite, smoke and plaster permeated the entire second floor. A blanket of choking dust appeared at once in all of the rooms obscuring vision. Matt reversed his position on the floor, leaving a sweep of blood on the planking. He swung his head and shoulders through the doorway, angling his body to present the smallest possible target. The .357 was anchored against the doorjamb.

The second one came in a rush, screaming as he came, his face contorted as he charged up the last of the steps and slid to a halt, straddling, almost tripping over his dead companion. The AK-47, tucked into his hip in assault position, bucked with recoil as the terrorist sprayed the room with automatic fire.

Matt shot him twice. The second assassin from the *Compass Rose* lurched as the bullets slammed into his body, ripping and gouging their way through heart and brain tissues. He was dead before he hit the floor.

Silence replaced the pandemonium of the earlier seconds. Stillness sprinted throughout the house—a deafening, total, and absolute silence that slowly returned to a sound of ringing in Matt's ears as the only resonant legacy of what had transpired. Seconds ticked by, but time was distorted. The interval could have been ten seconds or ten minutes. There was no way of knowing. The absolute quiet was unnerving and disorienting.

The situation was, at best, a temporary standoff. But the noiselessness was beginning to unravel Sa'id's composure. The remaining Arab had no way of knowing if the second man had finished off the colonel. Both of the *fedayeen* who had climbed the steps were either seriously injured or had died, for neither had answered his calls.

Time was both Sa'id's friend and his enemy. The assassin had a hostage and each minute that passed brought the *Compass Rose* closer to her destination. The colonel could do nothing to help his people, not even warn them, even if he had been aware of the presence of the *Compass Rose*. The American was trapped, alone, wounded or dead, here in his residence. But Sa'id had to get free and the longer he delayed, the poorer his chances of returning to the boat and escape. Sa'id still had time—he could wait for a bit, but the colonel had to die. Salal had made that very clear. The American could not be permitted to sound an alarm.

As long as I have the woman as a hostage he will not get past me, Sa'id reasoned. All Americans, it was known, were sentimental fools, with stupid codes of gallantry. The colonel, he was sure, would not dare to risk her death.

Sa'id held Megan before him, his knife to her throat, pressuring against the skin with its razor edge. For a better grasp, the terrorist shifted the brutal grip of his left arm on her from around her neck to across her breasts, maliciously compressing and twisting the tender flesh of her right breast, bringing tears to her eyes.

"Call your man, filthy cow. Do it now," the killer ordered. Sa'id bore down, squeezing the nipple and mass of tissue in his hand. The point of the blade bit into Megan's throat, neatly puncturing the skin. A tiny trickle of blood escaped down her neck.

A sound—half groan, half squeal—escaped from Megan's throat, against her will. She struggled against the pain in her chest. She had felt far worse pain than this before. If Matt were still alive, she thought, she would not be a party to sacrificing him to this animal.

There was no sound from the stairs. Still only silence—yet Megan knew that he was alive. "He must be, must be," she whispered, the words never passing her lips. If he were there, listening at this very moment, he would have no way of knowing that there was only one of them left. Somehow she had to tell him.

"You coward," she mocked at Sa'id, getting her breath back. "If he were alive do you think he'd let you put your foul hands all over me? The three of you may have killed him but you haven't the courage to even find out. You're not even man enough to go up there to try to finish what your moron lackeys began."

She surprised herself at the control in her voice.

"Let me go. Do you make war on helpless women? Are you as afraid of me as you are of the dead up there?" she said rolling her eyes toward the stairs.

There was a half moment of hesitation. The pressure of the knife lessened but the knife itself was not withdrawn. "I am afraid of no man, whore," Sa'id replied in a hoarse whisper. "Come, we will see if this man is still alive and if he is, if he is man enough to watch you die slowly before his eyes."

Sa'id pushed Megan toward the darkened steps, keeping her fully in front of him, a protective shield between him and the sharp crack he had already heard from the American's weapon. They started in an awkward dance up the steps toward the first landing, Megan taller than her captor, a step in front of him. The knife had been removed from Megan's throat and was now pressed against her spine, at the small of her back, Sa'id's other arm, the left, still clutching at her breast.

Six steps up the first flight, Megan took her chance. Bracing herself against the next higher step, she pretended to stumble forward, and twisted to her left while lunging backward, into her captor. She bent forward at the waist, and reached to grab Sa'id's left arm, ignoring the knife at her back in his right fist. Sa'id, in losing his balance, instinctively shot out his left hand to grab at the railing but Megan had held it firmly in place, throwing her total weight on him.

"Bitch!" he screamed.

He sliced upward, but she had already twisted to the left and the point of the blade sliced along her right side, cutting deep but not stabbing into the vital organs. The knife sliced a twelve-inch gash, perhaps a half an inch to an inch deep, on a diagonal up her right side and bounced off of Megan's ribs as they both tumbled rearward down the steps.

They hit the bottom together, Megan on the top of the slighter man, struggling, grasping at the hand that still clutched the stiletto.

"Bitch! Whore!" screamed Sa'id, in a frenzy, as he shook loose from her reaching grasp. He kicked out at her as she again lunged for the knife and he caught her in the ribs with the heel of his boot. She sagged and rolled onto her stomach, moaning from the pain, the fight gone out of her. Sa'id scrambled to his feet, dominant over her prostrate form. A sob of frustration and despair escaped from her throat and she pounded the carpeted floor weakly with her clenched fist.

"That's right, whore," Sa'id screamed at the crumpled body. "Cry. Just as our women, the women of Palestine cry for their men, and for their children. Just as they begged for mercy before they were used and butchered, now you can beg. I send you to your betrayed and crucified Christian God. Perhaps he will give you mercy."

Sa'id reached out, grabbed her by her hair and yanked rearwards, extending and exposing her throat, his knee in the small of her back. He raised the wicked knife, extending it laterally behind him, then sent its polished, honed edge slicing through the air toward her naked, extended throat.

23
In The Name Of Allah

Salal had found the doctor and then seduced him with promises of an opportunity to amass wealth and perks surpassed only by Kadafy and Hussein. Well known in the nuclear physics community for his brilliance, Doctor Harun l'Alham was the architect of the Libyan nuclear reactor. The Israelis in a single air strike destroyed his creation. For the Jews he bore no love and had a debt to repay.

Harun was a man of the world, an elitist who, by virtue of his superior intellect, thought he was owed the accolades of merit, recognition and wealth. The doctor had no close friends and was also known for his excesses. An admirer of Dr. Josef "Beppo" Mengele, the Auschwitz Angel of Death, he lacked both moral compass and human compassion. He was an ice cube obsessed with his own ego, wealth, and power.

Doctor l'Alham was not born a Palestinian. As an Arab, he was neither a patriot nor even a practicing Muslim. He did not consider himself much of an idealist nor did he care about or subscribe to any Arab or religious cause. But if the price was right he would espouse any purpose; in short, he would do whatever was necessary to continue to improve his life of indulgence. At least for now.

The doctor's education and training caused him to view other living things analytically. With few exceptions, he saw his fellow man as inferior to him, living organisms, surviving, eating, reproducing, dying, void of soul or spark of true intellect, absent of any need or desire other than that required to survive. Harun gloated in the absolute knowledge that he was indispensable to the Arab scientific community.

Harun sat in the rear of the dry but humid ambulance under the rain dripping pine trees, petulantly waiting for the radio message; the message that had brought him all this distance from Libya. For his efforts in Jericho, Harun was to be well paid—more money than he had thought possible was to be his for just a very minimal risk to his personal safety. For this reward, he endured the hardships of two months at the Jericho training base. The effort was to ensure that should all else fail, he would be capable of his own defense.

Harun admired the manner in which Salal had bent Abdul's team to his will, the way he led and inspired all of them. He remembered the astonishment of his comrades when they had learned from him and Salal the true objective of Jericho. He was particularly impressed by the way the author of Jericho had fielded the several questions that had been asked after he announced that Sunny Point was to be only a very necessary, but secondary, diversionary objective.

The past week had been a hectic time. The week, he convinced himself, was full of danger. Certainly there had been more than an exaggerated degree of risk, he liked to believe, in being smuggled into the United States from London under an assumed name. There had been a sense of adventure as he was provided armed escort from the rendezvous in New York until he had arrived to meet Salal at the safe house in Caswell Beach. But now that was past and the real danger was about to begin. Without him and his assistant, Yuusuf, he knew that Jericho would fail. He, Harun l'Alham, was the key to the entire operation. And now it had all led to this moment, this waiting in the cold and the rain, waiting for the signal that would rattle and then destroy the walls of their oppression. The nuclear device sat on the floor of the van, between his feet.

He sighed and wished the rain would stop.

*   *   *

The first battle casualties of the attack on Sunny Point were two guards aboard the terminal's patrol vessel. As the *Compass Rose* swung from the main channel, the patrol craft was moored on the leeward, southernmost end of the North wharf. Jimmy Gore had been the first of the two to notice the altered direction of the ship.

"Say, Bobby Ray, we suppose to be getting any ships in here tonight?"

"Not that I know about," said Bobby Ray, glancing up from a crossword puzzle he had been laboring over in the dry and comfortable forward cabin. "Why?"

"Come on up here 'cause looks like we sure got company comin'. You recognize that big bastard?"

Bobby Ray wiped at the fogged window and peered into the darkness at the closing silhouette of the *Compass Rose*, some two hundred and fifty yards in the distance, illuminated by her running lights and an occasional hatchway or portal light reflecting into the night. The guard snapped on the one and a half million candlepower searchlight mounted on the patrol craft and played it across the hull and superstructure of the approaching ship.

"Ah, I don know, but the profile from what little I can see sorta looks like the Atlantic Express but the Coast Guard don't let no ammo ships up the channel at night— 'specially on nights like this. Let me see if I can raise them on the radio."

"Unknown freighter, unknown freighter, this is Sunny Point Harbor Police. Sir, you are in restricted waters. Please identify yourself and return to the main channel. I say again, please identify yourself and return to the main channel of the river. Over."

No response. Twice again he sent the message. Still no response. The *Compass Rose* maneuvered to come broadside to the center wharf stern to the wind, bow upriver.

"Slip that bow line Jimmy, and we'll crank 'er up, then run on down to see if we can get somebody on the bull horn. Get on the radio back up to security and tell them to get a patrol down to the center wharf. Looks like that dumb bastard wants to try to dock that hummer."

Bobby Ray hit the starter buttons of the patrol vessel and heard the deep throated growl of the twin Cummings marine diesels which were his private pride. They settled to a purr of power as he throttled the boat out from behind the protection of the wharf. Punching on the running lights, Bobby Ray twisted the wheel hard over to starboard and flicked the button activating the flashing blue lights mounted above his head as he jammed the throttles forward, feeling the boat come up on plane, cutting through the low swells. Vaguely he heard Jimmy on the radio behind him as he threw the power to the engines and raced down on the bulk of the cargo vessel now some 150 yards from the embrace of the center wharf.

A 90mm recoilless rifle, one of only two in the assault teams, was positioned at the bow of the *Compass Rose* and manned by two experts in its use. They had waited until the patrol boat was a mere fifty meters off of the starboard side and then fired. Almost at the same moment the military radio mounted above Bobby Ray's head squawked to life.

"Sunny Point Harbor Police. Sunny Point Harbor Police. This is Army Blackhawk 68471." The crackle of radio static was the last thing Bobby Ray and his partner ever heard.

The shaped-charge warhead, designed to pierce the armor plating of a tank, hit and exploded at a downward angle of about forty-five degrees, just at the juncture of the cabin to the hull above the 250-gallon fuel tanks. Molten metal, wiring, and insulation were driven inward and downward, rupturing the tanks. The diesel fuel did not explode but rather began to burn with an uncontrolled white-hot heat, burping blazing splashes onto the water, streaming it over what remained of the deck. The fire licked and dribbled down over the sides of the hull to leave a fiery trail in the erratic wake of the unguided vessel. The hull remained intact and the engines, miraculously untouched by the explosion, continued their powerful growl until, at last, starved of fuel they sputtered to silence. Fanned by the buffeting winds the boat burned and rolled in the downpour of rain, a slow drifting column of fire, a beacon of conflagration, caught in the current of the ebbing tide.

Machmued looked at the luminous hands of his watch.

The second hand ticked around the face of the clock, eroding away the minutes without respite. A furtive face appeared briefly at the door of the bridge, visible for an instant and then a voice.

Machmued stepped out into the night onto a wing of the small bridge. Four grim faced men—strong, fit, serious young warriors—entered the bridge, each armed with automatic rifles, grenades hanging from their belts, all dressed in identical dark camouflage fatigues. Machmued deposited the Walter PP into the flexible nylon holster tucked inside the belt loops at the center of his back.

"Casualties?"

"None of our men."

"Send this message to Salal. 'We have sounded the trumpet.'"

The wind snatched away his words and blew them down across the river and out across the open Atlantic.

Al-Rashid acknowledged his instructions and sped to the radio room. Machmued turned to the remaining three men, the sub-force commanders. "Remember, my brothers, we are *fedayeen*—Freedom fighters," he said to his subordinate commanders. "We carry this holy war to America, here in their homeland so that their children and their wives can feel and be touched as ours have been touched. We may not see our homelands again. If such is the will of Allah, we bow to it. When your children and your grandchildren sit in peace in the new state of Palestine they will sing great songs of your courage."

"Now go. Do as you have been instructed," he said, clasping each one to him and kissing him on both cheeks. "Rachada, you and Haffar, release the assault teams as planned. We will meet again in the next world. Salaam, my brothers. Allah go with you." Pride filled his eyes and determination marked Machmued's clenched jaws.

The final phases of Jericho had begun.

24
Into the Eye of the Storm

There were two reports, deep, barking sounds that deafened and obliterated Megan's sobs. They were separated it seemed by no more than a second although it must have been longer.

Matt's first shot took Sa'id in the right elbow, shattering the joint and breaking both of the bones that bound the forearm to the remainder of the skeletal structure. The impact picked Sa'id up and spun him, off balance, into the camel colored couch positioned against the front wall of the house. The knife skittered from the nerveless, useless fingers of his right hand. Matthew stood on the landing, a specter horrible, a *djinn* smeared with a gory paste of blood, grime, and plaster dust. An unquenchable determination consumed the hurt man behind the gun. Megan's lover grimaced in pain as he leaned against the wall, supporting his weight it seemed on one leg, but the large black eye of the .357 Colt Python in his right fist was unmoving and was centered on a spot between Sa'id's eyes.

Sa'id searched desperately for the 9mm Grach, but it was across the room, too far to reach. In one continuous, fluid motion Sa'id dove forward toward Megan and the knife on the floor, expecting to take Matt by surprise, placing Megan's half risen, dazed form directly in the line of fire. The Arab grasped the knife, blade first, with the fingers of his left hand and rolled to a kneeling position. Sa'id's arm blurred forward in a continuance of the motion, releasing the knife.

Simultaneously with Sa'id's first sign of movement Matt thumbed back the hammer of the double action revolver. The cylinder rotated, locking a fresh hollow-point cartridge between the barrel and the firing pin with a metallic snicker click. The hammer hung delicately, in full cocked position, waiting to be slammed forward into the firing pin and the primer of the cartridge by two pounds of pressure on the trigger.

Matt squeezed.

The revolver boomed and punched back. The barrel bounced up and to the right in a short violent arc of recoil and then rapidly settled back to its initial point of aim.

The two lethal projectiles sped past each other in mid-air. The point of the knife dug into the mortar of the wall two inches to the left of Matt's throat, sprung out and fell with a clamor to the floor. The bullet smacked with a meaty "thwaap" into Sa'id, entering to the right and behind the clavicle. The expanding copper sheathed lead bullet nicked the aorta, rupturing it, and then sped through the soft spongy tissue of the left lung, exiting at and shattering the fourth rib on his left side.

Matt hobbled down the steps to hover over Sa'id, the pistol cocked in his right hand. Sa'id was dazed, his face a mask of uncomprehending shock and pain. The terrorist could not accept that he was a living dead man, but the look in the other man's eyes left no doubt. Sa'id felt fear. A cold hard clenched fist closed around his heart, staggering him.

Could it be that Allah would permit his death at the hands of the American? Could it be meant to be so? No, this was not to be his *kismet*.

And then, suddenly, he knew.

For a moment his eyes cleared and focused. Sa'id was in the end a Muslim, one who submits to the will of Allah. The Arab looked up into the face of his enemy.

"I die in *jihad*, in the holy war, and tonight I will be in heaven. *Enshallah*," he said in tortured whisper. "You have gained nothing and earned for me a warrior's reward. It is my destiny, my *kismet*. *Allah akbar.* God is great and I have won."

"No, Salal, you've lost," Matt offered as a fact.

Sa'id parted his lips in a grotesque, blood-frothing grin. His face was a gruesome deathhead.

"You are so very wrong, *Giaou* shit eater," he snarled

defiantly, using the derisive term while choking on the now massive flow of blood from his mouth.

"You fool. I am not Salal. Salal lives," he said in a final act of defiance. "You are defeated. Allah ordained it from the very beginning."

The jagged edges of the pierced aorta split under the pressure of the welling blood as it was forced out of the blood vessel. Sa'id was losing vital fluid, hemorrhaging to death, choking on his own blood. He sighed with a deep breath, his eyes searching for something as the light faded from them and he died.

Matt lowered the hammer of the pistol. He found Sa'id's discarded 9mm, checked the chamber and placed it within close reach on the floor as he turned to Megan.

"Meg. It's okay now babe, it's okay," Matt said, cradling the bleeding woman in his arms.

"Can you speak? How bad are you hurt?" he asked, applying pressure to edges of her wound, further stanching the diminishing flow of blood. The slash was deep but it had bounced off of the ribs rather than penetrating through them. The wound was painful but not life threatening. She trembled, the terror ebbing, as she fought to bring herself under control. From a vast distance he heard her voice, weak but understandable over the ringing in his head.

"Actually he cut me a good gash when we fell from the steps," she whispered in painful understatement. "It's bleeding rather terribly, isn't it? I'm a bit dizzy, lightheaded, but otherwise, I suspect I'm okay." Surprised at her own composure, she pulled herself to an upright sitting position.

"Matt, who are these people?"

"I'll get us some help. Got to use the phone in the kitchen. The one upstairs is shot to hell," he replied, ignoring her question.

Confusion and disorientation from the events of the past twenty minutes, as well as shock from her wound, began to affect Megan's coherence. She painfully rose and twisted into a sitting position. It caused the seam of her wound to gape

open and shed blood with a heavier flow. The entire right side
of her blouse had turned a deeper, wetter red and was plas-
tered to the side of her body.

"Matthew," she asked with childlike concentration,
"who were they? What did they want? Why did they try to
kill us? What's going on here?" Her voice seemed to come
from a deep hollow well. She heard but did not recognize
her own voice.

Matt dialed the switchboard at Sunny Point and listened to
the unanswered ring. "Islamic terrorists, Meg. Some of the ...
hello, yeah, this is Colonel Gannon. Operator, open a DSN
line to Fort Bragg. This is a flash precedence call," he said,
reciting the military code words that would give his call pri-
ority over all others on the military line.

He gave the operator the number and continued with further instructions. "As soon as you get through, break in and
plug the call into the line I'm on now—even if this line is
busy. I want to talk to Colonel Jack Dalton. Yes, that's right,
Dalton. Now, while you're making that call, switch me over
to the security desk there at the terminal."

The operator made the transfer and started to work on the
Fort Bragg linkup.

"Owens?" Matt demanded into the phone's transmitter.
"Don't talk, just listen. I expect you're going to have a security penetration at any moment if they aren't already there.
This isn't a drill, repeat this is not a drill, and you are to consider any incident as a hostile intent. No, no. Just listen to me.
I don't know how many men or where or what they'll be after
but they will be armed and dangerous. Get the reaction force
down to the docks. This is not a drill. These people are as real
as they can get. Got that?"

There was a pause. Exasperation and impatience showed
on Matt's face.

"Good, good, Mr. Owens. No, no Owens. Damn it, just
listen to me. Get one of our EMT medic teams out of the fire
department and dispatch them down here to Garrison House
right away. I'm shot up a bit. I've got a lady here and she's

hurt too. A knife wound to the ribs. There are three dead terrorists inside and I don't know who, if anyone, may be outside. Get the local cops over here but for Christ sake, tell them that the inside of the house is secure. I don't want them to pick up where these three just left off. Got it? Tell the medics to use the back door, on the side of the house away from the water. I'll meet them there—where the sedan is parked. Yes, that's right, at the back. Get the reaction force together and break out the M-16's and vests. Alert our duty patrol boat, and the Coast Guard but get the roving patrols geared up first. Get the..."

The operator broke in.

"Sir, I have your Fort Bragg number," she said and plugged the call into the open line.

"Thanks. Owens, drop off and get going on your alert notifications. I'll get back to you in a minute."

"Sir, this is Major Tenneth, the Staff Duty Officer."

"Tenneth, this is Colonel Gannon, down at Sunny Point. I need to talk with Colonel Dalton ASAP," Matt said recognizing the voice of Keith Tenneth, the number two man in the operations section of Jack's command.

"Sir, I'm sorry but Colonel Dalton is out on a live fire exercise here on the South base range. One of the companies is out for inclement weather insertions and battle drill. The colonel took off from here in a Blackhawk C-and-C ship about twenty minutes ago. Can anyone else help you?"

"Do you have radio contact with him?"

"Yes, sir, but I can't patch you through."

"Does he have a cell phone?"

"Yes sir, I believe he has his personal phone with him. Do you have the number?"

"Yes. I'll keep trying to get him from here. If you get him, tell him it's urgent! We need to execute Gambit. I say again execute Gambit ASAP."

"Roger. Understand execute Gambit. Is that correct?"

"Affirmative. Our friends are here earlier than we expected and I need him like yesterday. Haven't got a feel for numbers or targets yet but if he gets on the Sunny Point operations frequency we'll feed him all the info as we get it. Tell him to get his ass over here and not to spare the horses. Got it?"

"Ah, Roger, sir. Hold one please, let me see if I can get him."

Tenneth put him on hold and was gone.

The operator broke in. "Sir, I have Mr. Owens on the line. He says it's urgent. Shall I patch him in?

"Yes, go on, but don't break the connection with Bragg."

"Yes, sir. Here he is." A wave of nausea swept over Matt and his sight began to spiral into a tightly focused tunnel as his peripheral range of vision fled for a moment.

"Go ahead, Owens."

"Colonel, the patrol boat says they have a freighter coming into the restricted area and ... wait just a minute, Colonel. Got them on the radio right now."

"Shit!" Matt exclaimed.

"Owens again, Colonel. They've gone out to investigate."

Tenneth came back on the line.

"Sir, I have Colonel Dalton. He's airborne and diverting to your location. The colonel's flipping over to your terminal security radio frequency, not the ops frequency. Looks like we got lucky. Two platoons in the air. We've got the alert company loading now. The full force will be airborne in ten minutes. Colonel Dalton estimates thirty minutes until the first elements reach your location. He wants to know if you have any other information for him."

"Yes, tell him we've got an unidentified freighter entering Sunny Point's restricted waters. Tell him to contact my patrol boat on the security frequency. He can get a SITREP from the boat first hand. I'm on my way to the terminal and will be up on the security frequency in about two minutes."

"Roger, sir. Out here." The connection to Fort Bragg clicked dead.

"Owens, you still there?" Matt asked.

"Sure am, Colonel. EMT's rolled out with the ambulance about five or six minutes ago. They won't be long. Should be there in just a few minutes. Got the word to the Security Chief, sir, he's on his way and we're getting the reaction team together. Anything else?" he asked.

"Just get the alert drill going and listen to the radio. I'll give you further instructions there. Monitor both the ops and the security channels. Use the reaction team to cordon off the freighter's berth area as much as they can.

"Do not permit the reaction team to be drawn into a committed firefight," Matt instructed. "Tell them to give ground. Harass and snipe."

"Yeah, I ... hang on a minute Colonel, something coming in now." There was a pause and Matt could hear the static crackle of the radio in the background.

"Colonel, sounds like we got a stranger on our security frequency and wait..."

Another pause.

"Colonel, the patrol boat's on fire and all hell's breakin' loose down on the center wharf. What the hell is goin' on?"

"Shit! Okay, get the reaction team down there as soon as you can. I'm on my way, as fast as the ambulance gets here. Tell the reaction force to hold and harass as long as they can and then withdraw to the admin area and set up a perimeter. Hold there."

Matt hung up the phone and turned to Megan who had found her way into the kitchen and onto one of the three stools that lined the breakfast counter.

"Hang on, babe. Medics are on the way and will be here any second."

"I'm fine, Matt, just a bit dizzy and..." Megan slipped from the stool to the floor unconscious.

It was by sheer determination that Matt, too, was not overcome by the dizzy lethargy that threatened to sweep over him in stronger and more frequent waves.

Matt bent down and checked her pulse. Strong, slow and steady. The sigh of her breath was on his cheek and the rise and fall of her chest was regular. Loss of blood and shock had drained her but she was not in immediate grave danger.

Shock, he knew, was the most immediate concern. His bleeding had slowed and now the white-hot, nauseating pain was setting in. With large cushions from the living room couch, he propped up her legs and feet then slid a smaller pillow under her head.

Got to get some clothes on, he thought looking down at his bare feet. He picked up the .357 Python as he passed from the kitchen through the living room and tucked it into the waistband of the blood soaked trousers he had thrown on earlier. Straightening up, he headed for the stairs, stepping around Sa'id's body and over the remains of the two others that clogged the upstairs hallway. The smell of cordite was still strong in the air. As he entered the bedroom, he found himself yawning and realized that he was very tired. Matt knew he had lost a great deal of blood and now the numbness of the two wounds was beginning to wear off and the throbbing pain had begun anew. Gotta get the medics to dope me with some painkiller, he thought.

Pulling open the doors of the bedroom closet, he grabbed at the stack of handkerchiefs stacked within. Laying the handkerchiefs with caution into the wound on his side, he gathered one of the large heavy bath towels from the bathroom and wrapped it tightly over the handkerchiefs and around his chest. Although bulky, it was a comfortable temporary bandage. A second towel, smaller in size but devised in the same manner and secured with a strip of tape took care of the leg, at least for the moment. The gentle pressure of the makeshift bandages felt good against the wounds and the throbbing eased off a bit.

Matt cast a hurried eye about the room, spied a shirt and drew it on, twisting the buttons into place, letting the shirttail hang out. Snatching up the blue nylon bag from the floor, he drew out a dark maroon nylon windbreaker, which he pulled on over the shirt. Reaching once more into the backpack, he pulled out a box of .357 hollowpoints and two charged speedloaders. The cartridges, nestled in a protective Styrofoam packing within the cardboard box, he shook into the deep pockets of the windbreaker. Slipping his naked feet into a pair of rubber soled, leather boat shoes, Matt snatched up the pillows from the bed and a blanket from the nearest open box of shipped bed linens and started back down the hallway. The steps were the worst part.

Painfully he maneuvered down the seventeen steps. A blood soaked patch in his trousers stained a scarlet stripe along the white walls of the hallway against which he leaned for support. He held the blanket and pillows crushed to his chest by the encirclement of his right arm, his left arm bracing against the wall for support. He moved across the floor, able to put more weight on the wounded leg, dragging it a bit behind him.

Matt bent over Megan's still form. He listened to her rhythmic breathing, and noted with satisfaction that the flow of blood from the wound in her side had ceased. The rise and fall of her chest was still strong and without interruption. He wrapped and tucked the blanket around her body, piling the pillows in a bunker around her. For the moment, it was as much as he could do. Matt rose from beside her and withdrew the pistol from his waistband, kicked open the cylinder and pumped out the empty casings. From the supply of cartridges in the pocket of his jacket, he reconstituted each of the five fired chambers as he walked to the kitchen door. There had been a kaleidoscope of events compressed into less than an hour since the doorbell had rung.

The wind had diminished and the rain had slackened and all but died. The precipitation now fell in a silent mist. Somewhere off to the East and thirty miles at sea, "Kate" shook her sea foamed locks and rested before renewing and redoubling her rage. With malicious intent and increasing speed, the hurricane changed her direction and began to double back to the mainland, to aim the greatest of her unspent fury at the Cape Fear River and Sunny Point.

Matt could hear the wail of the ambulance siren as soon as he opened the back door of Garrison House. He crossed to the military sedan, noting with satisfaction flashing blue lights that announced the arrival of one of two local police patrol cars.

As before, it was from silence to sudden mass confusion. The two cops, weapons drawn, passed a wave acknowledging Matt's presence and warily began to search the immediate grounds of the house. Then the two medics were upon him, interrupting, as he snapped on the ignition and stabbed for the key button on the side of the microphone.

"I'm okay," Matt said, forgetting about the pain and reconsidering the decision to take a painkiller. "Just tape me up here. Quick. There's a woman in the house, knife wound to the right side. She's lost a lot of blood and is pretty shocky. Take care of her first and try to be gentle, for Christ's sake. There are also three bodies, two upstairs and one in the living room. They're beyond any help you can give."

A thick salve of antibiotic cream and a heavy gauze pressure bandage were applied about his chest, covering the wound to his left side, and another to his thigh. The engine of the sedan roared to life as Matt threw the car into gear and maneuvered it from its parking place onto the main street of Southport. Pressing the transmit button on the mike, he hoped that Jack Dalton would be in range to pick up the transmission.

"Anchor Six, Anchor Six, this is Carnival 6, Carnival 6, over."

The radio net erupted in sound as each of the guard patrols at the terminal recognized Carnival Six as the call sign of the terminal commander. For the moment they abandoned radio discipline, interrupting and cutting each other out in their effort to relay information but adding to the confusion of the moment.

Jack's voice filled the receiver's speaker. "Carnival Six, this is Anchor Six, go to alternate."

"Roger," Matt replied. "Carnival Six to alternate. Out."

The alternative frequency was one on which Jack and Matt had agreed during the Fort Bragg briefings. The frequency was secure from the point of view that it was known only to the two of them and so lessened monitorship or interruption from anyone else—friend or otherwise.

"Carnival Six, Anchor Six." Jack was on the alternate frequency.

"We're on the way, Carnival Six. Have a good situation report from the clandestine teams from the platoon we had spotted out at the terminal. Bastards used the storm as cover. Came in by ship. Traffic on the other net. Wait out."

There was silence for perhaps a minute as Matt maneuvered through a flooded and washed out portion of the roadway and made it to the intersection of the highway that ran past the entrance of Sunny Point. The receiver crackled back to life.

"Carnival Six, Anchor Six."

"Go, Anchor Six," Matt declared into the mike.

"Got some info on the ship, Matt. Vessel's name is the *Compass Rose*. Ring any bells for you? Your folks have just relayed that she is now clear of the center wharf and headed back downstream. We've made contact with your guard force. Your guards indicated that they saw many men, I say again, they saw many men, discharge and disperse across the wharf and move inland. Some are on motor bikes."

There was a pause in the transmission. Both men knew without saying that they were facing the worst-case scenario. The terrorists had gained access to the operational areas of the terminal and had done so without loss.

The radio crackled.

"Looks like more than just a simple hit and run," Jack said, confirming the worst that both had avoided verbalizing. "They mean to stay and do us some big time damage. Over."

There was another meaningful pause in the conversation.

"Coast Guard will be at the mouth of the river in one five minutes to handle the ship," Jack relayed.

"Roger, Anchor Six. No bells on the ship, but we'll sort it out later. Let's keep the civilians out of the line of fire. How long before your elements arrive? Over."

"First of my ground elements at your location estimated in

one zero to one five minutes. Additional two increments loading at present time. Do you need assistance at Garrison House? Over."

"Negative on assistance there. I'm enroute to the terminal now. Three KIA, no POW's at Garrison House. Salal not among the ones down but I have confirmation he is in the area, Anchor."

Matt glanced up at the sky. "Weather seems to be easing up a bit right now. Don't know how long it will be before it closes in again. Am clear to terminal security frequency. Over."

"Roger, your switch and weather report. Think it's just the lull before the main storm hits. We expect it will be touch and go to get our choppers in there, Carnival, but we'll do what we can. Good luck. Out," Jack acknowledged and the radio went silent.

The sedan cleared the flooded area and began to rocket down the road toward the Sunny Point terminal. Matt switched back to the terminal security net. Suddenly there was a rumbling wave of sound that came from the direction of the river's edge. A fireball leaped into the air illuminating a mushroom of smoke, announcing an explosion of some intensity. But it was not in proximity of Sunny Point's explosive storage areas. The explosion seemed to come from the river itself—more downstream from Sunny Point than any of the several ammunition pads surrounding the wharves.

"Carnival base, Carnival Six. Over."

"Go ahead, Colonel."

"Large explosion on the river. Looks as if it came from vicinity of South end of the terminal, down around the SEL&P compound. Have you got anyone down there that can tell us something? Over."

"Carnival Six, this is Patrol Three. I'm about five hundred yards inside the South Gate back off on the side of the road. That explosion was the freighter, the one that just left the terminal. The God damned thing just blew up—right in the main channel across from the power station. Damnedest thing you ever saw. She's settling fast, stern first. Looks like she's got the main channel blocked up tight. Wait a minute. I've got movement up the road. There's a group of men on the road, running toward the South Gate. I can't..."

A series of small explosions came over the radio mixed with the crack of small arms fire.

"Jesus H. Christ!"

There was what sounded like two reports from a small caliber weapon close by the open mike and then the radio transmission went dead.

"Patrol Three, Carnival Six." Matt paused, waiting, hoping for a response.

"Patrol Three, Carnival Six, over." Silence.

Matt pressed the gas pedal to the floor and raced past the main entrance of the nuclear power facility toward the terminal. The needle of the speedometer was pegged at the 80 mph mark on the face of the dial. Two more miles to the terminal's access road.

An orange striped, white ambulance, red lights blazing hurtled into Matt's vision, lighting the night, charging down the vacant highway, at and then past him. The vehicle screamed by, a flashing specter of light and wailing siren hellbent for somewhere. Matt shot a glance into the rear view mirror and noticed the brake lights of the retreating vehicle flash as it slowed at the entrance of the power plant and slid through the turn and into its entryway. Less than a mile to the terminal entrance road now. Matt leaned forward expectantly, somehow uneasy, somehow knowing that something didn't fit, but too preoccupied with the chatter of information coming over the radio to focus on whatever it was. Matt braked for the turn onto the terminal access road and then drove the pedal to the floor once again. The small six-cylinder engine screamed in protest but the car responded nonetheless.

Matt slew into the turn for the terminal's entrance. Less than a half-mile to the gate.

The ambulance didn't make sense and then in an intuitive instant, it did. The scheme came to him then, a blazing split second of infused knowledge. This was all wrong. The scenario was all too coincidental, too pat.

Matt stood on the brakes, locking the wheels and skidding the sedan along the wet blacktop, on the edge of losing control. At last the design of traction cut into the pattern of tire treads grabbed and the friction of the road brought the speed tumbling down. The car rocked to a stop, idling laboriously, like a spent horse.

The ambulance—it was the Goddamn ambulance. Matt sat there, stunned, his mind working, absorbing and analyzing. In cold logic he reasoned it through. First, there was nowhere to the north in reasonable proximity for the ambulance to come from. Boiling Springs, the closest town to the north, had no rescue service. Any emergency response would have been to Sunny Point, not the power plant. Any local emergency team could not have made a mistake on the location of the access road, mistaking one for the other. Medic support to the terminal or to the SEL&P reactor compound would have to come from either Southport or from the terminal itself. Still the ambulance had appeared on the scene just moments after the explosion. And then there was the report of men moving south across the terminal and the lost contact with Patrol Three. The glow of the burning superstructure of the *Compass Rose* appeared over the pine-spattered horizon just opposite the nuclear facility along the river.

What if the blast of the *Compass Rose*'s destruction had been both a signal and a diversion? Yes, that made sense. There had just been enough time between the blast and the appearance of the ambulance.

That was it. The attention of the security people at the nuclear power station was diverted and concentrated on the Sunny Point boundary to the North and to the riverside approaches on the East. There was a damn good chance that they would fall for the ruse. As they watched the action and the fireworks that appeared to the North and the East, the terrorists would put a sabotage team in through the main gate. Yes, that was it! The ambulance was their way to the reactor building. But why? At best any damage there would be of nuisance value. What large-scale damage could so few do? They could never gain access to the control room. The door was code locked and impenetrable without a large quantity of high explosives.

Matt couldn't reason to an answer, but the logic of it all was too appealing, too clear to reject. Salal was using a lure. Sunny Point had to be just bait, a diversion. Yes, it had to be, must be.

Time and events were moving too fast.

He had to decide. The terminal was his first responsibility. But, he argued to himself, they were already alerted and help was on the way. The power plant was, for all intents and purposes, open, unsuspecting, and ripe. If he were wrong, if Sunny Point were the objective ... it could be a wild goose chase. Could he dare to be wrong? More than just lives hung in the balance. Matt committed himself and snatched up the mike from the seat.

"Clear the net, clear the net," he heard his excited voice spill across the several conflicting voices which had been crashing across the speaker.

"Anchor Six, Anchor Six. The power plant, Jack. They're going after the fucking nuclear power plant, too. I'm going to divert. Put your force down on the south side of the terminal, I say again put them down between Sunny Point and the power plant. Acknowledge, Anchor Six, acknowledge."

The tires again protested against pavement, squealing and fishtailing the sedan to traction as Matt chased the bright tunnels that his headlights bore into the wet and foggy night, back the way he had just come.

25
Sunny Point
on the Cape Fear River

Machmued was the last man of the strike force to leave the *Compass Rose*. A skeleton crew of three, the captain and the pilot remained on board. The captain and crew would abandon the ship as soon as its final positioning was assured. The pilot would die with the ship. The sirens of the installation had come to life announcing their intruding presence while the ship was still ten feet out into the stream, unberthed. The moment was tense and this was their most vulnerable time, but they docked without further incident. The strike force debarked unchallenged and intact. The twenty security, assault and demolitions teams of four and five men disappeared into the darkness to do their work, burdened with rucksacks of explosives, ammunition and weaponry. The one hundred man covering force spread out in a fan before them.

The current tugged the *Compass Rose* back into the stream but it was after she cleared the wharf that the churn of dark water announced that power had been applied to her twin screws to aid her flight from the berth she had occupied. The maelstrom of gale had not swallowed the bulk of the ship as she departed. Rather, the wind had subsided and the rain abated, falling more softly as if in a reverent benediction for these, her last few minutes of existence. Machmued knew she was a dead ship, her fate already decided by the radio detonator that he held in his hand. The rounded stern of the *Compass Rose* slipped through the waters to the main channel and began her turn downstream, her bulk receding into the blackness of the night.

The running lights of red and green were visible through the gloom as the current took her and she began to turn. The port light blinked out, masked by the ship's bulk as she came about and lined up on the channel and range markers.

Machmued judged the ship, its shape now indiscernible, blurred into the surrounding darkness of the night, to be one-half of a mile above the power plant when he extended the antenna of the transmitter. Salal's friend flipped the power switch to the "ON" position and touched the first of the three buttons on the face of the device. The radio impulse traveled the short distance seeking and finding the matching receiver frequency deep in the bowels of the *Compass Rose*. There was a large flash of flame and a muffled boom as the black sky was lit with red orange flames. The bow of the ship settled in the water, a gaping hole where once starboard and port had joined at the creased edge of the steel plates. As the bow flooded, the *Compass Rose* began to settle, responding slower and slower to the corrections applied to the wheel, becoming unmanageable, impossible to keep on course in the channel. She began an indelicate yaw toward the far shore.

At that moment Machmued touched the button for a second time. This time the flash of light was much stronger but at the stern of the ship. The explosion lifted the entire aft section of the ship, which then disappeared sliding beneath the surface of the water. The boilers of the *Compass Rose* ruptured and exploded almost simultaneous with the detonation, testifying to the rapidity with which the engine compartment had flooded.

The twisted wreckage of ship settled to the forty-foot bottom of the river, angled across the deep channel, contorted steel squealing, hissing and cracking in tortured protest. She came to rest broadside to the sweeping current, her superstructure mocking, deceptive in being half submerged. Fire leapt from the sucking whirlpools and bubbles of fuel oil that broke to the surface to become tiny isolated ponds and then rivulets of fire coasting down the waterway, marking a trail drifting on the current toward the open sea. Machmued grunted with satisfaction and removed his thick, spavined thumb from the button. The main channel was blocked. The business of destruction had begun. The Arab turned and disappeared into the darkness of the terminal where his *kismet* awaited his arrival.

Salal sat in the jump seat of the ambulance that had been backed in among the pines, a short distance from the highway and four miles from the main entrance to the Southern Electric Power and Light, SEP&L, nuclear power station. The interior of the vehicle was hot and crowded, despite the fact that the clamshell rear doors were wide open to the weather and the windows in the cab of the vehicle were cracked far enough to permit the spatter of rain to invade the interior. Salal and Abdul were dressed in the white jackets of medical technicians. The other two men in the rear of the vehicle, Doctor l'Alham and his silent associate, were similar in their dress. In the center of the floor of the vehicle, resting beneath the legs of the nuclear scientist was a large black leather suitcase, its corners reinforced by brass colored flanges.

"The waiting is always the hardest," Salal whispered to the muggy air. He looked at his watch. Machmued was late, but it was not yet a matter of concern.

"Probably a delay caused by this foul weather," Abdul rationalized.

"We'll give him five more minutes and then go for the power plant," Salal responded with impatience. They had come too far to turn back now.

The Jericho commander looked at his watch again.

The dull thud of the first explosion was followed in what seemed like seconds by a louder, heavier report of a second explosion. Salal started. The heads of the three other men jerked up, alert, inquisitive, sensitized to what the splash of light on the horizon and the remaining dull glow meant.

Salal, sweating now despite the autumn wind and cold rain, turned. "So, now it is in our hands. *Enshallah*, as God wills," he said in a calm voice to his companions.

Abdul took one last deep drag from his cigarette, cast it into the rain and turned the key in the ignition. The engine sputtered to life. He tapped the gearshift marker to the Drive position and applied power. The ambulance moved over the sandy soil to the black hardtopped road, scraping its roof on the low hanging branches of the sheltering pines. As Abdul turned onto the highway, he levered the gas pedal to the floor and reached overhead to snap on the rotating emergency flashers.

The roadway and the cab were bathed in their pulsing reflections as he hurtled the vehicle down the road past the entrance to the ammunition terminal toward the power station. The rain increased in tempo and the gray drizzle again became splatters of sound against the roof and windshield. The headlights of a single oncoming vehicle racing toward the terminal stabbed at him, temporarily blinding him, just moments before he began to apply the brakes, allowing him to negotiate the sweeping entry to the access road.

Salal withdrew the twin to Machmued's 9mm automatic from the waistband of his trousers. Punching at the magazine release button, he felt the clip slide downward and out of the base of the pistol's grips. Checking the full magazine, he guided the clip back into its place, noting the click as it locked into position in the handle. Salal's hands were sweating. The brass of a chambered cartridge was displayed as he drew back the slide of the weapon a quarter of an inch. The Jericho commander lowered the weapon, semi-concealed between his legs; they were slowing for the gate. The team of bombers could taste the tension inside the van, tension that had built to an unbearable pitch.

Abdul braked to a halt and rolled down the driver's window.

The guard, bundled in a yellow poncho, peered out from the guard shack. Bending against the wind he emerged to stand next to the small structure, beneath its overhang, out of the resumed sweep of rain. A heavy metal flashlight swung from his left hand. Abdul lowered the window. The closed circuit surveillance camera ceased for a moment in its 180 degree sweep of the area, hesitated, recording on video tape the image of the visitor, and then ceased its silent patrol remaining fixed on the ambulance.

"What the hell you guys blow up down there?" Abdul asked with serious innocence.

"Isn't us," replied the guard over the gathering winds. "It's the ammo terminal over there. Got a call just a few minutes ago that they got a ship afire down there." He motioned toward the river.

"Yeah, that's why we're here. Can't get to it from the terminal side. Current caught the ship and has carried it and the casualties down past your place. They told us they spotted two badly burned guys on the bank right next to your inlet channel. We gotta' get down there to them," Abdul said, lying with conviction. "Open up."

"Can't do that without authority. Just wait a minute," the guard replied, disappearing back into the guard shack.

"Pig!" Abdul swore under his breath.

Salal looked around just in time to see the blue Tahoe, with the intelligence team, his covering force, rolling into the parking lot thirty feet away. He opened the door and dashed in front of the ambulance for the shelter of the overhang of the guard's shack that was located on the other side of the alarmed cyclone fence.

"Hey, guard, hey, guard," Salal hollered over the wind. "Let me talk to your supervisor; you're wasting time and people are in pain. Let's not play your bullshit games, man. Come on."

There was hesitancy in the guard's face, then indifferent decision. The guard placed the telephone receiver on the table within the shack, shrugged agreement, and moved outside to unlock the personnel access gate. The guard permitted Salal to enter the sally port pausing to relock the gate behind him as both he and Salal ran for the shelter and warmth of the guard shack.

Opening the door of the shack, the guard motioned Salal inside before him. Salal, sober and angry faced, strode past him and waited for the guard to enter the building and close the door.

Salal held the silenced 9mm Walther PP in his right hand. The two and one-half inch baffled silencer extension affected the balance of the weapon, but its principal effect was on the muzzle velocity of the 95-grain weight lead, parabellum bullet. But at the shooting distance of eleven feet it made little difference. The unsuspecting man had just begun to speak when Salal turned and fired once. A stuttered cough came from the silenced Walther. There was a gentle backward tug of recoil as the bullet sped at slightly under nine hundred and fifty-five feet per second toward its target. The guard, who had his profile to the door, had just turned his head toward the doorway when the bullet struck. The impact of the projectile splintered his skull, driving fragments of bone inward to become lethal missiles in their own gory right.

The guard pitched back and then forward to thud, head first, into the narrow console before the bank of radios and telephones. The electrical discharge of the man's brain stopped. A spreading stain in the crouch of his trousers accompanied the tremoring convulsions and then twitches of his extremities. Together they signaled the total relaxation of all muscle groups. The guard, a young man and the father of three, crumpled to the floor, blood from the wound above his eye coloring the yellow slicker, running down the sleeve and shoulder of the raincoat. The man was dead.

Salal picked up the phone.

"Hey, yeah. Disregard. These guys with the ambulance are pulling out and going back to the terminal. They just got word on the radio. Sorry to bother you."

He hung up. Perhaps it would buy them a moment or two more. Salal searched around to see the TV camera motionless, still pointed at the main gate. They would have to move swiftly now. In moments the controls in the guard shack would be overridden and the gates would be inoperable. Searching he found and depressed the button to open the first gate of the sally port.

Nothing happened. He punched it again. The gate began

to ease back and the tire shredding spikes retreated into their retracted position under the roadway.

Abdul gunned the ambulance forward into the cordoned space between the two independent locking gates and Salal punched the control button once again to close the first gate. The remainder of Abdul's security team stumbled from the Tahoe and raced across the open space and into the quarantined zone just as the gate slammed shut. Salal punched the control button for the inner gate and just at that moment the security sirens went off.

The TV camera locked on the area between the two gates. Salal knew that the central security control room would be overriding the guard post controls and electrifying the entire perimeter fence.

A gate identical in design to the one that they had just breached blocked the team's movement forward. The first gate had to be in the locked position before the second gate could be activated. Time was running out. They had to get through that second gate.

"Shoot out the camera," Salal ordered.

An immediate burst of automatic weapons fire replied to his orders and the camera flew in chunks from its pedestal. The siren's wail added to the din, making it difficult to hear, let alone relay orders. The siren was located somewhere in the darkness, unseen, half way up the seven stories of the closest of the two reactor buildings, only sixty yards away.

Salal punched the button for the second innermost gate again. The steel frame began to ease back from the heavy steel locks, almost to the width of the ambulance. The gate slowed and then shuddered as the electric motor whined down and clicked to a stop. The central guardroom had overridden Salal's controls.

"Abdul. Satchels. Quickly," he ordered.

Salal pointed at the motor, some thirty feet away and on the opposite side of the fence. There were two soft pops as the firing pins of the explosive satchel charges struck the primer fusings. The canvas bags sailed toward the motor just as the gate began to move to the closed position. One struck the electrified fence and detonated, spraying the motor with hot shrapnel. Two sailed over the fence in a high short arc, landing next to and under the motor, erupting in a barrage of noise and shrapnel. The gate shook and the cyclone fencing sung as the metal splinters zinged across its meshed wire.

The snap of a bullet whistled by Salal's ear, thudding into the building to his left. The bullet came from the direction of the watch office and not a constituted reaction force. Adrenaline pumped into his blood stream. The timing was beginning to unravel, a flicker of doubt smashed through a closed door in his mind.

"No!" I will not let it come apart," he said in a whisper. This would work, even if it cost all of their lives.

Abdul slammed the ambulance forward jamming it in protest into the gap. The gates bent and with a groan sprung from their concrete track, useless but still a barrier. The glistening white body of the ambulance was crumpled, gouged and torn as the vehicle struggled to break itself free of the heavy steel reinforced gate and force itself through the hole in the electrified fence. With a final lurch they were through.

Salal and the remainder of the covering force followed the ambulance through the inner security fencing, firing in disciplined assault as they fanned out inside the brightly-lit interior zone, taking up whatever covered positions they could find, dashing forward in bounds under the protective fire of their comrades.

A muzzle flash blinking from beyond the second gate identified one of the positions now being taken up by an increasing number of guards as they arrived on the scene. The new threats were taken under fire by Salal's team. There was a muffled cry and firing from the position ceased.

Abdul drove the battered ambulance across the fifty yards of open space. Salal and two others ran beside the conveyance protected by the shadows of the reactor building and vehicle's bulk. Abdul stationed it adjacent to the single steel access door set in the side of the reactor building and switched off the ignition. Salal and his two companions established a base of covering fire so that the second half of the team could leapfrog forward.

The first of Abdul's three men still at the gate burst from cover, dodging, rolling, ducking and firing as he ran for the cover of the ambulance and reactor building. The terrorist was greeted with an applause of pistol fire as he tracked across the open area. The meaty thwack, thwack, thwack of bullets striking his body tumbled him like a great pile of rags to the ground where he lay motionless, his blood washing across the rain soaked pavement.

A guard began a dash across the same area only to meet the same fate from the two Arab riflemen remaining near the gate.

It was a stalemate, a standoff. Neither of the forces could cross the no man's land. The fifty yards of well lit, rain swept, cleared space was a killing zone.

"Stay there. Keep them pinned down," Salal shouted in Arabic to his two distant riflemen, over the sound of gunfire. He turned to Abdul still in the vehicle. "Abdul, bring the suitcase."

To his two riflemen companions, Salal gave new orders. "Guard the door with your lives. Let no one inside of the building."

The fighter to the left of Salal turned to reply but instead grunted in shock and collapsed, a red stain spreading across his abdomen and chest. There was one man left to guard the door.

With a scurrying of footfall, Abdul, Doctor l'Alham and his companion jockeyed the suitcase from the ambulance. By half lifting it, half-sliding it across the rough finished concrete, they made it to the protective safety of the doorway.

A renewed firing was heard at the main gate. A heavier, deeper bark marked a larger caliber pistol joining the battle against Salal's men across the way. There was nothing he could do about that now.

Salal gestured Abdul toward the door with his AK-47 rifle

and spoke in Arabic. "Grenades and then automatic fire on my signal."

He waited to a slow count of three.

"Now," he exclaimed, yanking the unlocked, heavy door open.

The soft pop of fuses igniting followed by a trail of firefly sparks marked the grenades' path as they were pitched inside the building. There was the chunk of metal against concrete as they landed and skittered about on the thick concrete deck. Suddenly, there was a calliope of noise and concussion. In a flash of light and flame the multiple explosions of the grenades dwarfed the previous sounds of gunfire and reverberated across the interior of the reactor building. Air sucking concussion waves and steel splinters covered the expanse. Salal and Abdul assaulted through the door, spraying the interior of the building with automatic fire.

The silence that followed was loudest of all. There was no return fire, only the distant patter of running, retreating feet. They were in. The entire action, from front gate to present, had taken less than five minutes. But there was no time to celebrate their success.

Once inside the building, Doctor l'Alham hesitated to permit his eyes to adjust to the brightly lit interior and to orient himself to the room. Now inside the vaulted area, he dismissed the muffled sound of outside small arms fire as well as the scramble of plant employees away from the fringes of the reactor area.

By prearranged agreement, l'Alham now was in charge.

They were in a portico adjacent to the container vessel itself, in reality a story beneath the reactor, next to its base and separated from its core by a twenty-foot-thick wall of ferrous concrete.

"This way," he commanded to the laboring Yuusuf and Abdul who, together, struggled the suitcase forward, protecting it with their bodies.

The four of them, led by Doctor l'Alham, half ran, half stumbled forward into the depths of the building.

Matthew was, at most, five or six minutes behind the ambulance, yet he knew he was too late as he heard the sound of gunfire erupting from the SEL&P compound.

The Sunny Point commander drove to the gate, sliding the sedan to a halt broadside to the locked outer access area, levering the door open even before the vehicle had come to a complete stop. Matt drew fire, from both the guards and the two terrorists who were pinned between him and the guard force.

Crouching behind the sedan, Matt settled the front sight of the Colt Python on the chest of the fighter who was hosing the sedan with automatic fire. The heavy pistol leapt in his hand in recoil. Once. Twice.

The chatter of the AK-47 ended.

The man who had been crouching behind the heavy metal framework which housed the electrical motor for the gates, sat, splay-footed, on the ground, unmoving, his hand still wrapped around the pistol grip of the AK-47 which lay next to him.

Matt moved to the front of the car to get a better firing angle on the remaining *fedayeen* terrorist. Crouched in the shelter of the front wheel well, his legs were hidden from the view of his adversaries by the front tire. There was a momentary lull in firing.

"How many left?" Matt called out. His voice sounded tinny, hollow, and ineffective.

There was no response.

Matt darted up to view the second man. An immediate burst of fire punctured the thin metal bodywork and ricocheted off the heavy engine block.

The guards, now accepting their unidentified ally, redirected a renewed fire at the remaining two figures in the compound, the first at the gate and the second holding the door of the reactor building.

Both of the terrorists knew there was no escape and it was clear they were prepared to buy time with their lives.

Matt bobbed up and snapped off a shot, too quick to be accurate. Scuttling to the rear of the sedan, he stretched out on the cold, wet roadway and peered carefully around the rear end of the car. Matt cradled the .357 in a two handed grip, unable to position the pistol for a clear shot without exposing himself to the retribution of the rifle. With caution he edged forward, exposing his head and firing arm. Matt fired once, his own muzzle blast illuminating his position and then quickly rolled to his left. The ground where he had laid two feet distant was raked with 7.62mm jacketed bullets, ricocheting and puncturing the fuel tank of his sedan in several places. Raw gasoline began to mix on the cement roadway with the falling rain.

This was not a good place to be, he thought. One spark and Matt knew he would be history.

As he crept toward the front of the car, aware of his human frailty, his finiteness, the pain of the wound along his left side and in his left leg kicked in.

There was a flurry of fire. Matt exposed himself just enough to see two guards break from cover, distracting and redirecting the man at the gate's attention, as they darted into the open area, firing as they ran. Zayed popped up long enough from the gate's cover to establish a vicious crossfire with his companion at the reactor building. The two men were chopped down, stagger stepping into death, arms akimbo, falling as drunks to the pavement.

Too late, however, the terrorist recognized his error. His head snapped back in Matt's direction. The AK-47 came to bear and began to tat, tat, tat its spray of bullets toward the rear of the sedan. The Python barked three times, a deep booming echo, dispatching the hollow pointed bullets on their way. Two of them found their mark, neither fatal, but of sufficient shock to drive the man backward, exposing him to the vengeance of fire from the other side. The terrorist went spinning down, tiny spangles of water spitting about his fallen body. The Arab did not move as more bullets from the guards thudded into his carcass.

"Two down, one to go," thought Matt.

Trying to protect the pistol from the rain with the bulk of his body, Matt shook open the revolver's cylinder, shucked out the empty cartridges and replaced them with six fresh ones from the speed loader in his jacket pocket. The luminous hands of his watch stared at him. A full twenty minutes had expired since he had started back toward the power plant and the terrorists had held access to the reactor building for at least ten of them. Muffled explosions came from the direction of Sunny Point. Dull orange glows marked the trail of the raiding party's uninhibited successes at the port. According to Matt's watch, Jack and his troops were still at least five, perhaps ten minutes out.

"Shit!" he exclaimed aloud in angered frustration. He was stymied. And there was nothing more he could do from the position he now occupied. The last of the terrorists was masked from his sight by the angle of the building. The guards would have to root him out alone. All he could do was wait—on this, the wrong side of the fence.

Doctor l'Alham moved with a purpose. Both he and Salal were confident, excited. They had advanced perhaps three hundred feet into the building and next to a small steel access door at the base of the concrete reactor shield. Doctor l'Alham looked up at the labyrinth of piping that covered the walls and overhead, seeking and finding the main cooling lines, which carried through the wall to bathe the nuclear core in cooling water.

"Here," the doctor exclaimed. Salal looked about and spied a large heavy metal table against a far wall. Two folding metal chairs sat beside it. Motioning to Abdul, the two of them slid the table over against the concrete wall and placed the chairs atop the table. Doctor l'Alham and his assistant opened the suitcase and were working on wiring within. Five silent minutes passed, the only sound that of the breathing of the men. Doctor l'Alham turned.

"It is fused," he announced.

Salal and Doctor l'Alham climbed to the top of the table and were handed the suitcase. With great care they stepped up onto the chairs, balancing and straining to keep their heavy burden on a level plane as they stretched, reaching it into a solid platform built by the mantle of pipes over their heads. Salal climbed down from the chair to the table, thence to the floor. Doctor l'Alham reached inside the suitcase and by touch rather than sight, removed the final safety. The clip he removed would activate a trembler sensor circuit in forty-five seconds. Once activated, the slightest movement or tampering with the suitcase would cancel the timer switch and detonate the device. Doctor l'Alham looked down at the three upturned faces below him. The nuclear physicist smiled and depressed the button that started the digital clock. The blue-lit seconds began to eat away at the sixty minutes that were displayed on the face.

"It is done," he said in triumph. Doctor l'Alham jumped from the table and the four men together slid it back to its original position. Salal knew that the suitcase would be spotted and hoped that the Americans would not be so foolish as to move it before he and what remained of the team were clear. But that was in Allah's hands. They raced for the stairway leading to the second floor and their escape route.

Except for the splatter of the rain and the moan of the rising wind that had replaced the now silenced wail of the siren, there was little other sound at the SEL&P compound. The occasional random shots of a guard went unanswered by the terrorist who still protected the door. The second hand on Matt's watch continued in its fruitless race to catch the time that was slipping by. His intuition told him that the enemy at the door had to be eliminated before major damage inside the reactor building could be accomplished. Brandt's protégé tried to puzzle out Salal's intent. Given the number of men in this attack, there was just no way they could carry enough explosives to damage the reactor. If Salal thought he could force his way into the control room, that would be equally an impossible task.

There was a sudden burst of fire as the remaining guards broke from cover and assaulted toward the doorway of the reactor building. Two fell, writhing on the pavement, at the bark of the terrorist's AK-47, but the three remaining made it across the open space. A grenade went off thirty-five or so feet to the left of the doorway. There was a second burst of fire and the detonation of a second grenade at the door itself. The terrorist who had held his position for as long as was possible had dropped a grenade at his feet, killing himself and one of the final two guards who was closing in on him.

Matt, soaked from the rain, chilled by the wind, painfully rose from behind the cover of the wreck that moments before had been his car. Running, limping to the fence, he shouted for any one of the guards. Jake Palmer, the SEP&L security chief who had given Matt his orientation on the facility's security measures earlier in the week, broke from the knot of men, spoke into his handheld radio and waved Matt forward. Palmer, as were many of Matt's own guards, was retired military and Matt remembered how he had been impressed with Palmer's understated, quiet confidence during his briefing on SEL&P security. The single remaining security gate that was still operational snapped to the unlocked position and rolled open. Matt, running as best he could, crossed the area and flattened himself against the reactor building with Jake as they surveyed the damage and pondered their next move.

"Appreciate the help back there, Colonel," Jake said, nodding toward the bodies in the vicinity of the gate. "They had us pretty well pinned down in that Goddamn cross fire until you showed up. But what in the hell are you doing here? Sounds like you got some trouble over at Sunny Point. Do you know what in the hell is going on?"

"Terrorists," Matt replied. "A boatload of them. We've got reaction forces inbound right now."

"We've got the county and state responding here. Should see some blue lights any minute now. We're going to wait for them to go after the ones inside."

"How much damage can they do in the building?" Matt asked.

"Not much. They're after the control room, but there is no way they'll ever make it. That's a sealed entry. There's just no way."

"What's the worst they can do?" Matt pressured, not waiting for Palmer to finish.

"They could bust up some of the plumbing, even cause us some serious damage if they got the right pipes, if they had enough time and explosive. But to rig it would take a hellava lot more explosive than two or three men could carry and a whole shit pot more time than they're gonna have."

"Jake, there must be more to it than just this. Now listen. The ones that we killed out here were just buying time for the ones inside. They're not after the control room at all. I think they are after the reactors."

"Colonel, there's no way. They'd have to get to the reactor core and that's behind twenty feet of ferrous concrete. There's not enough explosive in all of Sunny Point to blow through."

"We're just wasting time, Jake. We've got to get inside. The longer we wait the better chance they have of doing damage."

"Yeah, you're right, but I just can't afford to lose any more men. Christ knows we're thin as shit on the perimeter right now and that firing from Sunny Point is moving in our direction down by the river."

"Help's on the way to handle that chore," Matt replied. "But we've got to get into the reactor building now."

Jake nodded reluctant agreement. The two men moved back to the doorway and Jake deployed the remaining handful of guards behind them and issued instructions for placement and search zones once inside the building.

"Okay go, go!" Jake exclaimed and jerked open the door, rushing through it, followed by Matt and the remainder of the guards. There was no sound in the cavernous building. The guards leapfrogged forward as they had been trained. In a matter of five minutes they made a preliminary sweep of the first floor and found it to be clear. They came from behind their selected covers and worked forward up the stairs to the second floor.

Jake's radio announced that state and county police had arrived. The colonel acknowledged and gave instructions for them to secure the outside of the building, giving them a thumbnail sketch of what had thus far happened and their own progress in the sweep of the building. One of the guards still on the first floor suddenly called. Matt and Jake ran to his side. The guard had focused his flashlight into the pipework overhead and discovered the suitcase.

"Get me a Geiger counter," Jake ordered. A portable hand held device appeared instantly, brought from one of the screening stations scattered throughout the building.

Jake twisted the dial calibration to its most sensitive setting and poked the toggle switch to the ON position. The needle remained at the far left-hand side of the scale. The guard captain raised the Geiger counter toward the suitcase and the background buzz of the instrument and the needle on the scale rose. Radiation was leaking from the suitcase.

The meaning hit both Jake and Matt at the same time. Jake's eyes widened. "Get me a ladder," Jake demanded.

"No, wait," Matt directed. "They knew it would be found. Think about it for a minute. The damn thing has got to be booby-trapped. Don't touch it!"

"We have no choices, colonel. We've got to get the Goddamn thing disarmed and out of here. Any minute and it could go off."

"Touch it and it will go off," Matt replied. "Just hold on. First, let's get everyone out of here. No panic. Second, get some kind of scaffold over here so we can get to that damn thing without dropping it. I'll get an Explosive Ordnance Disposal team over here."

Matt turned and walk-jogged to the door of the building while Jake spoke into his radio.

The scene outside of the reactor building was different

from that which it had been when Matt had entered minutes earlier. The blue flashing lights of a half-dozen police cruisers illuminated the area. Two fire trucks from the SEL&P station stood by, their red lights reflecting off of the pavement as EMTs worked on wounded men. Huddles of people stood off around the edges of the area, out of the rain, staring and gossiping at the bodies lying about the area.

The thwupp, thwupp, thwapp of a Blackhawk announced the arrival of Jack's first elements as it made a low sweeping turn overhead and settled toward the perimeter of Sunny Point. Matt ran to his sedan, the smell of gasoline fumes heavy around it. Reaching inside he grabbed the microphone, praying that the military radio would still function.

"Anchor Six, Anchor Six, this is Carnival Six."

A flight of five choppers appeared in the darkened sky, chasing downward after their earlier replica, the roar of their engines drowning out Jack's response. The muffled boom of explosions, the distant rattle of automatic weapons fire, and the sharp small flashes of white, orange and red coming from the direction of Sunny Point increased. Green tracers from the AK-47's floated into the sky. Jack's voice broke the radio's silence.

"Send it, Carnival."

"I need an EOD team at the power plant ASAP. We've got a suspected tactical nuclear device here that has been armed. Over."

"Roger. Wait out." Less than thirty seconds later Jack was back on the radio. "Inbound your location, Carnival Six. Do you have status on Jericho leader? Over."

"Negative," Matt replied. "Believe him to still be in the area but no contact with Jericho Six at this moment."

"Wait out, Carnival. I've got traffic on the other net."

There was a silence for what seemed an eternity before Jack's voice came up on the frequency once again. "Carnival, bird with the EOD team just passed over you about a minute ago. Chopper's on his way back. Good luck, Matt."

"Roger, Anchor Six. I'm going to keep the bird for a while.

Good hunting. Out here."

As the Blackhawk settled to its concrete nest two minutes later, it kicked up a heavy swirl of spray and rain as the pilot released pitch from the blades and chopped power on the engines, diminishing their roar. The Blackhawk is a much bigger, heavier, more powerful helicopter than the UH-1 Huey that was used in Vietnam, and it greased to a landing without difficulty in the gusting, variable winds. A combat clad team of three men jumped from the bird. Matt greeted them, identified himself and led them with their gear past the reestablished presence of the gate security and into the reactor building and the suitcase.

Jake had left one of his subordinates to jury-rig scaffolding, having gone on to assist in clearing and then evacuating the rest of the building. The platform was supported on a total of four aluminum ladders which had been acquired somewhere from the depths of the building.

Matt pulled the Sergeant First Class to the side. Pointing to the suitcase he said, "We put a Geiger counter on it. There's radiation leaking from the suitcase. You can bet its boobytrapped."

There was no reply, just a nod.

The black sergeant climbed to the top of the ladder and began to examine the outside of the suitcase. With an ever-gentle touch he pried open the top and, flashlight in hand, peered inside. After a quick examination of the interior he closed the lid and with extreme caution made his way to the floor. The NCO was sweating profusely. Matt moved over and listened in on the conversation with the other two men of the team.

"It's got a digital timer," he was saying, "with thirty-seven minutes left to go. They did some fancy wiring, lots of false leads. The device is rigged with a trembler. Can't even breath hard or she'll go off until we get that trembler disconnected. I think I can get to it, but I can't see if it's wired into the timer or not. We'll just have to assume that it's on the same circuit. The trembler is much easier to get to, the way it's set up. I can bypass it but there's no way to get to the timer."

"If you take out the trembler, can we get the bomb the hell out of here?" Matt interrupted.

"If it goes right, yes sir, but either way it will still be armed."

"Take out the trembler," Matt directed. "We've got to get it away from here."

"You got it, sir," and up he went to the suitcase with a roll of tools and a second man.

Jake arrived back at the scene, watching the EOD specialist from a distance.

"Anything?" Matt asked with hope, but already suspecting the answer.

"Not yet, but we're still checking. They're out of the building, but can't be too far away. We've got roadblocks to prevent anyone from getting in or out, but the bastards are loose. What have you got here?"

Matt reviewed the situation and together they waited as the seconds slipped into minutes.

"Got it," was the final, relieved cry of the NCO on the platform. Between them they slipped the suitcase from its cradle of pipes and lowered it to the waiting hands beneath. The blue digital numbers of the clock inside the suitcase read twenty-three minutes.

"Get it to the bird," Matt directed and followed the explosives team to the Blackhawk. Climbing aboard with some assistance from the crewchief, he plugged into the intercom and radio net.

"Crewchief, out," Matt ordered. "Pilot, I've got a bomb sitting on my lap and the timer says twenty-one minutes until it detonates. Take us out over the Atlantic and we'll give it the deep six. Let's go." Matt strapped on the lifejacket that had been tucked under the crewchief's seat.

The Blackhawk's engine roared, spinning the blades at increasing speed until the pilot could apply pitch. The machine struggled into the air and gathered its forward momentum, bounced and blown sideward by the wind, rushing crablike toward the bank of the river and then buffeting, twisting to the East and the coastline. They climbed to 150 feet as the airspeed indicator wound up to read 180 knots. The blasting wind was on their tail and the pilot struggled to keep the nose pointed up and to the East as the airspeed indicator needle pegged against its stop.

The Blackhawk passed over the coastline amid the rainsqualls, through the vertical updrafts and downdrafts of wind, beating forward as the speed began to bleed off. The pilot clawed the big machine upward, fighting for altitude, trying to get away from the reaching trees and towers which threatened his aircraft and the men within. The blue numbers read eighteen minutes. They rocketed toward the open sea well past the design limits of safe flight for the Blackhawk, staying in the air by the will and skill of the two senior Warrant Officers who worked the controls.

Thousands of thoughts flooded Matt's mind. His mouth felt strange. Though lucid and aware, his mind was somewhere off in the distance, not participating in these events—patiently watching and offering a narrative for him to reflect upon.

"Buck up," he spoke to himself from the bottom of a deep well, his voice strange and somehow mechanical. The effort to form his words or sort out his thoughts was hard. Matt sat in the canvas seat, suffering, draining down, feeling himself beginning to drift off. Matt stabbed at the damaged leg. The pain had become a dull throb and didn't give him the spike of electric to bring him back. Matt recognized that he was on the edge, slipping over the side of reality, beginning to hallucinate. Punching again at his left leg, he felt the pain jerk him back to reality, attesting that he was still alive.

"Got to stop daydreaming. Got to stay on top of it," he rebuked himself. A voice announced its presence over the intercom.

"We're over water and a little south of the shipping channel now Colonel, you can kick that hummer out any time you want," said the pilot.

"Negative," Matt replied weariness in his voice. "Put her to the firewall and drop down on the deck. We want to put this thing in deep water and we only have thirty to eighty feet until we hit the continental shelf, about twenty miles out." Matt started to tell the pilots that the bomb was nuclear and then thought better of it.

"Doesn't make a difference anymore," he thought aloud. "Too late." The blue number was now an 8.

There was no reply from the pilot. The co-pilot muttered, "Jesus Christ."

"How much time left?" asked a disembodied voice through the earphones. It was an effort even to answer in monosyllables.

"Plenty," Matt lied.

Matt thought about Jack and the fight that was far from over at Sunny Point and what Rufus Brandt's reaction would be. The ICO had acted almost a month earlier than the latest intelligence had predicted. Thank God there had been the few weeks though. And thank God for people like Jack Dalton who had it wired all together. Perhaps the terrorists might make some political mileage out of the attack, but the bloody nose they would get would make them think twice in the future. Very few of them would see the morning light. Rufus had been right. It had been a one-way trip. But this would be one of those one-way trips that failed and wouldn't draw a crowd of new recruits. The radicals couldn't afford to lose a big one and they had put all their eggs in this one basket. They had come damn close but they had failed, they just didn't yet realize it.

The blue number was now a 6.

He thought of his unseen adversary, Salal, and felt his presence in the suitcase that rested on the deck in front of him. He drew a mental image of a faceless man looking down from on high, in the darkness, waiting for the land to erupt. Matt saw his look of triumph, the smile of success that he enjoyed as he laughed and the number flashed over to a blue 5.

Matt could not remember seeing the 6. Wasn't he supposed to do something when the number was 4? He couldn't remember. There was something important that he was to do. He squeezed at his torn left side. His ally, the pain, came back to rescue him. He remembered. It was time.

"Time to drop ... this monster. Get as low as you can and hover," Matt directed with a hoarse voice and obvious effort over the intercom.

"'Bout Goddamn time," the co-pilot's relieved voice whispered over the intercom. The pilot's voice came over the earphones.

"Can't hover. Wind's too high. Hard to see through the rain. We're on instruments now, Colonel. Can't get much lower and sure 'n hell no hover. Kick that mother out."

Matt forced open the door, sliding it back on its track to expose the interior to the full force of the wind and rain. The Blackhawk shuddered at the impact and pitched violently sideward and down in the air. The pilot struggled at the stick and collective controls to keep the ship under discipline.

"Get that son-of-a-bitch out! And get that Goddamn door shut before we eat our lunch," the co-pilot ordered, bringing Matt once again from the brink of unconsciousness.

Matt sat on the aluminum deckplating, his back braced against the forward jump seat, his legs drawn up close to his chest. Overcome with weariness, he just wanted to sleep. Taking a deep breath, he pushed, just as the chopper soared and cranked over to the right. The sudden change of the aircraft's attitude carried the suitcase clear of the door and tumbled it to the darkness below. Matt's legs dangled over the lip of the door, his body almost following the parcel into the sea. Exhausted, he reached for the door and struggled it forward, until, at last the latch popped back into the locked position.

"Get us the hell out of here," Matt directed and the bird spun alarmingly back the way it had come, the pilot again clawing for altitude, now fighting headwinds and racing away from the sea.

The detonation came in four minutes; it seemed to be a much shorter time. They were at best ten or so miles away.

Bright sunshine spilled over them, much like the sun rising as it did each morning from the sea. The explosion created a hole in the ocean and seared its bed, burning it to a dry scorched place before it permitted the waters to tumble back in and turn to steam in their cooling ministrations. The vaporizing white heat of the blast transformed itself in an instant into a column of superheated air that rose from the seabottom on its own familiar mushroom stem. The blast sucked the moisture from the air, creating an instant fog that materialized in the flash of an eye from the primary site outward to a distance of eight miles and more. The waters erupted behind them, chasing after the fleeing helicopter. A wall pursued them with a green white sheen of liquid—eighty feet high— to race with increasing momentum across the storm tossed ocean toward the land. There was no sound, at least no sound he remembered.

The tidal wave raced down on them in agonizing slow motion, coming closer and closer.

Then came the shock and concussion wave.

The convulsion hit and shook the Blackhawk like a rat caught in a terrier's jaws. The pilot pitched forward striking his helmeted head against the instrument panel, dazed. The Blackhawk held together but the co-pilot was at the edge of panic, his reflexes raw, jumpy, overcompensating for the directions received from his brain. For a few brief instants the co-pilot struggled in vain to bring the craft under control as it tumbled nose down over its own axis, round and about, no longer a part of its element, but something alien and foreign not belonging in the sky.

In the Blackhawk's final moments, just as it settled to the outreaching sea, the co-pilot let it go. Throwing up his hands to ward off the impact, the warrant officer struggled to rip off his helmet and harness, succeeding at neither effort. The helicopter hit nose first and tumbled end over end, ripping off its rotor blades and huge pieces of its fuselage, coming to rest on the surface behind the crested eighty-foot high tidal wave that rolled the remaining flotsam of wreckage.

There was no longer an up or a down, just a crazy spinning world of bright flashes and terrible darkness as the Blackhawk plummeted down, end over end, into the sea. Matt fought toward the door to open it, to escape from the doomed aircraft. The door slid open as the latch was ripped from its housing.

In a surreal world, Matt remembered wrestling himself forward through the opening, doing combat with the sea that rushed up to greet and take him. He yanked at the circular clip that would release CO_2 into his life vest that was designed to buoy him back up to the surface. The effort was pure reflex, an unreasoned instinct, an unplanned, final attempt at survival. Suddenly Megan appeared in the water opposite him, floating just out of arm's reach. Matt scrubbed at his eyes with a fist. She did not disappear. How did she get here he wondered?

"Megan, what are you doing here?" he asked aloud in childish wonder, trying to reach out and touch her. She vanished just out of reach.

I should talk to her, he thought. Tell her that I will make it up to her, tell her that I love her.

The last thing he remembered was a terrible pain that ran through his left leg. The pain was the worst he had ever experienced. Matt was sure that he must have been dying because then the pain left, and there was in its place, black emptiness.

26
Distant Demons

Matt came swimming up from the dark, murky depths of unconsciousness to the watery distortion of images, floating in space and time, receding and expanding, vivid and opaque. How many times, for how many days, Matt did not know. He heard voices, both close and from a distance, detached from them, observing yet seeking to be a part, close enough to wash through his mind, penetrate his thoughts. There were shifting lights and pain and dullness in his left leg and then pins and needles and more pain. There were hot sweats and cold sweats and demons most terrible which had haunted him last when he was a child. And then finally, one sun-lit day, his eyes opened and there was stillness and peace.

Matt sensed rather than felt his hand in the hand of another; a warm, soft hand that held onto him. His vision expanded from the one spot high up on the wall, from the blank eyed television set that hung in a frame set into the ceiling and tilted toward the bed, until he broke through the surface of silence to the quiet of the room. Megan was there with him, smiling down on him, holding his hand. She brought it soft against her lips. Matt felt their velvet on the back of his hand, saw the tear that slipped from her eye, felt the sparkle of her smile.

"Welcome back, Yank. I missed you," she said her eyes brimming.

Matt smiled weakly. His face felt cracked, swollen and stiff in its movement of skin.

"Where have I been and for how long? How did I..." he asked in a hoarse, cracking whisper.

"Sush. It's not important now. You're back and where you should be. That's all that matters," she replied.

Just that fast he was drained of all strength. Tired unto

very death itself. Struggling, he tried to concentrate, to form the words. His mouth was full of glue and mush.

"I love you, Megan. You must—it's important that you … it's so very …" He slipped back into the world from where he had come.

Each successive time thereafter when he surfaced, Matt was stronger. The sense of unrealness and panic that had clung to him earlier receded and was lost. There was one bad fright that the patient in him remembered. He swam up to consciousness for the second time and it had been at night. There had been a man in the room, an orderly or an attendant. Matt had felt trapped, threatened, overwhelmed by the shadowy presence. He panicked and screamed out in terror, and then slipped back into the safety of unconsciousness.

Three mornings later, around five or so if the bedside digital clock was accurate, Matt awoke from the muted dimensions in which he had existed. Hungry, alert, and alive for the first time since that night in the chopper, he knew the worst was past. Whatever had happened to him was over now and he knew he would make it.

His left leg, just below the knee, itched terribly, but neither could he see it, nor could he reach it from the restraints that bound his arms to the sides of the bed.

Shit, he thought and wiggled the toes, twisting the calf against the stiff sheets seeking relief. He realized that while all the sensations were as they should be, something was wrong. He pulled and contorted himself to a sitting position, surprised by his weakness and the vast effort it had taken just to reposition his body on the bed. By the illumination of the bed lamp he looked down at the flattened blanket overlaying where the leg should have been. The thought settled in.

Where it should have been.

The limb from below the knee was gone.

He fell back upon the pillows. A wetness welled up in his eyes and a single tear escaped to channel itself down his cheek, past the squarish jaw, to his throat. In a short time he drifted off again, but this time not to unconsciousness but to resting sleep.

By nine the next morning he had completed a regime that he could not remember having been through before. A cheery blond nurse had shaved and bathed him and in doing so had passed the warm soapy cloth over his loins. The reaction had been immediate and startling. The nurse noted the incident without embarrassment though not complete innocence. With a mischievous, tempting laugh, she pronounced, "Colonel, you are recovering much faster than expected and there is no doubt as to the question of your returning strength."

At nine-thirty, having been poked, prodded and visited by several physicians who said little but gave a tight smile at him in approval, Megan's form danced through the door. She lit up with a grin and marched over, without a word, to plant a searing, passionate, tongue seeking kiss on his sore, dry and cracked lips.

"Meg, the gash in your side ... how are you?"

"All sewed up, no great damage and healing nicely, thank you very much. It will be a grand story for our children," she said, lightly dismissing her own injury.

"Well, Yank," she said, smiling down on him, "you do know how to show a girl a good time."

"How long?" he asked.

"How long, what, darling?"

"Since they decided to take off the leg?"

He had said it with a sense of curiosity, not seeking sympathy nor pity, rather just acknowledging that he had been physically altered and accepting the condition as part of his reality.

"Today is the twenty-sixth day you've been in the hospital," she replied in a matter of fact voice. "You gave us quite a scare, you know. They told us that you would not make it. You were touch and go for the first twelve days."

"How did I get here? Where did they find me?"

"Jack found you out there in the ocean, darling. God knows how he did it, but he did. He stayed here for a week

hovering over you, talking to you even though you didn't
respond—and threatening the doctors. Your heart stopped
twice and you've been put under the knife a total of five times.
You are a sight, don't you know. And your parents have been
here, too. I've had several long chats with them and we now
know each other quite well. When you were pronounced out
of danger they went back to Florida, but they will be back in
a few days. We speak every day on the phone."

"My parents? Jack, huh? I can't remember. It's all just a
blank," he said with a troubled face. "Where is Jack?"

"He had to go. Couldn't stay longer, but he calls. I told
him you are out of danger. He said to tell you that just
because he fished you out of the ocean he will not be responsible for your life," she said smiling.

"What about the others, the pilot and co-pilot," Matt
asked.

"They were found in the wreckage when they recovered
the helicopter from the ocean's bottom." Megan paused.
"They never made it out of the aircraft."

Matt silently stared out of the window and off into the distance. "Two good men," he said emotionally and stared off
into the distance out the sole window of the room. After a few
awkward moments, he coughed back the quiver in his chin
and made a feeble attempt to lighten the mood rubbing at a
missed patch of stubbled beard on the underside of his chin.

"Guess I'm a mess. A face that only a mother could love,"
he tried to joke.

"A face that only a mother or a total nutter could
love," she corrected with smugness. "I suppose that
makes me a nutter."

She had said it in a brave voice as if well rehearsed, but now
that it was said her chin began to quiver and the tears welled
up in her eyes. She turned away so he would not see the tears.

"Meg, come over here," he said.

She moved to the right side of the bed, sitting upon it,
next to his right arm that he raised and wrapped about her
waist. Her eyes puddled again.

"Knock it off," he demanded in a rough voice, squeezing her about the waist."It's okay. We're alive. We're together and, hell, it was the bad leg anyway. Besides, if I'm not mistaken ma'am, I believe that I'm in love with you. And as soon as I get out of here, if you'll still have me, I'm going to make an honest woman of you."

She wiped the back of her hand to her cheeks, sniffed, and regained her composure.

"Bloody, stupid twit. Of course, I'll have you. Why do you think I came over in the first place if not to lure you permanently into my bed?"

Matt smiled a painful smile, laughing in spite of himself. "Always did suspect you of being a Goddamned Black Widow spider out to devour me."

Two more days of returning strength and increased awareness to his surroundings passed. Megan seemed to always be there to brighten his spirits, but provided no answers to his detailed questions on the attack.

"All in good time," she would say, "All in good time." Then on the morning of the third day of his conscious recovery there was a tentative knock at the doorframe and General Rufus Brandt entered.

Brandt smiled and nodded politely in Megan's direction.

Megan shot him a look of pure hatred and anger. There was little doubt where she placed the blame for Matt's condition. Matt caught the exchange in spite of the efforts of both of them to conceal it. He squeezed Megan's hand in protest of her act as well as to reassure her that it didn't matter any longer.

"I'll just be outside, darling," she said icily to Brandt rather than to Matt. "He shouldn't be tired or excited by your adventures of daring-do, general. So please, do be brief."

"Oh, we won't be too long. Miss Felton. And I'll try not to get him excited," Rufus responded in out of character submissiveness.

Megan bent and pecked at Matthew's cheek and then stuck her British nose in the air and sailed from the room.

"She's quite a woman, Matthew," Rufus chuckled. "Been raising hell with the staff here ever since you arrived and God help them if you weren't taken care of to her standards. How you feelin' son?"

"Pretty sore. Leg itches like hell sir, but otherwise, guess I'll live," Matt replied.

Rufus grunted an acceptance. "Had some doubts about that, glad to see I was wrong," the general allowed.

There was a moment of uncomfortable silence.

"It was a setup," Matthew asserted. "You knew where Salal was going to attack. You weren't just speculating on Sunny Point; you knew, you just weren't sure when."

"Without his knowledge of course, we did try to make his decisions easier for him. We did not, however, know about or anticipate either the nuclear device or the attack on the power facility. Neither of those events was part of the scenario," Rufus said.

"You had someone inside of Salal's organization, didn't you?" Matt asked.

"You'll get a full debriefing when you get out of here, but yes, we had someone who wanted peace as much as we do and was tired of the killing. We had a very helpful source at the very beginning," Rufus admitted. "Much to our dismay and consternation, he disappeared early in the operation. When he did, we lost our access to Salal's plans and timetable. We didn't know that Salal was going for the power plant or that he was bringing his force in by boat. Other than that we had his entire effort pretty well wired so yes, you're right, Matt, it pretty much was intended to be a setup to hook Salal."

The general moved to the window and looked out on the lawn below. "Remember when I told you it would be a dangerous operation and that it could change the lines they draw on the Middle East maps?"

"Yes sir, I remember. Back when you first briefed me in D.C. ... when I got back from the Sinai."

"That's right. What I could not tell you then, Matt, was that the President, Malcolm DeFore, and I were the only

three who knew the whole scheme. Part of the watershed
from Desert Storm was the fracturing of a single Arab vision
regarding Israel and the Palestinians. That was unfortunate
because Desert Storm contributed to Arafat's inability to control the PLO and he was the Arab horse we've been backing
to pull it all together on the Arab side. You must remember
that the basic coin of the Arab world has always been distrust.
Arab politics and culture are byzantine in their structure. The
whole configuration has a pragmatic pyramid base—me
against my brother, my brother and I against our cousins, our
family against the tribe, the tribe against the neighboring
tribe, and so on. The foundation of their society is based on
distrust and revenge. That attitude, that cultural trait fractures
any permanent stability in the Arab world ... that and their
ability to hate."

Rufus returned from the window and closed the door to
the hospital room as he spoke. "In an indirect fashion our success against Iraq has given rise to even more splinter groups
and radicals in the Arab world. Lots of personal ambitions that
laid claim to the spokesperson leadership for the Palestinian
cause, but it wasn't the cause they were promoting. To most
of them, it's personal self-aggrandizement—power."

He crossed the room and settled into the single chair next
to the bed. "I don't know if you remember, but when Arafat
had his ass kicked out of Lebanon, he had to settle for Khadafi
as sanctuary. Despite appearances to the contrary, that's when
it all started to unravel for Arafat. Libya was not the PLO's
first choice of sanctuary. The signs of Arafat's demise were
there long before then if you start to look for them. Unlike
Lebanon, Arafat found that being in the geography of Libya
made logistics support of operations inside of Israel, Gaza and
the West Bank too tough. Besides, Arafat was getting old.
He's tired of looking over his shoulder for the Mossad or an
assassin from his own people. He wanted political legitimacy,
something they could put on the base of a statue or memorial to him. Terrorism was not accomplishing anything except
piling up bodies. So he sinned."

"You mean he started talking compromise and began negotiating; he began to accommodate Israel," Matt offered.

"Yep, that's about the size of it," the general responded. "When he did that, he lost the support of a huge slice of the PLO and the control of several of his key subordinates—witness his open split with Abu Nidal and his faction. He also lost what little control he had over the PLO's *Fatah* militiamen, their quasi-military arm. After he indicated a willingness to negotiate the Israelis let him back inside Gaza and the West Bank."

"And the radicals saw his return as a betrayal of the PLO," Matt interjected.

"Events snowballed and it got more and more out of control. Several of Arafat's lieutenants defected. Oh, he still retained power within their circle of leadership," Rufus said, gesturing, "but he was on the way out."

"Just a question of time before he was retired by one of the young turks?"

"Best guess was that someone like Nidal or bin Ladin would have taken over unless we somehow put the militants out of business first. So like it or not, we had to find a way to prop Arafat up, had to find a way to quiet down the militants and reduce their influence."

"And show the Arabs in the street—who want peace and the chance to move on with their lives—just how radical the militants are and how far they would go to destroy the peace process," Matt added.

Rufus nodded in the affirmative. "At the same time we wanted the moderates, now represented by a reformed, more pliable Arafat, in a stronger political position." Rufus heaved himself from the chair and began to pace.

"All we had to do was first, find something that would unite—at least for a time—all or most of the worst of the radical elements, both Arab and Islamic. Second, we had to then seduce them into an action that would strip them of their terrorist gunmen, make them look foolish and then by that action fracture them to a point of political insignificance, at least till we could get a peace treaty signed. So that was our mission from the President."

"Let me see if I have it right, sir," Matt said. "You distract and isolate the Arab terrorists and the Islamic radicals by suckering them into a united action outside of the Middle East. You set up an operation that takes away the best of their fighting forces, and disenfranchises their leadership by their pre-programmed failure. Simultaneously, you also take some of the pressure off of Arafat from the militant and radical sides in the peace negotiations and give him more wiggle room."

"Malcolm DeFore and I found it necessary at that point to bring in other intelligence assets to find Salal's force, track it to the target and bring it down before any damage was done. The first plan was to take down Salal's force at their assembly point here in the US. But, as you know, they never had one. We didn't find that out until it was almost too late. We planned to put his folks under surveillance as they crossed the borders into the USA. We thought that was working and had four of them covered. They were, as we later found out, the intelligence and surveillance team that was put in early. We estimated that Salal had between fifty and seventy men that he would infiltrate and assemble somewhere close to the target. We didn't want a gun battle; but if it came to that we wanted to physically isolate them with an overwhelming force. That was Jack's preemptive mission."

"And that was the why of Sunny Point?" Matt concluded, seeking confirmation.

"On the button. Sunny Point was the best choice for several reasons. The terminal was easy to watch, it is located in a rural area, small local population near by. Any sudden increase in Middle Easterners or strangers would be seen and easy to track. Although isolated we could get to it quickly and we didn't have to worry about a great deal of collateral or civilian damage out in the boondocks if it came down to any shooting.

Rufus paused. The admissions he had to make were painful to him.

"Two hundred men coming in by ship gave us a jolt," Rufus continued. "That's a sizable force, more than we expected. And we didn't go that one step further and look beyond Sunny Point. The assassination attempt at Garrison House on you, well – just totally unanticipated. Incomplete intelligence and dumb assumptions on our part; my fault and responsibility. Part of the *fog* of battle that Clauswitz wrote about."

There was a moment of awkward silence, both men buried in their own thoughts.

"Well sir, how'd we do?" Matt asked, his curiosity evident, his interest piqued. "That's why you're here isn't it? To tell me, I mean."

"Yes, that's the most of it, Matt, that and to see for myself how you're doing, how you've come out of it."

The general walked to the window and gazed down onto the long stretch of lawn and the busy street beyond. He turned and propped his hips against the windowsill. "Jericho was a damn close thing, Matthew, much closer than we had planned for, and bigger than we had expected. Too damn close. We've clamped a Top Secret on the entire incident. We don't want to panic the American people. Were John Q. Public to know that the terrorists had acquired a nuclear capability, well ..."

The thought went unfinished. In a moment Rufus resumed the discussion. "We believe the attack on the power station and the tactical nuclear device part of the operation was kept from the ICO backers. That was Salal's doing—we think."

Rufus paused as Matt tried to heave himself up higher in the bed.

"It sure 'n hell changed the ante, didn't it, general?" Matt responded. He paused waiting for an answer, knowing that there was no simple one. Rufus grunted.

"What happened after I checked out? Did we get Salal? How bad was the damage at Sunny Point?" Matt asked, changing the subject. A dozen questions gnawed at his mind as the memories of the events came flooding back.

"Salal disappeared. We missed him and they tore the hell out of Sunny Point," the general replied. "They took out the center and southern wharves, dumped these big port container cranes into the river and blew up a hellava lot of munitions, but it could have been a lot worse. When you're a bit stronger, I'll have Max come down and fill you in on the details. He and Jack would be here now except that I've got them running on some other things right now."

Matt raised an eyebrow.

"Besides, Jack's frequent presence here would add fuel to the fire of speculation by our friends in the media once they found out who he was."

There was a pause as Rufus fished out a cigar from an inner jacket pocket and stuck it, unlit, in the corner of his mouth. Chewing the unlit cigar seemed to relax him and the general continued.

"You may not know it, Matthew, but you are somewhat a local celebrity around here. We didn't ah, repress, the details of the action over at the Garrison House. We had to change the circumstances around a bit, but so far, it's been bought and the smart asses in the media haven't been able to get through the misinformation that's been generated over the whole thing. They've been their own belligerent selves, but cooperative with us to this point. There was quite a bit of speculation on the six o'clock news at first, but it's died down now. We told them that you came across some suspicious activity in your first few days at the terminal and that it looked like drug smuggling and that you had reported it on up through channels. Your three visitors were described, very colorfully, I might add, as "hitmen" hired by some heavy drug folks to take you out of action. Quite inventive, I thought, given the time we had to come up with something."

"How did you cover up the action at Sunny Point and the ship sunk in the main channel?" Matt asked.

"That, I'll admit," replied the general, "did take a bit more inventiveness. We wrote a good bit of the terminal damage off to 'Kate.' The sinking of the *Compass Rose*, we attributed to a deliberate scuttling by the crew as the result of a fire that got out of control. The story that she was driven aground by the wind and hit a snag that opened her up and started the fire wasn't too hard to sell. We've been able to reopen the channel to limited traffic."

"We stuck to the drug cover story pretty much. We tied it in with the Coast Guard and came up with a plausible story about a large delivery right off of the terminal."

"What about the device we carried out to sea that went off right as planned? What was the cover story there?" Matt inquired wearily.

"I can see that I'm tiring you out. I'm told the NOAA confirmed a shifting of two of the land plates just off the continental shelf the night that 'Kate' was off the North Carolina coast. The result was a significant underwater earthquake but it brought no damage to the mainland. Earthquake reports are not unusual. Happens up off of Alaska all the time. Story didn't get much media coverage; 'Kate' got more. Radioactivity was pretty well dissipated by the offshore winds so we dodged a bullet there."

The general crossed the room, his hands clasped behind his back, the unlit cigar clamped in his jaw.

"We've been pretty lucky so far, Matt. The shit hit the fan during a good news week and there were enough stories elsewhere not to make this one a major attraction. Drug busts are not big news anymore," Rufus waved an arm. "Oh, I'm not so naive as to believe that a few of the media heavy hitters couldn't make things hot for us or that they haven't figured out what went down there at Sunny Point. I expect they've agreed that it's in the public interest not to raise too much hell about it right now."

"Just like what goes on at Area Fifty-One," Matt commented ruefully.

Rufus just laughed.

"But you can bet we'll hear about Sunny Point later when it fits the media's needs or when they figure it all out—and they will, one of these days," Rufus responded.

"But how much of it will come out, general, and whose head rolls when it does?" Matt asked.

"The Sunny Point side of it will come out, but no one, Matt, no one," he added, "but the NSC has been privy to the specifics on the affair at the power plant or the nuclear implications. So far as anyone else knows, a splinter group of eco-terrorists just ran amuck and unsuccessfully tried to break in to the power station. The knowledge of what really happened there is just not in our national interests. The implications are just ... well, monumental."

"But what's to stop them from trying again, general?" Matt asked. "We caught them with their fingers in the cookie jar, for Christ's sake. They make an armed military attack against a government installation in the United States. They plant a nuclear bomb at a civilian nuclear reactor and just about blow ten square miles to hell and we can't even tell the world what these crazy bastards have done, what they're capable of? That sucks!"

Matt was visibly angry. "What the hell does it take? How many Goddamned free swings do they get?"

"We need to think in terms of measured response," Rufus explained in a calm, soothing voice. "There are just no grounds that justify turning a quarter of the world into little more than a glowing pile of nuclear waste. There is no sense in it."

Matt opened his mouth in protest and shut it, the muscles of his jaws clenched in frustration.

"We're not out to destroy the world, only a cancer. Selective and elective surgery, not escalation, is the way to do it. Our turn at bat will come. There's a rather physical message in the works now. We'll be sending it to the ICO in a few days, just to let them know that they can't intimidate us. We'll make them think twice. And if that doesn't do it, well, we'll just keep tapping them on the head until the Arabs decide to take care of their own problems and throw the bastards at the top out. Prudent action measured with restraint, Matt. That is how we are going to respond. That's the key."

Matt listened and said nothing, his face displaying neither emotion nor reaction.

Rufus smiled and glanced at his watch. He crossed to the bed; his hand outstretched and took Matt's into his own, gripping it tightly. He looked down on the younger man intently, his face a sober mask.

"Matt," he said, "we've had this conversation before I know. I've asked you to trust me before and it's cost you half a leg. But I'm going to ask you to trust me again, son. You've got my word that we'll get Salal and the rest of them as well. We'll stop the insane butchery and they will pay; that I promise you. We'll balance the books in the fullness of time. We'll end the story on Salal and his backers."

Matt looked into the eyes of the older man, caught up in his earnest resoluteness, but reluctant to concede without condition.

"I hear you, General, but I want something for me before I back you up on this one," he said.

"Name it."

"Until we nail Salal, I'm still an active player. Don't let them throw me out because of this," he said gesturing toward the stump of leg beneath the covers. "Don't bullshit me on it, General. I'm not talking about some piss-ass clerk job. I mean in the field and with no special privileges. I can hack it," he added.

"I wouldn't have it any other way, tiger. You have my word. You'll be in on it—all the way. Now I'd better get my ass out of here before your British Florence Nightingale decides to turn this room into another Battle of Bunker Hill."

"Okay, boss," Matt replied, with a new familiarity toward the old soldier, squeezing the older man's tough, leathery hand. "It isn't over yet, so I guess we'll just hang in there together until it is."